Wish You Were Here Yet?

Do They Know It's Christmas Yet?

Book Three

James Crookes

Also by James Crookes

Do They Know It's Christmas Yet? (Book 1)

Did They Steal A Million Yet? (Book 2)

All titles also available on Audible, read by the author.

For my brother.
And for every brother and sister.

Chapter One

"It's not bloody blasphemous!" said Tash, trying badly to perform a *Ctrl Alt Del* on Maureen before letting out a little: "Jesus!"

She'd managed to upset her in record time.

"You're a dirty Doreen," said Maureen. "Potty mouth."

Jamie and Tash held in a giggle.

"I just think *Maur-mond* sounds like Mormon." Tash handed the business card back to Jamie.

"It's an anagram," said Raymond.

"It's not really an anagram, is it?" said Tash. "It's the end of your name and the start of Maureen's."

"Snazzy though, isn't it?" said Raymond, pleased with his gifts from Jamie.

Raymond had been keen to show Tash the early Christmas gifts he'd received from her brother. One hundred business cards printed with his new business name and contact details.

"Very nice, very kind of you, Jamie," said Tash, glancing at the card one final time.

Maurmond Storage Facilities
Shad Thames, South Tower Bridge
London

"You missed your phone number."

"It's on the back," said Jamie.

She flipped it over, to confirm, then looked at the front again.

"I really like the..." she was desperately trying to change the mood, "the font."

"What's a font?" asked Raymond.

"A font's where you christen a baby, Raymond, in a church," said Maureen, folding her arms.

"No. No. It's the typeface," said Tash. "I like the way it looks. Look, I'm trying to be nice!"

Jamie squeezed his nephew tightly. The baby had only seen his uncle last night, but it had been two months of separation for Jamie. Well, thirty-six years and two months, but happily, the bulk of that had passed in a heartbeat when he accidentally travelled back to 1984 with his sister. Thankfully she had finally come back to take him back to 2020.

"You dropped Gabriel, Jamie," said Tash, casually picking up the family heirloom teddy and placing it on her son's chest. Gabriel was probably approaching his eighty-fifth birthday when Tash and Jamie's mother, Andrea, fetched him from the loft and handed him over to her newborn grandson in hospital. Tash had burst into tears immediately. It was July, she was hot, had stitches, lost all feeling below the waist, and now her mum was presenting her with the teddy their great grandfather had brought home during the war. It was probably German and had the kind of filling that would make the EU shit themselves, all horsehair, straw, and curved wires. He had once boasted glossy golden blond fur but having been adored by three generations of babies (Dorothy, then George, then Tash), this little fellow looked like one of those inside-out cats people pay a fortune for.

Jamie looked up at his sister and realised she was distracted as she placed the tiny bear with his new owner. Tash had seen a bright fire burning in Maureen's eyes when this beautiful baby bundle arrived in her home.

"Do you want to say hello to Auntie Maureen?" said Tash, hoping this distraction would help improve the frosty atmosphere. She gently rubbed her son's cheek and smiled at Maureen, who paused before replying.

"Well, if that's alright with you?" she said begrudgingly. "Should I wash my hands?"

"Don't be daft," said Tash, as Jamie gently handed the precious cargo to Maureen. "Just don't breathe on him."

Maureen paused and looked over.

"I'm kidding! Go and warm him by the light bulb."

Maureen ignored the insult about her chilly home and instead muttered something about babies not being called Raymond once more, but her joy was plain to see as she walked back into the lounge, followed by her husband. Tash started to follow, but Jamie blocked her path.

"You went home without me?" said Jamie in his best whisper.

"Only to fetch Raymond," replied Tash, unable to maintain eye contact with her brother.

"I don't understand," said Jamie.

"We don't always need to understand everything, Jamie," muttered Tash and brushed him aside. He followed her into the lounge, and they all sat or perched on some Draylon. Dixie Peach was still playing the biggest hits of the year.

Raymond was smiling happily at the baby in his wife's arms, as she gently swayed him to 'Last Christmas.' Tash was the first to speak.

"So, what have I missed?"

"Martha was just telling us she's got a job in a cheese factory," said Raymond.

Tash nodded in a way that beautifully encompassed sheer indifference and faux delight.

"And she's wanted for double murder," added Raymond.

"But only in America," added Martha.

"But only in America," reiterated Raymond.

"I didn't do it," said Martha dismissively, like you might say, "it's just a scratch."

"And she has a plan," said Raymond.

"Yeah! I have a plan."

"Not in front of the baby," instructed Maureen, gently rocking him on her chest.

Tash looked around the room, waiting for the sign of a smile on anyone's lips. When none came, she heard her voice.

"Is this a joke?"

Lots of voices muttered ...

... "no,"

... and "afraid not, actually,"

... and "yeah, double murder," whilst all simultaneously examining the swirls in the carpet.

Tash took an exasperated deep breath.

"Sake."

Chapter Two

"Last call for Iberia flight IB3163 to Madrid, please proceed urgently to gate number seven. Final call Iberia IB3163."

The faceless lady's voice was followed by the mechanical chime that reverberated around the lofty ceilings of Heathrow's Terminal Two, including the smoky Sky Bar's observation deck. Jamie had ordered two margaritas as they seemed to be the porn-star martini of 1984, but the flustered lady behind the bar had looked blankly back at him, so he settled for two double vodka-and-Um-Bongos. (Um-Bongo was pretty much the only pre-blended apple, lemon, passion fruit, mandarin, apricot, guava and mango on the market back then). He hadn't told Martha that these weren't margaritas, so was happy when she asked him for the same again after planting some cash in his hand. Jamie finished his second and felt his cheeks glow with the rush of alcohol.

Martha lifted a folded brown leather wallet open and delved inside to produce her final twenty-pound note. Happy that she had exhausted all the currency within, she slid out an Access credit card and read the name on the bottom.

"Are those finished?"

Martha and Jamie looked over at a cleaning trolley.

"Did that trolley just speak?" asked Martha.

Jamie nodded.

Then the shortest adult Martha had ever seen peered over the top. She held a cloth in one hand and pushed the trolley with the other. With a smoking cigarette hanging from her lips, she gestured at four empty cocktail glasses on the table between them.

"Sorry, I didn't see you down there," said Martha.

"Are those finished?"

"Yes," replied Martha. "Same again, please." She held out the purple banknote displaying William Shakespeare leaning on a wall. He looked like one of those rarely present self-conscious fathers waiting at the school gates, unsure if he was in the right place.

"You need to order at the bar," replied the lady, stacking the glasses on her upper tray and attempting to wipe the table-top between two pairs of elbows, oblivious to the obstruction they caused.

"You'd think they would give you a lower trolley," said Martha to the cleaner.

The cleaner lifted one elbow to wipe under them at a time, and both Jamie and Martha allowed it, like kids at the dinner table.

"Why?" asked the cleaner.

"So you can see over the top," replied Martha. "It can't be fun driving that thing blind."

"Or bigger heels," said Jamie, "that would do it."

"Are you taking the piss?"

Both looked mortified.

"No," they replied in unison.

"I was just thinking if you hit a lost suitcase or something, then that Marlboro's going straight down your throat," said Martha.

"It's Benson and Hedges," replied the cleaner. She was particular about her tobacco.

"Whatever. An accident just like that is what killed my mother."

The cleaner stared at her for a moment, removed her

cigarette, and then tried to reach the ashtray at the other side of the table. Jamie leant over to her.

"Would you like me to lift you up?"

"Piss off!"

Martha offered to take it off her, and the cleaner handed it over. She was surprised to see Martha wipe the filter with a napkin and take over the cigarette. "Shame to waste it."

Jamie started to shuffle in his plastic moulded seat.

"I think these are twenty-minute seats," he said.

"Excuse me?" said Martha.

"These chairs, they're twenty-minute seats."

Martha realised she was holding the wallet. She offered it to the cleaner, who was about to walk away.

"What do you want me to do with that?"

"I don't give a crap. I found it; I'm just being a good citizen," said Martha exhaling smoke and tossing the leather purse onto the cleaning trolley, causing two glasses to fall into one another and smash. "Sorry."

The cleaner started to tidy up the shards of glass and then shuffled the trolley away.

"The name on the cards is some kind of double-barrelled crap," shouted Martha. "Maybe look for a guy in a crown or a chick with some horses."

"I still feel a bit bad about that," said Jamie.

"What the height thing?"

"No. Stealing the money."

"We found the wallet, Jamie. It was lost. Besides, he had Amex Gold, a BA Executive Club Lounge card; he ain't gonna miss a few bucks."

Jamie shrugged. He was feeling warm and happy in the company of this extraordinary American woman. Maybe half a bottle of champagne and then those two Vum-Bongos helped. And yes, that was what he would call them when he introduced them to Tash in 2020.

"Shall we arm wrestle to see who queues for the next drink?" said Martha, nodding at the line of impatient passengers waiting for their departure stiffener. She stubbed out the remnants of the cigarette into a disposable foil ashtray.

"Okay," said Jamie, placing his elbow on the wet table and offering his open hand. Martha slid her palm inside his. Her skin felt silky soft, and a knot tied itself instantly in Jamie's stomach. He hoped this match would take forever, so decided to go easy on her.

"On your marks," said Jamie, "get set."

Before he said 'go', Martha slammed his hand back onto the table in a heartbeat.

"Best of three?" He asked.

She smiled, and they repeated the challenge with the same result.

"Best of five?"

Martha laughed and shuffled in her seat. "What was the twenty-minute seat thing? My ass is killing me."

Jamie sat up and became quite animated. He loved it when he knew stuff which interested other people. This sort of thing didn't happen much to him.

"Public seating has like kind of ratings. Depending on how long they want you to sit there. So, if you sit somewhere like the Hilton on Park Lane, you're good for a few hours. If you sit in McDonald's, you might be in a ten-minute seat or something. Designed to be uncomfortable after you finish your meal, so you don't hang around."

"Well, these guys fucked up then," said Martha with a laugh, "we've been here hours."

She looked over at the clock above the Departures board.

"I can't read that! What time does it say?"

Jamie glanced over and squinted at the clock.

"Seventeen forty-three."

"What's that in English?" said Martha.

"Nearly quarter to six."

Then Jamie froze.

"Quarter to six!" He repeated.

Martha stared back at him. "What? What does that mean?"

"It means Tash has been waiting for me at Tower Bridge for thirteen minutes!"

"Crap!" said Martha, "you gotta go. Take this."

She handed him the twenty-pound note, and he curiously declined it with a shake of his head whilst simultaneously stuffing it into his trouser pocket; his Asperger's was being overloaded.

"I'm good, Raymond gave me a few quid for the bus," said Jamie trying to stand up and pull back his twenty-minute chair simultaneously.

Martha copied him, and soon everyone looked at this curious couple who both appeared to be fighting the Formica topped table between them. Jamie fell first.

"I'm okay!" he shouted from somewhere out of sight.

Martha went to help, but her coat sleeve caught on her chair back, and she fell too. Her forehead struck Jamie's chin so loudly that the family at the next table winced. The mother leaned over to look down. "Are you alright?"

Martha was lying flat on top of Jamie, her nose touching his. Jamie breathed in the Vum-Bongo fumes from her open lips and felt the warmth of her on his chest. She stared into his eyes. Jamie tried to stare back, but he was never very good at holding eye contact, so he blinked a lot and then answered.

"We're on the floor."

"That would explain the lack of ceiling," said Martha. "I think one of my knees might be drunk."

Martha's impossibly long eyelashes suddenly hypnotised Jamie. Eventually, he spoke. "This is actually comfier than Maureen's sofa."

"Certainly smells better," she replied, and they both laughed like teenagers.

Chapter Three

Jamie and Martha raced out of the Departures door to see cars unloading lucky passengers and driving away.

"I suppose the Arrivals exit would be better for a cab," said Jamie, glancing down at his watch. Three whole minutes had passed since Martha's nose had touched his.

There was an almighty screeching noise that caused Jamie to cover his ears. It was Martha summoning a taxi that had just dropped off an elderly couple and their suitcases. It had already started to drive off, so wasn't in a hurry to stop at this busy intersection. That didn't bother Martha; she just paced out into the road and blocked its path.

"You got a fare, dipshit." She shouted.

Jamie tripped off the kerb, still holding Martha's stolen twenty inside his pocket.

"London Bridge," shouted Martha to the driver.

"Tower Bridge," said Jamie opening the back door.

"Same place isn't it?" said Martha.

"No," said Jamie sliding onto the still warm seat.

He slammed his door closed and watched Martha walk alongside the glass. She gestured to roll down the window, and he did.

"It's really two different bridges?" she said.

Jamie nodded. All of a sudden, he felt immeasurably sad.

The taxi driver stared impatiently into his wing mirror for a gap in the traffic, the indicator clicking momentarily in time with 'Hard Habit to Break' on the radio.

"Thank you for all your help," said Martha. Her voice sounded quieter now. Anyone other than Jamie might have identified it faltering too.

Jamie nodded. He wasn't wired to thank people back for their thanks. Some people took it as ignorance, although it certainly wasn't. If someone thanked him, that was because they wanted to thank him. Why would he need to say anything back?

Their eyes locked again just like they had under the bar table, and Jamie managed to blink considerably less than before. My God, this woman was confusing; scary, assertive, funny, intelligent, clumsy, and the most beautiful human in the world.

Martha rested her hands on the lowered window and started to lean in.

Was she going to kiss him? What? Now? His first proper kiss aged thirty-three? Through the window of a taxi that was about to take him to his sister so he could travel thirty-six years into the future?

And then Jamie could smell Martha's alcoholic breath once more.

She was close.

And closer now.

Time stood still for Jamie.

Sadly, not for the taxi driver, who spotted his gap in the traffic and skidded away with no word of warning. The door frame nudged the tip of Martha's nose as it left her life forever. The taxi, not the nose.

That, thought Jamie, was the best kiss I never had.

Chapter Four

"Can't stop here, mate," said the cab driver as they waited for the lights to change on Tower Bridge Road.

Jamie ignored him and tried to open his door, but it was locked and controlled from the front of the vehicle to prevent people doing a runner without paying. The sensory overload of the stranger talking, the traffic noises and Huey Lewis singing 'If This Is It' on Radio 1 had neutralised all logical brain power, so he continued to try the door.

"You can't stop here; the lights are changing!"

Jamie pulled down the window and started to climb through it.

"Bleeding hell! What are you doing?" shouted the taxi driver.

His voice was lost amongst the beeping car horns from traffic passing in the opposite direction. Jamie was half in and half out, facing the cold tarmac beneath. With one final drag, he slid into a heap on the ground and then leapt up.

"I'm okay!"

Then he ran across more oncoming traffic into the darkness of the damp clusters of pedestrians making their way across the bridge.

"Oi!" shouted the driver.

He wasn't expecting Jamie to come back, so was amazed to

watch him walk straight in front of a Talbot Sunbeam that slammed to a halt with inches to spare.

Jamie thrust the twenty-pound note through the driver's window and ran off one more time toward the flood-lit mighty Tower Bridge.

He was one hour and twenty-one minutes late for his big sister, and she was going to be livid.

All he needed to do now was find a cross lady in a heavily modified Sinclair C5. That shouldn't be difficult even in the dark, as she would be swearing very loudly by now.

Chapter Five

"Nah, I've not seen anyone like this, pet," said Kenneth in his hushed Geordie tone.

Kenneth was starting his night shift when he first spotted Jamie frantically pacing Tower Bridge over and over. His job was based in the control office, usually staffed by Technical Officers whose job it was to raise and lower the iconic bridge. At 7.00 pm, he had swapped places with Lloyd and sat himself alongside the antique switches that controlled the counterweights that lifted and lowered the mighty bascules. After the third hour of watching this distressed young man, he'd realised that he was now crying, so had offered him a seat and a cup of tea from his overnight flask. Jamie had tried his best to explain his dilemma whilst attempting some seven-eleven breathing to calm his nerves. He had refused to avert his gaze from the window that overlooked the bridge and continued to scan every single figure and every single vehicle that passed by. Inside, any surface without glass or painted steel equipment had amateur photos of birds blu-tacked onto it. Kenneth was a keen spotter and loved the variety of vertebrates that he could photograph every day, despite the inner-city location of his office, as he called it. The river attracted all kinds of exciting Aves, some more common than others, and many had surely made the trip from warmer climes on the decks of boats passing through the famous bridge. His Olympus Trip

35 was always primed and hanging around his neck. The TV ads featuring celebrity photographer David Bailey in the late seventies had convinced him this point-and-shoot was worth his hard-earned cash. The fact that his hero Phil Daniels from the film Quadrophenia was in the commercial clinched the deal.

Kenneth had agreed to join the lookout on the understanding that Jamie gave him some indication of who he was looking for. In the absence of any photos of Tash, Jamie had agreed to draw her, like the artists' impressions he'd seen Nick Ross introduce on BBC's Crimewatch when he was growing up. Nick Ross fascinated Jamie, as the more Jamie lost his hair, the more he was bewildered by men who had hair options but retained the same shit hairstyle throughout their life. Who chooses a flat side parting?

Kenneth squinted again at the hand-drawn sketch in his hand, and Jamie leant in to look too. He realised Kenneth was holding it upside down, so he adjusted it accordingly, and Kenneth looked once more.

"Nah, man. It's not really helping to be honest. Are those glasses?"

"No, they're curls. She has curly hair."

"I see now. Yes. Lovely. And these are freckles, are they?"

"Paint," explained Jamie. "She had paint on her from Grandad's loft."

"I'm with you," said Kenneth kindly.

"Although she might have washed that off, so try to picture her with or without that."

The picture displayed Jamie's dyspraxia perfectly. The effort was there, but his unorthodox coordination skills meant the execution was very different to the intention. To an unkind eye, this might be the work of a seven-year-old.

"Maybe it would be better if you did a sign with her name on it and a little message where she can find you, like? I could stick it up in me window."

"You think?" Jamie looked hopeful and blew his snotty nose.

"Worth a go, man? Come on; I'll get you some more paper."

"You'll keep an eye out whilst I write? Out there?"

"Of course."

Kenneth was a man of his word, and this little guy was confused and distressed. He hated what London did to some people. He'd seen it countless times since he moved down here in the seventies. He was increasingly convinced that this lady didn't exist. This man smelled of alcohol and looked like he'd lived in his clothes for weeks. They were stained and creased. He didn't know Jamie had borrowed them from some hotel laundry just a few days before.

"Can I interest you in a Pacer, young man?" He offered the square tube of chewy mints to Jamie, who took one and set to work on his new poster.

Kenneth stepped in from the cold, and as the door closed behind him, Jamie's poster wafted in the breeze and settled back in place on the window. In heavily scrawled biro, it read:

TASH! It's JAMIE. I'm in here or will be back soon.

Sorry I was late.

JAMIE (your brother)

Kenneth hadn't mentioned that the double Jamie was possibly overkill. And the 'your brother' line, too. But if she did exist, maybe she was a bit simple, too.

"Looks champion that, man. I put one in the other office too. On the other side of the bridge, like."

Jamie smiled and held up another drawing. The gentle giant of a security guard took it from his cold hands and examined it further.

"Lovely. What's this? One of the shoes she was wearing? It's very pretty that, but."

"No," said Jamie, tapping the drawing. "That's what she's driving."

Kenneth glanced up at this pathetic figure and decided to indulge him.

"I'm with you. Like a magic slipper?"

"No. That's our time machine."

Kenneth suddenly had the expression of a man who'd invited a psychopath into his child's birthday party.

Chapter Six

"Jamie, come on, man. It's time to wake up."

Jamie had dreamed of sleeping in a hut in Dusseldorf with a bunch of builders. He'd been cold but felt secure and could still taste the sugar from the Pacers and the cocktails on his lips.

Kenneth's gentle tone had broken his slumber, and he realised the thinly sprung bed that dug into his back was actually a set of keys in Kenneth's coat pocket which he'd kindly wrapped around his homeless visitor when he curled on the floor to rest.

"You missed a canny yellowhammer an hour or so ago." Kenneth tapped his Olympus.

Jamie either didn't understand or didn't care.

"Any sign of her?" said Jamie sitting up too quickly and banging his head on the control desk.

"Ooh! Steady man! You alright?"

Jamie ignored him, oblivious to the imprint of the steel rivets that had made an impression on his creased forehead.

"My sister, any sign?"

"Nah, man. I'm sorry. But I'm sure she'll find you. Here..." Kenneth handed over the final cup of tea from his flask. Jamie thanked him and then spilt most of it down his front. He dried himself off with Kenneth's jacket.

"Listen, my shift's over, and you cannot stay here all day. The tech officer's a bit of a stickler for rules and all that. Yer know?"

"Okay, yeah, no, yeah," said Jamie, finding his feet and stretching. "Thanks for your help, Kenneth."

"It's nay bother, mate. I just hope you get yourself sorted soon."

Kenneth offered his hand to shake, which Jamie always struggled with. He sort of held it for a bit and then let go before opening the door onto the bridge pavement.

"And take care of yourself, yeah?" said Kenneth kindly.

"Take care of yourself," repeated Jamie as he stepped outside into the chilly morning air.

"Have you got somewhere to go?"

"Yes," replied Jamie.

"Where?"

Jamie scanned the ground. "There," he said, pointing to the pavement one metre away from the office.

He took a sideways step, leant against the painted sky-blue railings, and then waved at Kenneth from his new home. His wafting arm knocked a pedestrian in the face.

"Ow!"

Jamie looked up to see Sab squinting from the surprise assault. She pulled off her Walkman headphones and rested them around her neck. The two orange sponges spilt 'Footloose' into Jamie's kaleidoscope of confusion.

"Sab?" said Jamie.

She looked scared and confused; then recognition filled her face.

"Video tape thief!"

She smiled, and Jamie did too.

"Are you alright? They threw you in a car!" She looked concerned. The last time she'd seen this man was outside Woolworths when he'd been dragged into the back of a Mercedes and kidnapped with his sister.

"I'm fine," said Jamie, realising it would be too much to change history yet again. "I'm waiting for my sister."

"You look terrible," said Sab, fumbling for the stop button on the Walkman suspended on a nylon belt around her waist.

"Thank you," said Jamie. "I've been sleeping on some keys and need a poo."

"You've been sleeping rough?"

"Sort of," Jamie said before waving awkwardly at Kenneth through the glass.

"Listen, I'm going to see Maureen's husband. He needs some help with his books. Why don't you come with me? Get yourself warmed up?"

Jamie was about to protest but then spotted his poster proudly displayed in the office window.

"Okay," he replied. "But I can't be long."

"No problem," said Sab as they set off together towards the south of the river.

"I've lost my sister. We were supposed to meet here."

"I'm sorry to hear that."

"I need a poo."

"Yes, you said."

They walked in silence for a moment.

"I've only had one poo in 1984."

Sab glared at him as they continued their walk, and he continued to talk.

"How do you know where Raymond works?"

Chapter Seven

Over the coming days, Jamie became a familiar sight to the locals, commuters, and tourists on Tower Bridge. He spent many hours pacing the length of it, stopping for teas and coffees with Kenneth on the night shifts. The posters changed once Jamie had access to Raymond's stationery drawer; he was becoming quite creative with his use of green ink. He used this pen for his flyers too. He handed these out to anyone that agreed to take one from him, which weren't many. He soon realised that you became invisible if people perceived you lived on the street. Raymond and his wife Maureen became regular visitors and soon convinced Jamie that he could afford some time off his search. His posters in both offices on Tower Bridge remained in place, and his sister would surely have to pass at least one of them when she finally arrived to take him home. They both expressed concern about the onset of winter and the inclement weather for sleeping outside until she did. He eventually relented and accepted their kind invitation to spend one night in the box room at Gaywood Close.

He never moved out.

Chapter Eight

"To Bombay, a travelling circus came..." sang Michael Algar from the Hitachi speakers. He was probably known better as Olga, his nickname in the Toy Dolls, his punk band. Olga was a talented musician, earning royalties from Ready Brek breakfast cereal commercials and the theme tune to the ITV kids' music show *Razzmatazz*. However, 1984 had seen his band's biggest commercial success with a cover version of 'Nelly The Elephant'. The appeal was undoubtedly the "wooooooooooooah!" crescendo from silence to euphoria at the start of each chorus. It was hard to dance to at a school disco but ensured absolute chaos when the drums arrived. Many flailing arms had caused fights on dance floors at Christmas parties across comprehensives all over the UK.

"Turn this down, Raymond. It sounds like a building site," said Maureen. "He won't sleep through this."

"Don't worry about me," said Jamie.

Raymond leapt up and lowered the volume on the music centre.

"I was talking about your nephew," replied Maureen, gazing at the baby sleeping by his mother's side.

Raymond inched back to his seat.

"More," said Maureen.

Raymond returned to the Hitachi one more time to dip the volume further.

"It was the Moray Eel, by the way, Tash," said Raymond.

"What?" asked Tash.

Raymond gestured to his opened Encyclopaedia Britannica before leaning in to read. "They have a pharyngeal jaw. I think that's how you pronounce it." He tried again. "Pharyn-geal."

The room fell silent.

"What even is that?" Tash's irritation was rising in her voice.

"I'm not sure; there's usually an illustration. But it means that if you got your hand stuck, you'd really struggle to get it back."

Tash stared at him, so he felt the need to say it one more time.

"Pharyngeal."

"How hard could it possibly be to just come back in time thirty-six years and spend a nice Christmas with some new friends?" said Tash.

"You need to stop playing the victim here, 'cos I'm the one with my life on the line," replied Martha, keeping one suspicious eye on a slender box of dates with 'Eat Me' printed on the lid.

"Well, it's not really your *life*, is it?" Said Tash. "Worst case scenario will be a bit of prison, no?"

"No," said Martha. "The CSI report states double homicide on the most southern of the Four Brothers, Lake Champlain. So, they could send me to the chair."

"Nope, none of that makes any sense," said Tash. "Do you have any wine, Maureen? I'm suddenly regretting trying to be a nice person."

"You're welcome to my piss?" said Martha offering her an almost full glass of Pineapple Quosh that sat alongside her untouched Anadin tablets. She glanced at Jamie. "I didn't get used to the taste. Sorry."

"The chair?" asked Maureen.

"Electric chair," explained Jamie.

"They can electrocute you if they arrest you on a lake?" asked Raymond.

"They can if you're one mile west over the county line," Martha replied. "They say I murdered two people just inside New York State border. If they stitched me up in Vermont, I'd be looking at a life stretch, but as it stands, they want to send me to the chair."

"I thought they all stopped that nastiness? Years ago?" said Maureen.

"Nastiness?" said Martha.

"Killing prisoners, all the states ditched it didn't they?"

"Yes," said Martha, with a tone that suggested a caveat. "But some states want it back, and New York state is one of them."

"Well, it doesn't mean they will," said Jamie.

"Great. Maybe I'll just die in prison of old age, then."

"Who did you kill?" asked Tash.

"Nobody! I was in bed!" said Martha.

"On the island?" asked Jamie.

"I've never been to the island. They set me up."

Tash absorbed this news and then turned to Maureen. "Any developments on the wine front?"

"We're not big wine drinkers, to be honest," replied Raymond. "I can put the kettle on?"

Tash delved deep into her red holdall, and after a lot of rustling and clinking sounds, she held up a bottle of Pinot Grigio Blush. "Corkscrew?"

Raymond squirmed. "Erm...."

"Tell me you have a fucking corkscrew! That's a staple! Tell me you have a corkscrew?"

Tash looked more shocked by the corkscrew developments than any amount of murder revelations.

"No, we do have a corkscrew... Don't we, Maureen?" He started opening drawers in their wall unit and stared inside.

"If you were in bed, why do they think you killed someone?" asked Jamie, his heartbeat still thumping in his ears since the return of this beautiful American. He could remember the nights he smelt her ever-fading perfume on his stolen eighties suit.

Martha took a deep breath and looked into the eyes glaring

back at her (and Raymond's arse cheeks as he delved into his spacious storage facility).

"It was the day I came home from London," said Martha.

"Back in October?" asked Jamie. "That's when the murders happened?"

"Bingo!" said Raymond, and he stood up, holding a bright red Swiss army knife.

"Fuck's that?" asked Tash.

"It's a Swiss army knife," said Raymond. "Everything you'll ever need on there," he added with a smile before handing it over to a confused Tash.

"You need to open it up a bit," Raymond gestured with his hands.

"Can everyone shut up for a moment?" Maureen decided enough was enough. She even clapped her hands when she said it. The meandering nonsensical chatter had finally pushed her over the edge, and The Toy Dolls weren't helping. Happily, they were about to give way to Alison Moyet, and Maureen's fingers always clicked to 'Invisible'; she liked the bells, so she would surely soon be cooling down. "It's two days until Christmas, and this is all a bit much. We've got nothing in the fridge, we've got nothing wrapped, and we've just survived an assassination attempt."

"Interesting order there," said Tash.

"We've got cheese in the fridge, darling," said Raymond, remembering the crate of Canadian imports they had rammed in there since Martha reappeared.

"And you can't wrap anything because you haven't got any wrapping paper," said Jamie, "nor any gifts."

"Helpful?" said Tash to her brother with a questioning face.

"What's your point?" asked Martha.

"My point is, our lives have been turned upside down over and over since we met these two," said Maureen, and she pointed to the siblings, "and now you," she pointed at Martha at this stage, "you, are about to get us all arrested – again!"

She managed to say "again" in a pitch that surely woke any sleeping residents of Battersea Dogs home four miles north of them. There was a respectful silence at the outburst. Then Tash broke it.

"The fuck's this?"

She held up a slotted screwdriver amongst an ensemble of small knives she'd unhinged from Raymond's Swiss army knife.

"That's a slotted screwdriver."

Tash looked at it and then at the bottle of wine in her hand.

"But you can use it to remove stones from horses' shoes too." Raymond genuinely thought this information would help.

"Right. As it's Christmas, you get ONE benefit of the doubt," said Maureen to Martha. "Take us back to the beginning. And DO NOT LIE."

It wasn't often that Maureen's face went quite so crimson, and everyone seemed to respect this fact. Her folding her arms added even more drama. She'd seen Krystle Carrington use this confrontational body language to significant effect on Dynasty last week. She had innocently asked Raymond if he thought the actress who played Krystle was pretty, and he'd struggled to convince her that he didn't. In fact, he had stammered for the rest of the evening, so that pissed her off too.

"I never lie," said Martha.

She realised this was quite a bold statement, given the suspicious faces glaring back at her.

"I never lie when cops are involved," she added.

The low hum of muttering filled the room with things like...

... "not completely true, really,"

... and "you smuggled yourself abroad in some cheese,"

... and "well, no smoke without fire."

"I never lie about killing people!" shouted Martha.

Chapter Nine

"The white zone is for the immediate loading and unloading of passengers only," came the clinical female voice over the speaker system outside the arrivals hall at Burlington International Airport, Vermont.

Martha yawned as she dragged her bags across the concrete sidewalk that led to the taxi rank. She had flown through the night to JFK in New York and then transferred for her final journey home after the strangest trip of her life. A quadruple Bloody Mary had helped her descend into an uncomfortable five-hour sleep, where her anxiety dream – something to do with a stalker – proved less horrific than her actual life when she awoke and remembered her failure in London. How the hell had her rendezvous with Bee gone wrong? She couldn't possibly have failed at her task. Her grandfather's will had made her errand clear – although not perfectly clear, and certainly not perfectly simple – but nonetheless, she had followed the instructions to the letter. Why wasn't the lawyer where she said she would be?

And now she had the headache from hell.

Her outbound from Heathrow had an eleven-hour delay, which meant she missed her connecting flight at JFK, so she could drive six hours to Burlington or wait six hours for the final flight out of New York. She chose the latter and now found herself dehydrated, bloated and strangely hungry at 8.15 pm in her hometown.

She'd hoped to get a cab to Eikenberry and Lowe to have things out with Harvey and Bee. Why on earth hadn't she met her? And why were they STILL not answering their phones when she tried them from JFK?

Now she was resigned to another night without answers. She walked to the front of the line of yellow cabs waiting for fares. She opened the back door, tossed in her bags, and slid along the long bench seat before closing the door shut.

"Where to?" asked the driver, barely glancing over his shoulder.

"Five Sisters," replied Martha, as a UPS van cautiously mounted the wide walkway beside her and blocked the glaring light from the arrivals foyer.

"Street?" asked the driver, punching his fingers on his pay meter.

"Golden," but before she could say "Place", the opposite rear door opened, a man climbed in, and the door slammed shut.

"Wait up," he instructed the driver, who complied.

Martha looked like she'd seen a ghost.

The man grinned stupidly before reaching into his pocket, then fell off the bench seat into the footwell. He was trapped, but after some considerable fumbling and muttering, he managed to lift the metal in his hand and hold it towards Martha. Her reaction wasn't what he had expected.

"You gotta be fucking kidding."

Chapter Ten

"You have a boyfriend?" asked Jamie before blushing and feeling suddenly hot, despite the loud clicking of the single radiator as it cooled in the lounge.

Tash allowed herself the tiniest of smiles.

So, he does like her.

"Ex," replied Martha before naming him. "Louis."

"What was he pointing at you?" asked Raymond in a voice that suggested he didn't really want to know as this sounded too much like an episode of *Tales of The Unexpected* that had haunted him since the summer. A hitchhiker befriended a driver, and they both drove deserted streets whilst the radio news revealed a murderer was on the loose. It had been too much for Maureen; she'd insisted on watching *Pot Black* instead. There was no way she would sleep after watching something so scary; she much preferred fat men with fags spilling beer on a snooker table. But Raymond had already pieced it together. The hitchhiker was the murderer.

Or the driver. One of them was. Probably.

Either way, he didn't like the sound of this curious man that leapt into Martha's taxicab.

"An engagement ring," answered Martha.

"You're engaged?" Jamie didn't mean for his voice to falter when he said this, but what could he do?

Martha took a slug of her Quosh and immediately regretted it.

"Are ANY of these corkscrews?" asked Tash, holding up a myriad of steel blades and attachments in her hand.

Raymond squinted over at her.

"He said he was sorry he'd missed my birthday," said Martha, "Jerk."

"Well, it's quite normal to forget a birthday from time to time," said Raymond.

The look Maureen gave him said it all.

"No, of course it's not," said Raymond. "Terrible business."

"He had an excuse," explained Martha.

"See?" said Raymond, suddenly perking up. "He had a reasonable excuse, Maureen."

"He was in jail."

"Oh," said Raymond before silence landed again.

"Raymond," whispered Maureen badly. "Raymond."

Raymond looked over at his wife, who whispered again. "Ask her what he was in for."

"Well, she can hear you, Maureen. Why don't you ask her?"

Maureen had more expressions than Dulux had colours. And the one fixed on Raymond right now was brutal, so Raymond cleared his throat and started stammering at Martha.

"What was he er, what was... What did he... You know.... Why was he...?"

"Wow! This is going well, Raymond," said Tash. "You've asked difficult questions before, haven't you?"

"The papers said DUI," said Martha.

"Oh God," said Raymond with a high-pitched shriek. He silenced himself with the back of his fist in his mouth.

"What's that? What's DUI? Is that bad?" asked Maureen.

"Well, it's ... dead on arrival, isn't it?" replied Raymond, shocked to hear his own voice say the words.

"Is that the American spelling?" said Tash. "Seriously, is there a fucking corkscrew on this thing?"

"Driving under the influence," said Martha. "Weed."

Maureen must have further scrunched her already crumpled

forehead as Martha expanded on this.

"Cannabis."

"Isn't that what Paul McCartney from Wings got arrested for?" asked Raymond, before adding, "Marijuana?" He pronounced the J, which tickled Jamie and Tash. "It was on John Craven's Newsround."

Martha shrugged.

"Wings!" snorted Tash under giggles.

"Stop showing off about drugs, Raymond!" said Maureen. "You're giving out all the wrong impressions. What if we're bugged?"

"Bugged?" replied Raymond, peering under the frame of their G-Plan coffee table.

"You're engaged?" asked Jamie again.

"No," replied Martha.

"So, you turned him down?"

"Kind of."

"What does *kind of* mean?"

"He drove us to a diner," said Martha. "I was sleep deprived and hungover. But mostly hungry and broke. So, I thought I'd let him down gently after he picked up the tab. So that's what I did."

"My kind of girl," said Tash before lifting her fingers out of the way of a blade that snapped back into the Swiss army knife.

"And then I kind of slept with him."

Maureen looked at the floor. Jamie shuffled in his chair and swallowed.

"He took it well then?" asked Tash, examining her nail gels to ensure the blade hadn't chipped them. "The turn down?"

"Maybe I was a little obtuse," shrugged Martha. "I'd had a few martinis."

Tash slammed her bottle down on the glass-topped coffee table and delved into her massive Nanny McPhee bag once more. Clinking noises ensued.

"I don't mean to be rude," said Raymond, "but does this have anything to do with why you're here?"

Martha nodded. "It has everything to do with why I'm here. Everything."

Chapter Eleven

Martha's headache was pounding in perfect synch with an unabated knocking. Opening her eyes, she lifted her head to read the digital alarm clock. Then she realised that the winter storms were back, with the torrents of rain pounding on the sidewalk outside. Along with the knocking and the hangover, this was a tsunami of disorientating noise.

She peered between the Venetian blinds covering the small window by her bed and was surprised to find herself squinting in the morning sunlight.

Then she remembered last night, and things started to make sense.

The rain wasn't rain. That was Louis in her shower. The knocking was someone at the front door. Maybe Harvey? Maybe Bee?

She pulled herself out of bed and slid on her dressing gown before tiptoeing to the front door to prevent her brain rattling in her aching head.

"Enough with the knocking. I'm coming!"

The knocking didn't stop.

Martha walked past her discarded clothes that lay on top of the mail she'd kicked out of the way on their amorous route to her bedroom. She started to undo the many locks on the unloved door, struggling with the bolt at the top.

"I said enough with the freaking knocking! This better be important."

As the door flung open, she could only muster the energy to whisper, "Frankie?"

Lieutenant Francis Duffy stood on her doorstep, his face bloated and red from crying. Tears continued to fall down his ample cheeks.

"Frankie? No. Tell me no?"

"I'm sorry, Martha," he replied and then sobbed like a baby.

"Come on in," she said kindly and placed an arm gently around his shoulder as he stepped inside.

"Now face the wall and keep your hands over your head against the wall," sobbed Duffy.

She did as he asked. "You need to get better at this, Frankie; you're gonna give yourself a heart attack. And you said wall twice."

"Martha Hobson, you are under arrest. You have the right to remain silent. Anything you say can be used against you in court..."

"Are you still reading this shit?" said Martha, interrupting his flow as she spotted a little typed card in his hand.

He placed the card behind his back and tried to continue without it.

"Anything you say," said Duffy.

"You missed a bit," said Martha.

"No, I didn't."

"You missed the attorney part."

"I said that part."

"You didn't. Get your script back," said Martha gesturing behind his back.

He casually glanced at it and then placed it behind him again, wiping his nose with the back of his hand.

"You have the right to talk to an attorney..." He was interrupted again.

"What's the charge, Frankie?" Martha was genuinely amazed to see him.

Duffy took a deep breath to calm himself and then stammered his reply. He was more nervous than her.

"I can't say."

Martha turned around to face him. "I'm clean, Frankie, you know that."

"Against the wall," said the policeman, hoping Martha would comply. She did.

His hands reluctantly fumbled around her loosely tied robe to identify any weapons secreted about her person.

"Should I light some candles first? Set the mood?"

"Sorry, I need to do this part." He sounded mortified.

"I know you do. I know. But you gotta stop crying every time you arrest me."

Martha turned around and opened her robe fully, causing the overweight father of three to avert his eyes in any direction he could think of. After trying the Springsteen poster next to the wall-mounted phone, the pile of discarded clothes by his feet, then the single lightbulb hanging from the cracked ceiling, he settled on his scuffed leather shoes.

"No weapons, no drugs, no panties." She was exasperated by the developments but knew this behaviour would stop Duffy in his tracks.

"Understood, ma'am. Please dress."

As she tied her robe up, she walked back to her bedroom, muttering over her shoulder.

"Quit calling me ma'am. You make me feel sixty. You want a coffee? Some water?"

"Stay where you are," said the lieutenant, resting his hand on his gun.

"It's me, Frankie. It's me! What's this all about?"

"I'm sorry, Martha, but it doesn't look good this time. You did something bad, something real bad."

"What? Tell me what? What the fuck's going on?"

"It just doesn't seem like you, Martha. I can't understand why you would do that."

"What did I do?"

She handed him a tissue, and he blew his nose.

"That filled up quickly. Need another?"

"I have enlarged mucus ducts. It's a family thing. I just had a CT scan to confirm it."

He blew into the second tissue that Martha gifted him.

"You mean glands?" she asked.

"I do mean glands, excuse me. It wasn't my intention to mislead you. I'm a little overwhelmed right now. I believe the glands feed into the ducts."

She handed him a third tissue; his eyes were red. He was unmistakably crying.

"Where did this happen?" said Martha.

"The UVM Medical Center."

"The what?"

"The University of Vermont Medical Center," said Duffy.

"When?"

"About seven or eight weeks ago."

"Are we talking about the crime you're arresting me for?"

"No. The CT scan. For the glands."

"Frankie, I'm trying to look like I give a shit about your fucked up nose, but you just accused me of some kind of serious crime."

"I'm sorry, I misunderstood."

"Is this drugs, again?"

Duffy looked at his shoes again.

"Where was this?" she asked.

There was a pause.

"May I borrow another tissue?"

"Borrow? I don't want the fricking things back!" said Martha as she tossed the Kleenex box at him.

"Thank you."

"Frankie. For the love of God, where did this happen?"

"I can't say until we interview you," he replied, examining the inside of his latest tissue. "Jeez, that's a lot of mucus. I think this may be a dairy issue too."

"When was this?"

"Overnight."

She released a massive sigh of relief.

"You scared me there, Frankie!" said Martha, slapping him around the head. "You scared the shit out of me! Why the hell did you do that? Do you want coffee?"

He glanced around the room for a trash can to place his snotty collection of tissues.

"Excuse me?"

"I was here all night. I have a witness and everything."

"You need to be careful what you say."

"Follow me," said Martha, and for the first time, the police officer dropped his guard and walked behind her manic pink hair into her bedroom, turning to look at the bathroom and the sound of running water.

"Check the shower," said Martha.

"Pardon me?"

"My fiancé is in there. I was with him all night."

"You got engaged, Martha?"

"Well, I kinda turned him down, but the jury's out. Just look in the bathroom, Frankie!"

Duffy considered this for a moment and then looked at his hands full of tissues. Martha opened both her palms, and he placed them into them. She grimaced as the mound of mucus and paper wet her skin, so she decided to let them drop onto the rug by the foot of her bed. Duffy knocked on the bathroom door.

"Vermont State Police Department. Please come to the door."

"Just go in," said Martha, annoyed by the procedures. She opened the door and shoved him towards it. "Nothing you haven't seen before."

"Coming inside, sir, please raise your hands," he said reluctantly. He rested his palm firmly on his gun and slowly shuffled towards the sound of the waterfall.

Martha dropped down onto her bed, dried the snot off her palms onto her unmade bed sheets and let out a massive sigh. At least she would soon be sipping orange juice and feeding her hangover with pancakes.

Duffy peered his head back into the bedroom.

"Is this a joke?"

Martha sat up straight. "What?"

"Get dressed; we're taking you in."

"What?" Martha was on her feet now, walking over to the bathroom. Inside she saw lots of steam, lots of water, and lots of emptiness.

"Louis?" said Martha before spinning around a few times. "Louis?"

"Your ex, Louis?"

"Yes!"

"Martha, you know he's been in jail since July."

"No, they let him out! He came to meet me at the airport, and we went for dinner."

Duffy stepped back into the bathroom and turned off the faucets that fed the shower head.

"He proposed to me! He proposed! I'll get the ring!" She was frantic.

Martha remembered the moment Louis fell off the back seat of the taxi and offered up a golden ring with the tiniest solitaire diamond she had seen in her whole privileged life.

She spotted the leather box by the side of her rumpled bed and grabbed it.

"You coming out?" she asked Duffy, who was still in the bathroom.

"The steam is good for my sinuses. You mind showing me in here?" he replied.

Martha walked through the tiny bathroom and joined Duffy, sitting on the side of her bath with a towel over his head. He was rubbing the side of his abdomen.

"You OK?" asked Martha.

"Grumbling appendix," he answered. "Stress and mucus make it worse."

"Don't let it explode in my bathroom."

"Thanks for your concern. People can die from an exploded appendix; did you know that?"

"I did not know that."

"You get appendicitis in jail... they take that very seriously.

You could be hospitalised within ninety minutes."

"I'm not going to jail."

"I hope not."

"And I don't got appendicitis."

"No," replied Duffy before snorting in a chest full of snot. "That's got it."

Martha looked repulsed. "Here," she said, handing over the jewellery case.

Duffy fumbled around in mid-air with both hands, unable to see from his resting place beneath the towel. Martha guided his hands towards the box and pulled it into his vapour tent.

"Are you taking drugs again?" he asked.

"What? You know I'm not! I might have got drunk last night, but martinis are still legal in Vermont, right?"

Duffy lowered his towel. His face was red, and his thinning hair was now wet and sticking to his head. In one hand was the opened leather box; in the other was a steel can ring-pull.

Martha stared at it.

And then stared some more.

Then she grabbed the jewellery box and pulled out the lining. Still no ring.

"No. This isn't right. Louis! Louis!" she continued shouting his name as she walked back into her bedroom.

"He slept next to me. His clothes are... His clothes... Where the fuck are his clothes?"

Duffy followed her back into the bedroom.

"He parked his pick-up outside!" said Martha, opening the wooden Venetian blinds by her headboard. "He kerbed it, we laughed, and he parked it on the grass!"

Outside was a rogue dog arching his back to take a difficult dump in the middle of her tiny lawn. No pick-up. Just Duffy's police car.

"Martha, he's been inside since July."

Martha sat down on her bed, and Duffy started to examine the floor, bending to look under the bed.

"What are you looking for?" asked Martha.

Duffy spied something by the doorway to the hall and walked over to pick it up. It was his cue card.

"Martha Hobson, you are under arrest. You have the right to remain silent. Anything you say can be used against you in court..."

Martha placed her hands over her ears and started to cry. Duffy began to sob too.

Chapter Twelve

"You said you were going to make trifle?" said Tash, looking over at Maureen.

"And?" replied Maureen.

"How do you make yours?"

"Why are you asking me that now?" replied Maureen. "We're hearing about Martha's murders."

"I didn't do any murders," replied Martha.

"Oh, Maureen's is a very nice trifle," said Raymond. "Swiss roll soaked in sherry at the bottom, custard..."

"You had me at sherry, Raymond," said Tash. "Where is it?"

Raymond looked at Maureen, who considered the general mood.

"OK, I'll get the QC," she said. "But don't go crazy with it."

Maureen left to find her hidden stash in the kitchen pantry as Michael Jackson's 'Beat It' filled the brief silence. Despite being released in 1982, 'Thriller' had been the best-selling album of 1983 and now 1984 too, and any of his nine singles from it were rarely far from any radio station. Raymond had never heard the record's second half, as Maureen always switched it off whenever Eddie Van Halen started his 'horrible' guitar solo in the middle. So it was a bit of a change for him.

"So, you're NOT engaged?" asked Jamie. Suddenly he seemed far happier.

"I'm not engaged," replied Martha.

"But he did propose with a diamond?"

"Maybe not a diamond. Looked like some piece of shit from the Stop & Shop gum machine. But I didn't dream that part. He proposed. All part of one massive plan to steal my money and silence me forever."

"He set you up?" asked Tash.

"No, that bitch did. The one who took my inheritance when we found your little go-kart thing."

"Who?" asked Jamie.

"The one who asked me to take your Polaroid. She took it off me in that basement."

"The friendly one in TV Centre?" asked Jamie.

"You'd be friendly if you were about to become eleven million dollars richer."

"So, she killed someone and framed you?" said Tash.

"She killed my grandpa's lawyer on his boat and some other lady too."

"Who?" Jamie was inching to the edge of his seat now.

"Well, the cops say it was *her* body. They say she's dead and Harvey's dead. And I did it."

"Why would you do that?" asked Raymond.

"Harvey told me I had to come here and meet Bee in a café. I did, and she told me I had to take a Polaroid of these two and you so that I would get my inheritance. That's all I know."

"But you did it," said Jamie. "We did it."

"Not according to Virginia State Police. The records show I must have failed cause my grandaddy's inheritance went to an unknown charity. They say I was so pissed I came home and murdered both lawyers."

"Did you?" asked Jamie.

"I can't believe you asked that." Martha looked hurt.

"You were with your fiancé," said Tash, peering towards the kitchen. "Where's Maureen? Is the wine cellar far?"

"Raymond!" shouted Maureen coldly. "Come and reach the glasses for me."

Raymond leapt to his feet to join his wife in the kitchen. He whispered to Maureen. "I'll sort that now, darling; you go and sit down."

Maureen stomped back into the lounge and sat down.

Tash smiled at her. Maureen folded her arms.

"Turn this racket down, Jamie; we'll have no head banging in here. What a terrible noise."

Jamie did as he was told, just as M.J. started to sing again.

"Coming," shouted Raymond, pushing the door open and wheeling in a golden-coloured cocktail trolley. The solid rubber wheels kept snagging on the carpet pile.

"Raymond! What on earth are you doing?" said Maureen.

"Well, I thought we said we'd get the sherry, darling?"

"Not the trolley! This isn't a soirée!" Maureen was absolutely appalled.

Tash leant over and grabbed the bottle of QC that sat amongst some tiny sherry glasses with coloured hand-painted polka dots on their sides. QC was sold as English sherry for years in the seventies and eighties before the Jerez region of Spain put their flip-flops down and insisted only Sherry from Jerez could be called Sherry, and the British stuff must be called fortified wine. Maureen loved the TV ads every Christmas with an arrogant aristocrat and his comedic butler sipping Croft Original, so she had placed that on her shopping list. Sadly Croft Original wasn't on offer for £2.35 when Raymond went to Victoria Wine shop, so QC it was. Maureen hated it when Raymond went off list and let him know by swapping his towel for a flannel the next time they went swimming at Clapham baths. He wouldn't make substitutions again if he realised the knock-on effects. He had to learn somehow.

Tash couldn't care less if it was from Andalucía or Accrington and was madly tugging at the metal foil still wrapped around the cork stopper.

"Got any peanuts on there, Raymond? Or Duty-Free scratch cards?" Tash was lifting a lace cloth to peer at the empty lower shelf. "Doors to manual."

"I thought as we were having a social gathering," said

Raymond before Maureen interrupted his attempt to explain his momentary madness.

"We are, but those are the soirée glasses!" said Maureen.

"Are they?"

The sound of the small cork popping free from the QC silenced everyone.

"I'm good from the bottle if everyone else is?" Tash raised it to her lips.

"You'll do no such thing," said Maureen. "Just pour it, Raymond; we'll discuss this later."

Tash handed the bottle over, and he lifted the first glass to his eye line and gently poured. It took no time to fill as the glass was tiny. As he was closest to Tash, he handed her the first glass. She upended the contents into her mouth and held it out again, empty.

"Fill her up."

Raymond looked for Maureen's permission, but she simply closed her eyes in despair. He refilled Tash's glass and started on the others.

"Are these for kids' cocktail parties? Or?" said Tash holding up the miniature drink.

"I thought you said you didn't accept the proposal?" Jamie was back on track with Martha.

"I didn't, but I was with him through the night. Or so I thought," she looked briefly sad. "He did a sunrise slink."

"But the policeman said he was in prison?" said Jamie.

"An inside job. Louis was in on it, probably on Bee's payroll. The cops found the remains of two bodies and pointed their fingers at me. And my alibi is bullshit cos my ex was in prison the whole damn time."

"Should we get my Parker pen to make some notes?" asked Raymond handing a QC to Jamie. "This is all a bit confusing. I'm better when I see things written down."

"The woman lawyer stole her money," said Maureen pointing at Martha.

"Bee," Martha nodded.

"And paid her ex to distract her whilst someone else killed two people. One was the man lawyer..."

"Harvey," said Martha.

"And the other was some poor innocent woman that the police assume is this Bee woman."

"Correct!" said Martha, accepting a glass from Raymond before sniffing the intensely dark drink. "Jeez. How long has this been in the bottle?"

"Then they got someone to say they saw her doing it," Maureen pointed at Martha again, "and arrested her."

"That's excellent, Maureen!" said Raymond. "Thank you!"

"That is quite a nice summary, actually," said Tash, holding out her glass for a third top-up. Raymond spotted and complied before pouring a drink for his wife.

"Well, I have seen every episode of *Crown Court* bar one," said Maureen, and if she hadn't been cradling the smallest glass of fortified wine known to all of humankind, she would have certainly folded her arms at this magnificent boast.

The three younger people all looked bewildered by this revelation.

"She was at the chiropodist for her bunions," said Raymond. "We tried to change the time, but we couldn't." He thought this might clear up any confusion. "So she missed the final episode."

"They don't need to know that. Stop talking."

"Why do you assume it wasn't Bee that was found with this Harvey guy?" asked Jamie, spilling his sherry down his front.

"Don't get any of that on the chair, Jamie," said Maureen.

"I don't think it will make it down that far," said Tash. "I sneeze more than these things hold."

She really did hate these glasses.

"Bee's not dead," said Martha. "I'm sure of it."

In a moment of beautiful serendipity, Simon Le Bon sang 'Every minute I keep finding clues that you leave behind.'

Chapter Thirteen

"Second from the left," said the taxi driver with absolute confidence.

Duffy looked crestfallen.

"You sure?"

"Course, I'm sure, the pink hair and the cussin'. Definitely second from the left."

Duffy was in a police viewing room with the taxi driver, who hadn't stopped chewing his blueberry gum since he arrived. The warm sweet smell was infused with some garlic from whatever this man had chosen for lunch, and Duffy didn't want this to take longer than needed. Martha was standing in a row of twenty-something women on the other side of a large window. Duffy looked over at Martha and back at the driver.

"And when you say left, do you mean,..." but he was interrupted.

"You saying I don't know my left from my right? You think I drive cabs because I'm dumb?"

The blueberry smell was very close to Duffy's face now, as were the garlicky lips.

Duffy leant backwards and stammered a little.

"I'm not saying that. I just know a lot of people get confused."

"Confused? So, I'm confused now? Who's under investigation here, fat boy?"

Martha laughed at this insult, and the driver glanced over at her.

"She can hear us?"

"Erm, yes, we had a problem with the glass, and it er..." said Duffy looking at some notes on the desk beside them. "It's getting refitted on Tuesday."

"What?" said the driver, holding out his palm to rest it on the glass, but instead, it passed right through the window frame into the line-up room. Now the other women were laughing too.

"She can see me?" The driver's voice was getting higher now.

"Well, it's no big deal, really," said Duffy. "And you're saying that's left?"

With this, Duffy pointed to the right of the line-up.

"No! It's her!" The driver was almost kissing Duffy now as he barked in his face. "Pink hair lady!"

Duffy leant down to press an intercom button and spoke into a tiny microphone.

"You can all leave now," reverberated through some muffled speakers above the ensemble. "Exit left, please."

"Which is left?" asked Martha, causing more laughs from the line-up.

Duffy didn't bother using the intercom for his reply.

"Your left," he said, pointing to the door. The women set off through it.

"You know he's talking out of his ass? I was with Louis; we ate enchiladas, drank martinis, then did some squat thrusts in the cucumber patch," said Martha before being silenced by the friendly but assertive guard who looked like she believed her. The door closed as she was taken back to her cell.

"You picked her up at Burlington Arrivals and drove her where?" asked Duffy as he turned to the fruity stench.

"We drove east to Austin Drive, South Side."

"You didn't stop?"

"We didn't stop."

"You remember the address? The destination?"

"1920 South Cove Road. Some piece of real estate. Pool. Lakeside. There was a boat."

Duffy wrote down the address needlessly. He knew it already.

"Was that the boat?" asked the driver. "The one they died in?"

Duffy looked like he'd been hit by a greyhound bus. The phone alongside his notes started to vibrate as the single shrill bell sounded. He picked up the grey receiver.

"Duffy."

He listened intently to the voice on the other side, then spoke.

"That's bullshit! I don't believe anyone would watch a DUI the whole night. Why the hell would they do that?"

He paused.

"Hello?"

He looked at the phone in his hands.

"Hello?"

"I think they hung up," said the taxi driver.

Duffy glared back at this witness, now happily smiling at him.

"Yes, thank you. You can go now."

His face was pale now. He'd been told to arrest Martha for arson and criminal damage. Why had this taxi driver said someone had died? And why the hell would a cop watch her ex-boyfriend through the night?

Chapter Fourteen

Tash stifled another yawn.

"Am I boring you?" asked Martha.

"A bit, if I'm honest," said Tash with the brutal honesty she saved for those moments when she realised she'd made another terrible decision and just wanted to move things on a bit.

"Tash," protested Jamie.

"I'm just saying, there's a lot to take in, so can we just get the top line? Why is she here and all that?"

"Harvey had told his wife, his widow, that Bee had arrived at their house for a meeting. The meeting was on his boat with a new client."

"Sounds like a big boat," said Raymond.

"This was a fifty-three-foot Burger," said Martha.

"Sounds like a Big Mac," said Tash.

"It was found burnt out on the Four Brothers Islands. Just the steel shell of the yacht and smoking crumbs of bone. The killer used an accelerant."

"How do they know it's them? DNA?" said Tash.

"D.N. what?" said Raymond.

"Is that not a thing yet?" Tash looked surprised. "Is it still just fingerprints and stuff?"

"They found Harvey's gold tooth," said Martha.

"And what about the woman?" Maureen surprised herself that she was getting hooked on this little story.

"They found her..." she concentrated as she said this from memory, "Vitallium prostheses."

"Well, that's a triple word score at Scrabble if ever I heard one," said Raymond.

"A hip replacement," said Martha before something caught her eye.

Jamie raised his hand.

"Question coming in from the man on the front row," said Tash before topping up her glass from the QC.

"If they identified both bodies, including Bee, how can she have done it?"

Martha turned to him and smiled.

"That's why I'm here," said Martha.

Chapter Fifteen

The visitor's meeting room was cold and smelled of antiseptic cleaning fluid. Martha's white jail suit was stiff and made creases in her legs no matter how she repositioned herself on the black plastic moulded chair. A guard stood behind her at the only door in and out; in front of her was an empty room behind a glass screen. She was getting used to her new life behind bars. The guards were hardly friendly, but they were fair. The food was probably better than she could make for herself in her tiny apartment, but the company was a long way from the petty criminals and low ambition no-hopers she'd surrounded herself with back home.

A buzzer sounded, and she jumped in her seat. These infrequent meetings were rarely people she wanted to see. They were definitely never friends or family. Her friends had fallen away after her arrest, and her family were all dead. The steel door opened in the room behind the glass, and she could just about make out the colours of yet another police officer's uniform before she took a sharp breath.

"Frankie!" she shouted with joy.

Duffy didn't hear her but smiled as he walked to the other side of the glass and sat down. A taller police officer had plainly used his stool as it was set down very low. His eyes were only just visible over the desk between them. He started to crouch over it and swivel, much like he did every ten years when he needed to take his passport photograph in the Walmart automated machine. Martha couldn't hear the squeaking from the seat or Duffy's grunts as he continued to adjust his seat.

He sat again.

No. He was still too low.

The process began again. He was frantically going for it now and was surprised just how many turns this was taking. Soon it would spin no more, which was probably best because when he tried to sit down, he had to climb up a little. He was now too high but decided this would suffice. He smiled through the glass and picked up his phone handset. He gestured for her to do the same.

"Frankie!" repeated Martha.

"How you doing, Martha?" said the lieutenant.

"I'm doing fine," she lied and burst into tears. "You know I didn't do this. You know I didn't, Frankie!"

Duffy glanced at the guard by the door, eavesdropping on Martha's side of the conversation. He knew this exchange might be wired and recorded, so he carefully chose his words.

"Martha, I'm here because Vermont State PD are now handing this case over to these guys." He gestured around them when he spoke.

"No!" said Martha. "No, Frankie! You know I didn't do this. You've known me since I was a kid! I played with your kids! Me and Katie were best friends! You know I didn't do this!"

"Martha, Four Brothers is over the state line. You know that. These are their charges. It's out of my hands."

Duffy was using every muscle in his wobbly body to stop himself from weeping too. Both had snot pouring from their noses; he wiped his on his sleeve, she let hers flow.

He turned to look over his shoulder and then whispered into the handset.

"I thought I was arresting you for burning a boat out of spite. I swear to God."

"So, fix things then!"

"They want to make an example of you, Martha," said Duffy, his voice faltering.

"Don't say that, Frankie, no!" Her ears were ringing now.

"I did all I could, but this was a premeditated double homicide."

"I can't spend the rest of my life in jail!"

Duffy looked at his feet. It was a safe place to look at times like this.

"That is what we're talking, right? They don't have the death penalty? Tell me they don't, Frankie?"

"Of course not, no," said Duffy. "They don't have the death penalty."

He pondered for a moment.

"I mean, they keep trying to get it back, you know? Like more than many other states. Like *really* trying. They recently got it past the Assembly and the Senate, so never say never, you know?"

She started to sob, and he realised his musings weren't helping.

"But no, a couple of Governors keep batting it back, so you probably don't need to worry."

"Probably?"

"Calm down, calm down. You're just looking at life."

She stared at him in despair. He said the words so casually.

"I mean there is a one per cent, maybe, more, maybe like, I dunno, maybe like, I wanna say seven. Maybe eight per cent chance, that you know, they bring back, you know..."

"How long do I have to prove this? These things take like ten years, right? We can get an attorney. The most expensive. Help me get a good attorney, please?"

"You have no money."

"I do have money! I did what they told me; don't you see? I went to London! I just need to find it!"

"They want this to go to court next month. They want to pass sentence by fall."

"No! They can't do that. These things take forever!"

"They don't need to, Martha. The crime rates on this side of the border are rocketing. They want to make an example of you."

"Stop saying that!"

"I'm sorry."

She couldn't comprehend what was happening.

"It's their state laws, Martha. They make their rules."

"They want to send me to the chair?"

He tried to laugh. "We talked about this. It's just the rest of your life in jail. And if they bring the death penalty back, they probably won't use the chair anymore. It's not the best method. One guy's head set on fire."

"Frankie! Why are they doing this to me?"

"It's because it happened on Four Brothers. I have no jurisdiction. We're in New York State!"

"Don't you see? That's why they did it there. They set me up! You gotta believe me!"

Duffy smiled as kindly as he could but struggled to look her in the eye.

He slowly hung up the phone, then clutched his side, just as he had in her bathroom. Martha stared at this distressed man; she watched his hands squeeze and massage his ample side and then realised only one hand was massaging. The other was pointing at the pain. She looked up and realised he was staring at her with eyes wide open and eyebrows raised. He pointed again and then pointed at her.

Martha took a moment to consider what was happening. Then the penny dropped. She mouthed back at him as he slid off his stool.

"When?"

He looked over her shoulder at the guard, examining something they had just removed from their nose. Duffy pressed his hands onto his chest, one with all his fingers open, the other with his thumb tucked beneath.

He rippled his fingers to draw attention to his nine digits and then quickly moved his hands away before placing his palms together and resting them on the side of his face like a parent mimics sleep to a toddler. This caught the guard's attention behind Martha, so he tried to seamlessly turn this into a sort of yawn, stretch, and hand clap like a knackered flamenco dancer.

Chapter Sixteen

"Are you crying, Raymond?" asked Tash.

"Well, it just seems so unfair, doesn't it? What if she didn't do it?"

"I'm in the room!" said Martha. "What do you mean *if*?"

Raymond then surprised everyone by downing his drink and shakily pouring himself another whilst simultaneously choking.

"Wrong hole," he explained. "It's an unusual taste, isn't it?"

"I'm seeing a new side to you today, Raymond," said Tash.

Maureen raised an eyebrow, so Tash explained, "He was on the turps earlier."

"Cover your mouth when you cough, Raymond," said Maureen, then asked Martha, "so, what happened?"

"Well, they sent her to the chair, didn't they?" said Tash.

Raymond looked mortified. "Did they?"

"Well, of course they bloody didn't. She's here!"

"This is terrible," said Raymond. "Someone needs to do something about this. This is terrible."

"The sherry? Or the burning two people to death and then denying it thing?" said Tash.

Martha stared at her.

"Kidding!" said Tash.

"What happened?" repeated Maureen.

"I got appendicitis," said Martha. "They had to transfer me to Champlain Valley hospital."

"Ooh! Appendicitis! That's very painful. I can vouch for that," said Raymond.

"Kept Raymond up all night," said Maureen.

"You had it?" asked Martha, in a manner which didn't quite convince anyone she gave a crap about his answer.

"Well, no, not me, personally, so to speak. Someone got it on *The District Nurse*. The lady from *The Liver Birds* did her best, but it didn't end well," said Raymond. He was a fan of any TV show with that lady in it. Nerys someone or other.

"Neither of us could sleep that night. It was very unsettling," said Maureen.

"I had to make us a milky coffee," said Raymond. "Do you remember, Maureen?"

Maureen shuddered at the memory. "I do remember; it was terrible. We were out of milk, and you used Five Pints."

The three younger people just stared.

"Five Pints," said Maureen. "Powdered milk. Unpleasant business. We bought it during the Falklands Crisis in case London had another Blitz."

"We'll not see that twenty-nine pence again, shall we, Maureen?" Raymond was enjoying agreeing with his wife. They didn't do this nearly enough, he thought.

Jamie turned to Martha. "Did they have to operate?"

"Who?" she replied.

"The hospital?"

"No. I never got to the hospital."

"Should we get you checked out, then?" Jamie was confused.

"I think she means she wasn't ill, Jamie. Keep up," said Tash.

Chapter Seventeen

The ambulance came to a halt, and Martha massaged her pain. The paramedic had been excellent during their seventy-mile journey. She was conversational and undoubtedly unaware that her patient was in prison on suspicion of double homicide.

The rear door banged and swung open. Martha could see the entrance to the A&E Department glowing through the drizzly night. She could also hear the voice of an officer at the rear of the ambulance.

"Could you step outside for one moment, please, ma'am?"

The paramedic walked to the open door to protest. "They said to go to the blue bay?"

"That's correct; I'm afraid protocol means I must ensure you are unarmed," said the voice.

"Excuse me?" The paramedic was baffled.

"Ma'am, for your security, you have been unaware that your patient is suspected of two counts of first-degree murder. All staff moving to the blue bay must be checked."

The paramedic glanced at Martha, who did a self-conscious wave before rubbing her side again.

"This way," said the man.

"Of course."

The moment the paramedic stepped into the rain, she was

ushered to the side of the ambulance. Instantly the doorway was darkened by the silhouette of another body stepping in. Martha saw the outline of another prisoner. As she came closer, Martha couldn't believe her eyes.

"Katie?"

She hadn't seen her friend since they were teenagers when Martha offered her some grass on the way to the prom. That was the end of the prom and their friendship. Katie Duffy's dad had seen to that. Martha could see now that it was a bit of a questionable decision to roll a joint in the back of his police car. She should have waited until he dropped them off at the school hall. But hindsight was a wonderful thing. Hindsight and freedom. And money. Hindsight, freedom and money were wonderful things.

Katie pressed her finger to her lips, so Martha repeated in whispered disbelief.

"Katie?"

Katie gestured for Martha to stand, and she did. She then pointed to the open rear door and took Martha's place on the stretcher. She pulled a pink wig from her sleeve and placed it over her tied-back hair, then lay on her side and buried her face into her pillow.

"Katie?" said Martha one final time.

"Go!" whispered her old friend.

Martha paced cautiously to the rear of the ambulance and peered out. To one side, her paramedic was leaning against the ambulance side, being frisked by the police officer. He turned to eye-ball Martha and nodded to the rear of a van alongside them with wide open rear doors.

This guy looked like a seventies porn star, with a massive bushy moustache and impossibly curly hair. If he put a red sweatband around his head, he'd look like John McEnroe had swapped his tennis racket for nipple clamps. He nodded again, still chatting to the paramedic.

Martha leapt from the rear of the ambulance into the path of a passing Buick, which sounded its throaty horn. The paramedic turned just as Martha jumped into the Dodge Sportsman with painted-out side windows.

"Face the front, please, ma'am," said the policeman.

"Sorry," she replied.

"OK, I'm going to need you to re-enter your vehicle, and I strongly suggest you engage no further with your patient. Please do not stop until you are parked safely outside the blue zone."

"Aren't you going to frisk my driver?" she asked.

"Yes, I am. Please return to your patient, and lady, do not look her in the eye. The last person that did that ended up dead."

She swallowed.

"And the person before that did too, actually. So, the last person and the second last person," said the police officer, to avoid doubt. "Both dead."

The paramedic did as was told and climbed into the back of the ambulance. The officer walked to the driver's door and gestured to the driver to roll their window down. He did and rested his eye on this mightily hairy-porn star apparition.

"Sir, we were tipped off about a rogue paramedic embezzling funds and medication from the Champlain Valley Physicians Hospital. This lady has been positively identified in the back of your vehicle, and you are now forbidden by state law to communicate with her in any way. Please drive in silence to the blue bay and remain seated. You understand?"

"Yes, sir," nodded the driver. "Is she in trouble?"

"She will be if you speak to her. She's already in deep. Do her and you a favour. Proceed to the blue zone and remain seated. Do you understand?"

"I do," said the driver before rolling up his window and driving away.

The officer paced back over to the brown Dodge, slammed shut the rear double doors and climbed into the driver's seat. It took a few attempts to start the engine, and a lot of smoke puthered from the exhaust. He was soon on the freeway.

"Are you a friend of Frankie?" asked Martha, cautiously from the darkness behind his seat.

She could see his eyes look back at her into the rear-view mirror.

"You gotta do exactly as I say," replied the man.

"Where are we headed?"

"The border, there's a bag back there."

"Canada?" said Martha, fumbling in the darkness until she found a heavy zipped-up holdall. He simply grunted in the affirmative.

"What's in the bag?" She had unzipped it and was trying to hold a bottle up to the sporadic shafts of streetlight that successfully made it through to the back.

"Should buy time." His had a curious accent, and he was surely trying to disguise his voice.

"Is this hair dye?" Martha had unscrewed the lid and was grimacing at the scent of ammonia that filled her nose.

"And some sweats. And a uniform."

"Excuse me?" She didn't like the sound of that.

A logo lit up on the collar of the white overalls as a Kenworth lumber truck approached ahead. "Saputo", she read.

"Are you putting that voice on? 'Cos, you've done like five different accents since we set off."

He ignored her, and they drove in silence. After another mile, the van started rocking from side to side. Martha tried to steady herself, but the latest swerve impacted her head with the unlined interior of the truck.

"The fuck's going on up there?"

She strained to look at the driver, who seemed to pull at his moustache. Not in a contemplative way, in a manic way. He held a cluster of thick acrylic hairs in his hand, examined them and then pulled again, occasionally stopping to check his reflection in the rear-view mirror.

"What are you doing?" asked Martha as this mad man released a bone-shaking howl.

"Ooooh, that hurts like hell!"

"Frankie?"

"Owwwwwwww!"

"Frankie? What the fuck is happening here?"

"She said it would come off."

"Who did?"

"Katie. She said it would come off."

He was tugging away now with only one hand on the wheel and narrowly avoided a tractor coming head-on in the opposite direction.

"Don't tug. You're gonna hurt yourself," said Martha, edging forwards so she could offer help.

He stopped tugging at his raw upper lip and decided to remove the wig.

"Ooooooooooh!" he shouted.

"She stuck the hair, too?" asked Martha before smiling.

"You have zero empathy. Zero."

"She's getting her own back for prom night." Martha laughed.

"You brought a joint to prom night," he replied. "Any other father would do the same."

Duffy was sweating now. Maybe the glove box had some de-icer that might dissolve the hair bond. This was going to be a long trip. He hated his life right now.

Two hours later and the Dodge van idled away at the Canadian customs. Duffy had taken a risk showing his I.D., not just because he was a U.S. cop. The fact that his driver's licence photo looked nothing like the monster driving the van was surely going to scupper his plans. Happily, the border guard was enjoying *Airwolf* on a portable TV in his kiosk as the truck rolled up and away.

"Stay down," muttered Duffy.

Behind the driver, the van was in darkness, and the cursory beam of the guard's flashlight had barely settled on the mound in the back beneath a dark blue tarp.

"I ain't going nowhere," replied Martha.

"Not strictly true."

"Excuse me?" said the bump.

"You," said Duffy, with the unmistakable sound of a grin on his lips, "are going to work."

"Work?"

Martha's shrill response had made the van's shell vibrate, and soon Duffy's tummy was shaking, too, as he laughed at the thought of her finally putting in a proper shift.

Chapter Eighteen

"He helped you escape?" asked Jamie.

"This guy has an impeccable police career. Unblemished record for thirty-two years. He's received a commendation award no less than three times."

"Is that three times?" asked Jamie.

"Yes."

"OK. Why say no less than three times? If it's three times?"

"He makes a good point," agreed Tash. "Just say three times."

Martha glared back at the petty siblings.

"This guy has a family; this guy has a reputation, and this guy has a shit hot pension fund. He's not about to risk his career unless he believes I'm innocent," said Martha.

"We need more people like that in the world," said Raymond. "That sounds like the kind of policeman I'd have been."

"Wait, you were going to be a policeman?" asked Tash. This was news.

"Well, I decided I wanted to pursue other ambitions," he replied.

"You were too short," said Maureen.

"And I was too short," said Raymond. "So, it all worked out for the best, in a way."

"Did you achieve the ambitions?" asked Jamie.

Raymond looked a little hurt. "Well, of course, lovely wife..."

Maureen might have blushed at this.

"Ahhh," said Tash.

"Lovely car," said Raymond.

"Sorry about the car," said Jamie, and Raymond remembered how it now looked like Metal Mickey had lost a fight with a skip lorry.

"Lovely home," said Tash, trying to raise his spirits again.

"Thank you," said Raymond.

"If you're really into this sort of thing," she added, gesturing around the wall units and swirly carpet. "Which I am, by the way. In a way."

"Well, yes," said Raymond. He was never sure when people meant things, especially Jamie's scary sister. Did she mean it?

"And on the plus side, you have got fuck loads of cheese in your kitchen!" said Tash. "Who else can say that, hey?"

Maureen glared at her.

"Did I say *fuck* again? Sorry, Maureen."

Maureen tutted and tried again: "I sound like a skipping LP, but I'll ask again, why are you here?"

"Frankie drove me over the border and hooked me up with a job," said Martha.

"Was it in the cheesy sector, by any chance?" asked Tash.

"Bingo," said Martha.

"Do you get free cheese?" asked Jamie.

"It's an unusual question, but yes," replied Martha. "I was in the packing department. Nice people, hard work, shitty pay."

"Well, we all have to start somewhere," said Jamie. He was always glass half full.

"I don't think it was a career decision, Jamie," said Tash.

"No, I shipped myself here when I figured out their export process. Your address was in my socks. Been in there since I got arrested. You guys are my lifeline."

With this, she delved into her sock and produced a sweaty creased piece of paper with smudged ink smeared across it. She offered it to Raymond, who inspected it without touching it and smiled. He wasn't too excited about holding it.

"No, it's OK. You can keep that," he said.

Maureen leant in to look.

"Is that your handwriting Raymond?" she asked accusingly.

"Yes," he replied.

"Why are you sticking our address in ladies' underwear? You've turned into some kind of yobbo."

Tash caught Jamie's eye at the use of this word. They both smiled.

"No, we gave it to her when she left in October. She was going to send us the er," said Raymond. He tried to finish the sentence. "She was going to send us the, you know, the erm."

Tash looked at Raymond's crippled face, then at the others.

"You can say the word, Raymond," said Tash. "Money."

"Well, yes, that," he said. "I didn't want to be rude."

Martha was confused now. "What's wrong with his face?"

In fairness, Raymond was now glowing red at the unwelcome attention he was receiving.

"Raymond doesn't like talking about money," explained Maureen. "It's uncouth."

"OK," said Martha.

"Whereas I do remember that you said you would give us fifteen thousand pounds," said Maureen, before adding, "each,"

"That offer still stands," said Martha. "I just explained the problems I'm having."

"We went out of our way to help you," said Maureen. "We even toileted in a field."

"Toileted?" said Tash.

"It was a garden," said Raymond; accuracy was the cornerstone of his integrity.

"It was humiliating," said Maureen.

"It was dark," he replied in his most appeasing tone. "No one saw anything."

"We did all see Maureen's bum when I lit it up with that torch," said Jamie.

"That's one of those 'keep it to yourself' type memories, Jamie," said his sister.

"See? And now you want us to help you again!" said Maureen to her American guest. "Well, I'm sorry to say this, and please excuse my language," Maureen was very loud now, "but not on your nelly!"

"Steady on, potty mouth!" said Tash.

"Who's Nelly?" Martha was baffled.

"Really?" said Jamie. "We're not going to help her?" He looked shocked. For Jamie, the right thing was the only thing. "They want to electrocute her!" Then added, "To death!"

"I thought it was mostly injections in the seventies and eighties?" said Tash.

"Oh, I hate needles," said Raymond, visibly recoiling, "couldn't bare that."

The room stared at him. "I'm a fainter," he explained.

"You're worried about fainting before dying?" said Martha.

"Look. Whether it's death by electrocution or injection..." said Jamie before he was interrupted by Tash.

"Or fainting."

Jamie added this to his list. "Or fainting... We have to help!"

Tash's brain was filling with contradictory arguments. She could hear her own voice talking over itself in her overwhelmed brain.

I shouldn't be here.

Jamie and Martha are going to fall in love.

Nothing I have done has changed anything regarding their relationship. So, whatever does happen next, it must have nothing to do with me.

I was only here to spend Christmas with them.

I didn't know they weren't going to have a normal Christmas.

That QC is positively sticky.

I'll keep quiet.

Just say nothing.

Nothing, Tash. Let them talk it through without you.

Her internal monologue was interrupted by some wafting. Jamie had his hand up again.

"What is it?" said Tash with a sigh.

"Who says we take a vote on this?" said Jamie.

Raymond looked at Maureen, who shrugged a little, and Jamie looked at Tash, who did the same.

"Could we maybe, have a minute? You know, to talk things through?" asked Raymond.

Martha looked at all these tired English faces. She was exhausted and smelt of cheese, but deep down in her gut, she knew these were good people.

"Of course," said Martha.

"Shall we, er...?" said Raymond. He stood up and gently gestured that the four of them move out of earshot of Martha.

Jamie, Tash and then Maureen rose to their feet and followed Raymond. He surprised them by walking to the window next to the Christmas tree. Probably four or five feet away from where they had been sitting. There wasn't enough room for the four of them next to the Christmas tree, the 22-inch Ferguson television and Maureen's Toby Jug. They reminded Martha of a group of tourists rammed into a tiny vintage elevator with those see through walls.

"This is too tight, Raymond. I can still smell your sick breath," said Maureen, just inches from her husband's face.

"I think she can probably hear us, too?" said Tash, glancing over her shoulder at Martha, sitting right behind her. Martha offered a self-conscious wave.

"What if we whispered?" said Jamie. Loudly.

"Was that you whispering?" whispered Tash.

Jamie nodded.

"It's no use. We're going to have to move somewhere else," said Maureen.

All four looked around the box room festively lit by the modest Pifco Cinderella lanterns twinkling on the tinsel tree.

"We could go over there," said Jamie. "By the cotton wool thing."

"It's a snowman," said Maureen. Her homemade table decoration was probably more like a reception class goodie jar than Olaf, but she had spent a long time Gloy glueing the snowy facade to the empty jar of Tom Thumb Drops. She wasn't having anyone call it a cotton wool thing.

"I think that's a great idea, Jamie. Shall we vote on it?" said Raymond.

"Sake, just get the fuck over there," said Tash, marching past the mahogany effect nest of tables towards the dining area. The floor shook under her stomping, causing the glass cupboards in the wall unit to rattle.

Soon the four of them were nestled around the calver dining chair that came with the other three armless ones. MFI usually sold the Tudor Cromwell teak range with two dining chairs and two calvers, but these weren't from MFI, and Raymond was forbidden to let on.

"Can you hear us over here?" Raymond was smiling politely over at Martha.

"No," replied Martha.

Maureen was displeased. "Well, this hasn't worked, has it?"

"I have an idea," said Raymond.

Chapter Nineteen

"Can we just spin this along a bit?" said Tash, hunched up alongside her brother.

A single lightbulb hung from beneath the stairs and wobbled whenever Jamie moved his head.

"Get another duster, Raymond. I can still smell your breath," said Maureen.

As Raymond bent down, he head-butted Jamie, who recoiled and inadvertently clicked the cupboard door open again into the hall.

"No," said Jamie before closing the four of them in again.

Raymond stood up, twatting Jamie's face again, and the door popped open once more.

"No," said Jamie before closing it.

Raymond now had two dusters tied around his face like a poor man's *Dick Turpin*, which was no bad thing as Richard O'Sullivan's Dick was his favourite TV character until getting axed a couple of years ago. Maureen had once said O'Sullivan was handsome whilst watching his sitcom *Robin's Nest,* so right now, Raymond was feeling pretty cool indeed.

"It's a good look, Raymond," said Tash, inches away from the other's faces. "You remind me of..."

Raymond's eyes creased, suggesting a smile beneath his highwayman's disguise. He was willing her to make the comparison to his hero.

"Oh, what was that show with the guy with the mask?"

"Dick Turpin?" asked Raymond.

"Elephant Man," said Tash before being nudged in the nose by Jamie's rising hand.

Jamie couldn't quite raise his arm fully, as the stairhead ceiling was lower than the hallway's, but the other three got the gist.

"What is it, Jamie?" asked Maureen.

"Why didn't we ask Martha to wait here so we could have the secret meeting in the lounge?"

The inside of the stair cupboard went quiet, and then Raymond sneezed, causing his double duster mask to flap up like a matador's cape before dropping back into place.

"Shall we just have the vote and get on?" said Tash, remembering to abstain from voting if her presence changed the outcome. Then she remembered that in the original version of 1984, the one she travelled back to change, Raymond had been dead by now, so whatever brought Jamie and Martha together was the outcome of a decision made by Jamie and widowed Maureen.

Sake. How the hell did Doctor Who get her head around this time travel shit?

"I'm good with that," said Jamie.

Maureen and Raymond nodded.

Chapter Twenty

"Are you kidding? Is this a joke?" Martha wasn't expecting this, especially after her trans-Atlantic journey in a cheese crate in a climate-controlled freight hold.

"We just feel it's all a bit much. We've already taken too much on today," said Raymond with the kindest explanation he could muster. "Would you like some more QC?"

He raised the bottle as a pathetic olive branch.

"I didn't want the first QC," she replied.

"I will," said Tash grabbing the nearest empty glass and holding it up to Raymond. "Unless you have any Night Nurse?"

"Have you any idea what you are doing to me?" said Martha.

Jamie looked at his feet. This was awful.

Tash was doing maths in her head. Had she changed the outcome of the vote? Had Raymond changed it? And why wasn't he filling her glass?

"They want to execute me for a murder I did not commit," said the American.

"Two murders," said Jamie. "Two people were barbecued and identified by dental records or hip replacements."

Martha glared back at him. "You done?"

"Didn't we say it would life in prison?" said Raymond. "They haven't actually brought the death penalty back yet. And even if they do, people wait for years before they, you know, before they get around to doing it."

"Great. Maybe you'll come visit?" said Martha.

"I wonder if they double the voltage?" said Jamie.

"You know you thought that out loud?" said Tash.

"Pardon me?" said Martha.

"As it was a double murder," said Jamie. This made good sense to him.

"Not the right time for that kind of chat, Jamie," said Tash.

"Sorry," he replied. Although he wasn't sure why he was supposed to be sorry.

"Actually, they should lessen the voltage, so it takes longer," he said.

"More pain?" asked Tash.

Jamie nodded. "Longer to die."

"What if someone had killed ten people?" asked Tash.

"I'd probably suggest you forget the electrocution and use something really slow," he replied.

"Like an acid bath?" asked Raymond.

"Raymond! Stop it!" said Maureen.

"Sorry, Maureen. I was thinking about that film Barry Norman reviewed last week on *Film '84*. The one with those Chinese monkeys, it seemed to do the job."

"It wasn't acid. It was water," said Jamie.

"No, water wouldn't do that," said Raymond.

"It was a film," said Jamie. "And they weren't monkeys. They were *Gremlins*."

"Well, it looked terrifying. I can't believe people watched on and let them melt like that."

"It was a film," said Jamie.

"Why are we planning slow deaths? I thought you were my friend?" said Martha, her eyes fixed firmly on Jamie.

"I am. I didn't vote for this," he explained.

"Shush! It was a secret ballot!" said Maureen. "People died for the secret ballot!"

Jamie looked at the Christmas tree as his face started to glow red. Some of it was the reflection of the scarlet Pifco Lilliput bulbs, but most was his humiliation.

"What does it take with you freaks?" asked Martha. "I already promised you fifteen grand each!"

"It's not about money," said Maureen. "Tell her, Raymond."

"She can hear you."

"Tell her," said Maureen.

"It's not about the money."

"I'll double it," said Martha.

Everyone heard Raymond let out a little whimper.

"No, thank you very much," said Maureen.

"Hang on, where are we at?" asked Raymond. "You know, vis-à-vis money, so to speak?"

"I make it thirty K each," said Tash. "Not that I want to get involved."

"Why don't you want to get involved?" asked Jamie.

"Raymond, we made a decision," replied Maureen.

Martha wasn't leaving it there.

"One hundred grand. Each"

Raymond whimpered at a higher pitch and placed his fist in his mouth.

"No, thank you," said Maureen, sitting down on the settee in her customary demure way. She'd once seen Princess Anne sit down onto a sumptuous palace sofa in a kind of side-saddle way and, from that day on, had decided that she would do the same. "And that's the end of it."

The sound of Raymond's next whimper was certainly muted by his clenched fist but not silenced.

Martha stared at them all, one at a time, then slowly nodded.

"Well, what can I say? I misread our relationship. I thought we had made a connection."

Jamie's face had an expression Tash hadn't seen since their grandparents' dog Pepper died.

"Let's all have a festive drink and relax for a while, you know, clear our heads. It's been a tricky sort of day, what with me being attacked by an owl and Jamie being shot," said Raymond, topping up the miniature sherry glasses with fortified wine.

Maureen was the only one to protest. "None for me, thank you."

"No, right."

As he finished topping up his glass, she spoke again. "Or you."

"No, yes, of course."

"You're forgetting the trifle," she explained.

Raymond started to pour his tiny serving back into the bottle.

"Come on, Maureen, you don't need fun to have alcohol," said Tash.

"The saying is: you don't need alcohol to have fun," said Jamie.

"And the saying, like every fucking fridge magnet and car sticker, is wrong."

Suddenly Martha dropped to the floor and fumbled beneath the Betamax video recorder on a shelf under the TV. Seconds later, she leapt to her feet and pointed a gun at them. Tash noticed it was the same white-handled pistol she'd had when they first met.

"Sorry," was all Martha said.

Maureen looked mortified. "Has that been under there since October?"

Martha nodded coolly.

Maureen turned to her husband. "You told me you moved the TV stand every week to hoover underneath it!"

"Did I? I mean, yes, yes, I did. I mean, I do."

"How long has this been going on?" asked Maureen.

"Erm," Raymond said as he started counting on his fingers. Maureen's expression grew even more hysterical.

"Are you doing underneath the sofa?"

"Well, it's tricky with the angle of the hoover bag, it sort of catches when you," he was interrupted.

"Excuse me!" said Martha. "Gun!"

She wafted it around.

"Well, you're not going to use that, are you," said Maureen rhetorically. "An innocent prisoner wouldn't commit the very crime they're trying to defend!"

"I still think we should take her seriously, darling." Raymond's nerves were getting the better of his mouth.

"She shot at me in the car," said Jamie, remembering the day they met.

"She did shoot at Jamie in the car," said Tash, which wasn't very helpful.

"Really?" Maureen was confused.

"A warning shot," said Martha, assuming a lie would increase her credibility as a thug. In truth, the gun had fired by mistake.

Jamie was secretly delighted that Maureen was taking things a little more seriously.

"That's right. A warning shot," said Jamie.

"What's a warning shot?" asked Maureen, glaring at Martha.

"Don't ask her that, Maureen; she's a busy lady," said Raymond turning to Martha. "You don't need to answer..." But before he could say "that", Martha pointed the gun into the dining area and pulled the trigger. There was a loud crack and thud, and the dining table displayed a gap where the snowman once stood.

Blimey, she's a hard person to read, thought Jamie.

Maureen swallowed. Raymond swallowed. Then they raised their hands above their heads, followed by Tash and Jamie.

"I need help," said Martha, with pitiful despair.

Raymond started stammering again. "I'm sure we can sort something out."

Chapter Twenty-One

"I don't know what to say to you, Frankie," said Martha.

Lieutenant Duffy looked at the young lady before him. Her eyes were bloodshot from crying, and her nose ran into her open mouth. Her shock of newly purple hair continued as stains across her forehead and onto the wet towel around her shoulders.

"Let me see you. Spin around." He had the tone of a benevolent uncle trying to cheer up a niece with a grazed knee.

She did, tripping on her legs as she went.

"You look like the best cheese packer this town had ever seen," said Duffy.

His eyes were getting wet now too. She had the same cheeky smile he remembered from her childhood. Her overalls fit her very well, and her porcelain white legs disappeared into black safety boots.

She threw herself at him and squeezed tightly.

"You did a good thing, such a good thing. I'm so grateful."

She started to sob again. He returned the embrace.

"No more tears, Martha. You're on your own now. You gotta toughen up, yes? Where's that dope-dealing little girl who slashed my tyres for fun?"

She laughed, and he remembered having to replace his tyres.

"Actually, that was a very irresponsible thing to do. And you still owe me for those."

She squeezed him again. Duffy prized her away and straightened her collar. "You start work at 8am tomorrow morning."

"Are you kidding? 8am?" The old Martha didn't disappear for long, not ever.

She had pushed things too far, as Duffy looked hurt. "Don't do this, Martha. Don't be like that."

"Okay, okay," she nodded.

"Ask for Carla Barnes. She'll take care of you. And this place is paid for fourteen nights."

Martha looked around them at the faded motel room. Steam from the unvented shower was still spilling out of the bathroom, and the smell of musty dampness hung in their noses.

"You have to pay for this shit? I thought this was a detention centre."

Duffy managed a half smile. He made his way to the door, stocked with many slide bolts and twist locks, then unlocked the primary latch and turned to the pathetic-looking young woman across the room. His hand felt inside his pockets and extracted a handful of dollars which he placed on the table at the foot of the queen-sized vibrating bed.

Martha couldn't thank him. If she did, she would burst into tears again. She just smiled, but he knew she was thankful. They were both surprised that his voice faltered quite so much when he spoke.

"You never saw me. Whatever happens, you never saw me, understood?"

Martha nodded, then found her voice.

"They set me up, Frankie. Why are they doing this? Someone set me up."

Duffy took a long deep breath and then sighed.

"I got bills, Martha. I have a mortgage. I have a pension. I have too much. You understand? Too much at stake. This is bigger than us. I can't get involved."

She reluctantly nodded. He had been a tremendous parent to

his children after his wife had died in a traffic accident in the early seventies. He hadn't remarried, he was a firm believer in finding a soul mate, and he'd been blessed to find his. His heart carried the love for both of them every single day. Martha knew he was a man who would always do the right thing if he could.

Duffy reached into his coat pocket and produced a business card.

"That day you flew back to the states. I checked the passenger inventory for Heathrow outbound. Twenty-four hours before your scheduled flight and twenty-four hours after."

"Jesus, how the hell did you do that?" Martha looked suddenly alive.

Duffy just glared at her and then continued.

"There was no record of a B. Fernandez on any international or domestic flights."

Martha looked shell-shocked. She had been sure the lawyer was behind this and had spent countless sleepless nights on a paper-thin mattress staring at the painted brick walls of her cell, listening to the echoes of fighting, screaming, and crying that unfailingly followed lights-out. Each hour had been spent picking apart her demise, and soon each hour had been made more bearable by the utter conviction that she had found an avenue of explanation. Bee had stolen her money, faked her own death and emigrated.

And now this.

Martha dropped down onto the bed and placed her head in her hands. The theme of *Fraggle Rock* resonated through the hessian papered walls from the room next door. Then Duffy spoke again.

"But there was a Martha Hobson."

She didn't look up. "No shit, Sherlock. That would be me."

"No. There was another. She flew first class KLM to Curacao."

Martha looked up, a flame burning in her tired eyes.

"That's all I got," said Duffy.

He held up the business card.

"A private cab card?"

He flipped it over to reveal handwriting on the reverse. Martha walked over to take it from him. It read:

Miss Martha Hobson. London Heathrow to Curacao. KLM Airlines. Dep: 14:55 GMT

"What the fuck?" said Martha. "This is proof! This is proof! You gotta help me!"

Duffy was shaking his head. "You'll figure this out. I know it."

"What? What? How?"

Duffy opened the door and stepped through it. "Take care, Martha. And if you want my advice, keep moving. Get yourself together but keep moving."

He slammed the door and walked over to the silhouette of the brown Dodge parked alongside a sheeted-over swimming pool. He blew his nose noisily as he went so he didn't hear the motel room door open behind him.

"*Keep fucking moving,* shit for brains? What the fuck? I have nobody! Everyone's dead!"

"We just had a nice moment there, and you ruined it!" said Duffy. "You ungrateful little..." He thought for a moment but went for it. "... junkie!"

"I'm clean! You know I'm clean. And get a life, Frankie; it was just grass."

"Don't you got friends any place other than Vermont?"

"No!"

He was fumbling with the keys in the van door. "Well, get some! And do it soon!"

He climbed into the driving seat and slammed the door. The engine growled into life, and the lights lit up the gloomy stained brick façade of the motel walls. He blew his nose again, wound down his window and set off.

"Keep moving."

"Can't believe you're abandoning me, you piece of shit!" shouted Martha.

"You're welcome!"

As the van drove out of the motel parking lot, Martha shouted one final time.

"Thank Katie for me! I love you, Frankie Duffy!"

Chapter Twenty-Two

"How did she fly under your name if it wasn't on her passport?"

Jamie had been first to ask a question after Martha's latest instalment, and all were sitting now. Martha had relaxed the 'arms-above-your-head' rule, but he'd raised his to ask the question.

"If she can steal my identity to take eleven million dollars out of the country, I'm guessing a fake passport wasn't too difficult," said Martha.

"I thought she was dead. They found her hip, didn't they?" said Raymond.

"That could have been anybody's. She killed Harvey, torched the boat, then stuck a skeleton and prosthetic next to him."

"Where would you get a skeleton from?" asked Raymond.

"A grave?" said Martha.

"Euw," said Tash. "Bit nasty."

"Do you know this, or are you guessing?" said Jamie.

"It's more than a guess. It's my theory. Cos I sure as fuck didn't kill anybody, and my money sure as hell isn't in my bank account."

"Could you mind your language, please? Maureen doesn't like swearing," said Raymond.

"Who swore?" said Martha.

"You did," said Raymond.

"Did I?"

Tash nodded. "You said fuck."

"Yeah, you did," agreed Jamie. "Twice."

Then Raymond joined in, and before long, the four of them were muttering to their American captor; things like...

... "yeah, you did,"

..."I heard it too,"

..."really doesn't like that sort of thing,"

..."definitely heard a fuck,"

... and "double fuck," filled the room.

"Okay! Okay! Sorry!" said Martha, interrupting the hum.

Jamie's hand was up again.

"Christ-sake, Jamie, you don't need to raise your hand to ask a question," said Tash.

"Tell her I don't like that either," said Maureen in a stage whisper to her husband.

"I think she heard you, Maureen. You're closer to her than I am."

"Tell me she doesn't like what?" said Tash.

"Maureen doesn't like blasphemy either, I'm afraid," said Raymond.

"How exactly do you want us to help?" said Jamie. "You're in England now. You've escaped. What else could you need?"

"Let's call it an early Christmas gift," said Martha.

"What is it?" said Maureen.

"I want to clear my name, convict the actual killer, and find my grandaddy's money," said Martha.

"Quite a big gift," said Tash. "Would you settle for an M&S voucher?"

"Disgusting," said Maureen to her husband. "She always lowers the tone."

"What? M&S?" said Tash. "Marks and Spencer."

"Oh! It stands for Marks and Spencer, Maureen!" said Raymond, "I think Maureen was confusing the letters for that other sordid business."

"Which one?" asked Tash teasingly.

"You know," said Raymond before clearing his throat, "the one with the leather stuff."

"Nope. Lost me there, Raymond."

"Whips and zips and things." Raymond's collar was suddenly quite prickly. "And oranges."

"Oranges?" Tash was confused.

"Oh! S&M," said Jamie. The penny had dropped.

"Oranges?" said Martha.

"I'm not sure what they do with the orange, actually," said Raymond. "Maybe they have a portion at halftime, you know, like football."

"Half time?" said Tash. "You two have an interval?"

Raymond looked at Maureen. Maureen looked at the carpet, and then her tummy rumbled.

"Excuse me," said Raymond.

"Before I got clean, I used to sell a bit of weed," said Martha, ignoring the weird Brits.

"You sold weeds?" Raymond's mouth was wide open. He looked at his wife. "Mrs Wong could make a fortune, her patio's full of them."

"The type you smoke," said Martha.

"Don't suppose you have any on you?" asked Tash.

Martha ignored her. "And some clients still get nervous when the cops feel my collar. They're kind of relying on me to keep their identity to myself."

"Rich people?" asked Jamie.

"And powerful people," said Martha. "Cut to the chase, someone who will remain nameless was surprised to get a call from me before I left Canada. Someone in corporate banking."

"Ooh, this sounds exciting now," said Tash, leaning in. "Developments."

"Eleven million US dollars were deposited in Sint Anna Bay Bank on October twenty-third in the name of Martha Hobson."

"Wow! There's your money!" said Raymond. "Sorted!"

"Why can't you just get that, then?" said Maureen.

"It's not that simple. Claude says the account was closed two days later, right after the funds were transferred to a Swiss bank," said Martha.

"Who's Claude? Is he the guy who's remaining nameless?" asked Tash.

"Forget the name."

"Claude?" asked Raymond.

She nodded. Raymond nodded.

"Do you know the name of the Swiss bank?" asked Jamie.

"Échap Bank," replied Martha. "But Swiss bank accounts have numbers, not names."

"It's almost like this criminal doesn't want anyone to catch her," said Tash.

"Do you have the number?" asked Jamie.

"Yes," replied Martha. "But that account closed three days later."

"Can we just get to the end part where you tell us where the money is and what you want us to do?" said Tash. "Skip the ads and stuff?"

"We need to identify an amount of eleven million dollars being deposited into Banco Hispano Americano sometime around October thirty-first."

"That's Hallowe'en," said Jamie.

"What does that mean?" replied Martha.

"Well, you know, trick or treat and stuff like that."

"I know that part. I wondered what the relevance was with banks?"

"There isn't one," replied Jamie.

"So why did you say: 'that's Hallowe'en'?"

"Because you said October the thirty-first," replied Jamie. He wasn't getting confused at all. "That's Hallowe'en."

"It's begging if you ask me," said Maureen.

"What is?" asked Martha.

"Trick or Treat," replied Maureen.

"We turn the lights off and lie on the floor, don't we, Maureen?" said Raymond. "Pretend we're out."

"Sounds perfectly reasonable behaviour for a couple of pensioners," said Tash.

"Pensioners?" said Maureen.

"Last year, I hadn't closed the curtains properly, though, and they spotted my slippers through the gap," said Raymond. "I won't make that mistake again. Cost us a banana and our last tin of Carnation."

"I'm guessing no one came this year?" said Tash.

Raymond thought. "They didn't actually, no."

Martha clapped her hands to get back on point.

"So, all I need is someone who can access the SWIFT banking system. It handles international payments between banks and should be hackable by someone with access to a head office branch of a major bank, or someone with like cutting edge computer skills."

The room fell silent. Then Raymond spoke.

"The Cubs' Akela, Mrs Higginbottom, has a Casio scientific calculator. She's very adept with it, isn't she, Maureen?"

"I'm not getting her involved with the mafia," said Maureen. "She's in charge of our next bring and buy sale. What if she took a hit?"

Martha glared at her. "I'm not the fricking mafia!"

"I think a Casio scientific calculator and a central banks computing system might be a little different," said Tash.

"Why can't he-who-can't-be-named find out?" said Raymond.

"Voldemort?" asked Jamie.

"Claude," whispered Raymond.

"Something to do with European banking systems. He can see that it left that account for another but can't trace it without someone physically inside a European bank to help."

"We need a computer geek, some smart teenager that can hack into stuff like that film *War Games*," said Jamie. "Like Uncle David said he was."

Tash stared at Jamie.

"Uncle David, who works for Midland Bank?"

"He's a vicar, Tash."

"He is in 2020, Jamie. Right now, he's nineteen and working at Midland. And he's always been our go-to for computer stuff."

Tash immediately regretted speaking. Why had she got involved?

Chapter Twenty-Three

Number 538 Gaywood Close should have been enjoying the serenity that any home around the UK expected at 2am so close to Christmas, yet it wasn't. They had all retired to bed, but the sound coming from the settee in the lounge was extremely loud.

"What the hell is wrong with that woman?" said Tash from beneath Jamie's quilt. He'd offered up his bed, and she'd portioned off an area for a makeshift crib for her baby son, now blissfully oblivious to the epic snoring from the American downstairs.

"Even when she's asleep, she's selfish," said Maureen, flipping her pillow again and then placing her fingers in her ears.

"I don't remember her snoring like this when we slept together," said Jamie.

"Woah! You slept together?" replied Tash, flipping her quilt down so she could hear this revelation as clearly as possible.

"We shared the sofa," said Jamie. "In October."

"It'll be all that cheese," said Raymond.

"Cheese gives you nightmares, doesn't it?" said Jamie. "Not snores."

"Oh yes. What am I thinking of?" said Raymond.

"If you remember, can you keep it to yourself?" said Tash.

"Are you sure Uncle David works at the Midland, Tee?" said Jamie.

"No."

"And you're sure he was into computers at nineteen?"

"No."

"But you think he'll help us?"

"No."

"Goodnight, then," said Jamie.

"Goodnight," Raymond said, turning over and kicking Jamie's face.

The two men had top and tailed in Raymond's bedroom, as Jamie had given up his own. Maureen had offered the sofa to her captor, and so of them all, she had been the least compromised by sleeping in her own bed in her own room. Except she had been woken countless times by the snoring.

There followed lots of...

... "goodnights",

... "sleep tights",

... and "night all" type exchanges, which were brought to an abrupt halt by an American voice from downstairs.

"Can you shut the fuck up?"

The phone rang.

"Who could that be?" asked Maureen.

"We're all here," said Raymond.

"Someone wants to speak to us," said Maureen.

"It sounds like it," said Raymond, as the shrill bell rang from the Trimphone on the hall table.

It continued ringing.

"They're not hanging up," said Maureen.

"No," said Raymond. "I would imagine it's a wrong number."

"Very late to be ringing anyone," said Maureen.

"Is anyone going to answer the fucking phone?" shouted Tash.

Then it stopped ringing.

"It's stopped ringing now," said Maureen.

There was silence, and then Raymond spoke. "I wonder who it was?"

"Sake!" said Tash. "If you'd answered it - you'd know!"

"I would imagine if it were serious, they would call back," said Maureen.

"We have caller display in 2020," said Jamie.

"Jamie!" said Tash.

"What?"

"Not now. We need to sleep."

Chapter Twenty-Four

It had been ten minutes since the shrill school bell announced the end of term. The schoolyard was mostly empty but for a few clusters of chatting parents being dragged away by impatient children desperate to start their summer holidays. Car doors slammed, and engines fired up as drivers wound down windows to let out the baking heat of the July sun. Glenn Frey's 'The Heat Is On' disappeared into the distance with a pale green Volvo estate.

Tash looked at her watch. Eleven minutes since the end of school. A flash of light caught her attention, and she looked over to see the reflection of the brilliant sunshine in a swinging door. Behind it was Mrs Horvat, trying to waft some fresh air into the stuffy classroom. Tash set off over to her.

"Hello, Mrs Horvat," said Tash.

"Hello, Miss Summers." Mrs Horvat looked hot and flustered, yet at the same time blissfully happy about the six weeks of freedom that lay ahead of her. "Is he not out there?"

Tash looked around the tarmac expanse, partially painted with hopscotch squares and snakes and ladders, and then beyond to the school field and prefab classrooms that sat on the edges of sun burnt grass.

"I can't see him," replied Tash.

Mrs Horvat raised her hand to her brow to block the sun and peered over to the steps leading to prefab B.

"I spy legs!" she smiled as she gestured over.

Tash followed her gaze and smiled back. "Thank you! Little shi-," she stopped herself and tried to turn shit into sausage, but they both knew it was too late.

"Have a lovely summer," said Mrs Horvat.

"You too," replied Tash, pacing over to the little legs in the distance.

Her skin was prickling in the heat, and as she continued on her way, she delved into her shoulder bag to pull out sun cream. The plastic lid was greasy, so she struggled to flick it up. Turning at the timber stairs, she saw two children giggling at something hilarious.

Except it wasn't hilarious.

A nine-year-old girl had her back to Tash and was proudly lifting her skirt for her audience of one, whilst her pants rested around her ankles. Her classmate was enjoying his favourite last day of term ever. In fact, he was resting his hands on his freckly knees as he squatted to get a better view.

"Raymond!" shrieked Tash.

He looked up in horror, and the girl instantly dropped her skirt back down, pulled up her pants and glared at this bossy mum. Tash squirted a perfect stripe of Boots Soltan up the centre of her own face and hair in absolute horror.

Staring back at her was her son.

Exposing herself to him was her nine-year-old self.

Tash sat bolt upright in bed and gasped for air. She felt her face – it was dry. No sun-cream. Some sweat, but no SPF 50. She looked over to see her son Raymond, fast asleep in his makeshift cot in Jamie's bedroom in Gaywood Close.

"What the fuck was I thinking? I can't stay here."

She leapt out of bed and started to cram her discarded clothes into the red holdall.

Chapter Twenty-Five

Tash tiptoed down the stairs grasping the holdall in one hand and her son in the other. She had fed him just before her stressful dream, and he was freshly changed. There was no time for goodbyes. She'd messed up with that kind of thing too many times. As she reached the foot of the stairs, she placed the holdall down and gently unzipped it with her free hand. She awkwardly extracted a carrier bag laden with gifts and quietly paced to the lounge door. The handle squeaked as it turned, as did the hinge as it swung open. As she stepped into the room to leave the gifts under the Christmas tree, she was surprised to hear voices.

"Morning, mommy, coffee?" asked Martha.

Sitting around the table with her were Raymond and Jamie.

"Sake," said Tash under her breath.

"We didn't want to wake you," said Jamie.

"What time is it?" asked Tash.

"Quarter past nine," said Raymond.

"We found out who was calling," said Jamie.

"It was the police!" said Raymond.

"The police?" Tash sounded shocked.

Martha caught her eye. "That was my reaction."

"They were calling from the warehouse to say they'd repaired the phone line. The baddies had cut it."

"That's very nice of them."

"It is. Although they said they'd be commandeering the place from Boxing Day as a crime report suite. So, they probably did it more for themselves."

Tash just nodded. She wanted this boring chat to end.

Maureen entered the room carrying a teapot. "Toast or cereal?"

"I haven't slept past seven since he was born," said Tash.

"That'll be the cheese," said Raymond.

"No, still wrong," said Jamie.

"You know we didn't eat any cheese, don't you? You just have a kitchen full of it?" said Tash.

"Toast or cereal?" repeated Maureen patiently.

Tash sighed and sat on the spare dining chair, briefly examining the bullet hole in the super fresco wallpaper next to the condensation-dripping window. Jamie offered to take baby Raymond, and she handed him gently over.

"Do you have any cornbread?" asked Tash.

Maureen stared at her.

"Corn flakes?" she replied, hoping to make sense of this irritating lady.

"Cornbread," said Tash.

"No."

"Sourdough?"

"I don't know what that means."

"Brioche?"

"Pardon?"

"Bagels?"

"No."

"Banana?"

"I've got a banana, but I'm not peeling a whole one."

"Banana bread?"

"Are you making things up now?" asked Maureen. "Just to be clever?"

"Soda bread?"

"No."

"Spelt bread?"

"No."

"Rye bread?"

"It might be quicker to ask what bread Maureen has," said Jamie.

"What bread do you have, Maureen?" asked Tash.

"Sliced."

Tash waited, but that was the end of the list.

"I'll take that then, please. It sounds delicious."

Her eyes landed on a knitted festive tea cosy, most likely the product of Maureen's handy work.

"What's that?"

"A tea cosy," said Maureen, stopped in her tracks. "Why?"

"No, nothing, I just wondered," said Tash. "Gonna be lovely when it's finished, that."

Maureen shook her head and went to get Tash's feast.

"Are you cold?" Raymond asked, looking at Tash's coat zipped up to the top.

This latest delay was a significant inconvenience but hadn't surprised her. She'd been hoping to leave without being seen. Nothing had been straightforward since she'd first sat on the C5 in Grandad's garage loft.

"A bit," said Tash. In truth, it wasn't a lie, as the house was usually just the wrong side of bearably comfortable when it came to temperature.

"We're all cold. This is part of the British charm, right?" said Martha. "Unheated homes, bathrooms with no lock, crappy teeth, every drink is brown."

Jamie glanced over at his sister for a moment longer than he might normally. Tash hoped she hadn't triggered any suspicion. She hated the idea of leaving again but needed to stick to the original plan. Hopefully, she hadn't impacted the version of 1984 that saw Jamie fall in love with Martha, regardless of whether she was caught again. Tash knew for a fact that Martha wouldn't fry. After all, she had seen her at Jamie's side in 2020.

And as Tash saw it, even if Raymond had originally died, Martha would still have shipped herself to this address, and Maureen and Jamie would still have found her at some time or other. Tash needed to stay out of their plans and felt comfortable that Raymond wasn't the kind of guy to impact decision-making in Gaywood Close.

Yes, she was confident she should just piss off home with her baby and leave things be.

"We've just been talking about Uncle David. He moved to London after his A levels, didn't he?" said Jamie.

"That's what they told us. Why?"

"And he was skint, so lived with Mum and Dad and you. But you'll have gone to Sheffield for Christmas, right?" said Jamie, his eyes still scanning the waterproof coating on his sister's coat.

Oh Christ, thought Tash. I just need to get out of here anyway I can.

"I don't know, why? You're not planning on going to Mum and Dad's flat, are you? That would be mental."

"Well, we can't wait outside every branch of Midland bank, can we? On the off chance, he rocks up for work. And there's no point anyway if he's gone to see Grandma and Grandad."

Tash rubbed her head, now pounding with an ache that felt a match for any tablets, even Maureen's Anadin.

"Well, no banks are open today. It's Sunday," said Maureen walking back from the kitchen with a slice of toast on a plate and placing it down in front of Tash, who tentatively lifted it to see if it was hiding another one beneath.

"What?" asked Maureen, questioning Tash's curious reaction to her food.

"Nothing, it looks delicious," said Tash, before muttering: "I just thought toasts travelled in pairs."

"They'll be open tomorrow," said Maureen.

"Christmas Eve?" asked Jamie.

"It's not a bank holiday," said Maureen. "We've worked every Christmas Eve, haven't we, Raymond?"

"Yes, Maureen," said Raymond, upturning the Denby milk jug over his teacup, hoping there might be a drop left. There wasn't. "Shall I top this up?"

"Top this up? Who are you trying to impress? We don't top anything up in this house. You start topping this up, and what next? He'll be topping up baths." She nodded at Jamie, who opted to stay out of things.

"I was speaking figuratively, I just meant put a splash more in, so some comes out when you tip it up. You know, like most other milk jugs."

"We always travel up on Christmas Eve, don't we? We always have," said Jamie.

Maureen looked Jamie up and down like she was seeing him for the first time. The disdain on her face was easy for all to see.

"Took Christmas Eve off, did they? Your parents? Every one?" Maureen hid her envy badly but nodded to indicate she was fine with it. "Well, I suppose that's fine if someone else is happy to take that shift. Like me and Raymond."

"I'm not actually working tomorrow," said Raymond. "The police said that the warehouse is still a crime scene, so I can't move much stuff about, sort of thing."

"Well, some of us are working," said Maureen.

"Yes, no, I know," said Raymond and immediately regretted adding, "until twelve."

"It's still working! And I've done you a list of jobs. I know how much you hate being bored."

Maureen handed Raymond a handwritten note with numbered errands taking up all of one side.

"Yes, I do hate being bored," Raymond said to the assembled faces around the table. He took the note and read it before looking over at the sofa. "That's quite a lot of hoovering."

"Well, some parts of this carpet haven't seen the hoover since October, have they?"

"So, we go to the flat today," said Jamie, ignoring the cleaning faux pas.

"Jamie, I hate to blow smoke up your arse, but if someone were to ask me what your biggest strength was, I'd probably say your lack of self-awareness when dancing," said Tash.

Jamie looked confused.

"It takes real balls to break dance at a funeral wake," said Tash.

"Thank you," said Jamie. "But why tell me now?"

"Because if that same person were to ask me about your weaknesses, making decisions would be top of my list. And yes, I do have a list."

"Why is going to Mum and Dad's flat a bad decision?"

"What's the plan? How do you see us moving forward with things? We need to gain access to Uncle David's bank? How is visiting our parents two months after I was born going to help?"

"What's your plan then?" said Jamie.

The room fell silent.

"Just tell me the address, and I'll take it from there," said Martha, waving the gun around her head.

"No guns at the breakfast table," said Maureen. Martha took on the look of a chastised child and placed the pistol on the window ledge behind her, alongside a pair of painted Staffordshire china spaniels facing outwards, probably for the benefit of the binmen. Their necks were adorned with green tinsel collars, a seasonal embellishment that lasted for Maureen's sacred twelve days.

"Please don't take a gun to Mum and Dad's flat," said Tash.

"Got a better idea?" said Martha.

Jamie knocked over his tea. His foster family reacted calmly. They'd seen this a hundred times before.

Chapter Twenty-Six

"You're paying for this call," said Maureen to Martha.

"Add it to the thirty G," said Martha, staring at Raymond as he walked through the hallway. "Or hundred G, whichever you want."

He looked confused, and so did his wife.

"What does she mean by G?" whispered Maureen.

"I think it's something to do with horses," said Raymond.

"It means K," said Tash, sitting at the bottom of the stairs, with Jamie behind her.

"Oh," said Raymond before explaining to Maureen. "It means K."

Maureen just wrinkled her nose at him. He shrugged.

"Grand!" said Jamie. "Thousand."

Raymond and Maureen both did a sort of "Oh! That makes sense!" noise. Raymond started to crouch down and then stopped.

He turned to the others.

"Could I ask you to close your eyes, please?"

"What?" said Jamie.

"You're asking a woman with a gun to close her eyes?" said Tash.

"Oh, shoot. I left the gun through there by those pot monkeys," said Martha but made no attempt to fetch it.

"Those are bone china," said Maureen.

"Well, a kind of ceramic," said Raymond. He couldn't lie about that sort of thing, especially if this woman were an outright criminal. She might steal them.

"And they're dogs." Maureen was offended. "Royal Doulton." She hoped.

"Maybe. They look more Shaker Maker," Martha had received these toy-making kits every Christmas as a little girl.

"Why do we need to close our eyes?" Jamie asked, already scrunching his tightly closed.

"Please?" said Raymond.

They all reluctantly complied, except Maureen, who nodded to her husband that the coast was clear.

He crouched again and lifted the edge of the carpet off-cut that they'd had professionally edged with tape to sit beneath the door mat but on top of the actual carpet. They were taking no chances with this Axminster blend. It was like a coaster for the carpet.

As the corner upturned, it was plain to see that the floor beneath was a deeper, richer colour as it had been protected from sun damage since 1973. It was also plain to see a small flat key that Raymond snatched and stood back upright, causing his knees to crack.

"Nice hiding place," said Tash. "Don't you normally hide a key outside?"

"I can't believe you looked!" said Maureen.

"Don't worry, Maureen, I have another idea for a hiding place," replied Raymond as he slid the tiny key into the phone lock and twisted it a few times to loosen the handset and allow a call to be made.

"Is that a lock for a phone?" asked Martha.

"Has everyone opened their eyes?" said Maureen.

They had.

"We never gave the all-clear." Maureen wasn't letting this go.

"Do you remember the number?" asked Martha, glaring expectantly at Tash.

"From when I was two months old?" replied Tash.

"Can anyone hear me?" said Maureen. "I just said something."

"We'll just use the phone book," said Raymond.

"Raymond!" It was one thing being ignored by idiots, but something else for her husband to blank her.

"Sorry, Maureen," said Raymond as he dropped the lock from his trembling hands.

Tash stepped over to the telephone bench seat and bent to pick up one of the directories on the shelf. She took the blue one labelled London Postal Area, surnames S to Z.

"This is so fucked up," she muttered as she sat back down and flicked through to Summers. There were fewer than she thought, and her forefinger was resting over a listing in moments. Her heart started to race, and she felt a lump in her throat as she read her father's name and address.

Summers, G, 16B Sancroft House, Lambeth

Her eyes prevented her from reading the phone number at the end as, for some reason, they had started pouring water onto her cheeks. Jamie didn't notice until she snorted very loudly.

"Wow, that's quite a snort," said Martha, as Jamie leant forward and wrapped his arms around his sister, who sat on the step below.

"What's wrong, Tee?"

She didn't answer, and the room fell silent but for the occasional snorts of snot to clear Tash's airways.

"I'm in that flat," said Tash. "I'm only like eight weeks old, and I have no idea how Mum is doing it. She thought she was bringing two babies home."

Raymond and Maureen looked at one another. This was news to them, and they felt a curious affinity with this weirdo's parents. It was as if they silently realised that effortless parenthood wasn't necessarily the gift everyone else seemed blessed with. Everyone has their story.

Maureen gestured to her husband with a nod, and he interpreted her perfectly.

"We don't need to do this, Tash, not if it upsets you," said Raymond, almost resting his hand on Tash's shoulder, then awkwardly placing it back by his side.

"We absolutely fucking do," said Martha. "I don't know what this weird shit is, but my life is on the line."

Everyone except Tash started back at Martha, surprised by her harsh timing.

"She's right," said Tash from behind her palms. She wiped the tears from her eyes and dried them on the net curtains next to the front door. If she'd been looking at Maureen, she would have seen the thoughtful biting of her lip to hold in her abject horror at this thoughtless vandalism.

"You need to do whatever you think is right, Jamie," said Tash, "and Maureen."

Raymond looked around in the vain hope that someone might point out that he was in the room too. When they didn't, he picked up the telephone and started to fumble in his pockets. When he found nothing, he saw Martha handing him his script on a single ripped piece of *Love Is...* paper that Maureen had donated from her pad by the phone.

This torn-off stationery displayed the naked cartoon couple hugging under a full moon with the phrase *Love is... being partners for life.* Beneath the print were some bullet points in Martha's handwriting.

"Are you sure you want me to do this?" Raymond's voice sounded suddenly dry.

"Come on, out of all of us, who sounds most like a bank manager?" Martha said the words bank manager like most people say, 'utter wanker'.

"We do have a lady Prime Minister, you know," said Maureen, folding her arms across her chest again.

"Step up, Iron Lady," said Martha.

Martha gestured to the phone.

"I'm not doing your dirty work," said Maureen.

"Just do it, Raymond, please," said Tash, handing him the

phone book after pointing out the printed number that listed a direct connection to her younger parents.

Raymond held the phone handset under his neck and lifted the phone directory close to his face, with his little script resting on top. He started to dial the Trimphone.

The silence in the hallway was broken only briefly by Maureen's tummy rumbling, followed by Raymond apologising for it.

They waited again.

"It's not connecting," said Raymond. "Oh no, it is. It's connecting. It's ringing."

He was swallowing a lot now.

"I thought it wasn't connecting, and then it connected."

They waited.

"It's ringing."

They waited again.

"Still waiting for them to pick up."

"We got it," said Martha.

Raymond's body jolted upright, and he went very red as he stared at his notes.

"Yes, hello. Yes, sorry. Hello. Erm, is that George Summers?"

Everyone waited.

"Sorry, Mrs Summers, yes, hello. Hello. Yes. What it is. The thing is..."

Tash gestured for him to breathe and calm down. She was fascinated to see someone talking to her younger mum but didn't want Raymond to scare her or blow the whole plan.

"I need to speak to Uncle David, please."

"Sake, Raymond!" whispered Tash.

"I mean David Summers. David Summers, please. If that would be OK, sort of thing. Sorry,"

They waited again.

"Me? I'm his boss, actually. From the bank where he works. I'm his bank boss," said Raymond.

Raymond listened and then placed his hand over the mouthpiece before whispering to his crowd.

"She says his boss is a woman called Linda."

"See!" said Maureen.

"You speak to her then!" said Martha, shoving Maureen towards her husband, who instantly froze to the spot.

"Sake," said Tash, leaping up from the carpeted stairs and snatching the phone from Raymond.

"Thank you, Raymond," was the first thing she said before projecting firmly into the Trimphone. "Hello, yes, this is David's boss, Linda, that was my PA. We need to speak to David, please."

She listened down the phone and her eyes filled with water again. She was talking to a lady thirteen years younger than her, a lady that was also her mother.

This was bizarre, freaky, but most of all, unfathomably emotional.

The tears were plain for all to see, and Jamie walked over to give one of his best Asperger's hugs. His nose was squashed on her shoulder, and his arms locked her in a vice.

"No, there's nothing to worry about," said Tash in a hushed voice, "I just wondered if he had a moment to talk," but she was interrupted.

"Oh, of course, yes."

She listened more. And then she heard it. A baby crying in the background. Herself, thirty-six years ago. Not much younger than her baby was now.

Everyone disappeared, and everything. The woodchip wallpaper, the teak telephone seat, the swirly carpet, the smell of cheese. She was with her parents once more. How could they be younger than her but so much more like parents? Her mother still sounded like her mother, but how she used to sound. As a younger mother. There was a higher pitch to her voice. A lack of self-confidence. A naivety. And then her mum spoke again.

"No, I'm still here, sorry..." replied Tash.

And then she gained some poise.

"No, I'm fine, Mrs Summers. I just have a cold."

She listened again.

"No, that won't be necessary. I'll talk with him later. Thank you."

Her eyes closed now, and the heat of the tears beneath her eyelids made her open them again.

"Yes. And you. Merry Christmas..."

Tash gently reached down to press the black button on the phone to end the call before adding... "Mum."

Maureen produced a tissue from nowhere and handed it to Tash, who might have thanked her. It was hard to tell.

Raymond was the first to speak. "Well done. She sounds just like you!"

Tash managed a smile before blowing her nose. Clearly, this wasn't the man-sized tissue she was used to as it filled quickly, and her fingers were soon covered with overflow.

"Oh," said Raymond.

"Jesus," said Martha.

Maureen offered another tissue which Jamie intercepted and tried to help with a clean-up operation.

"I mean, who gives one fucking tissue?" said Tash.

"This is everywhere," Jamie said as he started rubbing the tissue between his sister's fingers, making things worse.

"Where is Uncle David? What's the plan?" asked Martha.

"He's at the head office Christmas party. An afternoon thing for the sub-branches or something."

"Do we know where that is?"

"Yes. We do," said Tash, taking the tissue from her brother, screwing them both up and throwing them into a round black bin adorned with painted flowers around the perimeter. A whimper from Maureen followed this.

"Get those, Raymond," said Maureen. She couldn't keep it in. Raymond bent down and emptied the bin, visibly uncomfortable about the gooey balls of tissue in his grasp.

"We don't really use this," said Raymond.

"You don't really use a bin?" asked Tash.

"It's a talking point," explained Maureen.

"It's a talking point," said Raymond.

"It's a bin," said Tash.

"Where's the party?" said Martha.

"If it's the head office, it's The Ned," said Jamie. Referring to its luxury reincarnation since 2017.

"The what?" said Raymond.

"Got a pool on the roof. Dead posh. They filmed Goldfinger in the basement. It's a posh hotel," said Jamie.

"Best get our swimming cossies!" said Raymond, only half joking.

"Don't be disgusting," said Maureen.

"You might get arrested in your two-piece, Raymond. Right now, it's the Midland Bank head office. Just down the road from St Pauls," said Tash.

"Let's go," said Martha.

"We don't all need to go," said Maureen. "We've got plans."

"We all gotta go," said Martha. Her expression reinforced the point. "All of us."

"How do we get there?" said Jamie with his hand in the air and one eye watching with interest as Raymond pocketed Tash's spent tissues. "We destroyed Raymond's car."

This remark landed with maximum impact.

"Yes. How do we get there?" said Raymond, wiping his sticky hands down the side of his trousers and maybe, just maybe, holding back a tear for his knackered Princess.

"What sort of plans?" said Tash, wondering if she'd identified a window for her to sneak back to 2020 once and for all.

"I've got to help Maureen with the cubs Christingle parade," said Raymond.

"Woah, the cubs-stingle-what-the-fuck?" Tash was interested.

"Parade," said Raymond. Maybe he'd not said it clearly the first time. In fact, he went for a third. "Parade."

"Like on a vehicle? A moving thing?" asked Martha.

The penny dropped quickly with Maureen.

"We are not diverting the Brixton, Clapham and Streatham Scouting packs to St Paul's Cathedral so she can rob a bank!"

"I'm not robbing a frickin' bank!" said Martha. "Have you listened to anything I said? I just need to get into their computer to find my money. Our money. Your money."

"Well, it's not such a big detour, really," said Raymond.

Always way too honest for his own good. "If we head back through Holborn, we could just tootle along the A40 and do a loop back across Tower Bridge."

"Stop describing routes, Raymond," said Maureen.

"What's tootle?" asked Martha, lifting her cup and spilling tea down her front.

"I can't take my son out in this weather," said Tash.

They all looked through the open door into the kitchen and outside through the window. The sun shone brightly in a clear blue sky.

"You're gonna need to do better than that," said Martha.

"I'm not leaving the C5 in the garage. There's no way. I am never going to let that leave my sight."

"You can't see it now," said Jamie.

"No, I can't see it now, but I do know that I locked it in the garage."

"So, it's locked then it's safe," said Martha.

"What if we never come back?"

"This is crashing a Christmas party so we can hack a computer," said Jamie. "It's not a flight on Apollo 13."

"I'm not leaving it," said Tash defiantly. "End of."

"Then we bring it with us," said Martha. "End of." She turned to Raymond. "What time does this thing kick off?"

Raymond looked at his chrome Casio watch and pressed the side button to illuminate the screen. He squinted to read. "I'm glad you asked, actually. Six minutes ago."

"What?" said Maureen. She hated being late for anything. How embarrassing. "They'll be waiting for us! Get changed NOW, Raymond. NOW!"

Chapter Twenty-Seven

Tash pulled the cotton hat gently over baby Raymond's ears and zipped up his coat. He was snuggled up in a papoose around Jamie's chest, who looked utterly delighted to be in his company. They stood in the hallway, ready for their mini-mission. Martha joined them next, sneezing as she descended the carpeted stairs with a highly solemn look on her face. She had no choice but to blend in with the British public, and her cheesy overalls didn't achieve that in the slightest, so she now stood before the brother and sister in a borrowed combo from Maureen. Tash flashed instantly back to her horrific episode around BBC TV Centre dressed as Margaret Thatcher. Martha had been dealt a similar blow and was squashed into Maureen's second favourite wool blend twinset and skirt. Maureen didn't have a fourth favourite, and Tash had trashed her third. Martha scratched an itch for the hundredth time and asked the question most people of a certain age were asking in 1984.

"The fuck is this material? Cat?" She followed this with another sneeze.

"You look lovely," said Jamie, prompting Tash to laugh. She was surprised to see that Jamie wasn't laughing back at her. His gaze was firmly fixed on this purple-haired vision of confusing wonder. Martha didn't take kindly to Tash's snorts, so she shot a question her way.

"Did you get your weird shit moon buggy?"

Tash raised her eyebrow and calmly lifted her hand to show the key to Raymond's garage. "We can get it on the way."

"You're going to have to take the blame for this, Raymond." Maureen's voice spilt down from the landing and announced her appearance at the top of the stairs.

They were all surprised to see her legs were covered in green tights, tucked into pixie boots. Each step she took down to the hallway revealed more of this apparition. A thick plastic belt. A horizontally striped red and dark green jumper. A wide green knotted scarf.

But it was her make-up that surprised everyone the most.

Well, the lipstick.

It was a much brighter shade of red than anything she had ever worn before. And it wasn't on her lips. It was forming two mightily rosy cheeks.

Her ears had pointy tops, which may have been attached to her ears, or, more likely, were fixed to the elf hat that covered her hair.

"Anyone order a leprechaun?" said Tash.

Jamie knew better than to smile. Martha giggled and then spoke. "I like what you've done with your make-up. Takes years off you."

Maureen blanked her and continued down the stairs until she was alongside her house guests.

"Actually, it was the distance that took years off you," said Martha. "Now you're closer; you look the same age." Like Jamie, she was inclined to tell the truth, regardless of how this might land.

"Well, I don't think the day could get much stranger now," said Tash with a polite smile.

Then Raymond came down the stairs. Much faster than he'd hoped. He'd been unable to see the top stair, so he overestimated his footing, and things just went tits up from there. Luckily, he fell on his arse, so he bounced all the way to the bottom in a seated position. It wasn't elegant, and it looked painful, knocking the wind from him as he came to a stop on the hall floor.

"Sorry about that. I'm not used to the shoes."

With that, he clambered to his feet and straightened his clip-on beard. He was dressed head to toe in a 1970s department store Father Christmas outfit, including a pillow strapped around his waist, a hooded fur-lined red coat, and black wellies.

"Never wear wellies in this house again, Raymond," said Maureen, unconcerned for his free fall. "Do I make myself clear?"

"They're not muddy," said Raymond.

"Did I say anything about mud?"

"No."

"So why are you?"

"You're right, sorry," said Raymond.

"I don't know if anyone remembers a few moments ago," said Tash, "just before Freddie Krueger's mum came down the stairs," she gestured at Maureen's striped jumper, "I said, I don't think the day could get much stranger. Well, I'd like to retract that. I *now* think that the day couldn't get much stranger."

Chapter Twenty-Eight

"Okay. I'm going to retract my earlier retraction and say that *now* I don't think the day could get much stranger," said Tash, as the chilly breeze blew her hair from her face, grimacing at the smell of the Shire horse in front. Bertie, for that was his name, was pulling something akin to a rag and bone man's carriage. And he was a very big boy. He needed to be, as he was dragging Father Christmas, his elf helper, two-time travellers, and an absconded convict wanted by the FBI for double homicide.

Not to mention all the other stuff.

Mountains of parcels (mostly gift-wrapped selection stockings containing Mars bars, Marathons, Bounty bars and Opal Fruits), a plastic Woolco Christmas tree smothered in every colour of tinsel known to humanity, and an odd pink-coloured mountain range.

This was, of course, Maureen's oldest candlewick bedspread that was reserved for emergencies. Emergencies that would necessitate the use of a twenty-three-year-old candlewick bedspread, like today, for instance, when it was just about covering Tash and Jamie's extended Sinclair C5 that sat hiding in the middle of all the festive paraphernalia.

And there was one final thing on the cart:

Anthony Pritchard-Gittins.

He was what Maureen might charitably call "plump" and was the most decorated London cub scout south of the river in 1984. And if you were in any doubt about the specific detail of this accolade, you needn't worry, as Anthony would tell you at great length in his eight-and-a-quarter-year-old Welsh lilt until one of you died.

That's when he wasn't boasting about mummy and daddy's indoor pool at their second home on the outskirts of Cardiff. Which surprised Tash, and she said as much. Her observation that "most rich folks don't live around here," was lost on him.

"Maybe there's a waiting list at Chelsea cubs?" went over his head too.

He didn't hear her final thought on the matter, as she managed to keep it on the down low: "Or perhaps your parents enrolled you in the Brixton pack cos they just don't like you. I get it."

In fairness, he was one of those people that are difficult to like. Maybe his entitled upbringing, lack of manners or trail of golden caramel down his chin from an endless supply of Mackintosh's Golden Cup that he kept helping himself to from the stash of gifts didn't help. His parents had purchased a Kodak Ektralite 400 camera for him to commemorate the event. Every few minutes, he'd unzip his massive camera case that hung around his neck, then extract the tiny camera. It was a geek's dream. An outer protective case became a carrying handle for the 110 compact camera, and he'd debate whether to use another of his twenty-four exposures. His father had suggested the Hanimex as it did the same job and was under six quid. But young Pritchard-Gittins had learned about labels from his mother. So, the £19 Kodak it was to be.

He'd already got the wrong side of Tash by asking what was wrong with her son's teddy bear. That didn't go down too well.

Tash, baby Raymond, and Jamie sat on fold-out camping chairs that kept sliding to the sides of the cart, causing considerable angst as the drop to the road was a big one. Their expressions were hard to read as Maureen had painted their cheeks to match hers, and they both wore elves' hats. Except Maureen didn't have any spare ones, so Tash sat beneath the festive tea cosy she'd been so rude about earlier, and Jamie's face was being lifted by one of Raymond's hiking socks that were cutting a line around his forehead. Behind them, Martha sat on a sack of gifts, apparently unconcerned for their welfare, and in front of them, Raymond and Maureen were seated on a fixed wooden bench, with Anthony perched on one end. Raymond held the horse's reins like a professional.

A professional plumber.

Or doctor.

Or any profession other than one that involves horses.

Maureen was flicking through some stapled pages of foolscap paper with copied handwritten notes in purple ink from the scout hut Banda machine. Photocopiers were slowly replacing these basic printers, but schools across the UK still used these old Rexograph spirit duplicators well into the eighties. The smell of the alcohol-based solvent filled the noses of disinterested pupils as teachers handed out the mostly purple worksheets.

"Maybe he's not called Bertie," said Maureen.

"What makes you say that?" replied Raymond.

"Because he's not listening!" said Maureen. "NEXT LEFT, BERTIE! LEFT!"

The shouting made no difference, and the cart continued straight along Newington Butts.

"Did we know there wouldn't be a driver?" said Raymond from beneath his sweaty white nylon beard.

"You said you could do this," said Maureen, frantically flipping back and forth at the pages in her gloved hands.

"I said I could be Father Christmas," he replied. "I didn't realise I would be driving."

"Well, who else drives the sleigh?" said Maureen. "Rudolph leads it, but Father Christmas steers it!"

"Yes, but I'm not actually him, am I?"

"Pardon?" said little Anthony, his ears pricked by the revelation from the man dressed as Father Christmas. "Are you not really him?

"Of course, he's him," said Maureen, looking over at the boy who had now opted to pace around the slowly moving float. "Sit down, Anthony. How many times!"

"I told you! It's Anthony," he replied, making the *th* sound soft like in *Thursday*. "You keep getting my name wrong, stupid elf!"

Maureen looked mortified.

"How much longer? This is taking bloody ages," he added.

"Sit down!" shouted Maureen, her face glowing red as she flipped another page.

"What are you looking for?" shouted Jamie from behind.

"We need to turn left," said Raymond.

"And?"

"Well, Bertie just seems to want to go forwards."

"Can I look?" said Jamie, leaning over to take the paperwork from Maureen.

"You have instructions for a horse?" said Tash, peering at the notes.

"Missed another one," said Raymond, sadly as another left turn passed them by.

The problem with taking the wrong route didn't only inconvenience Father Christmas and his team; It was proving a bit of an annoyance to the ninety-three cubs that were following on their bikes, brought up the rear by Akela in her 1971 Hillman Imp. Many thirteen-year-old cars in 1984 were considered naff and antique but, most of all, unreliable. And Akela – aka Mrs Lynch – was driving an olive-green model with an overused manual choke. She had no need for the heater today, as the anxiety of applying the brake pedal and nudging the accelerator simultaneously every time she slid into neutral meant her adrenaline levels were working superbly as nature's radiator. Too often, she'd been left with a stalled engine at traffic lights and stop signs, so during stop/start processions like this, she literally was not taking her foot off the gas, causing considerable fumes, heat, and anxiety. This distress was made worse as the procession ahead had unfathomably strayed half a mile off the planned route.

Sadly, it wasn't the horse that stopped and started. Raymond hadn't sussed that either. No, Mrs Lynch's intermittent pauses were caused by the tired, cold legs of cubs, all keen to reach their destination and hand out sweets and surprises to underprivileged children. But credit to them, they hadn't stopped singing as they pedalled at varying speeds. Although Martha was enjoying that part the least.

"Go tell it on some other fucking mountain!" she shouted over her shoulder, and everyone on the sleigh hoped this hadn't made its way to the sensitive ears of the angelic cherubs behind. She turned back to Jamie impatiently. "What's the problem up there?"

Jamie turned to her. "We don't know how to steer."

"Really? Is there no steering wheel?"

"It's a horse," said Tash.

"I figured that, with the swishy tail and smell of shit. I was talking about this yard sale on wheels."

"It doesn't work like that," said Jamie. "You need to steer the horse." He was flicking through the notes again.

"Daddy says I'm an excellent coachman," said Anthony, peering under the bedspread.

"I bet he does," said Tash. "And I can think of some other things starting a "C", too."

They looked over their shoulders at the cub, struggling to get a clear line of sight beneath the pink cover at the curious white machine beneath. "You've driven one of these before?" said Jamie, gesturing at the vintage wooden cart.

Anthony looked up and around the curious sleigh, disdain forming on his face above his woggle. "Not like this. Ours has leather seats, it does. Use it at the Royal Show every year in Llanelwedd."

Tash and Jamie looked at one another. Then she couldn't help herself.

"Did you get a badge for that, too?"

"Did you hear that, Raymondo?" shouted Martha, eavesdropping on this last exchange.

"Father Christmas," said Raymond, correcting her.

"Did you hear that, Father Christmas?"

"No. I can't hear much up here, actually. I think it's the hood. Or I might be getting a cold."

"Don't sneeze in that beard, Raymond. I borrowed that from work."

"No, of course. Sorry, Maureen." Raymond followed this with a sneeze, coupled with an unexpected fart. He immediately looked at his wife to see if he was in trouble; the fear in his eyes was visible behind the beard and droopy hood. "I'm sorry, it's because I was trying to keep the sneeze in." She glared at him.

"Hey, Tony," said Martha to the cub, now fiddling with the Christmas tree.

"My name's Anthony," he replied, with the soft *th* again. He repeated it for good measure. "Anthony."

Martha nodded at this revelation. "You might be confusing me with someone who gives a shit. Put that candy bar down and swap places with Santa."

He'd never really been spoken to like this, so took a while to absorb the essence of the message.

"Do I get paid?" he asked.

"No," replied Martha. "But I have a gun. Say no, and I shoot Santa in the knee."

Anthony swallowed and looked over at the man at the helm. "But it's totally your call," she added.

"Blazes! We've just missed another left," said Raymond.

"Don't swear in front of cubs," said Maureen.

"Sorry, Maureen."

Chapter Twenty-Nine

"Can't you hold it; we'll be there in a bit?" said Tash.

"You've been saying that since the Elephant and Castle," replied Anthony, keeping a tight grip on Bertie's worn leather reins.

"When you gotta go, sis, you know what it's like," said Jamie.

"I've pushed a nine-pound baby out. I have an excuse!"

"He's eight!" said Jamie.

"Eight and a quarter," said Anthony.

"Sake," said Tash.

"When you get to my age, you stop adding on the quarters," said Maureen.

"How old are you?" asked the inquisitive cub.

"No. You don't ask a lady her age," said Raymond from beneath his beard.

"Why?" replied the cub. "Can't she remember?"

Tash and Jamie smirked at one another.

"See! It's not just me!" said Anthony, delightedly pointing at Wyndham's Theatre coming up on their right. The magnificent stone front displayed signs for the new musical *The Secret Diary of Adrian Mole, Aged 13 ¾*.

"Is that Buckingham Palace?" he added.

"Anyone got a 'thick as pig shit' badge?" said Tash.

"Pardon?" said the boy.

Raymond turned over his map of London and squinted again at the tiny, printed words. He had lived in London all his life, so the route should have been simple, but the authorities had advised the cub group to stick to minor streets wherever possible. Their current position on Charing Cross Road was causing him a few problems with his acid reflux. It might have been a Sunday, but a horse, cart and just under a hundred cubs on bikes tested the patience of even the most charitable cabbies.

"We've only got a bit further to go, and you can choose from hundreds of toilets," he said.

"How much further?" asked Maureen, not even attempting to read the map.

"Well, erm, if we risk Shaftesbury Avenue, we could probably tootle along..." but he was interrupted by his wife.

"Stop saying tootle."

He looked up and saw her serious face. She meant it.

"Sorry." He thought for a moment. "How about pootle?"

"Stop describing routes and tell the boy when he can go to the toilet."

"Erm," Raymond lifted his beard to scratch his chin beneath. The owl scratch marks were still visible on his face. Maureen slapped his hand instantly. "Put that back this instant."

"I think I might be allergic to the fibres," he explained. In fairness, the brief appearance of his face did seem to display a puffiness that wasn't there when he got out of bed with Jamie this morning.

"How long?" said Maureen.

"About a mile?" Raymond pitched this as a question to see how it landed.

"I need to go now," said Anthony.

"Well, make the bloody thing go faster, then!" said Tash.

"It can go faster?" said Martha. "Hey, munchkin!" she shouted at the cub. "Do what she said!"

And he did. The acceleration caused the Christmas tree to fall over and half a dozen presents to tumble into the road.

"Leave them," said Martha. "Leave them!"

Maureen glared at her, so she explained.

"Collateral damage, keep moving."

The cubs behind picked up pace admirably and continued to sing about eleven pipers leaping as they weaved in and out of the discarded Doodle-Art tubes and He-Man action figures.

Chapter Thirty

"I don't understand," said Raymond. "We should be there by now."

They had stopped on Old Gloucester Street to take stock, and all the adults gathered around his *1972 OS Map* of central London, even Maureen, and this time she had a question.

"Where is it?"

"The hospital?" replied Raymond.

"Yes."

"Well, it's at the end of my finger, isn't it?" he asked rhetorically.

"Don't get clever with me. I don't know how maps work, do I?"

"Well, they're an aerial view of all the roads," Jamie said, trying to be helpful. "And they also have little brown markers to show you where boring people like to visit. Here look, *Bloomsbury Square Garden*," he squinted to read. "*London's oldest square laid 1665.*"

The singing from the cubs waiting patiently on their bikes was getting louder.

"Why you don't have a block system amazes me," said Martha, clearly baffled by the spiders' webs of roads and alleyways. "We never have problems getting places."

"Maybe we should all just climb in a cheese crate and post ourselves where we want to go," said Tash.

"Stop pointing at that tennis court now, Raymond. Everyone can see your dirty fingernail," said Maureen.

"It's not a tennis court. It's Holborn Police Station."

Maureen leaned in to look. "Why's there a Nazi on it?"

"No, that's a policeman, look. He's stopping the traffic." Raymond lifted his arm to mimic the symbol on the map. "It's just a symbol."

"Stop it. You look like Hitler," said Maureen, pulling his arm back down.

"Woah, man down!" said Tash.

They looked over to see Anthony lowering himself off the sleigh.

"What are you doing?" asked Maureen.

"I really need to wee!" replied the cub.

"This is technically abuse," said Martha.

"Will one of these houses let him use their loo?" asked Jamie, pointing to a row of three-storey townhouses alongside them.

"It's a good question, Jamie," said Tash. "Good luck asking."

Everyone looked at one another. Then at Father Christmas.

"Raymond, knock on that door," said Maureen.

"Not that one," said Maureen, just as Raymond's knuckle was about to strike number 47. "They've got a CND sticker on their car." She nodded to a powder blue Austin Maxi parked outside.

"How do you know it's their car?" asked Jamie.

"Can you pick that Christmas tree up, please, Jamie?" replied Maureen. She wasn't open to questions.

Raymond and Anthony walked to the house next door, and Raymond lifted the heavy door knocker and then let the brass slam down to the base plate.

"What's wrong with CND?" asked Tash.

"What is CND?" asked Martha.

"There's nothing wrong with it," said Maureen, blanking

Martha's question, "but they're not the cleanest of people. They spend most of their time camping in fields, so there's no way they'll have Cleen o-Pine'd their loo."

"Clean up what?" asked Tash.

"Cleen o-Pine," said Maureen. "When it comes to cleaning, you can't beat it. It's double action." Maureen was an advertiser's dream.

"Can't argue with that," said Tash, wishing she'd not asked.

The door knocker reminded Anthony of the one that changes shape in *Mickey's Christmas Carol*. His parents had taken him to see the film when it was released last year as a double feature with the re-released *Jungle Book*, which meant he got two King Kones. One for each film. On the way home, his mum asked which he enjoyed most. His answer was strawberry. She had meant which film but wasn't listening to his answer, so it didn't really matter.

Raymond was about to knock again when they spotted a curtain being drawn back from the large sash window enabling someone indiscernible to peer out. The curtain slid back into position, and then there was silence.

The sound of a heavy latch made them both jolt upright. The dusty black door opened to reveal a diminutive elderly lady with eyes that twinkled behind tortoiseshell spectacles.

"Well, hello, Father Christmas," she said, her voice gentle and reminiscent of a St Trinian's teacher.

"Oh!" said Raymond with a laugh. "No, I mean yes, of course, yes. I do apologise for intruding, but I wonder if we might beg a bit of a favour? So to speak. This young man is in desperate need of a lavatory, and he's been cycling across town to help poorly children."

The lady looked both her visitors up and down. Raymond fumbled in his trouser pockets beneath his Santa suit and pulled out a bent business card.

"This is me," he said, proudly handing over the card to the cautious homeowner who took her time to examine it.

"You're Mormons?"

Raymond immediately leapt in to point at the creative spelling. "No, it's Maurmond. You see, my wife is Maureen, she's with the cubs, and I'm Raymond. It's a clever play on words, sort of thing."

The old lady looked at the card and at Raymond.

"I don't think so," she said doubtfully.

Raymond shuffled uncomfortably. Mainly because he was uncomfortable in this Santa suit designed for a man one foot taller in 1977, but also because he feared he'd blown their toilet window.

"You're Father Christmas, surely?"

Raymond visibly melted.

"You're based at the North Pole, aren't you?" she asked.

"Oh," said Raymond, "good one!" He winked at her to seal their adult deceit for the sake of the youngster. "Yes, but we have some storage by Tower Bridge now."

"Well, of course, if I can't help a cub scout at Christmas, what sort of a person would I be?"

She smiled at Anthony, dancing from one foot to another whilst grabbing his trouser zipper to keep the wee in.

"Up the stairs, it's straight in front of you, don't worry about your shoes." She opened the door widely for her guests.

"Well, that's very kind indeed, madam," said Raymond watching Anthony race past the old lady and pelt up the stairs.

"Come on in, Father Christmas. We're letting all the heat out."

Raymond muttered his thanks, followed by an apology, then some more thanks. He looked around the grand Georgian house, which was a curious mix of antique furniture, brass lamps, opened drawers and piles of bags. A few stained rectangles on the ornately plastered walls suggested paintings had once adorned the space beneath wall-mounted brass picture lights.

"It's a beautiful home you have," he said.

"Thank you," replied the old lady as they both tried to ignore the sound of Anthony unleashing a few pints of blackcurrant Cresta that he'd enjoyed before his expedition.

"Are you having a bit of a tidy-up?" said Raymond, nodding

at the black bin bag by the door to the living room. Immediately he regretted asking such a personal question. Had he upset her? What if she lived like this all the time?

"Not that it needs a tidy-up!"

She was smiling back, but maybe she was upset?

The brass door knocker interrupted the silence, and Raymond was happy for the distraction.

"I'll get that," he said, turning to twist the dull oval brass knob that displayed a patina only seen on old doors.

The lady started to protest, but the door swung open to reveal Jackson, a nine-year-old cub who had been riding his early Christmas present, a lime green Raleigh Strika. He'd been singing louder than all the others, so Raymond knew his name. His bike wasn't new but was new to him, and he was living his best life.

"What is it, Jackson?"

"Can I go as well, please, Father Christmas?"

"Well, I don't think we should really be asking this kind lady..."

"Of course, you can," said the lady. "Come on in."

With that, she gestured up the stairs, and Raymond closed the door again. It made a clunk and thud unlike any door he'd closed before. He felt like he was in an episode of *To the Manor Born*. Maureen loved that show as the lead character reminded her of herself. In fact, she'd mentioned that every time they had watched it. Every time.

Anthony was coming down the stairs now, two by two.

"Did you wash your hands, Anthony?" said Raymond.

He was corrected again about the pronunciation and repeated the question, but overdelivering on the soft *th* sounds, entirely by accident.

"Did you wath your hanths, Anthony?"

"Yes," replied the cub, opening the door to leave. "Hello, Michael."

"Hiya," said Michael, another cub, stepping inside as Anthony stepped out.

"Hang on a minute," said Raymond in protest.

"It's alright," said the old lady. "Come in."

"Are you the last one?" asked Raymond, leaning to peer outside through the open door.

"Oh no."

The line of cubs queueing patiently for the loo stretched around the corner and out of sight. Beside them was a seamless line of shining metal and black rubber tyres as ninety-three bikes lay abandoned on their sides.

Chapter Thirty-One

The old lady waited at the foot of the stairs, supporting herself on the glossy oak newel post. Footsteps followed the sound of the flush upstairs as the final visitor departed the bathroom.

"Sorry about that. I think it was knowing they'd all been, and I hadn't that sort of brought it on, if you know what I mean?" said Raymond as he descended the squeaky steps. As he reached the kind lady, he smiled and offered some helpful news. "Oh, by the way. You're out of toilet paper."

She nodded at the news.

"I don't suppose you could help me with a bit of a favour?" he asked.

"Would you like a bath?" she asked.

The humour was lost on him. "Oh, no, no, thank you. I had a bath on Thursday."

She examined the owl scratches that peeked above his white beard and nodded philosophically. He carried on with his request.

"I'm having a spot of bother with my ordinance survey map. We're trying to find Great Ormond Street Hospital, and I'm embarrassed to say it's defeating me!"

"Of course," said the lady. "In fact, I can show you."

"Goodness! That's very kind!" Raymond was delighted with this outcome.

The lady fumbled in her deep cardigan pockets and extracted some car keys.

"Oh no! You don't need to do that. You can just tell me where to go."

"It's no problem. I need to drop some presents off with my grandsons anyway. You could help me with them?" replied the lady.

"My pleasure!"

Raymond opened the door and stepped outside. The cubs were all in place on their bikes, and Anthony was in position holding the reins. Everyone stared back at him.

"Have you just sat on a stranger's toilet?" said Maureen. She looked appalled.

"It's spotless," said Raymond, like this might neutralise her despair.

"You know, had you asked me yesterday how long it takes ninety-three cubs to take a piss, I would have struggled," said Tash. "But now, I'm just hoping that's the final question on *Who Wants to Be A Millionaire*.... if I ever get on it. And I get all the others right first."

"You'd need to deduct Raymondo's crap," said Martha.

"She's going to take us to hospital!" said Raymond cheerily, ignoring the nonsense from his cart.

"She threatened you?" asked Jamie.

"No. The children's hospital."

"That does make better sense," said Tash.

"Could you take these for me?" said the old lady, standing in her doorway and pointing at a large black bin bag she'd dragged to the mat.

"Of course," said Raymond, picking up the bag, which was far heavier than he'd anticipated. He hauled it over his shoulder and started to walk off like Father Christmas doing his first delivery.

"Where are you going?" shouted Maureen.

"Just helping her to put some gifts in her car," said Raymond.

Maureen tutted, then realised the old lady had spotted her, so she turned her frown upside down. She watched as the OAP slammed the front door and set off after Raymond. She stopped at the Austin Maxi with the CND sticker and unlocked the boot.

Jamie and Tash looked at one another and then at Maureen, who pretended this wasn't happening.

As the hatchback lid swung slowly open, it revealed a car rammed full of chaos. Suitcases and boxes and rugs and blankets. Clearly, this lady had little order in her life, Raymond thought. He'd spotted that in her home.

"Anywhere you can find a space," she said as she walked around and unlocked the driver's door and slid onto the brown vinyl seat.

Raymond plopped the bag on top of an upholstered shopping cart and then forced the boot lid closed. It took a few attempts before it clicked.

"Follow me, then," said the frail voice through her now opened window.

Raymond dashed to the sleigh and pulled himself up to the flat back, using the front wheel as a step. It wasn't stylish. It reminded Tash of the way Jamie climbed out of a swimming pool. One arm, then a kind of leg over attempt, which eventually caught some traction, allowing him to horizontally roll the rest of him up and out of the pool. Or onto the cart, in this case.

"We're going to follow that car," said Raymond to Anthony. "But just wait for me to get seated."

The Austin Maxi set off, and so did the sleigh. Anthony was never one for detail. The jerking motion caused Raymond to roll the entire length of the carriage and off the back onto the tarmac. The cortege of bikes squeaked as emergency brakes were applied, most to good effect, other than Jackson, who didn't realise he had to backpedal to use his, so instead, he found himself parked on Father Christmas. It was difficult to tell who was crying most, but given the sleigh wasn't stopping, Raymond was soon on his feet again and running to catch up. Jamie was now at the back with his arms outstretched, and Martha held his legs for support. Raymond's second attempt to board the sleigh wasn't helped by the sound of laughter from the cyclists up the rear, but he was soon back alongside his wife. The wholly unpleasant affair had only lasted about fifteen metres but had knocked the wind from him and the pillow from his trousers.

"Stop showing off and sit down," said Maureen.

He did.

"We'll be there in no time now," said Raymond, like a man still in control.

"How long?" asked Martha.

"Oh, erm," said Raymond, looking into the sky as if his brain was doing some computations. "I'd say maybe ten minutes tops."

"We're here," said Anthony, skilfully bringing Bertie to a halt.

Sure enough, the Maxi in front had stopped, and the delicate finger of the driver was pointing to their right.

Great Ormond Street Hospital for Children adorned signs on a myriad of limestone, red and grey brick buildings around Queen Square and beyond.

Their convoy had stretched one hundred yards, give or take.

"Okay, we're here," said Tash, clapping her cold hands. "Let's get on with this."

The Maxi gave a little beep of the horn and continued onwards and out of sight.

Raymond was the only one to wave back.

Great Ormond Street Hospital was enjoying the 47th year of the death of a British author.

Well, maybe *enjoying* is a little harsh. Still, *benefitting from the altruism* of a British author is more accurate.

Author, J.M. Barrie, had donated the copyright (and so the income) to his Peter Pan works to the hospital in 1929. When he died in 1937, the UK Copyright laws meant the hospital would enjoy these funds for fifty further years until the work entered the public domain. After that time, Peter Pan would be free for anyone to read and do whatever they wished with it.

This period would ultimately be extended, but that was unknown in 1984, so with three years of guaranteed income remaining, the hospital was immeasurably grateful for the phenomenal efforts and contributions from benevolent, charitable souls. Including the cub scout movement of South London. Who were in fine voice, despite their fifty-five-minute cycle ride across the capital.

Now they were about to enjoy the purest pleasure known to humankind.

Selflessness.

Father Christmas would lead the way around the wards of poorly children, and the cubs would share the magic of Christmas with souls less fortunate than them. A moment that would last in their hearts forever.

Unless they wanted a He-Man.

And unless Martha and Tash got their way, and they just dumped the delivery in reception.

Chapter Thirty-Two

"How long does it take to hand out some gifts to sick kids?" asked Martha, sitting alongside Tash on the emptied sleigh. Bertie patiently stood up front, dreaming of sprawling fields carpeted with buttercups and bees. His reality was a 1960s external staircase leading to one of the loading bays in the rear courtyard of the massive hospital campus. Anthony had capably tied the horse's reins to the railing before helping his cub mates and Father Christmas unload the goodies onto porters' trolleys. Head elf Maureen and helper Jamie had joined Mrs Lynch as the procession entered the labyrinth of corridors that would lead them to the wards. Tash had point-blank refused to leave the C5 unattended, and Martha had refused to leave Tash, so it was a stalemate. They waited in the cold, with baby Raymond tucked warmly inside his mother's coat.

"At least the singing has stopped," said Tash. "Who knew there were nine verses to The First Noel?"

"Well, in fairness, they stopped at six," said Martha. "Anthony took the last three."

She had finally nailed the correct pronunciation.

"Little thwat," said Tash.

Martha laughed but added: "That doesn't really work. It would be," she thought for a moment, "lithle thwath."

"Less impact," said Tash. "I need a swear word to have some attack."

"I hear you," said Martha.

They waited in silence for a while.

"That's a lot of sick kids," said Martha, scanning the monumental expanses of concrete and brick surrounding them and disappearing into the gloomy sky.

Tash nodded sadly, then tweaked her son's hat. He was still snoozing from his horse-drawn sleigh ride. "Heartbreaking," said Tash in a faltering voice. "In here for Christmas, too."

"Kind of puts things in perspective, doesn't it? All our problems. They're kind of insignificant," said Martha.

Tash nodded. "Although your problems are worse than most. If you don't find that woman who stole your inheritance, you will be executed. You know. Maybe. Probably not."

"Shit, I forgot about that," said Martha.

They both smiled.

"What do you think of my brother?" asked Tash.

"Excuse me?"

"Do you think he's weird?"

"Why would you say that about your own brother?"

"Answer the question."

"Of course, I don't think he's weird. Why would I think he's weird?" Martha was shocked.

Tash stared at her for a moment, then smiled and replied.

"Good."

"Seriously though, how long does it take to give some gifts? We need to find your uncle."

"What's the plan?" asked Tash. "You're not going to threaten him, are you?"

Again, Martha looked offended. "We have met, right? You do know I'm not an actual felon?"

"So, what is the plan?"

"I just need to get into the computer room. Once I'm in there, I call my contact. Should take minutes."

"What should take minutes?"

"He'll talk me through a few buttons and shit, and then I find out where my money is."

"Then what?"

"Then we go get it," replied Martha.

This made Tash sit up. "Woah! Rewind the 'we' part. We never agreed to that."

"Okay, cool. That's fine. I hear you. I just thought you might want to do the right thing."

"I've been doing the right thing for about seventy-five hours now, and it keeps leading to the wrong thing. I just need some sleep."

They were interrupted by the echo of a door banging open and the sound of children singing, followed by footsteps on a concrete staircase, then a familiar Welsh voice.

"I never actually pressed it. I just wanted to show how you could increase the heart rate with electricity," said Anthony.

"That child was sleeping," said Maureen.

"Well, he is now," said Raymond, trying badly to lighten the mood.

"We're going!" said Jamie. "We're going!" He was appealing to the nurse who had opened the fire exit for this spontaneous eviction.

Anthony started to descend the steps, attempting to photograph the view of the yard below but deciding against it. He was followed by Maureen, Raymond, and then Jamie. Next came the cubs, all fully committed to The Twelve Days of Christmas. Mrs Lynch made up the rear, looking mightily humiliated, loud hailer still in hand and silent tears running down her cheeks.

"It's a long carol, isn't it?" said Raymond as he pulled his hood from his eyes for the millionth time. "Do you think we could pick it up later, sort of thing? Maybe have a bit of quiet?"

"Don't talk to me," said Maureen.

"What did you do?" asked Tash as Anthony approached the front of the sleigh and effortlessly pulled himself onto the seat.

"You should never touch machines," said Maureen to the indifferent cub. "Never!"

"That was quite a jolt," said Jamie, cradling a mince pie in both hands.

"What did he do?" asked Martha.

"Come on, everyone. Calm down. They said he'll be fine," said Raymond, "when he wakes up." Raymond always tried to make the best of appalling situations.

"I can never show my face here again," said Maureen.

"Well, that's good, cos that nurse said we're banned," said Jamie, taking his first bite and watching as the rest of the crust and filling dropped onto the cold ground.

"Everyone shut up and answer my question!" said Tash.

Sure enough, the crowd did as they were told. Even the Twelve Lords stopped A-Leaping. Jamie's hand went up. Tash sighed and nodded at him.

"How do we shut up AND answer your question?"

Tash ignored this perfectly reasonable logic.

"Has our visit improved the quality of life for more children in *that* building than not?"

She had a leading tone to her question, which everyone considered as she continued to point assertively at the hospital wall. Then they all simultaneously muttered their responses in hushed tones whilst avoiding eye contact with Tash. Things like...

... "Without a doubt."

..."I'd say so."

..."The kids loved seeing Father Christmas."

..."Can I go to the toilet?"

..."Magical, really."

..."Their little faces lit up."

..."Certainly."

All whilst nodding at one another in an upbeat way.

"And it was a very low voltage," said Anthony.

They all waited for her response.

"Right," said Tash. "Let's get going."

"Thank God for that," said Martha, sitting on one of the

garden chairs behind Anthony, who was already holding the reins tightly.

"Right," said Maureen, in a loud tone, "get out of the way of the back of the sleigh and do it without talking!"

"Righto," said Raymond, setting off as instructed.

"She was talking to the cubs," said Jamie.

"Oh," said Raymond, before double-checking with his wife, just in case. "Were you?"

Maureen had clearly decided that this was a moment of her life that she never wanted to revisit, so she was highly focused on the job in hand. Subsequently, as often happened in their marriage, she ignored him.

"You need to get your bikes and wheel them – not cycle them – wheel them to the side over there so we can turn this cart around," said Maureen.

Raymond was impressed by his wife's assertiveness and the instant response it elicited from every single cub. He'd not seen her in action with her pack before. She reminded him of a slightly younger Barbara Woodhouse off the telly. But maybe not as obviously sexy.

"Oh, hang on a minute now," said Anthony, his voice had lost its customary confidence.

"What?" said Tash, as Raymond repeated his swimming pool style ascent onto the timber carriage floor. He made lots of grunting noises as he stood up straight and reattached his beard. Jamie was already back in position and holding the Christmas tree upright.

Anthony looked nervously over his shoulder at the adults staring back at him and Bertie, the magnificent Shire horse still waiting patiently in front, inches away from a mossy 1960s wall. His bridled nose exhaled a cloud of carbon dioxide into the cold, damp air.

"I've never actually done reversing," said the cub, offering the reins back to anyone who would accept them.

"Sake," said Tash.

Chapter Thirty-Three

"This is why the eighties are shit," said Tash.

"Don't swear in front of the children," said Maureen.

Maureen was the only adult still sitting on the carriage, cradling baby Raymond. The sleigh was lighter now as the gifts had been delivered, but it was a vintage piece, and the seasoned and weathered timbers were a substantial load on the antique wheels. The extra nine stone and ten pounds of Maureen and baby Raymond, the extended Sinclair C5 and the plastic Woolies Christmas tree weren't adding a significant amount of weight.

The cubs had laid their bikes on their sides and now formed a sea of green caps around the front of the carriage, worryingly close to the rear of the horse. Anthony was busying himself unhitching the shafts and holdbacks that attached the carriage to the horse. Tash thought he was surely worthy of a badge in horsey-type-stuff but wasn't about to tell the precocious little prick.

"Why do you say that?" asked Jamie, genuinely intrigued by his sister's remark. "The eighties are wicked."

"Because if we had phones, we could YouTube our way out of this!"

"What does any of that mean?" asked Martha.

Tash sighed and looked at the American.

"You think of any crazy shit scenario that could ever happen to anyone at any time – and someone else has already thought of it, found a fix and then posted a video of them showing you how to solve it," said Tash.

"Posted it where?" asked Martha.

"Not posted it like you post stuff. I mean posted to the internet."

"Stop talking about space and help the others," said Maureen.

"Space?" asked Tash.

"Whatever it was you just said," said Maureen.

"The internet?"

"I mean it. You're like a walking episode of *Dramarama*! Just push!"

Raymond decided to break the tension again. "I'm sure it's a lovely place, Tash. Maybe we can hear about it all later."

"What's a lovely place?"

"The spaceship thing, inter-wotsit."

"Internet."

"Yes."

"Three, two, one!" said Martha, and once again, the cub collective all strained to create enough force to start the steel-rimmed wheels of the cart rolling backwards. The two-inch-wide flat faces of rubber tyre began to hum with the motion.

"It's moving!" said Jamie. "Keep going!"

Sure enough, the cart started to inch backwards. It was hard to see at first, but soon the movement of the shaft away from Bertie's sides was apparent, and Anthony ensured nothing caused the beautiful animal any anxiety. The cart slowed to a halt.

"Now then, a one-horse open sleigh!" came a shout.

They looked behind to see two cleaners standing on a raised platform above an industrial bin. Behind them, double doors opened into an industrial kitchen overflowing with cooks, cleaners, and mayhem. A radio was playing 'So Near to Christmas' by Alvin Stardust.

"Ho ho!" said Raymond, remaining in character and waving to them both.

"Stop showing off," said Maureen.

One of the cleaners tossed overflowing bin bags into the vast steel refuse chamber, and the other lifted tray after tray of food waste and slopped the contents onto the bags. There was no doubt that a Christmas lunch had been in full flow, every tray erupting with a volcano of left over lumpy pink custard, gravy, and sprouts.

"Good job, fellas, let's go for a bigger push this time, step it up," said Martha, returning to the job in hand. "One, two, three."

The cubs made no extra effort, despite the encouragement from their American coach.

"You counted down last time," said Jamie.

"And?"

"Nothing, just saying," said Jamie, blushing a little. "I think we got confused."

"No one's confused," said Martha. "Who's confused? I'm not confused. Any of you guys confused?" she asked the mass of red-cheeked kids. None were brave enough to admit if they were.

"I think down or up will work," said Raymond.

"You do the countdown, Raymond," said Maureen, gently rubbing the cheek of the sleeping baby in her arms.

"Ten, nine," started Raymond.

"Not from ten," said Maureen.

"Sake, not this again," said Tash. "Everyone push... NOW."

And they did.

Once the wheels had made one full rotation over the smooth tarmac, the children's joy was visible on their faces, and another revolution soon followed.

It was Jamie who panicked first.

"Bins! Bins!" he shouted, unable to form a more coherent warning.

"What about them?" asked Tash, trying to peer behind the cart.

"Bins!" said Jamie.

"Stop!" shouted Tash.

The cubs did as they were told and immediately grappled

with finding any available part of the carriage to prevent it rolling any further. Happily, it soon stopped.

"Excellent!" shouted Martha.

"Well done, boys," said Maureen.

"That was close," said Jamie.

They all turned to watch the C5 slowly roll from beneath the bedspread which was snagged on the carriage side, then off the back of the cart and into the bin and the abyss of pink lava and turkey gristle.

In a moment of vicious serendipity, the cleaners simultaneously pebble-dashed the inside of the bin with approximately forty pounds of turkey giblets.

From the bowels of the hospital kitchen, Alvin continued to sing that his heart was aching. Maybe a couple of Rennies would help.

"You can't put that in there," said the gobbiest of the cleaners. "It's for food waste."

"Yes, thank you, I wondered what that sign meant," said Tash, gesturing to the stencilled paint *FOOD ONLY* on the side of the bin as she frantically paced over.

"Oh no!" shouted Maureen before holding her mouth a little too late. She had woken the baby in her arms with her exclamation.

"What's the problem?" asked Jamie.

"We haven't set the video for Cliff Richard!"

"What?" said Tash, sadly examining her ride home which was now peeking from beneath a pink and brown slop mask.

"He's on the *Rock Gospel Show Christmas Special*. And Alvin Stardust."

The way Maureen said Alvin Stardust might confuse someone who hadn't heard of him. She somehow managed to elevate this seventies pop star to Pope-like status simply by the tone of her voice.

Tash removed a turkey neck from the nose of the C5 and dropped it onto the ground.

"This is why the eighties are shit," said Tash.

Chapter Thirty-Four

"Come along! These children need to get home. Their families are waiting for them," said Maureen, suddenly feeling far more relaxed about her nanny duties. She and baby Raymond sat at the front of the repositioned sleigh, with Anthony sitting up front in his driving position. The cubs all sat patiently on their bikes, one foot expectantly placed on a pedal, the other on the ground.

"Sake!" said Tash.

She and Jamie were at one side of the large steel bin, Raymond and Martha at the other. Together they had collectively failed to extract the C5, so they had waited for the cleaning staff to return to the kitchen, so they could set about rocking the bin to upturn it. So far, this had simply made them all extremely hot and irritable.

"We don't need them to wait for us," said Raymond. "We have our little errand, so to speak. So, why don't they just cycle home behind Akela?"

"What about me?" shouted Anthony. "I left my bike in Brixton, didn't I?"

"Yeth," said Tash. "You're forgething abouth Anthony."

"We need him to steer," said Jamie.

"Good point, actually," said Raymond before shouting over to the solitary cub on the sleigh. "We need you to steer."

"We'll still get you home, young man," said Maureen.

"I'll go and tell Akela," said Raymond. And set off through the gates to the road outside where Mrs Lynch was sitting patiently in her Hillman. She didn't need much convincing and was soon revving the balls off the 0.9-litre engine, still nervous that it might stall at the first set of lights.

Raymond stood in the middle of Guilford Street and proudly held up his hand to stop the oncoming traffic. Not that there was any, but he felt all man.

"When you're ready, Akela," he shouted. "Boys, follow Akela on your bikes, and thanks for all your help."

The Hillman Imp emitted a cloud of lead-coloured smoke and sputtered into action. Two by two, and three by three, the cubs exited the hospital service yard and followed their leader down the road.

Raymond gave the final boy a friendly Father Christmas wave and then walked back through the gates, stopping only to wave at his wife. "Shouldn't be long now."

"This is the worst day of my life," said Maureen.

"Yes, darling, sorry about that."

"After the day they got us shot at," she added.

"Yes, of course."

"And the day they got us arrested and locked in prison."

"Yes, that was a bad one too, but technically the same twenty-four hours."

"Don't try and be clever with maths at me, Raymond."

"No, I wasn't trying to be."

"Why are you standing talking to me? Get over there and help them."

"Well, yes. This is it," said Raymond as he rushed over to help retrieve the C5.

"There's a lock on that wheel," said Jamie, pointing to one of three wheels beneath the massive cylindrical bin.

He walked around and kicked it down to secure one of the spinning castors.

"We need to apply pressure from the top," he said, pointing to the elevated area where the cleaners had dumped the food.

"I'll get up there," said Raymond setting off around the back to a flight of rusting open tread stairs.

"I'll help," said Tash.

She didn't move.

"I said I'll help push."

She glared at Jamie.

"What?" he asked.

"You're supposed to say, no, it's heavy and dirty. You stay here and make sure the bottom doesn't move! I'll push."

"That's not very 2020, Tash."

"We're not in 2020, Jamie. We're in the worst year ever."

"Okay," said Jamie, following Raymond up to the top of the bin. Outside the double doors to the kitchen, they could hear joyful laughter and the clink and rattle of plastic plates and stainless steel cutlery over Paul Young tearing a playhouse down.

"After three," said Jamie.

"Shush!" said Tash. "They're just behind you."

Jamie looked around and through the glass at the top of the doors.

"They're not looking!" he replied.

"Shush!" said Tash.

"Sorry," replied Jamie in his usual crap whisper.

"What's the plan?" asked Martha.

"Well, I thought I'd check out the pool and then maybe grab a cocktail on the beach," said Tash.

"Excuse me?"

"Well, we tip over the fucking bin, don't we? What do you mean 'plan'? Sake!"

"She's right, sis. We need to know who does what," said Jamie.

"Oh my God, could you please try to be quiet, Jamie!"

"Let's rock it from the top, and then once we get it wobbling, we'll sort of nudge it over?" said Raymond.

"That's gonna twat it on the ground. We need to lower it, surely?" said Tash.

"Good luck with that," said Martha. "There's a half tonne of crappy English cuisine in there."

"There's nothing wrong with English food, I'll have you know," said Maureen. "We invented Eton Mess."

Martha looked at Maureen and then up at Raymond. "I don't even know what she just said."

"It's like a meringue with tinned fruit," he explained.

"I never used tinned, Raymond. You take that back!" said Maureen.

"Fresh fruit," said Raymond starting to stammer. "Meringue, fresh sort of berries and cream."

"I think I might have confused you," said Martha. "When I said, I don't know what she just said; I meant I don't give a shit what she just said. Shall we start?"

"Yes," said Raymond. "Ten, nine, eight."

"Sake!" said Tash. "After three, one, two, three, push!"

Jamie and Raymond started to strain in unison, and it was no surprise to Jamie that this caused Raymond to fart.

"Sorry about that squeaker, Jamie," whispered Raymond through clenched teeth as he continued to strain.

"I thought I'd trodden on a duck," said Jamie, trying out a joke he'd heard Bobby Ball use the other night.

"No, I did a squeaker," said Raymond. He couldn't push and get jokes.

The bin started to lean over towards the expanse of tarmac on the other side and then swung back their way. They took a momentary breather and then pushed again. It was hard work.

They did it a third time.

And a fourth.

And fifth.

"Keep going," said Martha.

They did, and on the sixth push, it's top overbalanced it's base, and the vast steel drum slammed down onto the ground.

The C5's front wheel was now on the tarmac, and on first appearances, it seemed to be in once piece. Although it was difficult to be sure beneath the gloop that covered it.

"Well done!" said Jamie. Really loudly.

"Shush!" said Tash as she forced herself to start removing split and sticky bags of potato skins, carrot tops, cold mash potato and endless other indiscernible foods. Martha stood back. She wanted to help, but watching Tash gag as she busily worked didn't really motivate her to join in.

"Are you going to help?" asked Tash, in her no-nonsense voice.

Martha grimaced and shook her head.

"Nah."

Jamie was soon alongside his sister and together they managed to free the C5 from the bin and wheel it towards the rear of the old wooden carriage. Tash found the plywood ramp that they'd used to get the Sinclair on the sleigh in the first place. She struggled to drag it off and Martha surprised them both by taking half of the weight and walking to the rear of the sleigh. They positioned it together, and then the four of them wheeled the time machine, and its portable mixed trifle, up the ramp and hid it beneath the candlewick camouflage.

"Good job," said Martha as she and Jamie climbed on. Tash appeared on the other side and sat alongside Maureen who gently handed over her son.

Suddenly, they all realised they were rocking.

"What's that? What is that?" asked Martha.

Behind them, they saw Raymond attempting his swimming pool exit routine to clamber up.

"I don't know why I didn't use the ramp, actually," he said, before rolling over and taking a breath before standing up and walking to sit on a chair behind his wife.

"I think that went really well," said Raymond looking back at the overturned bin and mounds of waste food and slop that covered much of the courtyard.

"Let's get the hell out of here, before they see all that crap," said Martha.

"Everyone sitting comfortably?" said Anthony, with the reins tightly gripped between his freezing fingers.

The replies came in unison.

"No."

"...Of course not."

"...Are you kidding?"

"...Just drive."

Anthony was clearly enjoying today more than his passengers.

"Off we go!"

He expertly flicked the reins, and Bertie's patchy flared trouser legs came to life, and then he was off!

So strong.

So graceful.

So unattached to the carriage.

"Oh. I forgot to re-attach us, didn't it I?" said Anthony.

They all watched in dumb despair as the horse set off happily down the road and turned left out of sight.

"You gonna clear this up?" said a doctor standing at the rear of the carriage, pointing to their mess on the ground.

Chapter Thirty-Five

"They left a lot, didn't they?" said Raymond in an upbeat conversational way as he gestured at the food scrapings.

The doctor wasn't particularly chatty. "You saying the food's bad?"

"No, oh no. Not at all," Raymond stopped shovelling it from the tarmac and held the laden dustpan to his nose. He breathed in deeply. "Mmmm. Smells smashing."

They had found out that his name was Robyn with a Y and that he was just finishing his shift as a consultant, although he didn't expand on that part. Martha had said that much as she was pleased to learn he was finishing his shift, she couldn't give a crap how he spelt his name. He was in his late twenties, and if pushed, Jamie would describe him as a bit pleased with himself. Raymond would probably describe him as a little bit assertive, as would Maureen. Martha would probably describe him as hard to understand, and Tash would call him fit. In fact, FAF.

"Are you not going to help at all?" said Tash, throwing handfuls of turkey carcases into the upturned bin and glaring at Martha.

"I have this gag reflex," said Martha. "Any poultry or, you know, whatever this shit is..." she pointed in the general direction of the remaining food, "...sets it off."

"Nightmare," said Tash.

"I'm the same with dairy," said Martha.

"Yet you flew eight thousand miles in a cheese crate," said Tash.

"Someone's having a bad day," said Martha.

"That would be all of us, surely?" said Tash.

"Let's all try and be friends," said Raymond, lifting a dustpan piled high with congealed turkey fat, then absentmindedly missing the bin and pouring it down Robyn's leather jacket.

"I think you might struggle with him," said Tash.

Jamie laughed. Robyn leapt backwards and examined the damage.

And that was when it hit Martha.

She remembered Frankie Duffy's words in Canada.

Don't you got friends any place other than Vermont?

She could hear his kind voice as if he were standing next to her, and she could remember the ball that hit her in the stomach when he said those words. An intense and instant blow that came from nowhere. She'd never been struck by a bullet and hoped she never would but guessed that the feeling was similar.

She had no friends. None. That was what she'd realised.

But now, his words didn't yield the same response. Confusingly, she felt warm.

She didn't want to get ahead of herself and would rarely admit to herself that anything was ever going right. After all, this would tempt fate, and then when things did go wrong, she would realise that it was because she allowed herself to believe they were going right.

However, she did allow herself one thought:

Maybe it's not accurate to say *I have no friends.*

Yes, she would allow herself that.

She bent down, picked up a handful of sprouts, and tossed them into the bin.

As she went to get more, she realised Jamie's hand was in the air, and he was standing a little bit too close to the sticky consultant, who was trying to flick gizzard from his GOSH NHS name badge. It read: Robyn Sanchez, Senior Consultant.

He stopped and looked curiously at Jamie. "What's up?"

"Can I ask a question?" said Jamie.

Robyn considered this. He's never been asked if someone could ask him a question before.

"Yes."

"That wasn't it, by the way," said Jamie.

"What wasn't it?"

"When I said – can I ask a question – that wasn't it, even though that was a question."

"Are you taking the piss?"

Jamie was confused. "No."

"Get on with it, then."

"You see that motorbike?" said Jamie, pointing to a Honda parked in the yard's far corner. It was glistening white and bright red, and Tash was surprised no one else had spotted it.

"Yes," replied Robyn.

"I think I might need to ask another question," said Jamie. "Do you know who owns that motorbike?"

"Yes," replied the doctor, offering nothing more.

"He's going for a third," said Tash.

"Who owns that motorbike?" said Jamie.

"Me."

"Can I borrow it?"

"No."

"Okay."

"How do you think that went, Jamie?" said Tash, kicking a potato under the bin. "In terms of a successful answer to question response ratio?"

Jamie didn't like it when Tash pointed out his failings, but he wasn't done yet.

"Shame, cos we were just having a bet, weren't we, Dad?" said Jamie to Raymond.

"What?" said Raymond. He'd not been called this before. He even looked behind him to see if Jamie's father had arrived.

"Dad was telling me about his old motorbike, weren't you?" said Jamie. "Dad."

Tash and Martha were now spellbound.

"What type was it?" said Jamie, "I can't remember?"

Even behind his white beard, Raymond was an image of confusion. Tash could see him trying different responses on his lips, but no words made their way through the little gap under the moustache.

"Dad. What type was your motorbike? The one we were just talking about?"

"It was a er, it was a ... Harvey Davison," said Raymond with very little conviction.

"Harley Davidson?" said Robyn.

Raymond nodded sheepishly. "Green one."

What was Jamie up to? What was happening? Was anyone else suddenly hot?

The medic wasn't sure if he'd ever seen a green one. "Green? You sure?"

Raymond nodded. Even Maureen was holding her breath now.

"Dad was just saying that your one over there is shit compared to his Harvey."

"Harley," corrected the doctor.

"Harley," said Jamie.

Robyn didn't like this one bit. He'd spent a fortune on his Interceptor, and when he wasn't cleaning it, he was talking *at* people about it. Not *with* them, *at* them.

"That's one hundred and sixteen horsepower, that is," he said in Raymond's face, "that 'shit' bike."

"Well, I don't remember saying those words, exactly."

"I said I reckon it could shift that wagon easily, and he said not," said Jamie, nodding to the sleigh. "Our horse had to go home, see, and we started asking about how we get to the next lot of kiddies."

"Your horse had to go home?" asked Robyn. He stared at Jamie for thirty years or so.

"Yeah," said Jamie, eventually. Then thought it might help to explain why. "Early night."

"Where do you need to be?" asked Robyn suspiciously into Raymond's face.

"Pardon me?" replied Raymond, still unsure if he was about

to lose some teeth.

"These kiddies, where do you need to be, Father Christmas? Where's next?"

"Oh, erm, yes, erm, well, it's erm..." Raymond looked to the others for help.

They all replied in unison.

"Midland Bank Head Office."

Chapter Thirty-Six

"It's faster than I thought," said Raymond, his upper face covered by his clip-on beard, which was blowing up and over his forehead.

"Pardon?" said Maureen, clutching tightly to the floor as tears of water were forced out of the sides of her eyes.

"This is ace!" said Anthony, still at the front and fully living his best life.

"She's holding him very tight," said Tash.

"What?" said Jamie.

"You haven't noticed? Are you kidding?"

Tash nodded to the Honda, which was capably pulling them along Gresham Street at a pace none of them had expected. The motorbike had taken some severe high-pitched revving to get off the mark as they left Great Ormond Street Hospital, but it had kept a tidy pace once in motion. Tash was centrally placed on the sleigh and had decided to sit on the timber floor with her son. Jamie regretted his choice of a foldable chair, but there was little he could do now.

Martha had happily accepted Robyn's spare crash helmet whilst they made a makeshift attachment from the carriage jockey wheel to the frame of the Honda. Robyn was concerned that the steel of the shafts might scratch his pristine paintwork, so Raymond had offered up his Father Christmas tummy, which had fallen out anyway, so two ripped and tied half pillows provided a buffer on each side. Anthony had offered advice throughout but had been regularly chastised by Tash about his previous faux pas when he forgot to attach the same pieces to the fucking horse. Her words.

Tash looked at Martha's back and the seamless continuation of material from her twin set to Robyn's Top Man suit.

"She needs to hold tight, or she'll fall off," said Jamie.

"Yeah," said Tash, looking again. "Well, there's holding tight, and there's giving a free back massage with your massive Chi-Chi's."

Jamie looked at his sister and then out to Martha, who was laughing at something they'd spotted in Bow Church. Something hilarious.

"Next left!" he shouted. And then he yelled it again. And again, until Martha heard. Tash and Jamie saw her squeeze Robyn's arm to point out their destination. He slowed their sleigh down with expert precision.

Martha was off the bike in no time, expertly removing her helmet whilst tossing her purple hair back into perfect shape.

She reminded Maureen of the lady off the Schwarzkopf Coromist shampoo advert on the telly. *Don't get it wet for anything less* was their song, and it was Raymond's second favourite tune after the Shake N Vac one. Although in company, Maureen would still deny watching ITV unless it was *World in Action* or maybe repeats of *The Professionals*.

"Nice landing, Rudolph," said Martha as Robyn removed his helmet. She did a playful prod of his nose.

Tash observed Jamie swallowing awkwardly as he watched this exchange.

"You gonna let her get away with that?" said Tash.

"What are you talking about?" said Jamie.

"Nothing," said Tash. "Just kidding." She wasn't. Bloody hell, how the hell did these two ever end up together?

"What's the plan now?" said Jamie, looking firmly at his sister.

"You must have me confused with someone who knows what the fuck is going on."

"Are you going to swear throughout that baby's childhood?" said Maureen.

"He's asleep," said Tash. "And I only swear in the eighties."

Jamie gave her an astonished face.

"I do! I do now anyway, new rule. In fact, I'll quit altogether."

"Okay, I need everyone to come with me," said Martha.

"You can piss off," said Tash.

"That didn't last long, did it?" said Maureen.

"Smile!" shouted Anthony, clutching his Kodak 110 to his eye. The crowd immediately switched to happy souls and waited until Anthony clicked his camera button before reverting to their mutual collective irritation.

"I'm staying with this. I said it from the start," said Tash, tapping the bedspread that covered the C5. Some pink custard and bread sauce seeped through the loosely knitted fabric and found its way onto her hand. She wiped it clean on her tea cosy hat.

"You said you wouldn't leave it behind," said Martha, "different thing." Then she turned to Anthony. "Nice camera." He looked genuinely proud.

"That is a different thing," agreed Jamie, realising fair is fair.

"Jamie," said Tash, "You know what happens if this gets stolen or lost?"

"I'll stay with it," said Anthony.

"Oh, thanks, Bear Grylls, but I might need someone who isn't wearing shorts."

"Why is she calling me a bear?" Anthony asked Maureen.

"Your guess is as good as mine. She once told me she had a walking wardrobe," replied Maureen.

"Walk in," said Tash. "Walk *in.* And I did until I moved back to my parents."

"What's a walking wardrobe?" said Raymond.

"Walk *in.* Walk *in,*" said Tash. "Can anyone hear me?"

"Walk in?" said Raymond.

"Yes," said Tash. "Thank you."

"Like Narnia?" said Anthony.

"No, not like bloody Narnia," said Tash.

"Can you walk out again?" said Raymond.

"Am I in a wardrobe now?"

"No."

"Then yes, you can walk out again! Sake!"

"Are we getting a bit distracted?" said Jamie.

"He's right. I want this nasty business done with as soon as possible. Geoffrey Wheeler's presenting *Songs of Praise* tonight, and I refuse to miss that," said Maureen. "I refuse!"

"I didn't have you down as the churchy type," said Tash.

"What does that mean?" she replied.

"No offence, just, you know, I didn't see you as a God botherer."

"Are you going to let her talk to me like that, Raymond?"

Raymond shuffled in his Santa suit. "I'm not sure what she said. Some of her sentences don't make sense."

"I just meant, I didn't think you were deeply religious. I wasn't being offensive. It was an observation," said Tash.

"We're both in agreement on this. Fervent advocates, to be fair," said Raymond, squaring up. He hoped he hadn't been too confrontational, but he wouldn't let this pass.

"Of God?" said Tash.

"Geoffrey Wheeler," said Raymond. "He's the voice on *Winner Takes All,* too. Very talented chap."

"He sounds like a great guy," said Martha.

"What time are all the kids coming?" said Robyn, peering around the empty streets.

"What kids?" said Jamie.

"The kids. Coming to see Father Christmas?"

"Oh!" said Jamie. "Yes! Those kids."

Jamie looked at his sister. And then Raymond. And then Maureen. And then Martha.

"They're inside the bank," said Maureen. "Already."

Ooh, thought Tash, she really does want to see *Songs of Praise.*

Tash realised how far things must have escalated to prompt Maureen to join in with the deceit. And it gave her a bit of a buzz. With Maureen on board, things would undoubtedly get moving now.

"How long will you be? Cos, I need to get home for my Sunday lunch," said Robyn.

"Bit late. Mummy leaving you a plate in the oven?" asked Tash.

"I left home years ago."

"Oh! Married, are we?" Tash was now trying hard to shut down any chances of a blossoming romance with their American friend.

"No. I live with my partner," said Robyn.

Tash fixed him with a Paddington stare. Why wasn't he revealing her name? Or his? Please can it be a man? He didn't provide any further information.

"How does fifteen minutes sound?" said Martha.

"I can live with that," said Robyn.

"Cool, you stay with dipshit, and mind that no one steals her shitty go-kart," she said, trying to pull some purple hair from her face and behind her ear.

Luckily Anthony had been dealing with a Hubba Bubba that he'd found in his shorts pocket, so this most recent put down had gone over his head. Like most things as he was four and a half feet tall.

"I'm not going anywhere," said Tash and folded her arms like Maureen. She'd learnt from the best.

"Only you and Jamie know what your uncle looks like!" said Martha.

"We know what he looks like in 2020. Not now," said Tash.

"Well, he'll look like he did on all the photos we have of your christening," said Jamie.

Tash gave him a cold glare, but he didn't realise. He never spotted that kind of thing.

"And my christening photos. And all the old Christmas photos. And that video of him being ordained. And..." but he was interrupted.

"Jamie, stop talking! Please! Whose side are you on?" Tash looked exhausted.

"Yours, of course," said Jamie. "Well, everyone's. I mean, I didn't realise we had sides. Do we have sides? Whose side are you on?"

Tash tapped the mound of the C5.

"Jamie. I can't leave this with Ken Boon and Jimmy fucking Krankie over there."

Anthony looked over his shoulder to see who she might be talking about.

"No offence, dipshit," she added.

"I'll wait with your silly spaceship," said Maureen assertively. "Now, stop swearing."

She looked at Tash with a face that displayed a myriad of thoughts and contradictions:

We don't like each other, but we both like Jamie.

We don't get along, but we always do the right thing.

We both wish our lives went along different paths, but we're making the best of what we have.

And neither of us takes shit from anyone.

"You can leave baby Raymond with me," she added, with the hint of a grandmother's smile.

Tash realised she was suddenly feeling quite emotional. She looked at Maureen, then over to Raymond. He was doing his squint thing again and trying to spit out a bit of nylon beard that had found its way between his teeth.

Tash shuffled over to Maureen and gently handed over her still sleeping son.

"Thank you."

"Spaceship?" said Robyn, as Raymond, Jamie, and Tash clambered down onto the pavement.

"I was joking," said Maureen firmly. This matter wasn't up for discussion. "Sit down with me, Anthony; we're going to hear a story about a reindeer. Would you like to hear it too, Robyn with a Y?"

He considered this, nodded, kicked down the stand to his bike and walked over to join her.

Martha led Raymond towards the main entrance. Tash and Jamie followed, stopping briefly to admire the carving in both sets of cornerstones that flanked the steps up to the glorious door.

Midland Bank Limited.

These had been covered with elegant signs displaying 'The Ned' the last time she had been here, in 2020, for cocktails beneath the five-star hotel. But that was all in the future (and Tash's past), and right now, as they approached the vast double-height arched oak doors, it was plain to see that this was a place of work.

"Wait, everyone, slow down. We need to talk about this! What are we going to say?" said Tash.

"We're just going to find Uncle David and ask him to show us the computer room, aren't we?" asked Jamie.

"No, that's absolutely not going to work," said Tash. "Can everyone stop right now and agree on a plan."

"I got this," said Martha, forcing the heavy door wide open and walking confidently inside.

"I really hope she doesn't get us arrested again," said Raymond. "Does anyone else feel a bit hot?"

Chapter Thirty-Seven

Immediately inside the cathedral-like interior was a temporary desk and plastic chair beneath a security guard, who was just about visible through the smoke from his Hamlet cigar. He was singing along to 'I Just Called To Say I Love You,' which played from a teak Fidelity transistor radio behind him. He couldn't reach the high notes like Stevie Wonder, so he dropped an octave when needed. What was most impressive, though, was his commitment to the song. He actually sang *at* his visitors as the song came to its crescendo.

"Of my heart, baby, of my hearrrrrrrrrt!"

"Hello," said Martha.

"Shhh", replied the guard before miming the three-chord "pah pah pah" synth that ended the song.

"Very nice," said Martha.

"It is a good song that, one of Maureen's favourites," said Raymond.

"You know where you stand with Stevie," agreed the guard, taking a draw on his Hamlet.

'Police Officer' by Smiley Culture started to play, and he fumbled with his ten-year-old radio to lower the volume to a more respectable level. The little desk itself was a miniature winter wonderland. He'd clearly busied himself with some drawing pins and twisted crepe ribbon.

"Not so sure about this guy," said the unimpressed man. "When did talking become a thing? Talking over music?"

"I'd love to chat with you; you're obviously an oracle when it comes to music and culture," said Martha, gesturing at his opened newspaper. Samantha Fox and Linda Lusardi stood back-to-back as undressed Mrs Christmases on the centre pages.

"And full marks for your seasonal display. Normally you'd need to visit a kindergarten for that level of skill."

He'd never heard of a kindergarten, so he nodded his appreciation as they glared at a green and red foil snowflake that he'd pinned to the ornate timber panels behind him.

"The bank is closed; this is a private event." He closed his paper, and his print-stained fingers revealed today's Sunday Mirror, which displayed a photo of Pam Ewing on the cover as "the UK's favourite soap star". Victoria Principal had "beaten the pants off Joan Collins' Alexis Carrington to the title in the "shock poll results".

The main headline was saved for Prince Charles, though. "Charles The Peace Maker: Phone call bid to cool Diana and Anne rift." Anne was reportedly absent from Prince Harry's christening on Friday.

"We know that," said Martha without flinching. "And please sit up straight. The photographer will be here soon."

The guard hid his newspaper beneath his seat. "What photographer? Who are you?"

He suddenly became very interested in this young lady dressed as a purple-haired Nancy Reagan and her two elf helpers. Then he clocked Father Christmas.

"Sorry," said Raymond.

"This is a private party for Midland staff," said the man, turning down the radio even more.

"Correct," said Martha, offering something to him.

Jamie looked down to see she was clutching Robyn's name badge. When the hell had she swiped that? The security man attempted to take it from her, but she gripped it tightly whilst he squinted to read the name badge.

Robyn Sanchez, Senior Consultant. Great Ormond Street Hospital.

"What's this about?" he asked, with his face creasing into the shape of a walnut shell.

Martha thought for a moment. Tash and Jamie stared at her, and Raymond stared at the almighty hall that lay before them. The vast interior went on forever in all directions, easily double or triple height with ornate painted plasterwork around the ceiling supported by marble and stone columns that stood on the highly polished oak floor. A wide walkway behind the security guard led to a grand circular desk at a suitably condescending height for visitors to be looked down on. Desks and chairs struggled to fill the palatial space, and all were eerily empty.

He asked again. "What's this about?"

"This," said Martha, "is about fifty thousand dollars."

"Pounds," said Tash.

"Pounds," said Martha without missing a beat. "Fifty big ones."

"Christ, she's not doing a robbery, is she?" thought Raymond. There was no way he could outrun this massive fellow, especially not in this Santa suit.

"The bank's closed." said the man. This was all he could say.

"I'm confusing you. I can see that," said Martha. "We are here to collect a cheque for fifty thousand pounds from Midlands Bank to The Great Hospital. The one on Osmond's Street."

She was struggling with names, so started to tap her borrowed security badge instead.

"Great Ormond Street," said Jamie. "We work there."

"For the kids," said Martha, "and we are very grateful, sir. Thank you."

"I don't know about no cheque," said the bewildered man, wishing he could carry on with his paper. Page fifteen had a story about fake gifts filling the Christmas markets, and he wasn't worried about the rip-off 'Feed The World' sweatshirts, but he was concerned about the Cabbage Patch Dolls. His wife had found one of these elusive toys for their daughter, and now he wondered if it would be full of nails and sawdust. But who pays twenty-five notes when you can pick one up for a fiver?

"Well, that's no problem, sir," said Martha. "We're from the hospital..."

"Great Ormond Street," said Jamie.

"And we're here to collect a cheque. They said you wouldn't know about it, and we were to ask for..."

She turned to Jamie and Tash, who looked at one another before the penny dropped.

"She means Uncle David," said Jamie in a terrible whisper.

"David Summers," said Tash.

"David Summers," repeated Martha.

"He works here, does he?" said the man.

"No, he works at one of your branches, but he's here for the party," said Tash.

The eyes of the security guard scanned the row of people before him. He slowly rose from his chair and leisurely paced towards the round desk behind him. His shoes squeaked much like Raymond's.

"Summers?" said Martha under her breath.

"What?" said Raymond.

"They said their uncle's name was Summers," said Martha.

"Yes," said Tash. "What of it?"

"So, you're Jamie Summers?" Martha was grinning at Jamie.

"Yes," he replied.

"Your parents named you after *The Bionic Woman*?"

"The what who?" he replied.

"You never saw *The Bionic Woman*?"

"I'm from 2020," replied Jamie, like this would clear everything up.

"It was that show with Zoe Slater from EastEnders," said Tash, remembering the reboot from 2007. "How do you know about that?"

"Lindsay Wagner, my first crush," said Martha. "I was too old, but I got her doll for Christmas."

"Rewind that part," said Tash. "Are you gay?"

"Tash!" said Jamie.

"What?"

"You can't ask that!"

"Of course, I can ask that. It's a simple question." Tash was confused. She was about to abandon her brother in the past so he could fall in love with this crazy American woman. She'd seen them together as pensioners. Love, babies, grandkids. Surely that was the timeline?

"Who knows what they are as a teenager?" said Martha.

"Lots of people," replied Tash. She remembered candid chats with her uncle about his adolescence.

"Well, I didn't," said Martha. "Besides, people change their minds, right? That's what makes us human."

"It's a can of worms in 2020," said Jamie.

"What does that mean?" asked Raymond.

"Everyone spends so long being seen to do the right thing that they end up doing the wrong thing," said Jamie. "When I was six, teachers asked me if I wanted sausage or spaghetti for lunch. Now I'd be asked if I'd prefer to use the girls' or boys' toilets."

"Lost me," said Martha.

"Yep, we're all lost – it's called progress," said Tash.

"I prefer to go sitting down, to be fair," said Raymond.

"What?" said Tash.

"I prefer a bisexual toilet," he explained.

"Unisex," said Tash.

"Same thing, isn't it?"

"Don't ever change, Raymond," said Tash, squeezing his elbow.

The security guard hung up the phone and retrieved something from deep inside his left ear with a folded-out paperclip.

"What if he recognises us?" said Jamie.

"Who?" said Martha.

"Uncle David," said Jamie. "What if he realises it's us?"

"Well, that's unlikely. I'm two months old, and you haven't been born yet," said Tash.

"But he might see Mum in you."

"You can fucking take that back right now."

"Hey, don't talk about your mother like that," said Martha.

"Do you get along with yours?" said Tash.

"Mine died when I was sixteen. And my father. Helicopter accident."

"Oh, I'm sorry," said Tash.

"That's terrible," said Jamie. "Did it land on them?"

Tash took a breath. "I'm guessing the odds are them being in it."

"Correct. He was flying it," replied Martha.

Tash caught a glimpse at Jamie. "Don't say it, Jamie."

"What?"

"Don't say what you were about to say," said Tash.

"What was he about to say?" asked Martha.

"I was just going to say that technically, there comes a time when you are no longer flying a helicopter if you are crashing it."

Martha considered this.

"He has a point."

Chapter Thirty-Eight

The Groundhog Day Gale had set records in 1976. Maine had suffered worst, but Massachusetts and New York State had seen record low pressures. In Vermont, February had the worst snowfall on record when six and a half inches fell on February 2nd. Yet last month, June, had broken temperature records at 93 degrees Fahrenheit. Today was only a little cooler and Dudley had loosened his top button beneath his black tie as his single concession to the dry heat inside the chapel. He must have been dreaming. It seemed just a few years since he and Florence had watched their son squirm as the vicar tricked holy water onto his forehead and named him Jack Patrick Hobson. Florence called him a gift from God. The kid, not the vicar. She was a staunch Protestant, whereas Dudley was subscription free when it came to religion. After giving up conceiving, this wealthy couple had resigned to life without kids, so Jack's arrival was met with pure euphoria. And now, the smell of lilies and damp oak parquet filled Dudley's nose. The bleak concrete architecture of the crematorium building seemed to be exacerbating the sheer horror of the day. Maybe that's what it was meant to do. Perhaps the funeral experience in the 1970s was designed to be so hideously unique that no part of the day could be familiar or warm. Maybe the brutality of the day was designed so that no shadows of the event would ever darken your door again. If we make everything fucking horrible and use materials and fabrics and lighting that mourners never see in everyday life – maybe we are doing them an unknown service? A 1970s crematorium service would provide no source material for emotional triggers in the remaining lives of the bereaved. Yes, Dudley concluded, that was why today was so vile yet so welcome.

He stood alone in the front row. The remaining seats were filled to capacity by the good, the great and the hangers-on. Dudley was fully aware of the whispers, some compassionate, some pretty ruthless, but all accurate. This was too late in his life to embark on the challenges that now lay ahead, and he knew people thought the same.

It was the first time he'd attended a double funeral. The glossy white coffins indicated he'd spared no expense for his son's final journey.

Sadly, Dudley had paid for Jack's penultimate journey, too. Jack had abused the Bank of Dad since he first understood the power of money, and taking his wife for a spin in his father's forbidden helicopter proved to be his final deceit. The Bell 47 was a handsome machine and had long been admired by Jack, so when his dad finally acquired one, he literally couldn't wait to fly it. Maybe he should have at least waited until he gained a pilot's licence. Naturally, Jack hadn't sought permission from his father. Why would he? Dudley wouldn't have given it. So just forty-four minutes after taking the keys from his father's office, Jack had written off Dudley's investment, along with a derelict barn and a rusty Gibson tractor. He also snuffed out the lives of eleven hens, a toad, two stoats, himself, and his wife.

But the views until then had been fantastic. Even better than he'd hoped.

Really, really good views.

The fields were all sun-scorched from the heatwave and expanded as far as the eye could see. Maybe he should have spent a little longer looking at the dials in front of him.

Music reverberated around the stark grey slab walls. The concrete monolith was briefly intersected by stained glass panels that no one had bothered to design. Marv Johnson's 'You Got What It Takes' had been his son's song of choice for the first dance with his new wife, Maya. They had married just sixteen years ago, and the two never failed to sing along to it whenever it got radio airplay in the following years. Dudley had suggested this instead of a hymn to end the service. Dudley's wife Florence might have had a more Christian suggestion given her strong religious upbringing, but sadly she had passed fourteen months before her son, so Dudley had his way.

At eighty-six years of age, he had only recently resigned himself to wearing eyeglasses, but he was proud that all his remaining faculties were in top form. His hair was still growing on his head, his knees and hips were doing pretty well, his hearing was extremely keen, and he had a sense of smell that could rival a bloodhound. And, as Marv brutally informed his betrothed that she didn't look like a movie star, Dudley suddenly became aware of a pungent aroma that caused his eyes to fill with water. Until then, he had been tear-free throughout proceedings, so he wasn't too unhappy as at least now he looked appropriately bereaved. He turned to establish the source of the familiar smell and was shocked but not surprised to see a hazy cloud emanating from the mouth of a teenage girl standing at the entrance. She was leaning casually against the opened door to establish without any doubt her indifference to the ceremony. Dudley was conflicted about her location. She should have been mourning her parents alongside him, yet she was dressed in a yellow and black baseball cropped t-shirt with the word 'Vultures' emblazoned across her bra-less chest. Beneath, she wore black sports shorts with white piping that rose to the high slits on either side of her legs. She had wanted to complete her look with some leather shorts but thought better of it. It was all in adulation of her latest hero: an ex-Playboy bunny she'd seen perform at CBGB music club in Manhattan's East Village in the spring, during what would turn out to be her last shopping trip with her parents. The vocalist was raw but beautiful, confident but edgy. She was called Deborah

Harry, and happily, someone else in the audience went on to sign her and her band to Private Stock Records.

The aroma of marijuana had not gone unnoticed by the rest of the congregation, and this belligerent teenager knew it. In fact, she was pleased. Extremely pleased. Grandaddy needed to know who was boss in the house now that her parents were gone.

Chapter Thirty-Nine

"That's really sad," said Jamie, attempting one of his awkward hugs, which Martha reciprocated in a similar style. There was a moment when Tash surely spotted more than four arms, and she lost count of the number of times noses struck shoulders.

"That is very sad, Martha," said Raymond, before picking some more Santa fluff from his lips

A single tear fell from Tash's eye. "I think I'm going back to sit with Raymond."

"No, I'll be fine," said Raymond. "I think I'm just a bit overtired. Is anyone else hot?"

"My son," said Tash.

"Yes, sorry."

"We need to rethink his name, Tash," said Jamie.

"Excuse me!" came a gruff voice. The security guard gestured for his visitors to come to his circular desk. Beside him was a nervous-looking young man, dressed head to toe in white and clutching a can of Taunton Special Vat cider. He might have been wobbling a little; it was hard to tell.

"Uncle David!" said Jamie, in what he thought was a whisper.

"Shh!" said Tash.

But Jamie had already set off to meet him.

"I thought you were going outside?" said Martha.

"Jamie!" hissed Tash. "I can't now, can I? Sake." She set off behind her brother. Martha and Raymond followed.

Every night since he missed his rendezvous with Tash, Jamie had dreamed of the moment he met his younger parents, and now he was about to come face to face with Uncle David. A smile was painted on his face.

"Jamie, Jamie. To quote you: don't say a fucking word," said Tash, grabbing his arm to slow him down.

"When did I say that?"

"When we met Dad back in that hotel!"

"I didn't say that. I just said be careful what you say."

"Well, can you do the same now, please? Let Martha do the talking, and keep your mouth shut, OK?"

"OK."

"Hello," said young David, blushing slightly at the unexpected summons.

"Hi, Uncle!" said Jamie.

"Christ!" said Tash.

"Uncle?" said David. His blond hair gelled up on his head like his hero Howard Jones.

"He means our uncle," said Tash turning to Raymond. "Come on, Uncle!"

"Oh!" said David, still looking perplexed and pissed.

"Sorry," said Raymond. "I'm dressed as Father Christmas, by the way."

"Yes, I thought that," said David. "I've been a good boy this year."

"We're from the er, the kiddies place," said Martha.

"Great Ormond Street Hospital," said Raymond.

"Look, I think there's been a mix-up," said David, taking a packet of ten Embassy Number Six from his trouser pocket and flicking a disposable Bic to light one. The security guard made his way back to his newspaper and cigar.

"Yeah, we thought you'd think that," said Martha.

Bloody hell, thought Tash. What on earth was she going to say?

"I don't have a cheque for you. I'm just here for a party. I don't even work at this office."

"We know that, David," said Martha.

"But he said you'd come to get a cheque." He gestured at the guard now seated by the door.

"Did he? What a prick," said Martha. "No, the cheque is in the computer room. We just need you to take us there."

David looked at the four people before him. One was holding out a Great Ormond Street security badge, two were dressed like shit elves, and behind them, Father Christmas squinted every three seconds.

"Who told you to ask for me?" said David, suspicion rising in his cider-fizzled brain.

Martha stared at him. How much white could one man pull off? Well, considerably less than this one. His white rope knit jumper was tucked into his white pleated trousers, held in place by a thin white leather-look belt. White leather shoes with cracked leather toes shuffled beneath his turn-ups—no doubt covering white socks.

The silence continued, interrupted only by the echoes of the mighty clock that hung beneath the cathedral-like ceiling chiming the top of the hour.

Then Martha laughed. Slowly to start with, but building until her rasps echoed around the tiled floors and marble pillars. It was impossible not to join in, or indeed would have been rude not to, so soon her colleagues had joined in, and David found himself smiling too.

"What is it?" he said, stifling a giggle and dragging on his ciggie.

"Well," said Martha, catching her breath. "We were saying all the way here, what if he doesn't believe us! We would be in serious trouble!"

She looked at Tash and Jamie, then Raymond. "Didn't we?"

There followed the usual confused but compliant agreement. Things like...

... "yes!"

... "we did, didn't we?"

... "bit worried about that actually!"

Then a "Sorry" from Raymond.

"It was Linda," said Martha. She let the name of his boss hang in the air.

"My boss?" That seemed to have sobered him up briefly.

"Yep. She couldn't say too much before now, but she thought you'd be the man for the job. She's pretty impressed with your work this year, by the way. Pretty impressed!"

"I only started in September," said David flicking ash onto the chequered tiles.

"I know. I know! What a guy!"

"Well, I'm flattered she put me forward for this," said David.

"You should be too, Daniel!"

"David."

"David," said Martha. "So, where's the computer room?"

"Well, it's not in this building," said David.

"Pardon me?" said Martha.

"It's in Cooper's Row."

"Where the fuck's that?"

"Pardon?"

"Where is it?"

"Near the Tower of London."

"Sake," said Tash, under her breath.

Martha glared at David for a moment, cogs turning in her head.

"That's right. That's right. It is. Good," said Martha, "We definitely know it's you, now. You passed the test."

"Did I?"

"Yep. It's definitely him, guys," said Martha to three unimpressed faces. "Off we go then."

"Right," said David.

"Your shoelace is undone," said Jamie, pointing at David's feet. Tash couldn't hide her frustration that Jamie had decided to flag this. What difference would it make?

"Oh, thank you," said David, wondering what to do with his can of cider.

Martha took it from him, and after placing his cigarette

between his lips, he bent down to tie a bow. Martha emptied the entire contents of the can into her mouth and then handed it back empty as he stood up.

"Come on," said Martha, leading the pack back to the main doors.

David followed Martha happily, occasionally pausing to correct his path as he seemed to keep swerving left. Maybe the fresh air would clear his head.

"Seems a nice chap," said Raymond.

"Don't talk to him," said Tash to Jamie as he set off to follow. "Not a word."

"Okay," said Jamie.

Chapter Forty

"Whatever I do, wherever I go, I'm never coming back to you!" sang David, immediately followed by "back to you!" from Jamie and then Anthony. Then they continued together: "Whatever you do, wherever you go, I'm gonna get over you!"

It was quite something that they all knew the dance routine *and* managed to perform it sitting down.

Robyn had been more than obliging to continue the final mile to Cooper's Row with Martha tightly behind him again. And now David, Jamie and little Anthony were living their best life singing Hazell Dean's second hit of the year at the top of their voices as the vintage drayman's cart trundled down the eerily quiet Leadenhall Street. They were in the Square Mile now, the original City of London, where businesses and offices were traditionally closed on Sundays, so the cart was progressing at a decent pace.

"What part of *don't talk to him,* didn't you understand?" said Tash into Jamie's ear. Her son was wrapped tightly on her lap, happily sucking on his soother, and tiny watery tears of joy trickled horizontally from his eyes as the cold air blew in their faces.

"I'm not. I'm singing," said Jamie before continuing.

"I stand alone..." The trio continued. Stock Aitken and

Waterman knew how to write a hit; this was only their second after Divine's 'You Think You're a Man' earlier in the year.

"I can't go back to that scout group. Not ever. We lost a horse!" whispered Maureen as the day's events settled in her mind. She sat alongside her husband out of earshot of the others.

"Bertie will be fine," said Raymond. "He was delivering beer in these streets for years before his retirement. He'll be home."

"We got ejected from Great Ormond Street Hospital!" said Maureen.

"They'll soon forget about us. They've got Jimmy Savile coming later!" said Raymond in his best placatory tone.

"Can we sing 'I Am What I Am' next?" asked Anthony.

David and Jamie considered this whilst sharing another can of Special Vat that David had procured from somewhere around his person.

"We saw *La Cage Aux Folles* on Broadway last year. Excellent music," said Anthony.

Jamie offered the cider to Anthony, who politely declined, being eight and a quarter and all that.

"Snowflake," said Tash, a little too loudly.

Chapter Forty-One

"Sometimes the ace, sometimes the deuces!" sang Anthony, far louder than the others, as the cart came to an abrupt halt, immediately followed by the singing.

"Smashing song that," said Raymond. "Not heard that one before."

"Gloria Gaynor," said David at the exact moment Anthony said, "Shirley Bassey."

They were both right. Gloria released it in 1983, the same year as *La Cage Aux Folles*, and Bassey covered it in 1984. Not that her version troubled the charts, but it was evidently part of this privileged cub's vinyl collection.

Martha dismounted as before, closely watched by Tash to see if her improbable courtship with the NHS consultant might have progressed to second base, especially given the cobbles over the final stretch. He, too, climbed off his impressive motorbike and removed his helmet. "This is where I bid you all Merry Christmas, I'm afraid."

"What?" said Tash. That wasn't the plan.

"Can you not spare just ten more minutes?" asked Raymond. "That's all we need, isn't it?"

Raymond looked at Martha, who nodded.

The consultant looked at his digital Casio Soccer watch and then up at the collective of expectant weirdos.

"Alright. Ten minutes, no more."

"Oh, thank you!" said Raymond, followed by lots of other polite "thank you!" and "that's great" and "can't thank you enough," type remarks, ending with Martha. "Thanks, Robyn."

"I thought you were Robyn?" said David, struggling to climb down from the cart and smearing a rust mark down the back of his white cotton trousers.

"What?" said Robyn.

Martha spun around to mouth "he's drunk," at Robyn.

"They both are," said Jamie, offering to help his sister down onto the road.

"I don't need to come this time. You've got him," said Tash, nodding at her pissed uncle. "We're staying here. He needs sleep." She straightened the hat on her baby's head and kissed his nose. "Besides. You're only going to be ten minutes."

Jamie considered this, then turned to go. "Okay. Come on, Uncle David."

"Sake!" shouted Tash before handing baby Raymond to Maureen again. "I can't leave you to do anything."

"Pardon?" asked David, emptying his can with one mighty gulp.

"Nothing," said Tash, climbing off the sleigh yet again. "Where are we going?"

"There," he replied, pointing to a dreary, anonymous-looking painted door set into a faceless stone building.

"Really?" Tash was astonished that the computer centre of one of the largest UK high street banks was in a shabby back street.

"Of course."

Martha paced ahead and waited patiently for David to stumble up the kerb to join her.

"What's the delay?" he asked, wondering why she'd stopped.

"I need you to let me in," she answered.

"Oh," replied David. "Sorry."

He twisted the black doorknob, and the heavy door swung open.

"It's not locked?"

"No." David seemed to think her question was very odd.

Martha thought for a moment. Then a moment more, before leaning back to the cart.

"Hey, kid," she shouted.

Anthony looked up.

"You're coming too."

He delightedly hopped down from the sleigh and joined the pack.

"Come on," said Martha stepping inside first, followed by David, then Anthony, then Father Christmas and his two elves. The second elf looked over her shoulder at her son, carefully cradled on Maureen's lap.

Chapter Forty-Two

Inside the building, a mature lady was sitting at an upright piano, with one arm holding a sturdy oak baton that projected from the opened top.

"We're here to take some photos for charity," said Martha, as she held up her stolen pass to the confused woman. "I'm from The Grey Mormon Street Hospital, and he's from here." She pointed at David, who held up his Midland name badge before sliding it back into his C&A Clockhouse trousers.

"No problem," said the lady, not looking over. "I'm tuning the piano."

"We thought you were security!" said Raymond. "Didn't we?" He was smirking in the way only the British do when a simple misunderstanding really isn't that funny.

"Do you do requests?" asked Tash.

"If I had a pound for every person that asked me that, I'd throw them all at you, really hard," said the lady, pressing middle C over and over.

"Do you know where they are?" asked Jamie. "Security, I mean."

Martha elbowed him in the ribs. Why ask for a problem?

"Having a piss, I think. She's called Brenda."

"Both extremely helpful pieces of information, thank you," said Tash, secretly impressed by the blunt reply.

"Great. Happy holidays," said Martha walking past her towards the hallway behind. The others followed tentatively. Raymond offered his customary "sorry" as he brought up the rear.

"Are you blind?" said Anthony, on his way past. He had been fascinated by the skilful way this lady did her job, simply by ear.

"I am."

Everyone impatiently stopped walking, so the child could finish his chat.

"What's it like?"

"It's interesting," she replied, before striking B flat, and grimacing.

"Can you watch TV?"

"Yes."

"Do you know braille?"

"Yes."

"Do you cook for yourself?"

"Yes."

"How do you know when you've finished wiping your bum?" asked Anthony.

"Anthony!" shouted Raymond, hoping she might answer despite his reprimanding the boy.

"You have a lot of questions," said the tuner.

"Cub scouts never stop learning," said Anthony.

"Do you know, I had a feeling you were a cub scout," said the lady, twiddling the baton inside the piano.

"Did you?" Anthony was enraptured. "How?"

"Anthony, leave this lady alone, sorry about him, madam."

They set off again.

"Dib dib dib," said the tuner, attempting a cubs' salute.

"Do you know it's spelt with a Y?" replied Anthony, standing still. The others paused again, and let out a collective groan.

"Pardon?" she said.

"It's an acronym for *Do Your Best*. D-Y-B," said Anthony. "And we reply 'we'll Dob dob dob. Which means *Do Our Best*."

"Actually, that is interesting," said Jamie.

"Yeah, I thought that," said Tash reluctantly.

"News to me," said David.

"No shits given," said Martha.

The piano tuner nodded her interest too, then plonked on F sharp. "Bye then."

They set off once more and gathered in the hallway. There were three doors off, all adjacent to one another.

"Which way?" whispered Martha.

"Down," said David.

"You know your way?" said the lady, still well within earshot. "She'll be back soon."

"Yes, thank you," said Tash, loudly. "We know our way."

"This one," said David before opening the door and leading them all through. The door slammed behind them. The handle turned again, and they all walked back into the hallway.

"Must be that one," said David, pointing to one of the two remaining options.

Raymond opened it, and a shriek filled the air. A Midland bank employee was sitting on a toilet with her skirt around her ankles.

"Sorry!" said Raymond before slamming the door closed. "That's a toilet."

Then he realised he was still holding the handle. It had come off, and the spindle that connected it to the inner handle was still attached. Whoever was in there was now locked in. He started to fumble awkwardly with the ironmongery in his hand and struggled to reattach it to the door. He failed.

"There was a lady using that toilet," said Jamie.

"She could use some *me-time*," said Martha. "If you know what I mean."

"I thought the same," said Tash. "That was quite something."

"Unless she was drying her guinea pig?" Martha smiled at her own joke. "On her lap."

"You should apologise to her," said Anthony, glaring at Raymond and wondering why the lady would take a guinea pig to the loo.

"There's no sign on the door!" replied Raymond, oblivious to the fact he was now arguing with a child. His attention was focused on fixing the bloody spindle back through the hole in the door. How come it didn't fit?

"You should apologise!" said Tash. "He's right."

Raymond passed the handle and spindle to Jamie and started to knock on the door.

"Erm, excuse me. It's me. Er, Father Christmas. Again. I wanted to apologise for opening the door. It was a genuine mistake."

"Go away," came a voice from behind the door.

"Yes, sorry," said Raymond. "You might want to think about locking it next time."

"I think she's got that covered now. She can't open it without this part," said Jamie holding up the spindle and then dropping it on the floor.

"That's why I was trying to repair it," said Raymond.

"What if she wants to come out?" said David.

"Do you want to come out?" said Martha, irked by the delay.

"No. Go away," came the voice from behind the door.

"That bar needs to line up with the hole in the latch in the door," said Jamie.

"Yes, I'm aware of that," said Raymond.

"Well, squat down and look at the hole," said Jamie.

"You should wait until she's ready to come out," said Anthony. "That's what a gentleman would do. Not stare through a hole."

"Right," said Raymond. He waited. Everyone stared.

"Really?" said Martha. "What if she's taking a crap?"

"Oh, my word," said Raymond. "Not in front of a cub scout."

"Sorry," said Martha. "I'm sure cubs do it too."

Anthony thought. "Is that American for poo?"

"I don't think she was... you know," said Raymond. "Number two-ing."

"How would you know? Were you looking?" said Tash playfully.

"No. No. I just mean she looked very, erm, peaceful."

"Peaceful?" said Tash.

"Like dead?" said David.

"No. I mean, she didn't look like she was, you know... pushing."

Tash and Jamie smiled at one another, trying to restrain belly laughs.

"Oh my. I can never show my face in here again," said Raymond, tortured by his indiscretion.

"You're not showing much of it now," said Tash, staring at the beard that covered his blushing face.

"Well, we're not coming in here again, are we?" said Jamie. "So, what's the problem?"

"He told me it was the way downstairs," said Raymond, nodding at David, whose eyes were half closed with the effects of daytime drinking.

"We can't wait here all day," said Martha before walking to the toilet door and thumping. "Hey lady, he's sorry. He's a nice guy. He just fucked up with doors. It happens."

The toilet flushed.

"I'll take that as an acceptance," said Martha. "Come on."

"Won't she want to come out now?" said Jamie.

"Come ON!"

Jamie took the prompt and walked to the final door, opting to knock first. After all, maybe this was the gents.

"Go away," came the voice from behind the toilet door again.

"No, sorry, we're knocking on a different door now," said Raymond in the general direction of the loo. "Sorry."

Jamie tentatively turned the knob and forced the oak door open. Behind was a descending stone staircase.

"This is us." He led the way, followed by the others.

"At least we know where the toilets are now," said Anthony.

"Why do they have a piano in reception?" asked Jamie.

"It was too big for the toilet."

"Is anyone else hot?" said Raymond.

Chapter Forty-Three

The mainframe computer room was a curious sight. Deep in the bowels of a Georgian-era townhouse, the servants' quarters had been bisected with panelled walls, glazed from halfway to the ceiling. A door in the centre was closed, and next to it was another unattended desk, with a leather seated swivel chair pushed back from its usual place. Everything on this side of the wall nodded to the vintage fabric of the building. Everything on the opposite side was a chaotic mix of the sixties, seventies and eighties.

Large tape reels hung vertically on vast human-height machines lining all of one wall. Countless screens protruded from cases surrounding more buttons, knobs, wires, and keyboards. Dull grey metal boxes and cabinets continued in offshoots onto the linoleum-covered floor.

Despite its importance, this place was eerily empty. One woman and one man sat staring at mountains of computer paper and large black computer screens flickering with orange text.

"At the risk of repeating myself," said Tash.

"Then don't," said Martha, interrupting. "You're gonna ask if I got a plan."

"I don't think that's an unreasonable question, actually," said Raymond, adjusting his beard to make sure his face was fully covered beyond all recognition.

"Kid, I need a favour," said Martha to Anthony, his eyes captivated by this spacecraft-like control room.

He stepped slowly to a panel of glass and took a deep breath. "This is like *the Starship Enterprise*."

"Kid, I'm talking to you."

He extracted his camera from his grey shorts pocket and unflipped the cover. He wanted a record of this. "This is like *The Search for Spock*."

Jamie wasn't having that. "They should have stopped at *Wrath of Khan*."

"Rubbish, *Spock* is the best film of this year," said Anthony, still beaming like a kid. Which is what he was.

"Oh my God, you've finally got a geek-buddy," said Tash. "Maybe you could play on the rec after this, and he could be *R2-D2*. He's the right height."

"That's *Star Wars*. We're talking *Star Trek*," said the cub, capturing the perfect image in his camera viewfinder.

"She knows what she's doing," said Jamie. "Don't bite. That's what she wants."

"Wait!" said Martha. "I'll take that so that you can be in it."

Anthony hadn't considered this. "Really?"

"Sure!"

He was delighted and handed over the camera, then started to try to direct the shot.

"Right, how about I stand here, and you," but before he could finish, Martha casually pointed the camera in his direction and clicked the top shutter button without even looking at him or the viewfinder.

"That's a keeper," she said before flipping the camera shut and placing it in Jamie's trouser pocket. Which was quite an intimate thing to do under the circumstances, so naturally, it rendered him speechless.

"Wait! You said," said Anthony, but again, he was silenced by her. This time with a palm over his face. She squared up, took a deep breath, and reached for the door handle.

"Let's do this."

Chapter Forty-Four

"Happy holidays, team! I will need to see your vaccination certificates before we continue."

Martha spoke with a calm, confident and authoritative voice.

The two Midland employees looked up at the visitors shuffling awkwardly into their humming computer room. The pretty lady with purple hair was dressed older than her years, not unlike Mrs McClusky from *Grange Hill*, thought Norman, a show that his children watched religiously. He would often look up from his Littlewoods football pools coupon if the headmistress came on. He liked the way she often placed her tongue in her cheek.

"Can we help you?" said Tessa, standing up from her seat and glancing at the empty chair outside the door. "Where's Brenda?"

The visitors looked at one another and started to mutter.

..."That'll be the toilet woman."

..."The woman you walked in on."

..."The loo lady."

..."He made me."

Jamie's voice was loudest. "That woman having a poo. She must be Brenda."

"She's nipped to the bathroom but showed us down here," said Martha. "I'm Robyn from the Great Almond Street Place for the sick kids."

She flashed her ID for a moment.

"And I'm sure you know Daniel."

"David," said Tash.

"David," said Martha.

Tessa looked at the pissed wannabe pop star in white who offered a self-conscious smile and possibly a wink, but it was hard to tell as his eyelids were closing.

"No," replied Tessa.

"Well, he works here, and his boss... I wanna say LLLLLL...?" she looked at David for a prompt.

"Linda," he said.

"Linda, head of branch, has sent him here for a photo opportunity because you guys have very generously donated fifty grand to our hospital for the kids for Christmas! Isn't that something?"

She started clapping in appreciation, and soon, everyone, including the bewildered computer experts, joined in.

"But I do need to see your vaccination certificates," said Martha, "erm..."

She nodded to the woman to get her name.

"Tessa," replied the lady.

"And..."

"Norman," replied the man.

"Such lovely names, Tessa and whatever you said," said Martha.

"I don't understand," said Norman. "What vaccination?"

"Oh my God, Jamie. Did you not tell them about the vaccination?" Martha was in full flow now.

"Erm," was all Jamie could muster.

"Quick, get out, get out, get out, get out," said Martha, clapping her hands at the confused man and woman. "This little guy's come along for the photo opportunity. He's a long-term patient with double measles. Very, very contagious."

"Contagious?" said Norman as he walked through the door.

"Where's your camera gear?" said Tessa, following Norman.

Martha nodded at Jamie.

"Oh!" he said before removing the compact flip-open Kodak

that Martha had slid there moments before. He held it upside down. "It's here."

"How contagious?" said Norman.

"It's very contagious actually, Normal," said Raymond. Before adding, "I'm sorry, Norman, I think I just called you Normal."

"And is it normal to send such a poorly child out for a photo shoot?" said Norman.

"Oh yes, it's quite norman, Normal," said Raymond before doubting himself. "Normal, Norman."

"Can you stop saying Norman?" said Tash.

"I'm sorry, Tash," said Raymond before turning to the man. "Sorry, Normal. Are you hot? I'm hot."

"What's double measles?" asked Tessa.

"Well, imagine measles," said Martha. "And double it."

"That sounds quite nasty," said Norman.

"It's double nasty, Normal," said Raymond. "I'm sorry, I think I did it again."

"He looks fine," said Tessa.

Anthony was perplexed, his face moving in the direction of whichever adult spoke next. He looked like the umpire on Wimbledon centre-court. He even removed his empty camera bag and sat down with his legs crossed.

"It mostly lingers under the cap and woggle," said Jamie.

Tash stared at her brother, her twitching nose struggling to keep in a smile beneath it.

"But what are you going to do in there?" asked Tessa, clearly more interested in her career than health.

"Couple of photos with Father Christmas and the cheque, handing it over to the kid on death's door," said Martha in a flippant way. "But I really would get well away."

"Am I dying?" asked Anthony.

"No!" replied Father Christmas and his elves.

"Of course not!" said Martha before nodding madly behind his back at Tessa and Norman, who were now standing outside the computer room.

"Best thing you can do now is get a tetanus shot," said Martha. "It sometimes works."

She crossed her fingers as she said this and then slammed the door on the Midland two. They shot up the stairs in seconds.

"I think that was a bit harsh," said Raymond.

"Should we have had jabs?" said Jamie.

"What's going on?" said Anthony, "I want my camera back."

"What?" said Martha, undoing the back of her twin-set top.

"She just told a few fibs so we can arrange a surprise for the hospital," said Tash. "You're fine."

Anthony seemed to accept this and started to pace around the flickering lights.

"What are you doing, actually?" said Raymond, mindful that Martha had started to undress from the waist up.

"Help me with this, Jamie," she said, turning her back to him to display the fastener on her bra.

"Help you do what?" he replied with a suddenly parched mouth.

"This has taken a turn," said Tash.

"Turn around, Anthony," said Raymond, who was already shuffling the other way around.

"Just undo it," said Martha. "Quickly."

Jamie thought for a moment and then exhaled loudly onto his hands to warm them. He slowly reached out his hands to her porcelain white back and froze just millimetres away from the clasp on her bra. He'd never seen a Playtex Cross-Your-Heart bra. In fact, he'd never seen any bra this close up unless he was helping his mum with the washing. He never dreamt that Martha would wear a white one. In his dreams, it was usually grey or brown. He didn't dream big.

"Can someone please explain what's happening?" said David as he dropped down into one of the vacated seats, quite indifferent to the sudden promise of nudity.

"We're gonna be out of here in ten minutes. I just need him to undo my bra," said Martha.

Jamie bit his lip and took the plunge.

Oh.

My.

God.

How the hell did these things work?

"I'm so torn," said Tash. "On the one hand, I'm delighted that Jamie's removing a bra, but on the other hand, I'm aware that it will be 1985 in a week or so, and we might still be here, cos he's so shit at it."

"What is happening, actually?" asked Raymond.

They all ignored him.

"Pull it beyond the catch, and that will release it," said Tash helpfully.

"That doesn't even make sense," said Jamie, starting to sweat. God, her skin was soft.

"They overlap. Take the top overlapping piece and slide it further over the one beneath. That releases the catch."

"Why am I doing this?" said Jamie, trying again.

"Do you want me to help?" said Tash.

"No! I can do this," said Jamie. He'd not expected to have an audience of his sister, his uncle, Father Christmas and an eight-year-old boy the first time he got his hands on a bra that was still being worn.

By a woman.

And an alive one at that.

He'd had many nightmares about removing his Grandma's if he needed to perform CPR. Still, maybe that episode of *Casualty* had been exaggerated by a novice scriptwriter with no medical training.

"How are we doing?" said Martha.

"I'm trying, I'm trying," said Jamie.

"Is anyone else hot?" asked Raymond.

"Done it!" said Jamie with a level of euphoria that he usually reserved for when he managed to fasten his seat belt on a plane. Usually, around the time the cabin crew were walking around with bags of rubbish for passengers to lob their empty miniatures of vodka and gin.

Martha held her chest to stop the bra from dropping and

reached for the receiver on a green telephone that sat alongside a flickering screen.

"Read it, read the number inside," she said.

Jamie squinted at the label.

"Thirty-four C."

"Really? You forgot your cup size?" said Tash.

"The long number, read the long number," said Martha.

Raymond started to turn around to see what was happening, confident that the nudity risk factor was significantly diminished.

"Oh, one, zero, erm, one," said Jamie, squinting at a long number written in red biro across the care label whilst trying not to rest his hands on Martha's back like some kind of perv.

"Don't do ohs AND zeroes, Jamie," said Tash. "That's so lame. Commit to one or the other."

"Which should I use?"

"Well, *oh* is actually a letter. I'd go with numbers," said Tash.

"Read the number!" said Martha, her finger having already spun 010 on the phone dial.

"Sorry. Oh one, wait, sorry, zero one zero, is that a three?"

"Jesus," said Martha, flicking her bra entirely off so she could read the label herself.

"Oh, my giddy aunt!" said Raymond, simultaneously covering his eyes and Anthony's.

In fairness, Martha had her back to the room, she'd only revealed her back, and as she continued to dial, reading from the label, she tucked the phone handset into her neck and slid the two-piece back into place.

"Panic over, guys. Starsky and Hutch are back in the Torino." She gestured at her chest and continued dialling but realised something was hovering over her shoulder.

Jamie's hand was in the air,

"What's with the hand?" asked David, opening another can of Special Vat. Just how deep were those pockets of his?

"He wants to ask a question," said Tash.

"Go," said Martha, mouthing numbers as she dialled. This was a very long number.

"Well, on behalf of us all, I think we want to know what's

happening? I thought you wanted to get to a computer, not a phone."

Martha finished dialling, turned to look at Jamie, and handed him her bra. She lifted the handset of the phone to her ear. Jamie took the still warm cotton lingerie and held it like it was fresh out of the arc of the covenant.

"I don't know shit about computers, but my guy does. He'll talk me through everything I need to... It's me." She interrupted herself to speak on the phone. Someone on the other side of the Atlantic had answered.

"No. I got no idea what time it is over there, and I don't give a shit. I'm in a bank in London, and I'm looking at their mainframe computer."

Her audience was spellbound.

"What's the bank again?" asked Martha.

"Midland," answered the whole room in unison. Even Anthony.

"The listening bank," added Raymond. Not that it helped.

"You hear that?" said Martha down the phone. "No, you won't. I trust every one of them. This happens right now. I have five minutes. The clock is ticking. Speak to me."

She pulled a chair beneath her and squinted at the orange letters on the black screen by her side. She gripped the phone between her neck and shoulder and used both hands to follow the instructions down the phone.

"I can see how she got that job at Great Ormond Street," said David, lighting yet another cigarette.

The others looked at him for a moment and then collectively agreed.

"Yes, she certainly gets things done," said Raymond.

"Want one?" said David, offering a cigarette to Father Christmas.

"No, no, thank you. Maureen doesn't like cigarettes."

"Who?"

"My wife, the lady outside."

"Oh," said David. "But Maureen's not here."

"It doesn't quite work like that," said Tash.

He offered her one, she declined, he offered Jamie one, he refused too, then he offered one to Anthony, who said he'd rather have sweets if David had any. He didn't, despite having pockets nearly reaching the top of his white towelling socks.

"When are we doing the photo?" said David, suddenly remembering why they were all there.

"Shouldn't be too long now, I would imagine," said Raymond.

"Yes, not long now," said Tash, still struggling to look her uncle in the eye.

"You can come back and join the party after if you want?" said David, his eyes fixed on Jamie. "You know, at head office. Drinks are free. It's very Club Tropicana."

Oh my God, he's asking Jamie on a date, thought Tash. And Jamie has no fucking idea, the absolute knob. How much more complicated could time travelling become?

"Just me?" replied Jamie, still clutching Martha's bra.

"Well," said David, drawing deeply on his cigarette, "do you lot do everything together?"

The room fell quiet for a moment but for the sound of Martha typing badly on the keyboard.

Then Father Christmas and his two elves spoke in unison.

"Yes."

Chapter Forty-Five

The snoring from David was surprising, given he was face down on an opened ring binder. It was not the fact that he could snore in a position usually prescribed to stop snoring that surprised the others, but the two open steel rings that were surely pincering his forehead and mouth.

Martha had complied with her instructions down the phone and continued to mutter to her American helper whilst typing random numeric codes from time to time.

Little Anthony was sitting at David's feet and practising his top five favourite knots on the loosened laces that hung from David's white shoes. They were a birthday gift from his mum from Rebina Shoes in Sheffield, and she had suggested changing the laces for a more sensible pair, but he'd insisted he wanted to stick with these curious square-profiled ones. The shape pleased Anthony too, as he was currently tying them in his third favourite knot: The square knot. The coincidence delighted him.

"Did that blind lady upstairs answer you, earlier Anthony?" whispered Raymond.

"What?" he replied, barely paying attention.

"No, I just wondered about the toilet question. It was quite a good one. I mean, a bit forward, but worthy of thought."

Raymond pondered the dilemma for a moment. "I believe the Queen has a bottom wiper."

"Give me the name of this place again," said Martha, suddenly raising her voice and making the others jump, although not enough to wake David with a belly full of cider.

"Cooper's Row," said Raymond.

"The bank, the name of the bank." She was clicking her fingers to see if this would hurry things up.

All but David answered in unison again. "The Midland Bank."

Followed by Raymond adding, "the listening bank."

"Why do you say that every time?" said Tash.

Raymond struggled not to stammer his reply, fearing he was being ridiculed.

"Because it, it, it, says it, on the, on the advert, doesn't it?"

Jamie started to sing, and Raymond joined in. "Come and talk to the listening bank."

Tash stared at them both for a moment.

"Right. And you thought singing that part would help Martha how?"

"Just a bit more information, isn't it?" said Raymond.

Jamie nodded. He was in complete agreement.

"Would you like to know a fact about that man that wrote that jingle?" said Raymond, tweaking his beard again.

"No. I'd rather adopt Anthony," said Tash.

"I would," said Jamie to Raymond.

"Sake."

"The man that wrote that little song, I've forgotten his name for a moment now..." He stared into space and tried a few shapes with his mouth to see if he could summon this critical information from his tired brain.

"We don't need his name," said Tash.

"Right, okay. I'm sure it will come to me."

"When it does, can you keep it in?"

"I can't remember where I was now."

"You'd just got to the point," said Tash, yawning and rubbing her eyes.

"The man that wrote the jingle," said Jamie. "You were telling us about him."

"Yes! Yes!" said Raymond. "Well, you would not believe which other jingles he wrote!"

Tash started to examine her nails, but Raymond could see he had an audience of two. Jamie looked very excited with things so far, and Anthony had even stopped tying knots.

"Go on," said Jamie.

His reveal so energised Raymond that he counted each tune on his fingers as he spoke:

"The listening bank; The wonder of Woolies; This is the age of the train," he was on a roll now, so he decided to sing the next one. "Milk has got a..."

He smiled at Jamie, who joined in. "Lotta bottle!"

Then Raymond continued as before, "I'm a secret R Whites lemonade drinker."

He was out of fingers now, so he raised his other hand and then stopped.

"You didn't need that other hand, did you?" said Tash.

"That's an amazing fact, Raymond," said Jamie.

"One man wrote all those tunes?" said Anthony.

"Yes!" Raymond was effervescent with joy. "Can you believe one man wrote all those tunes?"

"Yes," said Tash.

"Don't you think that's incredible?" said Raymond.

"Have you heard of Lennon and McCartney?" she replied.

"Yes," said Raymond. Why was she bringing them up?

"They wrote over a hundred and eighty songs," said Tash. "And you're excited about some fella knocking up five tunes that each lasted twenty seconds?"

"I suppose jingles are very different where you come from? I would imagine things have really moved on, sort of thing," said Raymond philosophically. The curious remark didn't seem to register with Anthony, now working on a sheet bend knot.

"They hardly bother with them at all, to be honest," said Tash.

"No. We don't have TV theme tunes either, do we?" said Jamie.

"No," said Tash. "Good point. It's not all progress, Raymond."

"No theme tunes? What about *Minder*?" asked Raymond in horror.

"Hate to break it to you, but it's not on anymore," said Tash.

"I love that song. Do you know everyone thinks Dennis Waterman wrote it because his name's on the titles at the end? But it was his wife, and she only wrote the words. Gerard Kenny wrote the music. Waterman Kenny, it says. Or is it Kenny Waterman?"

"Remind me never to get in a lift with him, Jamie," said Tash.

"Why do you say that?" said Jamie.

"In case it breaks down. I'd hate to have to kill him with my bare hands."

"Waterman Kenny," said Raymond. "I'm sure of it."

"Thanks for clearing that up. If I had a pencil, I'd write that down," said Tash.

"There's one here," said Jamie, picking up a yellow Staedtler pencil from a desk and handing it to his sister.

"Thanks," said Tash, not bothering to inflect any sarcasm. It would be wasted on her lovely brother.

"Oh, it's broken," she said, looking at the tip. "Too bad."

Jamie looked at the sharpened end. "No, it's not."

Tash snapped it in half. "Yes. It is."

"One hour or *I'll* be calling *you*," said Martha loudly into the phone.

The others looked at her in anticipation, except David, of course. His snoring had become white noise to the others.

"Well, if you don't want her to find out – you'll call me in sixty minutes."

With that calm but authoritative threat, Martha hung up the phone.

"An hour?" said Tash. "We can't wait here an hour. My baby's outside in the cold!"

"And those people will be back," said Jamie.

"And I need the toilet," said Anthony.

"He's not calling here; he has all he needs. He's calling me at your place," said Martha.

"My place? How does he know my phone number?" said Raymond, suddenly full of dread.

Martha held up Raymond's business card and smiled.

"That's not my home number," said Raymond.

"What? Where the fuck is it?" said Martha, her buoyant mood sinking like a concrete Rubik's cube.

"It's the warehouse," said Jamie.

"Well, where the fuck is that?"

"It's nearer, actually," said Jamie.

"Cool!" said Martha. "That's great!"

"It was crawling with police twelve hours ago," said Tash,

Martha thought for a moment.

"That's okay. We've done nothing wrong. And they're not US cops. We're all in the clear!"

Raymond and his elves looked at one another and realised there was little they could do to prevent another journey in the cart.

"Let's go," said Martha.

"Had we better wake him up?" said Raymond, nodding at David.

"Jamie, wake him up," said Tash.

Jamie tiptoed to the bundle of pure white clothes snoring over the lever arch file, and gently tugged at a loose sleeve.

"Uncle David."

"Sake, Jamie!" said Tash.

Her shrieking exclamation caused David to sit bolt upright in his chair, bringing the lever arch folder with him, attached to his face. He started to flap his arms to release it, and the blue folder and all its contents dropped heavily onto the floor. His forehead and bottom lip each displayed a pair of red dots where the opened metal rings had slowly pierced his skin.

His hair now reminded Tash of Boris Johnson's, on a good day.

They all stared in shock at his face.

"Did you take the photo?" he asked with a confused expression and fumbling in his deep pockets.

Everyone replied "yes" in unison except Anthony, who simply glared at the cuts on this man's face. He'd not got his First Aid badge yet, and now might be the perfect time.

"We're going to get off, actually," said Raymond.

"Hmm?" asked David as he lit a cigarette and exhaled deeply, pausing to wipe his wet chin with the back of his hand. Luckily, he didn't see the smear of blood it left behind.

Raymond swallowed. "We need to skedaddle."

"To what?" asked Martha.

"I wouldn't smoke in here," said Jamie. "There's a lot of papers and stuff."

"What's the worst that could happen?" asked David, drawing deeply again.

Then, the sprinklers started to douse them all with freezing cold water, and an alarm sounded upstairs.

"Come on!" shouted Tash, and they dashed to the door. Uncle David rose to his feet and attempted one step, but his shoes were tied together, and he dropped like a sack of Smash.

"That doesn't look too good," said Anthony, staring down at the unconscious man on the ground. He walked over and felt his pulse. "He's fine. Just knocked out. You're gonna have to carry him." His cap kept most of his head dry, but water dripped off his nose.

"Well, yes, yes, that's one idea," said Tash. "But my mum is a nurse."

Jamie interrupted her. "Mum's a GP receptionist." He was the only person who seemed oblivious to the water soaking them all to the skin.

Tash glared at him. "Yes, but she is also a nurse and taught me nursing."

"Is she? Did she?" Jamie was amazed.

"You all go, and I shall wait with him," said Tash, wiping water from her face. The downfall was carefully directed to avoid most electrical equipment, which surely defeated the object. Still, nonetheless, it was doing an excellent job of extinguishing David's Number 6 and Tash's will to live.

"Are you sure?" asked Raymond.

"Go!" shouted Tash.

And they did. Then Anthony stopped and turned around.

"My camera bag!"

"I've got it," shouted Jamie, and they set off again.

Tash started to pull every drawer in sight wide open until she found what she was looking for.

Chapter Forty-Six

"What on earth's happened?" said Maureen, looking terrified as she cradled baby Raymond on her lap. "You're all wet!"

"Spot of bother with the sprinklers," said Raymond trying to do a walk that didn't look like a run. "Get on, Anthony."

The young cub effortlessly leapt onto the cart and settled beside Maureen.

Martha dragged herself on and offered her hand to Jamie, who self-consciously took it and immediately felt a tingle in his tummy. With her help, his clamber was far more elegant, and they were seated alongside one another in no time, leaning on the hidden C5.

Everyone tried to look the other way whilst Raymond did his swimming-pool exit style climb onto the carriage, and the heavy sighs and occasional burst of involuntary wind from the exertion. Well, other than Maureen.

"Raymond!"

"Sorry, Maureen. I think I've been swallowing a lot of air. With the stress and everything."

"Let's go!" shouted Martha.

"No! Tash isn't here!" said Jamie.

"She knows where we're going," said Martha. "Go!"

"No!" Jamie surprised himself with his defiant tone. "I'm not being separated from her again."

Martha looked at Jamie for a little longer than he liked, given the expression on her face.

"Jamie, you don't need to be separated from her. You can just get off too."

Jamie considered this.

"But then I won't be with you."

"I need a wee," said Anthony.

"He needs the bathroom," said Martha, like this was the end of the discussion.

"Again?" said Raymond.

"We're not going without my sister." Jamie was adamant.

"Bye then," said Martha, waving in his face. "It's been nice."

Jamie considered his options and then shuffled to the cart's edge.

"Here she is!" said Raymond as he spotted Tash running from the building.

"Where's Uncle David?" asked Jamie, staring behind his sister.

"He's fine. He's going to wait around and sort things out. Absolutely fine," said Tash, effortlessly climbing up and sitting down alongside Martha.

Jamie cautiously sat down.

"Let's go!" shouted Martha.

Nothing happened.

"Where's Robyn?" said Martha, squinting at the front of the cart.

"You were longer than ten minutes," said Maureen. "And we did say, ten minutes. He's gone home."

The sound of the alarm rang out into the empty street. A street that couldn't possibly remain so empty for long, given the bank's alarm was scaring the pigeons.

"Sake," said someone behind Maureen.

David lay in the basement in the recovery position outside the computer room. Tash's handwriting was emblazoned in blue magic marker pen across the back of his shirt.

"He knew nothing of this. He is innocent. PS We took nothing. PPS Your loo handle is fucked"

She knew computer hacking laws were six years away. And there was nothing her uncle could be blamed for if he was an unwitting accomplice. Which he was.

All good.

Nothing to see here.

Chapter Forty-Seven

"Faster! They could be gaining on us!"

"Has she been watching *Miami Vice*?" said Martha.

"Faster!" repeated Maureen.

"Is there any speed you'd like in particular, darling? Or just as fast as we can?" said Raymond.

"Don't be facetious and stop showing off, Raymond," replied his wife.

Maureen, baby Raymond and Anthony were sitting at the front of the cart, watching Father Christmas, his two elves, and Nancy Reagan pull the cart behind them. They were crossing Tower Bridge, and the sound of impatient car horns and squeals of humiliating laughter from pedestrians reverberated around Jamie's head. Tash placed her hand on the back of his neck for a moment.

"You're doing well."

Jamie heard his sister but didn't reply.

"They'd have to overtake the convoy behind us first," shouted Tash back at Maureen.

"Nearly there," said Raymond.

"Nearly where?" said Tash. "Nearly not there?"

"Well, we're closer than we were," said Raymond.

"Jamie!" came a voice.

They looked over to see Kenneth waving from outside his office as he started his shift.

"Where's Rudolph?" he added.

Jamie smiled but didn't reply.

"Who the fuck's he?"

"Kenneth," was all Jamie replied. He was way too focussed on ending this awful experience.

Tash waited for more, but it wasn't coming.

"Did you know those top walkways were originally designed so people could walk across the bridge even when it was open?" said Anthony out of the blue.

They all looked at the vertigo-inducing walkway high in the sky connecting the two towers. "But they ended up attracting women of the night, so were closed soon after the start of the twentieth century."

"Quite a view," said Raymond. "I would imagine."

"Don't be disgusting, Raymond," said his wife.

"I meant of London."

"I know exactly what you meant."

"Ladies of the what?" asked Martha.

"You know, prostitutes," replied the cub scout, "I seen it on the telly."

"Blimey. *Blue Peter*'s changed since I last watched it," said Raymond.

Chapter Forty-Eight

The cobbles of Shad Thames made the C5 wobble on the back of the cart, which Tash had now mastered pulling whilst walking backwards. She wasn't going to take her eyes off her ride home.

"Did you know they filmed part of *The Elephant Man* around here?" said Anthony.

He'd been an encyclopaedia of observational facts on the journey back, and Maureen had run out of faux-interested replies.

"Try not to wobble us so much. There's a baby back here," said Maureen to the entourage in front.

"Well, you could always walk this last stretch, you know, don't let us force you to sit on your arse," replied Tash.

Maureen glared at her. "You need to take a serious look at your potty mouth. If not, this baby's first word will be... Well, you know. It will be..."

"Be what?" asked Tash. "I don't know what you mean?" She and everyone else secretly hoped to hear Maureen give an example of her limited vulgar vocabulary.

"I mean, how would you feel if this little boy opens his mouth one day and says something like..."

Again, Maureen couldn't bring herself to say anything.

"Nope, lost me there," said Tash.

"I mean a swear word!"

"You won't hear Maureen saying any swears," said Raymond from the front. He'd lowered his beard, which hung around his sweaty red face.

"Say one now, Maureen, just for shits and giggles," said Martha.

"I'll do no such thing, and you watch your mouth too."

"Have you never sworn in your life?" asked Jamie. "Not once?"

"Never," said Maureen.

"Not strictly true, Maureen," said Raymond. "You swore at me that night we got shot at in October."

"Well, that's understandable," said Martha. "I'll give you that one."

"You got shot at?" said Anthony, his little face full of horror and awe.

"No, it's just an expression," said Maureen. "You get off now, Anthony; you can walk these last few yards."

"No. You're alright. I'll keep you company."

Maureen looked suitably unimpressed.

"*Elephant Man*, wasn't that the one with thing in it?" said Jamie. "Whatsisname?"

"The guy from *Alien*," said Tash.

"Yes, him," said Jamie.

"Rod Allen!" said Raymond.

"No, it was John Hurt," said Maureen, although she wasn't interested in the slightest.

"That's it!" said Jamie.

"No, Rod Allen is the man that wrote all the jingles," said Raymond.

"What are you talking about?" said Maureen.

"Back in the bank basement," said Raymond. "We had an interesting chat about jingles in adverts."

"It was just a chat," said Tash. "We didn't vote on the 'interesting' part, but I'm prepared to stick my neck out and say we all thought it was just a chat."

"You could count his greatest hits on one hand," said Jamie.

"I said his name would come to me!" said Raymond. "And it did! He's from County Durham."

"And?" said Tash.

"That's where he comes from."

"But why are you telling us?" asked Martha.

"What do you mean?" said Raymond.

"Well, you already know that, and we don't care."

Jamie's hand was up again.

"You don't need to raise your hand to speak, Jamie," said his sister.

"But it's changing the subject," said Jamie.

"Great! Go!" said Tash.

"There's a police officer outside the warehouse."

Chapter Forty-Nine

For some reason best known to the police officer, they had their back to the gang of misfits. They occasionally looked up at the windows above them and then back at their watch.

The grunts of Raymond, Tash, Martha and Jamie attempting to turn the cart around in the narrow street soon became too loud to ensure a stealth-like getaway, and the police officer, less than fifteen yards away, turned around.

"Season's Greetings," said the constable.

No one spoke; they simply stood still in the darkness.

"Come on over where I can see you."

The others abandoned the cart, Raymond helped his wife down, still clutching Tash's baby, and they all walked over to the poker-faced police officer. Close up, he looked no more than seventeen or eighteen years old. His spotty nose threw shade over a fluffy moustache that he'd most likely been cultivating since he reached puberty, which was probably sometime last week. His authority was undermined by his slight difficulty pronouncing his Rs.

"I'm PC Pulfertoft."

"Hello, PC Pullitoff," said Raymond. "How can we help you?"

"Pulfertoft," said the PC.

"Pull the top?" said Raymond trying to follow his lips.

"Pulfertoft."

"Pull," said Raymond.

"Fer."

"Fur," said Raymond.

"Toft."

"Smashing,' said Raymond. "Got it. Sorry."

"You can't leave that there," he replied, nodding at the cart. "You're blocking the traffic."

"What traffic?" said Jamie. He was right.

"Any traffic that might want to come down here."

"Well, your lot left that here," said Tash pointing to the VW Campervan with Spanish plates that Jesus Morón and his kids had been forced to abandon after their arrest last night.

"That's evidence," said Pulfertoft. "That stays there."

"It's in the way," said Tash.

"A vehicle could get around it. Can you tell me your movements today?" said the officer.

"Pardon?'

"Your movements, sir."

Raymond looked around at the baffled faces staring at him. Then he leaned to the constable's ear and whispered as quietly as he could.

"I haven't been today. I've been a bit backed up. My routine's all over the place with all the guns, and owls and mice and what have you."

"Your geographical movements," said Pulfertoft. "Where have you visited today?"

Fiddlesticks, thought Maureen.

Sake, thought Tash.

Crap, thought Martha.

I hope he doesn't arrest Martha, thought Jamie. I enjoyed touching her back.

If my bowels fail, would my wellies catch everything? thought Raymond.

The silence hung in the cool December air. Raymond swallowed. Maureen's tummy rumbled.

"Excuse me," said Jamie, knowing that Raymond was too occupied to offer his usual chivalrous apology on behalf of his wife,

"I asked, where have you visited today? And don't miss anything out," said the young PC.

Then the phone started ringing inside the warehouse.

"Is that your phone?" asked Martha.

Raymond shook his head. "Ours is more of a bell, like *ring-ring."* He sang that part.

"It's lower," said Jamie. "You're doing the home one. Your work one is more *ring-ring."* He sang that too.

"That sounds like the home phone too, Jamie. You're doing it wrong," said Maureen before immediately singing in an operatic tone with a bit of vibrato thrown in. Admittedly, she was in a higher key: *"Ring-ring."*

Meanwhile, the phone continued to ring from inside the warehouse.

The PC struggled to keep up with the singing.

"That sure sounds like it's coming from inside," said Martha.

"Not mine that," said Raymond. "That's too electronic. Sounds like something off an American TV show."

And it did.

Then it stopped ringing.

"Well, it's stopped now anyway. So, where have you been today?" asked the young officer.

Chapter Fifty

The phone started ringing again almost instantly.

Martha stepped from behind Raymond and into the amber lamplight that had recently flickered on outside Raymond's shutter doors. Jamie noticed how the hue from the sodium lamp muted her purple hair colour to a sedate black, and her chalk-white skin now had a glow like the Mediterranean sun had kissed it. Lucky sun.

"It's your new phone! You got a new phone!" said Martha.

Raymond smiled. "Oh yes, they fitted a new one! I like the sound of that. Very modern!"

"I need to answer it. Now!" said Martha.

Pulfertoft considered this momentarily and then stepped to one side to let her pass.

"Is this your card?" said the PC, suddenly holding up one of Raymond's Maurmond Storage Facilities business cards and thrusting it into Father Christmas's face.

Raymond was torn. He was proud that these were now making an impact and had freely entered circulation of the London public; last year's brand-new pound coin took longer than that! But equally, he was not sure what he was aiming at. He was remarkably intimidating for a man who would need ID to buy a pint of Harp lager.

"Phone!" shouted Martha. "Keys, Raymondo, keys! Now!"

"Oh yes, of course!" he replied before looking at the PC. "May I?"

He nodded and watched as Raymond fumbled under his Father Christmas cloak to find his trouser pockets as Martha watched on, listening to his laidback muttering.

"Nope! Not that pocket!"

The phone continued to ring. How was it possible that it seemed to be getting louder?

"Get the fucking keys!" shouted Martha, launching both of her hands down his damp red cloak.

"Blimey," said Raymond.

This reminded him of the time the shop assistant at Austin Reed measured his inside leg for his wedding suit. Except he was a man and smelt of Golden Virginia. Martha was a lady and smelled of Canadian cheese.

"Take your hands off my husband's privates!" shouted Maureen.

"I think I can manage, actually, thank you," said Raymond as politely as possible. And with that, he extracted a bundle of keys.

"Come on! Open the frickin' door!" shouted Martha.

Raymond's hands were trembling as he finally presented the key into the lock and turned it. The shutter took some force to open, and when it was only three feet up, Martha dropped to the ground and rolled inside, running into the darkness, guided only by the ringing inside the caged office.

"Is everything alright?" asked the policeman, momentarily thrown off guard by this odd behaviour.

"She's fine," said Tash. "What's the problem with the card?"

He held it to Raymond's face again. "Do you recognise this?"

"Erm, let me see, erm," he took it and squinted to read it. "No, I don't think so. Erm."

"You do, Raymond," said Jamie. "It's one of those that I bought for you."

"Oh yes," said Raymond. "Thanks, Jamie. Yes."

"Help me find a light!" came Martha's voice from inside the warehouse.

"No. You wait here," said Pulfertoft, blocking Raymond in his path.

"A property on Old Gloucester Street was burgled today. Number forty-five. And your business card was found in the hallway. How do you explain that?"

"Light! Anybody?" came Martha's voice again.

"I'm not sure we passed there," said Raymond, staring into the sky to see if the heavens might jog his memory.

"Maybe that was the house we stopped to use the loo?" said Jamie.

"Oh yes," said Raymond. "Thank you, Jamie. Yes, I think we did."

The phone rang and rang from inside. Raymond smiled at the PC and then sighed.

"And she's been robbed, has she? That's awful."

"She?" said the PC. "The house belongs to an elderly gentleman. Retired from the military. He went to church this morning. Then visited his daughter. When she dropped him home, he'd been robbed. All his late wife's jewellery, his military medals, paintings, sculptures..."

"Not us. The house we visited was owned by an elderly lady," said Raymond.

"They even took all his loo rolls," said Pulfertoft, disgusted by this brutal crime.

Raymond shuffled awkwardly.

"And left a floater in his loo. Some kind of dirty protest."

Raymond felt his face blush.

"Weren't you last out?" said Jamie to Raymond.

"Can anyone fricking hear me?" shouted Martha as the phone continued to ring.

Jamie was struggling to remain outside on the street. Every inch of him was desperate to help Martha answer the call that might save her life.

"Hello," said a young woman's voice.

Pulfertoft looked over his shoulder at another PC. She had returned from her recce of the road.

"They're co-operating fully," he replied.

"Sab?" said Maureen, unable to believe this apparition in blue uniform. How many more surprises did this woman have?

Sab attempted a professional but sympathetic smile at her old friends.

"What's with the uniform?" asked Jamie.

"Long story," she replied. "But it's basically a professional bollocking."

Chapter Fifty-One

"This is the moment I usually ask for you to hand in your firearm," said Detective Chief Superintendent Hepplestone. "But that's why you're here, isn't it? You lost it."

Sab was broken. Just a matter of hours earlier, she had single-handedly prevented a gangland style murder in a Tower Bridge warehouse. And as three Spanish criminals were being handcuffed by her colleagues, she had stood tall and felt immensely proud. Raymond and his wife had lived to see another day, and a money launderer with links to the Brinks Mat investigation was off the streets. She could still see the glint of admiration in her boss's eyes as she'd handed her a new assignment in a brown folder. But now she was circling her dressed in a dusky peach St Michael dressing gown, and she looked beyond livid.

In the night, Sab had called her boss to confess the humiliating theft immediately. Her partner had betrayed her and stolen her gun. If she ever was her partner. Oh God, why was she just realising that now? She was never in a relationship with this woman. She had deceived her just to get close to her, so she could steal a bloody gun. Initially on the call, her boss berated her for waking her in the night but then as the conversation continued, she had summoned her to the mews property. The townhouse was a mixture of top-end seventies and eighties furniture and fixings, competing for space with many antiquities. Habitat chairs sat alongside a classic antique sofa. A chrome tubular framed coffee table with a smoked glass top struggled beneath a vast chess set with carved ivory pieces and an empty bottle of Asti Spumante, which surprised Sab, given the expensive tastes of her boss.

"So, I can't ask for that," said Hepplestone. "But I can ask you for the folder I gave you last night. Or did your boyfriend take that, too?"

Sab didn't correct the sex of her partner; she felt it wouldn't help move the chat along at all.

"Well, I think maybe it's at my flat," said Sab, lying to prevent this incensed woman from biting her head off.

"Bull shit!" said her boss.

"Hammond found this on Pentonville Road. That's near your hovel, isn't it?"

With this, she threw down the manila folder, knocking over the bishop on her chess set.

"It was empty, of course, but lucky for you, he found these too. On the fucking pavement."

More papers landed on the chess set. The top one was a photograph of a purple-haired lady and the words: *Classified: Federal Bureau of Investigation, USA. WANTED.*

Sab reached over and picked it up.

"You can put that down," said her boss, still circling her like a vulture ready to kill.

Sab did as she was told, noticing how the purple hair on the photograph glowed under the Anglepoise lamp that illuminated the abandoned chess game.

"I just need twenty-four hours," said Sab, the desperation apparent in her voice.

"You don't tell me what you need," said her boss. "You just listen. Sit down."

Sab looked behind her and cautiously lowered herself onto one of the black leather Habitat chairs.

"On the floor."

Sab slid onto the floor, her boss now looming over her. How

could someone look so demonic in a size sixteen Marks and Spencer wrap-around dressing gown?

"You will start work in four hours. That should give you the same amount of sleep I shall get tonight."

"Thank you so much, Ma'am," said Sab, breathing a huge sigh of relief. "I won't let you down."

"Quiet!"

She complied.

"As a constable."

"But..."

"You're stripped of your detective status. Your pay grade will be adjusted accordingly."

"But," Sab tried to speak again.

"Don't fucking speak!" said Hepplestone. "You say one more word, and you're off the force altogether. One. More. Word. Understand?"

Sab slowly nodded.

"Now get out of my house."

Sab climbed up off the floor, a pathetic figure, using the sofa seat to help pull herself up.

"Don't touch the furniture."

She let go, straightened herself up, nodded to her boss, and walked to the drawing-room door.

"You are very lucky," said the DCS.

Sab didn't feel it. She'd been cheated and humiliated in love, and now had her career crushed, all within a matter of hours. She nodded her appreciation.

"You're not going to thank me?" asked Hepplestone.

Sab considered this, then realising this was a test, she shook her head.

"You're not completely stupid then," said her boss, with a vicious smile.

Chapter Fifty-Two

"Are you on the beat?" said Jamie. "On your own?"

"I'm with him," said Sab.

"Help me! You bunch of pricks!" shouted Martha over the sound of the incessant ringing that continued to echo inside. Jamie looked concerned but also distracted.

"Can I go inside?"

"Not yet," said Sab, before turning to Raymond and then Maureen.

"I know things have been bad, but really? Why did you do this?" she asked.

"Do what?" replied Maureen.

"We've been visiting poorly boys and girls," said Raymond. "I'm Father Christmas."

"And you?" asked Sab.

"I'm an elf," said Tash to the ground as quietly as she could.

"Pardon?"

"I'm a pissing elf, aren't I?" said Tash before looking down at Anthony. "Sorry, I think I swore again."

Sab looked at the little boy. "Are you a munchkin?"

"No, he's a cub scout, isn't he?" said Tash.

"What's a cub scout got to do with Christmas?" said Sab.

"No, he's a real one," said Raymond.

"They say a woman was in the house," said Pulfertoft. "A pensioner."

"A lovely lady. She was going to deliver gifts to her grandchildren," said Raymond. "We helped her load the car."

"What sort of gifts?" asked Sab.

"Not sure. They were in black sacks," said Raymond.

"I'd stop talking now," said Tash. "If I were you."

"What sort of car?" asked Pulfertoft at Sab's side.

"It had a CND sticker in it," said Maureen with disdain in her voice.

"Maxi was it?" he replied, suddenly pleased with himself.

"No idea," said Maureen.

"Yes," said Jamie. "Maxi."

The young PC looked over at Sab.

"She's known to us. Betty Hawkins. It started with a bit of shoplifting, and she's been cautioned for breaking and entering. She doesn't need the money; she needs the buzz. They call her the greyhound."

"No!" said Raymond. "Are you sure?"

"Why do they call her the greyhound?" asked Maureen.

"She's grey-haired," said Pulfertoft.

"Is she fast?" said Tash.

"No."

"Slender?" said Raymond.

"Don't be filthy, Raymond," said Maureen,

"No," said the PC.

"Is she a bit of a dog?" said Tash.

"Tash!" said Maureen.

"Well, come on, *they* gave her that nickname."

"No, she's not a bit of a dog," said the PC.

"It's a pretty shit nickname, then, Pullitoff," said Tash. "You see, it needs to reflect a personality trait or something physical."

"My name's Pulfertoft."

"I know," said Tash.

The phone stopped ringing inside the warehouse, followed by an almighty "Noooooooooooooo!"

This was followed by a thunderous outburst.

"You pieces of shit bastards! Why the fuck can't you get in here and switch on a God damn light. I missed the call! I missed the call! I'll never speak to you again. Ever."

Then the phone started ringing again.

Her voice sounded immediately different and warm. "Hey, Jamie, would you come in please and help me? Please?"

"May I?" said Jamie to Sab, who nodded and stepped aside. Jamie crawled under the partially raised door and disappeared. Soon the flickering of the fluorescent strip lights illuminated the concrete floor inside the warehouse, and the ringing stopped as the handset was snatched.

"It's me. Is that you?" said Martha from the office inside. "Thank fuck for that. Hold on... Jamie, I need a pen."

"Are we in trouble?" said Anthony.

"I'm guessing you are Anthony Pritchard-Gittins?" said Pelfertoft, reading from a pad in his hand.

"Anthony," corrected the cub with the soft *th*.

"He's big on that part," said Tash.

"He's been listed as missing by the scout group," said the PC.

"I wanted to go with them. We've been to the bank!" said Anthony.

"South Bank," said Tash, then leaned and whispered to Sab. "Lives in an absolute dream world. Lovely kid but full of shit."

Sab glanced over at Anthony and thought.

"We gave some gifts to the kids at Great Ormond Street Hospital," said Raymond. "That's why I'm dressed as Father Christmas."

"That would explain the beard," said Pulfertoft. "Seems like he's telling the truth. It pieces together. Father Christmas has a beard."

Sab's face summed up the frustration of being demoted so mightily and paired with such a knobhead.

"Do we know where this Hawkins woman lives?" said Sab to her partner without looking at him. He didn't answer.

Sab looked over at him.

"Oh, are you talking to me?" said Pulfertoft.

"Yes, I didn't think the cub scout knew where she lived."

"It's just that you weren't looking at me."

Sab rubbed her tired eyes in frustration, then pressed her nose to his.

"Do we know where she lives?"

"Who?"

"This Hawkins woman!" shrieked Sab, causing a flock of seagulls to fly up into the heavens.

"Yes," said Pulfertoft.

Sab turned back to Father Christmas and his helpers.

"Don't go too far away. We may need you to identify her in the next day or so. Okay?"

Raymond's shoulders visibly dropped in relief, and he nodded crazily.

The others nodded too.

"Let's get you home, Anthony," said Sab to the yawning cub. "Call a car."

Again, Pulfertoft ignored her.

"Call a car, Pullitoff!" said Sab. Tash smiled.

"Yes. Will do."

Sab turned to Tash. She looked her clothing up and down, her elf make-up, the cart behind with a Christmas tree on its side next to some covered bundle of rubbish and litter.

"Don't you ever get tired of doing weird things?"

Tash found herself starting to well up with tears. The one time she'd tried to show the kind of altruism that Maureen and Raymond had shown her, and look at the state of things now. Her young uncle could get sacked; they'd probably knocked out the banking system of the south of England, they'd lost a horse and assisted a robbery.

"Yes," said Tash.

"You look cold, Sab. Are you going to stop for a cup of tea?" said Maureen.

Her kindness touched Sab.

"Thanks, but we need to be going. Don't touch that," said Sab, nodding at the cart.

"Why?" said Tash, suddenly feeling anxious. The C5 was hers and not up for any kind of negotiation.

"That's listed as missing too. We'll send someone for it."

"Of course," said Raymond before suddenly spinning around madly. "Wait! Where's the Princess? It was here! It's been stolen!"

He circled again, then rubbed his head.

"Didn't you move it?" asked Maureen.

"When?" said Raymond. "We all left together in that police car! Do you think I got up in the night and collected it?"

"I doubt it. You're too busy waking the house with your toilet visits."

"It's very normal for a man of my age to get up in the night."

"You sound like Niagara Falls!" said Maureen. "I've told you to get checked out, but no! You'd rather bury your head in the sand. You can't avoid it forever. It's just a finger up the bottom!"

"Well, this has taken a turn, hasn't it?" said Tash.

"I didn't move the car," said Raymond.

"It had no windscreen, mirrors, or tax," said Sab.

"No tax?" Maureen sounded like she'd been accused of hunting for ivory.

"I had a spot of bother with the tax, actually," said Raymond.

"What kind of bother?" said Sab.

"No money."

"Raymond!" Maureen was broken.

"It's been impounded. Don't worry, you'll get a few pounds for scrap," said Sab.

"Scrap?" said Raymond. Not his Princess.

"Should cover the tax," said Tash.

The roller shutters started to rise again, and Jamie's legs came into sight as he forced them fully upwards. Martha had her back to them, frantically making notes with the phone to her ear. The fluorescent lights were still flickering on and off and her purple hair flashed in synch.

Sab glanced in.

"Hi, Jamie."

"Hi!" He wasn't paying attention. He'd caught his sleeve in the roller guides and was trying to free himself. She could have been Beyonce, and he wouldn't have flinched.

"Who's the woman?" said Sab to Tash.

"We met her back in October. Didn't Jamie tell you about her? Martha. Mental. Completely mental. But a good heart." She paused. "I hope."

Sab nodded.

"She arrived in a crate of Canadian cheese!" said Tash, laughing.

Sab laughed too.

"Where shall we send the car? This road is blocked," said Pulfertoft.

"We'll meet them at the south steps of Tower Bridge," said Sab before turning to Anthony. "Come with me, young man."

As the two PCs and the cub scout set off along the cobbles, Raymond, Maureen, and Tash could hear Anthony muttering away.

"You know, prostitutes, kind of thing. So, they shut them down."

Chapter Fifty-Three

"Are we ready?" said Tash.

At the rear of the abandoned cart, two ramps had been placed side by side up to the Sinclair C5. Jamie had fashioned them from two long timber shelf boards, each about ten inches wide.

"Ready," said Jamie.

The rear of the time machine was at the top of the ramp. Jamie was at the front of it with both hands on its nose, ready to force it onto the planks and down onto the cobbles. Tash sat in the seat, with her hands on the handlebars by her legs.

"I don't like going backwards," said Tash.

"Well, swap then. You push, and I'll sit in it.

"I didn't say that."

"Just think of it as reversing."

"I am doing. That's the problem. I hate reversing."

"Just keep it straight, that's all. And keep pumping the brakes to slow it when it starts to roll."

"Okay."

"I'm gonna start pushing now," said Jamie.

"No, no, no, wait," said Tash.

Jamie paused.

"Okay, I'm ready," said Tash. "No, wait!"

"Come on, sis! The police will be here soon for the cart!"

"Okay, I'm ready."

"You sure?"

"Yes," said Tash. It was dark, and Jamie could only see the whites of her eyes when she lifted her head to him. But now, she was looking over her shoulder.

"I'm going to push in three, two, one...."

Nothing happened. The sound of Jamie straining got louder.

"Push then, Jamie!"

"I am bloody pushing. Do you have the brake on?"

"No!" said Tash with an aggressive tone.

She had, but she wasn't about to tell him.

"Go again," said Tash.

"Three, two," said Jamie but was interrupted.

"We don't need the countdown," said Tash.

"It's so you can prepare yourself," said Jamie.

"I'm prepared. The counting just slows things down!"

"I'd have started by now if you hadn't stopped me!"

"Just push!" said Tash.

And he did with as much effort as he could muster, unaware that he had been pushing against locked wheels the first time.

The C5 – and Tash – shot backwards off the cart onto the two ramps and started their descent. Sadly, Jamie hadn't positioned a central ramp and being a tricycle, the front wheel fell into the gap, and the whole vehicle abruptly stopped.

"Sake!" shouted Tash. "What's happened?"

"I forgot about the front wheel," said Jamie, leaping down to make sure his sister was okay.

"Do something, Jamie!"

He ran into the warehouse to look for some more wood. Raymond and Maureen looked up; baby Raymond seated on her lap. Martha sounded like she might be rounding off her phone call.

"What is it?" said Raymond.

"I need one more piece of wood," said Jamie.

A clatter and bang from outside stopped the conversation.

"Jamie!" shouted Tash. "Forget the wood. We don't need it!"

"Oh," said Jamie. "We don't need it now."

He dashed outside to see Tash still seated, but the C5 was now on its side on the cold cobbles. The downward force between the two wooden ramps had forced them apart until the Sinclair, and its driver dropped through the hole created in the middle.

"I sorted it," said Tash.

"Well done," said Jamie.

"You're welcome," she replied. "Prick."

Chapter Fifty-Four

"Why are you holding the tree?" asked Martha as she finally hung up her transatlantic call.

Jamie had closed the shutter doors and was standing alongside the Christmas tree that had accompanied them on their scavenger hunt around London. He'd realised there were fairy lights amongst its collection of primarily smashed baubles and knotted tinsel and thought it would be Christmassy to plug them in. It just seemed right, with it being Christmas Eve Eve and all that.

"We broke its trunk," said Jamie. "So I repaired it."

"Sit down, Jamie," said Tash, examining the new set of scratches and missing pieces of Grandad's C5.

"She's right," said Raymond. "You did a great fix. I'm sure you don't need to hold it. You just need to have faith in yourself."

He pointed to the collage of brown tape, Sellotape and little splints of wood positioned around the base. Jamie let go, and the plastic tree toppled slowly over onto its side to the sound of more smashing baubles. The coloured Christmas lights went off.

"Oh," said Jamie. He leaned in to tighten a bulb and recoiled as 240 volts leapt through his body. There was a crack and smell of smoke, but amazingly the lights flickered on, then off, then on again.

"Jamie. Are you alright?" asked Maureen, still clutching Tash's son warmly on her lap.

"Jamie?" said Tash, surprised someone had beat her with the first response.

"I think I might lie down for a minute," he replied.

The hair protruding from beneath his walking sock hat stood on end, and a glazed expression filled his face.

"Ok," said Tash.

"I think I might lie down for a minute."

They all watched as he started to undress.

"Jamie," said Tash. "What are you doing?"

"Going to bed."

"No, you're not. You're just going to lie down."

"I think I might lie down for a minute. The lights are pretty, aren't they?"

They all replied, hoping that Jamie would soon inhabit his body again. Things like... ..."very pretty",

..."they are!",

..."you've done a smashing job," and

..."Jamie, pull your pants back up."

Tash walked towards her brother and tenderly lowered him down to the cold concrete floor.

"Put your clothes back on, Jamie, just rest," she said, removing his hat.

"We needed a strategy," said Jamie.

"We did," said Tash, placing her hand gently on his head. "Can you turn some heat on or something? Why isn't this on?"

She pointed to a three-bar portable electric heater.

"Yes, sorry," said Raymond, and he walked over to a bank of plug sockets and went down them, flicking them on as quickly as he could; the heater came on right after the Sanyo radio. Van Halen's 'Jump', plus the one working bar on the heater, did their best to warm the massive room.

"Would a cup of tea help?" said Raymond.

"Help you. Or help him?" said Tash. Before immediately regretting it. She thought these people had become his family. Why was she the only one helping?

"I meant him," said Raymond.

"I'm sorry. I just need to know you'll look after him."

Damn. She regretted that immediately. Raymond tried to make sense of this curious remark.

"I have some excellent news," said Martha. "But I'm keeping it in, as it seems like we have a first-response-slash-family-feud scenario, so could someone let me know when it's passed?"

"You must be in the wrong place," said Maureen. "We never get excellent news."

"Try me," said Martha.

She now had everyone's attention. Even Jamie's.

"Jamie, you ready for some excellent news?" said Tash.

Jamie looked at her for a moment, then nodded.

"Is it about the Princess?" said Raymond.

"Diana?" asked Martha, very confused.

"The car. My car."

"No. Why would I have news about your car?"

"I was just joining in," said Raymond. "Sorry."

Jamie's hand was raised.

"A question from the handsome elf over there?" said Martha.

Jamie blushed beneath his fading makeup.

"Have they decided to let you live?"

"No." Martha suddenly looked sad.

"Regretting that one, Jamie?" said Tash.

"The money," said Martha. "Correction: My money. It was withdrawn from the Swiss bank nineteen days ago and deposited in a single personal account in Madrid, Spain."

She waited for a euphoric reaction but saw blank faces.

"Why do Americans do that?" said Tash.

"What?" replied Martha.

"I'm not having a go. I'm just asking," said Tash.

"Just asking what?"

"You never just say a city. You always add the country. Madrid, Spain. London, England."

"New York, New York," said Raymond.

"No, that's a song, Raymond," said Maureen.

"Yes," he replied. "Sorry."

"No, he's right," said Martha. "It's New York city in New York state."

"Wow! I never knew that," said Jamie.

Oh, dear. Raymond hated being right, especially if it meant that Maureen was wrong. Why had he bothered to join in? He'd pay for that later; maybe he'd be second with the tea bag. Or third, if Jamie wanted a cup. Or fourth. Or fifth! Oh God, what had he done?

"If I say, Los Angeles, I know where I mean," said Tash. "I don't need to say, Los Angeles, California."

"It's probably because we have so many towns and cities with the same name, so we include the state. Because our country is so big and yours is so tiny," said Martha, making the *tiny* sound undoubtedly patronising.

Tash nodded as she thought.

"But there's only one Madrid in Spain and only one London in England. So, save yourself some time, yes?"

"Are we arguing?" said Martha.

"You might be; I'm not," said Tash.

"It does sound a little bit like an argument," said Jamie. "I'm sure you didn't mean it to sound like that."

"This woman dragged us across town. We've been sifting shit through bins. We've robbed a house..." Tash was interrupted by Jamie.

"No, Raymond robbed the house."

"Pardon?" said Raymond.

"We abandoned our uncle – unconscious – in a flooded office," said Tash.

"Abandoned? You said he was okay and was going to clear things up?" said Jamie.

"I lied!" said Tash. "That's what she makes us do!"

She wasn't sure why she was attacking Martha. She knew that she was tired and that she regretted coming back to 1984. But she was also bewildered about Jamie's future. He was supposed to fall for this girl, but how and when did it happen? She had tried hard since yesterday to remain neutral in every aspect of every conversation and every decision. Other than the one leaving her uncle to fend for himself. But she resigned herself to the fact that she had made a judgement call on that one, and it was undoubtedly the right one.

At least now, she was simply waiting for the opportunity to distract the others, then climb back into the C5 with her son and head home.

She would have liked to have seen a flicker of a spark, something that suggested a fledgling relationship forming between the two, but what the hell? It didn't matter. She'd seen them together in 2020, so something would work itself out. She evidently wouldn't be executed in the USA, and Tash could look back on this visit and know she had made no negative impact on the outcome of their future together.

She turned to Martha. She looked confused. Not angry or confrontational. Just confused.

"I'm sorry," said Tash, walking to Maureen and scooping up baby Raymond. "I'm tired. We're all tired. I'm glad you have excellent news. Let's hear it."

Martha held up her hand-written notes and cleared her throat.

"The Madrid bank has a calendar request to withdraw two million US dollars in local currency – whatever the crap that is - from a branch in the Balearic Islands."

"Do you know which one?" said Jamie.

"Island or branch?" replied Martha.

"Let's start with the island."

"Menorca."

"And branch?"

"It's one of two." She squinted at her notes. "He knows it's in a town called Sant Lluìs. Banco Central or Sa Nostra. And she's fixed the time and date."

"She?" asked Jamie.

"Bee. B for bitch," said Martha.

"Is that normal?" asked Raymond.

"Maybe, given the amount of cash they're handing over. They'll probably invite the fricking mayor."

"Let me guess, 9 am tomorrow morning?" said Tash.

"Noon, July thirteenth."

"July the fucking thirteenth?" said Tash. She was not hanging around to be part of this charade.

"Bit weird," said Jamie. "Why wait so long?"

"I don't give a shit! But, I do know that I need to be at that bank to catch the bitch who's living my life."

"Catch her?" said Jamie. "That sounds risky?"

"I don't take risks," said Martha. "I just take a photo of her, prove she's still alive, and get it to my buddy in Vermont Police."

"You have a buddy now?" said Tash.

"Okay, acquaintance. But he's not bent. He'll do the right thing."

Everyone stared back at her.

"He tried to help me because he believes me."

They stared again.

"He knows I'm telling the truth."

Tash turned to Jamie. "Is she hoping these little speeches will rouse us into supporting her on her quest? She sounds like those shit memes on Instagram."

"On what?" said Martha.

"I believe her," said Jamie before looking at Martha. "But I don't see how you can do it."

"And why do you say that?" Martha looked ready for whatever he was going to throw at her.

"Well, there's only one of you but two banks," said Jamie. "Assuming they both have just one door, too."

"What does that mean?" asked Martha.

"Given the amount they're handing over, surely they'll have an option to meet her at the back door or something?"

"That's a good point," said Tash. "Let us know how you get on. In fact, thinking about it, don't bother."

"Come on, guys! You're not going to abandon me now!" said the American. "Besides, I can pay you your fee in cash! I'll cover the flight costs."

"What are you talking about?" said Maureen. "It's Christmas Eve tomorrow. What do you plan to do for the next seven months whilst we wait to do a Judith Chalmers over to Mallorca?"

"Wasn't it Menorca?" said Raymond.

"It's the same place, Raymond. And don't interrupt me when I'm speaking."

Jamie's hand was in the air.

Tash sighed. "Jamie. You're gonna have to stop it with the raised hand thing. How the hell do you expect people to take you seriously?"

"What is it?" said Martha.

"Menorca is a different island to Mallorca," said Jamie.

Raymond winced. Maureen wouldn't like this one bit. He decided to pick up his new phone.

"What are you doing?" said Maureen.

"Oh, look at that," said Raymond, slowly hanging up. "Did you hear it ring? They must have dialled the wrong number. It's a lovely colour, isn't it? What colour would you call that?"

Everyone replied in unison. "Brown."

"So, you think we need four people?" Martha asked Jamie.

"He didn't say that," said Tash.

"At least," said Jamie. "Four people with a camera each. In position at each point of entry at least ten minutes before the agreed withdrawal time. We shoot for half an hour. Maybe more."

Tash said nothing but realised that she was now looking at four people and a plan that involved her brother happily remaining in London for more than half of 1985 until he could help Martha. This suddenly felt very reassuring indeed. Maybe love was in the air after all.

"So, I just need three people to help me?" said Martha.

"Yes," said Jamie, looking at the others, as did Martha.

Maureen looked at her shoes. Tash looked at Maureen, looking at her shoes. Raymond fiddled with the phone again, muttering something that sounded like, "You can never really tell if they've properly hung up, can you?"

"Tash?" said Jamie.

"What?" she replied. "What, Jamie? Think hard about what

you're going to ask me because I've got a five-month-old baby with me. We came back to see you all, to spend Christmas with you, to be nice! But I can't return home with a one-year-old son as people might kind of notice!"

"You were being nice?" said Maureen.

"Yes, I was being nice!" replied Tash. Her voice getting shoutier all the time. "I realised you were nice, and I thought I should try to be nice, and look where the fuck it's got me!"

Raymond and Maureen considered this.

"Well, that's a very nice thing to say, actually, Tash," said Raymond. "Isn't it Maureen?"

"I suppose so," replied his wife.

"The thing is, we don't even know what this woman looks like," said Tash, grasping at straws.

Martha fumbled inside her knickers and extracted a tightly folded bundle of paper. She handed it to Jamie, who took it immediately, still staring at the body of this beguiling woman.

"It's warm," said Jamie.

"It's been next to my fanny since I left Canada," she explained.

"Oh, my word," said Raymond.

"She means arse," said Tash.

Maureen looked like she might fall over, so Tash doubled down on the translation.

"She means arse!"

Jamie slowly unfolded the contraband, revealing the ripped cover of a Canadian newspaper folded in half across the middle. Beneath the *Gazette* masthead were the words:

Montreal, 206th year, price 35¢. Wednesday, November 21st, 1984.

The main headline read: *Double killer escapes US jail, Canadian border on alert.* Beneath that were two large black and white photographs. The first of a balding grey-haired man in a professional pose, very much the kind of image Harvey Eikenberry had been keen to portray on the portrait in his office reception. Beside that was a smiling middle-aged lady, most probably a cropped close-up of a candid moment, maybe a party or social event.

"That's Bee," said Martha, taking the newspaper and folding it in half again to focus everyone's attention on the perpetrator of the crime.

"She's behind this. She stole my money. Your money. Remember her from London?"

"She's the one who appeared in the TV Centre basement," said Jamie.

There was a long pause.

"Well, can't you ask some friends to help you?" said Maureen, glaring at Martha.

"What do you think?"

"Well, you'll just have to find some!" said Maureen, as if Martha was a fool to have not considered this already.

"I have an idea," said Jamie.

"Is it Lemon Coke? Cos they already invented it," said Tash.

"No, it's not Lemon Coke," said Jamie before turning to Martha, "although I *did* think of that first."

"Lemon Coke?" asked Martha. "They make lemon Coke?"

"In fairness, he did realise it tasted better with a slice of lemon in it," said Tash.

"He's right," said Martha.

"So, he invented a mix with Grandad. Coke with lemon juice already in it."

"Nice idea."

"Then fannied around for years trying to cover his arse in case he pitched the idea, and they stole it."

"You never pitched it?" said Martha to Jamie.

He shook his head. "I wanted to protect my invention. They thought of it themselves a bit later, but I was first."

"I don't understand what they're talking about, Raymond," said Maureen.

"You should hear his idea for a tile shop!" said Tash.

"Harry's Tiles!" said Jamie.

"But you're not called Harry?" said Maureen.

"Do you sell tiles?" asked Raymond. "I thought you fixed bikes."

"It's a play on words," said Jamie. "Harry's Tiles sounds like Harry Styles."

"It's 1984, Jamie. Harry's not been born," said Tash.

"No," he agreed.

"Big thinker, our Jamie," said Tash. "Big on ideas, low on actions."

"Well, that's where you're wrong," said Jamie. "Cos, I have an idea."

There was a sudden dull metallic bang as the shutter doors appeared to fold up before their eyes and twist hideously before slamming to the ground, causing a cloud of dust to float up from the dirty warehouse floor. Martha screwed up the papers in her hand within a heartbeat and threw the ball straight at Jamie's face.

"Everyone on the floor now. Place your hands behind your head!" The voice resonated around the cold interior from a loud hailer outside.

Chapter Fifty-Five

Jamie had never seen a Police Range Rover before. It was the two-door model, and he concluded that this was probably to prevent criminals from opening their doors when they pulled up at traffic lights. The bright headlights lit up the timber cart, which had served them well all day but was now being fixed to the rear of a flat-back Ford van by two men in overalls, instructed by a WPC.

The blue strobe lights on the roof of the Range Rover illuminated the stark brick fronts that lined Shad Thames as far as the eye could see. And every flash also lit up the suspect in the rear of the car. The purple of her hair glimmered like a *Top of The Pops* dancer, and her mascara ran down her cheeks, helped on the way by a restrained trickle of tears.

Tash stood with her son strapped to her chest, her face covered by her hands. Maureen remained seated on her plastic chair, hoping that any kind of photofit image of her that might pop up on *Police 5 with Shaw Taylor* would be indecipherable because of her elf make-up. She'd not been interviewed yet but was prepared for the worst. She knew she had one phone call, so she would use it to offer her resignation at the cubs with the added caveat that this was on the condition that Peggy Stonehouse brought her a clean pair of C&A knickers into prison. Or she might go shit or bust and insist on a pair of St Michael from Marks & Spencer.

Raymond was trying hard to present his best concerned-face at the fate of his brief visitor whilst also establishing the damage the Met had caused by destroying his shutter to gain entry. Why didn't they just knock? This wasn't *The A-Team*.

Jamie had a feeling he'd not felt before. He wasn't sure if it was in his stomach or his throat. But his eyes felt a bit bulgy, and his cheeks felt damp. This may have been the first time in his life he'd maintained eye contact with anyone for more than a second. He'd also ignored his reflection in the car door window whenever the blue light dipped.

He was staring at Martha, and she was hurting too.

She leaned towards the driver's door and attempted to speak through the open window.

Jamie struggled to hear, but he was pretty sure she'd just asked a very personal question that he hadn't been expecting at all.

"Yes," he said. "I have balls."

"The ball, the ball," said Martha. "Jesus!"

"What?" said Jamie before being pushed aside by the driver of the vehicle, an imposing policeman with a high-vis over his uniform. As the officer slammed the door, he wound up the window, killing their *Brief Encounter* farewell.

Martha flopped back into her seat and seemed to blow Jamie a kiss through the window.

He blushed and blew one back as the Range Rover ignition fired to life. He wasn't great at blowing kisses, it took a lot of coordination, and even he would agree it looked more like he was rubbing his chin whilst spitting out an orange pip.

Martha was shaking her head and miming again; she was rolling something up and throwing it at him.

Jamie nodded like he understood and waved her off as the car drove towards the cart, now being towed behind the Ford, with the WPC waving them off.

"What the hell happened?" said Tash. "I thought she was only wanted in America. And how did they know she was here?"

She reached out and hugged Jamie as best she could, with her son gently sandwiched between them. She closed her eyes and felt the heat of her salty tears.

"She didn't do anything wrong," said Jamie. "She's being set up. It's horrible."

"We did all we could."

Tash's brain was melting. This must always have happened, even if Raymond had died. Somehow, in some way, things would work out.

Martha in prison again = bad.

Tash's impact on this timeline = zero.

So, her reasonable conclusion was that somehow, some way, the truth would out, and her brother would get himself a wife.

The sound of leather footsteps on the cobbles grew louder, and Tash opened her eyes.

A WPC stood in the lamplight.

"I'm sorry, Tash," said the officer, "but she is a very dangerous lady."

Jamie spun around. "Sab?"

Sab was motionless. She was torn between her professional career and her reluctant friendships.

Jamie started to panic. "They're going to kill her, Sab! They're going to kill her!"

"She's going back to America. She'll get a fair trial."

"They want to make an example of her." Jamie was spiralling out of control.

"What?"

"They want to send her to the chair by fall."

"By what?"

"By fall, it's American for autumn." In overwhelming moments, Jamie would revert to familiarity to control his despair. Often saying things that were irrefutable facts and comfortingly familiar. Regardless of being appropriate or not.

"They do a lot of that," said Tash. "They speak English but feel they can improve on some parts."

Jamie was nodding. "Diaper."

"Beg your pardon?" said Sab.

"Diaper means nappy."

"Thanks for that," said Sab. "Noted."

"Diaper. Sidewalk. Cellphone," said Jamie.

"What phone?" Sab hadn't heard of those.

"Not invented yet, Jamie. Ernie Wise is gonna launch them next month."

"Fanny," said Jamie.

"What?" Sab looked shocked.

"Fanny means arse," said Jamie. "In American."

"I've probably got enough American to get by now, thanks," said Sab. "You know if I ever go. Which I don't intend to."

"How did they know Martha was here?" said Jamie, gesturing to the disappearing Metropolitan Police.

Sab sighed and turned to Tash. "Your sister told me."

"Sake," said Tash.

Chapter Fifty-Six

"It's not quite Dixons, is it?" said Maureen, struggling to be heard over Alphaville's 'Big In Japan'.

Raymond had placed his deceased boss's Polaroid Instamatic next to Anthony's 110 flip camera and onto his leather inset mahogany desk, hoping to make a collection that would impress the others. He tilted his head to one side and decided to move the larger Polaroid to the left of the smaller model.

"It doesn't matter how you move them, Raymond. We only have two."

"One if you factor in the fact that we need to give that one back to Anthony," said Jamie, searching through the bottom drawer of a grey filing cabinet.

"Maybe we could borrow a couple from Woolworths?" said Raymond, smiling at Maureen.

She'd already spent far longer than she would have liked explaining why she had been inside the store in October after hours when the alarms went off. She wasn't going to take advantage of her job again.

"We're not borrowing anything," she replied.

"One more! You were right, Raymond," said Jamie, holding up a Kodak Instamatic 10 with magicube flash attached to the top.

"I knew it! I bought that in for our stock take in the summer," said Raymond.

"We now have three cameras!" said Jamie, sliding it onto the display with the others but haphazardly not quite letting go as he removed his hand. The camera dropped to the floor, and the third of the four flashes in the cube went off.

"Two," said Tash.

"Sorry," said Jamie, crouching down to pick up the camera before recoiling from the still fizzing flash cube. "Ow! That's hot!"

"What are you actually planning?" asked Tash, changing baby Raymond's nappy on an opened draw by the radiator that struggled to make any impact on the office area.

"Trying to photograph that baddie woman in Mallorca," said Raymond.

"It's Menorca, and are you really planning on risking a trip there in July?" said Tash.

"We all are, aren't we?" said Raymond.

"I never was. I explained that to Martha," said Tash.

"I need to go home too," said Jamie. "I'd love to help, but I don't see how we can. I can't remember the bank's name in Mallorca or the date the lawyer woman was visiting."

"Well, you need the right island to start," said Tash. "And does anyone remember the town?"

"Madrid," said Raymond.

"That's the intermediary bank," said Jamie. "She said it was then being transferred to Sant something."

"Shouldn't be too many Sant's in Mallorca, surely?" said Raymond.

"Menorca!" said Tash. "And yes, there should be. It means holy or saint, and they're a God-fearing nation, so you'll probably have twenty or thirty to choose from."

"You'd need the bank name too," said Jamie.

"Banco something wasn't it?" said Raymond.

"That narrows things down, Raymond," said Tash.

"Is your eye alright, Jamie? It's all red," said Maureen.

"Which one?" he replied.

"That one," she said, pointing.

Jamie reached to the wrong eye and gently rubbed it.

"Other one," said Maureen.

Jamie switched eyes and then froze. In seconds he was on his knees, fumbling around on the dirty concrete floor.

"How did they know Martha was with us?" said Raymond.

"Tash told Sab," said Jamie, making her tummy plunge with almighty guilt and a million questions.

She'd taken every precaution to abstain from decision-making, to ensure history played out as intended, and now she'd managed to get Martha arrested and deported.

"It wasn't quite like that," said Tash in a lame protest.

"I thought Sab was back on the beat?" said Maureen. "They don't get involved with international murderers."

"She's not a murderer," said Jamie with his arse in the air.

"She told her boss, the one that fired her last night," said Tash. "Told them she'd found Martha."

"Oh, and he arranged the arrest?" said Raymond.

"She," said Tash.

"She?" said Maureen and Raymond in unison.

"Women can be bosses too," said Tash. "We are capable. We can do stuff."

"We let them fly planes in 2020," said Jamie.

"They can fly planes?" said Maureen, as if Jamie had said, 'take a dump at the dinner table'.

"Yes," said Jamie.

"And can they land them, too?" asked Raymond, holding his breath.

"Yes, I think that's part of the training, Raymond," said Tash, staring into space for effect before nodding her assurance. "Yep, pretty sure they don't all crash."

"Get up, Jamie; you're getting yourself filthy," said Maureen.

He ignored her.

"Why don't we all stick with the plan and have a bit of a Christmas together? We can discuss how to help Martha over some sprouts?" said Tash.

Jamie leapt up.

"Got it! Got all her notes!"

"Oh, that's great news," said Tash. "Really, really good news."

"She threw them at my eye," said Jamie, as he unravelled the screwed-up ball and read Martha's handwriting.

"Yep, we have the date, the town and the two banks. And the time," said Jamie, smiling at Raymond and Maureen.

"You just need two friends to help," said Tash. "Ideally, friends with cameras."

Raymond swallowed.

"Where would you suggest we make friends? At my tennis club? At the cub pack?" said Maureen facetiously.

"The cub people will be fine," said Tash. "They'll understand. Stop worrying!"

"Understand we used their pack to burgle a house and then kidnap one of the cubs to rob a bank?"

"No one robbed a bank," said Raymond. "Well, I don't think we did. You didn't rob the bank, did you, Tash? Bank? Rob it? Tash?"

It no longer surprised her that she was now living in a world where this kind of question could be asked and received so casually.

"Nope," said Tash. "So that's decided then? We'll head to your place for Christmas. Then you two make some friends – good luck with that – then you all go on a photography course and then save Martha's life. Any questions?"

Jamie stared into space for an eternity and then involuntarily raised his hand.

"Oh God, what now?" asked Tash.

Jamie spun around to point to the C5.

"Let's all go now."

"Home?" said Tash, hoping he wouldn't say the one thing she feared.

But he did.

"To Menorca."

Chapter Fifty-Seven

"Jamie, it's a two-seater," said Tash, madly clutching at any straws that she could still get a grasp of.

"We took three of us back to steal that million," said Jamie, pacing around his Grandad's time machine.

"But there are four of us, five if you count him," said Tash, nodding to her son on her lap. She was warming a bottle of formula milk in a Radio 1 mug filled with boiling water from Raymond's office kettle. She'd ensured her holdall of essentials had been strapped around the C5 throughout the day.

Jamie was rubbing the thinning area on the crown of his head.

"It usually works when the nose touches something," he said, remembering the first departure from Grandma's loft, then the brick wall in the BBC basement, and the opposing garage doors on Abbot's Park.

"You have to collide with something for it to work?" said Maureen on hearing the worst news of her entire life.

"I think so," said Jamie. "And, in theory, if Grandad could extend the seat, there's no reason we can't."

"Don't change that machine in any way, Jamie, or I will remove your legs."

Tash wasn't smiling as she said this, not even slightly.

"I've no idea where our passports are, Maureen," said Raymond. "We didn't think we'd need them after Salou."

"You don't need passports," said Jamie.

"I'm not breaking the law for anybody," said Maureen. "Leave me out of this."

"We're going forward in time; we don't need to pass customs. We'll arrive straight there," said Jamie.

"We're not going anywhere," said Tash. "It's a two-seater."

"Okay, here's what we do," said Jamie, peering at the rear of the Sinclair.

"Nothing's what we do, Jamie. Stop talking!" said Tash, testing the formula milk on the back of her hand and then feeding her son.

Jamie reached over to a shelving rack and lifted off a three-feet-long cross bracing piece of steel.

"If we can attach that to the rear of the C5 under the extended seat housing," he leant again to look, "and yes, we can..."

"Don't you need pesetas?" said Maureen. "What about suntan lotion?"

"It's night-time," said Raymond.

"I thought you were heading to July," said Maureen. Her mouth was very dry now.

"Then, we just fix this to another C5," said Jamie, looking up at the empty shelves that had once held hundreds of Sinclairs ahead of their despatch to retailers.

"Good luck with that," said Tash, visibly relieved.

"Or the Princess," said Jamie.

"They took that," said Raymond.

"Any wheels, any wheels at all!" said Jamie in frustration.

"Jamie, it's a non-starter!" said Tash burping her son and simultaneously spilling milk onto the collection of cameras. "Shit, sorry."

"Don't worry," said Raymond. "I'll sort that."

He stepped over to the desk and searched through a messy pile of filing before he uncovered a mansize box of Kleenex tissues. As he pulled the top one out, a set of keys fell from the box onto the desk. He started to mop the milk with one hand and lifted the bundle of keys with the other.

"VW," he read as he stared at the keyring, then squinted to read the leather patch attached. "San Sebastián."

"Jesus' van!" shouted Jamie in delight. "We'll use Jesus' van!"

"That's a crime scene!" said Maureen. "You can't use that."

"She's right," said Tash.

But it was as if she'd never uttered a word. Jamie skipped around the twisted metal that he and Raymond had fashioned a makeshift shutter from, and sang that nothing was 'gonna break my stride', maybe because Matthew Wilder was singing it inside the warehouse, or perhaps because he meant it.

Chapter Fifty-Eight

"I told you it was a terrible idea," said Tash, trying to contain her delight that Jamie's plan was terrible.

They were all outside now on the cobbles. The Sinclair C5 time machine was pointing in the direction of Tower Bridge. One end of Raymond's storage shelf rack was attached to the underside of the pimped rear seat; the other slotted into the chrome front bumper that protruded from the dirty VW campervan which had brought Jesus Morón and his Mafioso family to the UK from Spain.

Jamie has powered up the Sinclair with an extension flex and tried to get it moving forward in any capacity. Still, the ton of German engineering attached to the rear rendered the small C5 Hoover battery useless. How the hell could it pull that thing?

"What if we pushed it?" said Raymond, still dressed as Father Christmas and sitting in the driver's seat of the T2 camper, which was on the opposite side to the British ones and confusing him terribly.

"How would that work?" said Jamie. "If it was successful, we'd all be gone, and you'd still be here. No, you need to be inside it."

"This doesn't have seat belts," said Maureen, dutifully seated across from her husband.

"Is anybody else hot?" said Raymond.

"Take the beard off," said Tash.

"Won't I look silly?"

"Let's chance it," said Tash.

"Don't lose that beard, Raymond. I need to give that back when all this is finished."

"I reckon we need to achieve something like fifteen miles per hour. Or at least accelerate with that in mind," said Jamie, still scratching his head.

"What if we started this up and pushed you in your one?" said Raymond.

"That's too risky. I think the C5 needs to be in control. It's the thing that got us here, isn't it? You might just drive us to our death."

Maureen let out a little whimper at this and opened her door to exit.

"Where are you going, Maureen?" asked Raymond.

"He said death. That's me done with this nonsense. We don't owe that American woman anything."

"No. But she does owe us. Imagine it. Thirty thousand pounds!"

"She said a hundred thousand," said Tash, in a curiously disinterred manner.

"Yes!" said Raymond. "Things would never be the same again, Maureen! Besides, Jamie was kidding, weren't you, Jamie? Kidding?"

"We need an incline. We need a hill," said Jamie. "Then the C5 could pull that thing or behave like it was."

"Nearest is probably Point Hill," said Raymond, rubbing his hood to think.

"That's bloody miles away!" said Tash.

"And what if traffic pulls out on us?" said Maureen. "Stop suggesting locations!"

Jamie didn't speak.

Suddenly the evening darkness got darker, and a chilling rustling echo accompanied this new gloom.

"Owl," said Jamie with unmistakable hysteria in his voice.

Tash instantly cowered over her baby. Maureen leapt back

onto her seat and slammed the door. The Spanish barn owl was heading for Jamie's head, and he knew it. He turned to run away and smacked straight into the driver's door of the campervan. Raymond covered his shocked mouth with both hands. The owl had landed on Jamie's head and was flapping its wings furiously as it settled its talons into his shoulder.

"Let him in, Raymond!" shouted Maureen.

Raymond struggled to form words. "Wh, wha, wh, wha, who, who? The owl or Jamie?"

"Jamie!"

"But the owl is attached to Jamie!"

"Help him!" said Maureen.

Raymond attempted to open his door but only managed to smash Jamie in the face with it. Raymond thought it would be a good idea to keep trying to open it. It wasn't.

"Ow!" said Jamie.

"Sorry!" said Raymond.

"Ow!" said Jamie as the door opened onto him again.

"Sorry!" said Raymond.

"Ow!" said Jamie, as the door struck him one more time.

"Sorry!" said Raymond.

Jamie was flailing his arms in the air in self-defence, but the massive wingspan of his attacker was mighty.

"Fuck offff bird twaaaaaat!" shouted Tash, suddenly right next to her brother, both arms wrapped around baby Raymond on her chest.

It was the loudest thing Jamie had ever heard in his life but miraculously did the trick. The owl set off up into the December night sky.

"Are you OK?" said Tash, rubbing her brother's head gently.

"It got my shoulder," he replied.

Just visible in the streetlight, tiny drops of blood appeared in the shape of an owl's talons on Jamie's jacket. Raymond wound down his window.

"That was close!"

"That owl hates you," said Tash.

"Well, he did get it in a bit of a neck hold," said Raymond, "to be fair."

"Is it the same one?" asked Jamie, peering into the night. "Really?"

"Owls never forget," said Maureen.

"That's elephants," said Tash.

"It's owls, too," said Maureen defiantly.

"Yes, I'm sure that's right too, actually," agreed Raymond. "Elephants and owls."

"No, it's just elephants," said Tash.

"It was on *Animal Magic*," said Maureen, as if this made the fact irrefutable.

"They're very much the pug of the bird world, aren't they?" said Raymond.

"What?" said Tash.

"The owl," said Raymond. "Very much the pug of the bird world, so to speak."

"Flat face," said Jamie.

"Yes, flat face," said Raymond.

"Much like Jamie after you twatted him with your door fifty times," said Tash.

"I was trying to help," said Raymond.

"Interesting way to help," said Tash. "Please don't try to help me if you ever see me drowning. I'll take my chances."

"Raymond's not a strong swimmer," said Maureen.

"His athletic build had me fooled," said Tash.

"Shh!" said Raymond.

"Don't shush me!" said Tash.

"Shh!" said Jamie.

"Nor you, prick!" said Tash.

"Shh!" said Raymond, Jamie, and Maureen.

They stopped arguing and listened.

Yes. That familiar sound was coming back—that unmistakable reverberating echo of dread and imminent attack.

"Run!" shouted Tash.

The shadow of the returning owl darkened the driver's door of the VW, and Tash darted to the C5 with baby Raymond blissfully sleeping through the whole sorry affair. Jamie dutifully ran in a different direction. As godfather and uncle to baby Raymond, he didn't want to put him at risk. Jamie made three full loops of the campervan with the owl swooping at him before deciding to make a run for it into the warehouse. As he hot-footed it into the gloom of the cavernous building, the owl did a stunningly graceful sweep into the skies before descending into Maurmond Storage Facilities.

"No!" shouted Jamie from somewhere inside.

"Help him, Raymond!" shouted Maureen.

Raymond climbed out of the campervan and made a rather unconvincing mercy dash into his workplace to save his colleague. Lots of energy and movement in his arms, less in his legs.

"Good bird!" shouted Jamie. "Calm down!"

"Get something to catch the owl!" shouted Maureen through an impossibly small gap in her passenger window.

"Like what?" said Raymond.

"A fox."

"A fox?" said Tash.

"Foxes catch owls!" said Maureen, failing to hide her annoyance that her advice should be questioned.

"Got any foxes, Raymond? Or do you want mine?" asked Tash.

"Have you got a fox?" asked Raymond, pausing in the doorway. Admittedly he did look surprised.

"Course I haven't got a fucking fox!" replied Tash. "Will a wolf do?"

"Raymond! Get the key!" shouted Jamie. "Key!"

"It won't be scared of a key," said Maureen. "I'd use a key to catch a magpie, maybe. They like shiny things. Not an owl. I still think the fox is the best idea."

"What about a fly to catch a spider, to catch a mouse, to catch a cat, to catch a fox... I mean, it's blue-sky thinking and might take a few weeks? Or we could call Owl-Busters?" said Tash.

"Key!" shouted Jamie.

Raymond leant in to switch on the warehouse lights, and as ever, they flickered like a lame nightclub, off, on, blue-white, black, off, on, buzz, off, on... until most of them remained lit. He should probably have left them on when he'd walked outside just moments before, but he was brought up to leave empty rooms unlit. In fact, he'd only just stopped unplugging the TV at bedtime. He'd had to convince Maureen that the risk of a house-fire was outweighed by having to reset the video clock every time they unplugged everything from the wall.

Jamie was standing outside the gate to the chain-link fenced office and holding it firmly shut. The fluorescent strip lights reflected in the dark red blood still glistening on his shoulders; a fresh owl shit sat on his head. The owl was sitting inside its new cage, on the office desk, clearly planning his next assault on this bastard who crept up on him yesterday.

"Lock it!" shouted Jamie, refusing to let go of the door handle, which housed a rusting 3-lever lock.

Raymond fumbled inside his Father Christmas outfit to find his keys and eventually did as Jamie asked, apologising every couple of seconds.

"He looks cross," said Raymond.

"How can you tell?"

"Well, he's got his hands on his hips, sort of thing."

"Hands?" said Jamie.

"Well, wings."

"Do they have hips? Owls?" Jamie meant it and stared at his attacker, trying very hard not to make eye contact.

"Is everyone OK?" said Tash, standing where the shutters sort of hung.

"We were just wondering if owls have hips?" said Jamie.

"Are you buying him pants for Christmas?" she replied.

"Is everyone alright?" said Maureen. She'd lowered her window by another couple of inches and was able to shout over to Tash from the safety of her Spanish crime scene van.

"Just planning a gift for the killer bird," said Tash. "Or do you think we should go with a chocolate orange?"

"You can take me home before you start any nonsense with your deathly Chitty Bang car," said Maureen.

"Not sure we'll have time for that, but I'll put it to the vote," said Tash to the irate-looking lady in the VW.

What happened next made them all leap at least six inches in the air, whether sitting or standing, other than the owl, who sat still ruminating his plan to scalp the balding elf.

"The fuck's that?" said Tash as the mighty horn reverberated around the warehouses and shook the very core of their skeletons.

"A boat at the bridge," said Jamie, calming himself down with deep breaths. "It wants to go through."

Then he looked up at his sister, outside at the campervan, and back at the owl.

Chapter Fifty-Nine

"When I seen you, I thought you were kidding, like!" said the warm Geordie voice.

Kenneth's eyes had never been as wide in his whole life, even when *It's A Knockout* came to South Shields and he met Eddie Waring. And now he was just metres away from a Spanish barn owl.

"I cannot believe it. They don't migrate, you know! How the hell's he got over here?"

"I know!" said Jamie.

"Fascinating, isn't it?" said Tash. She managed to say this in a way that indicated she thought it was anything but, yet Kenneth was spellbound. Raymond was standing behind Tash, self-consciously looking at the floor. Maureen remained seated in the VW.

"I cannot thank you alls enough," said Kenneth, unable to take his eyes off this mightily pissed-off bird. "I just wish I could stay longer. It's so beautiful."

The magnitude of the moment was improved by Joe Fagin singing 'That's Livin' Alright' on the Sanyo. Kenneth loved this as it was from a TV show all about Geordies. Life couldn't get any better.

. . .

When Jamie had run to Kenneth's office on Tower Bridge, the traffic had been nearly non-existent, something that happened only around this time of year and at this time of night.

Kenneth's "Back in 5 minutes" sign had been pinned to the window of his office, and he'd raced behind Jamie to the warehouse.

"Reckon I could get a little closer to take a couple of photos?" said Kenneth, his heart pumping in his chest.

"Of course!" said Tash, nodding at Raymond, who nodded back without moving.

"Key then," said Tash, and Raymond realised he was causing the hold-up.

He sauntered over to Tash and handed her the key, mindful of moving himself well away as soon as possible. Tash started to unlock the office gate door and stopped.

"Is that a point-and-shoot?"

Kenneth looked at the Olympus around his neck.

"Kind of, I suppose. There's a bit more to it than that, like."

"He's very tame," said Tash. "Isn't he tame, Jamie?"

Jamie nodded and tried to cover the dried blood on his shoulder.

"We were just saying how tame he is, Raymond?"

She turned to look at Raymond, still nursing talon-shaped scabs across his face from the recent owl attack under the instruction of Jesus Morón, happily mostly concealed.

"Oh, yes," he replied before coughing a lot and pacing further backwards.

"Why don't I take a photo of you? You just hold your hand out like this, and he'll hop on," said Tash, posturing her wrist into a position she'd seen on many episodes of *Countryfile* when dull people wearing oven gloves catch falcons or whatever.

"Are you kidding?" Kenneth looked amazed.

"Of course," said Tash, already removing the camera from Kenneth's neck.

Kenneth leant to demonstrate the focus ring on the lens and the automatic flash, but Tash interrupted him.

"Got the exact same model," she lied.

"Thanks very much, like!" said Kenneth.

"In you go," said Tash.

He smiled. "Are you gonna open it then?"

"Yes," said Tash. "Yes, of course, I'm going to open it."

She didn't.

"Is everything alright?" said Kenneth.

Raymond took a step back to the warehouse exit. Jamie followed.

"Yep," said Tash, nodding discreetly at Raymond.

"If you could get a couple, that would be amazing!" Kenneth gestured at the camera in Tash's hands.

"Of course! Three, two, one, in you go!"

At this, she opened the gate and thrust Kenneth inside the office, slammed it shut and locked it. The moment Kenneth was inside, the owl swooped.

Tash started to flick the shutter button randomly, and electric white flashes disorientated Kenneth as she ran to the warehouse doorway.

"We'll be right back," said Jamie, guiltily

"Sorry," said Raymond as he flicked off the lights.

Tash climbed into the C5 and started to steer as Jamie, Raymond and Maureen gently inched her forwards under the steam of the VW engine, adamant that they stay under five mph.

"I'm still not going with you. This is madness," said Maureen.

"No problem," said Jamie. "You can wait here for us to come back. Want to get out here?"

"In the dark? No, thank you."

"I think we should stick together," said Raymond. "Like in that film. All for one, and one for, you know, whatever it is they say."

"Which film?" said Maureen.

"That one with Raquel Welch in it." He pronounced every letter of Raquel.

"I knew you'd be thinking about her, Raymond. What's she got that I don't?"

"Nothing at all. She's quite plain actually; now I come to think of it."

"Am I pulling over or not?" said Jamie.

"You'll have to ask this pervert," said Maureen, nodding at her trembling husband. "Maybe he'd prefer Raquel Welch to go with him."

"Don't be silly, Maureen," said Raymond before turning to Jamie. "That's not possible with your machine thing, is it? We couldn't swing by and pick up Raquel Welch, could we?"

Jamie shook his head.

"No. No, I didn't think so," said Raymond. "No, we're staying as we are, Maureen."

Chapter Sixty

Jamie called it 'Gradient Resistance Force'.

Tash called it bullshit.

Tash was probably closer to the truth, given Jamie flunked his Physics GCSE.

"We have four cameras," said Jamie.

"Why do you get the good one?" asked Tash, looking at the Olympus Trip they'd recently borrowed from Kenneth.

"This has a strap! You know I'm better with straps."

Jamie was right. Attaching things to himself helped his coordination. A fact he was pleased to acknowledge after losing three passports, seven house keys, and two school hamsters. *

(*On separate occasions. The chances of lightning striking twice for him were exceptionally high, something the school staff realised too late).

"Can we not bicker, please? These lights will be changing soon, won't they?" said Raymond.

It was hard to take Raymond seriously with the Dalek head-on. The last time he'd time travelled, he'd insisted on wearing a slow cooker on his head in case of impact on arrival, but on this occasion, he hadn't found one in his sparsely populated warehouse.

"Can you see in that? Shouldn't Maureen be driving?" said Tash.

"I don't have a driving licence!" said Maureen, beneath the VW spare wheel that she and Raymond had fashioned into a crash helmet. It was difficult for her to keep her head upright given the weight of the 14-inch steel rim and rubber tyre coated in Spanish dust.

"They just steer straight; we'll be doing the driving!" said Jamie. "And no, Raymond. I'm controlling the lights; they'll stay at red on both sides until we're done."

"Handbrake off when I stick my hand in the air!" shouted Jamie from the door of Kenneth's office.

"Yes, understood," said Raymond, sitting alongside his wife in the campervan.

"What are we going to strike? He said the nose has to touch something?" said Maureen.

"Good question," said Raymond, then shouted out to Jamie. "What are we aiming for? You said the nose had to touch something after we set off?"

"I did, didn't I?" said Jamie.

Tower Bridge was very quiet at this time on the cusp of Christmas Eve, and now the only vehicle on the bridge was the VW camper coupled to the white go-kart. The VW's rear wheels sat on the road joint at the centre of the bridge.

Jamie flicked a few steel rocker switches in Kenneth's room, which set all approaching traffic lights to red and then slid the main lever to control the iconic opening bridge.

Amber strobe lights started to flash, and Jamie squinted to block out the distraction as he raced to sit back with his sister and nephew in the C5. He saw the folded-up roadblocks slowly concertina down as the road barrier lowered on both ends of the bridge, just like the level crossing gates.

"We'll aim for them. There's nothing to them; they're all flappy," said Jamie, pointing at the one they would surely hit once they set off. "Okay! I'll tell you when we're ready!" said Jamie.

He had fashioned a makeshift terminal at the end of the C5's extension cable that attached to the battery of the VW. They had tested its capacity for operating the Pye TV.

The ground was already trembling beneath them as the two

massive bascules lowered into their dungeon-like homes, causing the opposing road surfaces to separate and lift majestically into the air.

All Raymond had to do was fire up the campervan, and then Jamie would fire up the Sinclair Spectrum that controlled the C5. They'd practised typing in the destination, location and time, so the rising bridge would instigate the necessary momentum for the trike to tow the VW into July 1985.

Gradient Resistance Force.

Or just 'Sliding Down A Hill'.

Physics really did have its head up its own arse.

What could possibly go wrong?

"Start the engine Raymond," shouted Jamie.

Raymond did, and unlike his Princess, it started on only the third attempt.

Tash switched on the Pye TV screen, and the Spectrum prompts appeared. She started to type alongside the box that flashed *Destination Date*.

12 07 1985

"We're sure about going a day early?" said Tash.

"Let's not have this chat again. We need to have a good look around when we arrive," replied Jamie. "Do the time."

"Hang on!" said Tash and struck ENTER.

The screen went blank, and then another prompt appeared, *Time.*

"I don't think we need to get there so early. Why don't we arrive in the evening? It will be cooler for us all," said Tash.

"Type!" said Jamie, feeling the bridge rising them all in the air. She did.

21:30 hours

She struck ENTER.

"Right, remember double L in Lluìs," said Jamie. "See what options it gives us."

Tash waited for the screen to change, and sure enough, the final field appeared, *Destination.*

She started to type. She paused. "Nothing! There's no options!"

"What?" said Jamie. "None at all?"

"Just one. Sant Lluìs, Menorca. Nothing else!" replied Tash.

"Take it," said Jamie. "Quickly."

She struck ENTER, and again the screen went blank before reloading with the summary itinerary.

Destination Date: 12 07 1985

Time: 21 30

Location: Sant Lluìs, Menorca

ENTER TO TRAVEL

"This is the most fucking stupid thing I've ever done in my life, and that includes swimming with sharks in London aquarium," she shouted.

"I didn't know you could swim with sharks in London aquarium," replied Jamie.

"You can't," shouted Tash.

"You ready, sis?" said Jamie.

"Of course, I'm not ready," said Tash, and she hit the ENTER button.

Band Aid started to play from the little speaker, and the Sinclair C5 wheels began to spin, unable to move yet as the VW was anchoring them both to the rising bridge road.

They soon felt to be at an angle of ten degrees or so, but Jamie waited, despite the spinning of the Sinclair wheels on the tarmac.

"When are we going?" shouted Tash.

"In a bit," he replied over the engine noise of the campervan behind them. "Fifteen degrees gradient, I reckon."

Tash looked around.

"You've got your fucking eyes shut, Jamie! What are you doing?"

"I don't like the flashing."

The orange strobe lights continued to flash.

"You're in charge! Who takes charge of a sinking ship and then shuts their eyes?"

"Boris Johnson?" said Jamie.

"I'm being serious!"

The bridge was easily over fifteen degrees of an incline now and seemed to rise at quite a pace.

"Open your eyes!"

Jamie did and tried his best to establish if now was the time for Raymond to release the handbrake.

"What's he waiting for? Are we aborting?" whispered Maureen. She'd heard the expression in a repeat of *Secret Army* a couple of months ago and was secretly pleased she was able to use it.

"Pardon?" said Raymond. It was hard to hear under the Dalek head, and he suddenly had much respect for Stavros or whatever the Dalek chairman was called.

"Are we aborting?" shouted Maureen.

"I just need to wait for Jamie's hand," said Raymond, peering through the tiny slot the BBC props department had added for whichever poor sod had to act inside this.

"But we can barely see him down there. Maybe his arm is already up!"

"No, I can see his arm. He's using it to hold his sister off him. She looks quite cross."

"Go now!" said Tash. "Now!"

Sure enough, as Raymond and Maureen watched the siblings wrestle with one another, they also watched the surrounding landscape tilt at an alarming angle.

"Give the fucking signal, or I will!" said Tash.

"Calm down," said Jamie, still wrestling with his sister's arms, his eyes tightly closed.

They were approaching forty-five degrees and were high in the sky; the wind was filling their ears and chilling their faces.

"I wish he'd hurry; I've got a cramp in my leg from holding down the clutch," said Raymond.

"You said we weren't in gear," said Maureen.

"We're not, I don't think. I'm just being a cautious Caroline," replied Raymond.

"Jamie!" shouted Tash, still wrestling with him.

Jamie opened his eyes, saw their position, and instantly flung his arms into the air, immediately reminded of the time he rode Oblivion at Alton Towers, the last time he'd faced a death-defying drop into murky darkness. Freeing his arms gave Tash instant access to his face, so her fist struck his nose, something she regretted the moment it squelched.

"Sorry."

"Ow!"

"You moved your hands! It was your fault."

"Are those his arms?" said Maureen.

"I think so," said Raymond.

"They look quite short. Are you sure they're his?"

Then Tash raised hers too.

"They must be. There are two lots now," said Raymond, unaware that the plan was going tits up.

He started to wrestle with the handbrake, but it was stiff. "Blaming Nora, this is on tight."

"There's no need to swear, Raymond."

He squeezed tightly to release the handbrake and simultaneously lifted his foot from the clutch.

"We're in reverse!" shouted Maureen as the campervan leapt backwards.

The rear wheels of the T2 camper rolled back off the tarmac and into thin air, one hundred and fifty metres above the freezing water of the Thames. The underside of the camper slammed onto the bridge road with a bang. This was their own *Italian Job* moment, but with less money and considerably more soiled underwear.

Raymond needlessly slammed on the brakes and shoved the van into neutral. Jamie and Tash glared at one another in confusion, having been dragged uphill by three feet when the VW reversed.

The bridge continued to lift higher and steeper. It was approaching seventy degrees now.

"I'm going to have to select first gear to get the vehicle back onto the carriageway," said Raymond, much like he was talking to a learner driver on a test.

"I don't want to do this anymore!" said Maureen. "I can see why the Pope kisses the ground."

"Maureen, remain calm. I am in complete control," Raymond suddenly sounded very like James Bond. To him.

"You just reversed us off Tower Bridge," said Maureen hysterically.

"Maureen, that's a fair point. I am *mostly* in complete control. I was a little bit out of control then, but now I am back in control, so all things being equal," but he was interrupted.

"Raymond! What if we die?" Maureen was very shrill now.

Raymond channelled his inner Roger Moore and turned to his wife. His Dalek head didn't, as it was too big, so he could feel his nose crunch in on itself but continued with his inspirational speech.

"Maureen. We've got twelve empty bottles of Ben Shaw's Burdock under the stairs. That's £1.20 deposit. This is not our time."

Maureen nodded her spare wheel and tried to steady her trembling legs.

"Maureen, if anything happens, I want you to know that I love you," said Raymond.

"I'm still getting that smell, Raymond. Even through your helmet."

"Yes, sorry. I'll brush my teeth as soon as we get to Mallorca."

"Menorca."

"Yes, although I'm not sure about the tap water over there. Maybe I'll just squirt some paste in and kind of chew it for a bit."

The screams of Jamie and Tash were getting louder.

"Stop! Abort! No!"

But Bond and his Octopussy weren't listening.

"I'm going to get us through this, Maureen. Do you have faith in me?" He loved this alpha male character he'd just discovered.

"No, I don't. None."

Raymond's Dalek head nodded in reluctant acceptance.

"I'm not being unkind," said Maureen. "I'm just thinking about the outside light you fitted that keeps tripping off all the electricity in the street. And you pulling off the bathroom door handle and then breaking the door when you tried to refit it and couldn't."

The Dalek head nodded throughout. These were fair points.

"And the kitchen lino that you measured wrong, which means we have bare floorboards by the back door."

"We agreed that a larger door mat would cover that; we're just waiting for the 'Do It All' sale."

"And the man in Our Price records that you congratulated on his pregnancy," said Maureen.

The Dalek tried to interrupt but struggled. "Very long hair..."

"And when you stamped on that child's hand at the Odeon. On purpose. Twice."

"Maureen, when a severed hand appears on the floor during a horror film, you don't stop to think."

"It was *Never Ending Story*. He'd dropped an Opal Fruit."

"So anyway, I'm going to edge us forwards and then slide into neutral. And we can then wait safely until all this sorts itself out."

That seemed to stop the list of shame. Raymond took a deep breath, checked his mirrors and then looked over his shoulder.

"What are you expecting to see in the rear mirror, Raymond? God?" said Maureen.

"Maureen, you're being hysterical. Let's put some Radio 4 on."

Raymond fiddled with the radio, and the knob came off in his hands. Band Aid was playing on Radio 2.

"This isn't the shipping forecast."

"No. I've had a spot of bother with the knob," said Raymond before taking a deep breath and turning to his wife.

The bridge continued up to eighty degrees. It was a miracle that the VW tyres weren't yet sliding down the near vertical drop.

"This is too steep now, Jamie, stop him, this is too steep!" shouted Tash. "He's going to kill us!"

Jamie was struck dumb with fear.

"Don't do this, Raymond," said Maureen. "You've taken too much on."

"Nonsense. Just a little nudge forwards to stop us hanging off, so to speak. Off we toddle then."

Raymond swallowed beneath his helmet, selected first gear, and then nudged the gas.

Nothing happened except for a roar from the engine.

"What are you doing? Make it go," said Maureen. "Stop messing about."

"It's rear wheel drive!" said Raymond.

The sound of the rubber tyres squeaking against the lip of the bridge was getting louder. Smelly smoke started to gather around the van.

"I don't know what that means," said Maureen.

Raymond applied the brake once more, and then started to pull off again, slowly.

"It means I need to find the biting point and see if I can pull the rear wheels back onto the bridge."

The bridge continued to rise, and Raymond slowly lifted the clutch as he gently pressed on the accelerator.

The worn tyres continued to grind against the edge of the lifted road, but the steady motion started to cause traction, and the chassis of the VW started to squeak as it mounted the road.

The van lunged forwards.

And then, just as George Michael sang 'but say a prayer,' gravity took over.

Chapter Sixty-One

Chase McPherson had never drunk alcohol for twelve hours in a row, and she realised why at this very moment. Her boss had invited her to the Christmas Party at the head office in the City, and Chase had been delighted to see that wine, beer and cider had been free-flowing since the event kicked off at midday.

She'd made a few bad decisions that day, but then so had everybody, right?

The first was avoiding lunch and then forgetting to eat for the rest of the day. That couldn't have helped the alcohol levels in her bloodstream.

Then she'd told her boss that his hair was grey, something he'd denied until she clarified she meant the patches growing from his ears.

After that, she'd done a solo dance routine to Laura Branigan's 'Self Control' whilst demonstrating her party trick of removing her bra whilst keeping her blouse on. Something she'd learned from Jennifer Beals in last year's *Flashdance*.

On the plus side, she'd talked Emily Springer out of dropping a bottle of Cherry B down the full height of the magnificent spiral stone staircase onto the head of her cheating boyfriend, and she'd covered for her co-worker David Summers who had been accosted by strangers and dumped in the basement of another building before setting off the sprinklers. Together, they'd convinced bosses that this was the twats at TSB who annually took the cross-bank rivalry beyond acceptable levels of horseplay.

But now she was halfway across London Bridge just before 1am on Christmas Eve morning and the sprightly walk home, plus the chill of the fresh night air, had given her tummy reason to doubt her ability to consume so much from a free bar, regardless of the bag of sweet corn relish flavoured Skips she'd taken to line her stomach at breakfast.

She'd positioned herself at the side of the road and leant on the cold granite pillars that lined the bridge until the hideous nausea passed.

Happy that she was able to continue with her journey home, she stood up straight and took one final deep breath. It was then she spotted that Tower Bridge was open, and impossibly glued to the raised right deck at the highest point was the silhouette of a van with a tricycle at the front. It looked like a fairground ride. And then suddenly, they both plunged to the ground like a failed elevator.

However, just as the impending crash of twisted metal was about to resonate along the surface of the Thames, the curiously attached vehicles disappeared.

Gone.

Nothing there.

No bang.

No crash.

Darkness.

Gone.

They hadn't needed the barrier gates after all. The nose impacted with the horizontal road as the C5 hit the bottom.

Chapter Sixty-Two

"Sake!" shouted Tash.

The brief flash of light caused her and Jamie to close their eyes, and the intensity of the sudden July heat confused their senses beyond belief.

Maureen hadn't seen the brief flash of light as they flipped from December 1984 to July 1985. It wasn't the spare wheel over her head that prevented this but the fact that her eyelids were tightly closed as she muttered the Lord's Prayer. Raymond wasn't sure what he'd seen, as he had been focussing intently on the heads of the couple in front. Their vehicle needed to be in control of his, so he was tentatively tapping his foot on the brake pedal without severing the solid connection between the two vehicles. Outside the headlights were undoubtedly doing an excellent job of illuminating the concrete road ahead. Or perhaps half past nine at night in Mallorca or wherever was still light in mid-July?

Inside the VW, Maureen had tried to save her own life by bracing her arms firmly onto the dashboard, which had worked. It had also flipped Radio 2 to Jesus's favourite Spanish preset – Radio Popular, and now USA For Africa's 'We Are the World' filled the cabin through the crackling mono speaker.

"I hate this! I hate this so much!" said Tash from the C5 as she finally opened her eyes and gently applied the brakes that sat beneath her legs. Time travel really didn't suit her.

There was no mistaking that they had gone from 2 degrees Celsius to 32. Or 89 degrees Fahrenheit, as it was better known in 1985. Quite an uncomfortable temperature for the time of night.

Jamie lifted his hands in the air and tried to gesture slowing down, as best he could. Happily, Raymond realised he wasn't needed to do anything other than slow down, so he gently felt his way to decelerate both vehicles without causing any injuries.

In a moment, they were at a standstill.

Raymond wound down his window and attempted to lean out before remembering he was wearing a Dalek head. He sat back in his seat but shouted out into the night heat.

"We did it!"

Maureen let out a massive sight of pure disbelief and joy.

"Great job!" shouted Jamie.

"That wasn't so bad, was it, darling?" said Raymond. "We're quite safe now!"

Then a Monarch Airways Boeing 737 landed eleven metres in front of them.

"Shit!" shouted Jamie.

"Sake!" shouted Tash.

"We're on a bloody runway!" shouted Raymond. "That's why it was bright! The plane's lights!"

"Don't swear, Raymond!" said Maureen.

The heat from the aeroplane's rear remained even as the jet continued along Mahon runway with its reverse thrust blending with the ringing of fear in the visitor's ears.

Not for long. Next, the five of them were illuminated by a spotlight that emanated from the main airport terminal.

"Shift!" shouted Jamie.

"Yes, right," said Raymond, turning the VW engine off.

"Turn it on! Not off!" said Maureen, the hysteria rising in her voice.

"I tried, darling, but I got confused. I think it was the plane nearly crushing us to death."

Raymond started to twist the ignition key again frantically, and the camper engine roared to life.

"Push us!" shouted Jamie, ensuring the Sinclair Spectrum was switched off.

Raymond started to move both vehicles along the runway. "Someone needs to steer!" he shouted.

"I'll steer!" said Jamie, leaning around his sister to take control.

"Where the fuck are you going?" asked Tash as the entourage slowly turned into the darkness.

"Here, this way," said Jamie, oblivious of the advantages of any direction. Each way had the same weather-beaten concrete with occasional odd paint marks.

"They can still see us!" said Tash. "Cos we're being lit up by Charles and fucking Camilla in their Winnebago behind!"

They had successfully driven away from the fixed flood light that had illuminated them, but sure enough, the extended Sinclair, and its three passengers we now brightly lit by the yellow headlights of the VW camper joined to their back.

"Turn the lights off!" shouted Tash over her shoulder, and Jamie joined in.

"They want us to turn the lights off," said Maureen.

"Yes, I heard that too," said Raymond as water jets started to squirt up the windscreen, and broken rubber wipers screeched across the flat glass in front of their hot eyes.

"Well, turn them off then!" said Maureen.

"I am trying," said Raymond. "It's just this isn't our vehicle, you see, and I don't know which switch it is."

The full beam came on, briefly illuminating the heads of Jamie and Tash in front even more. Cyndi Lauper launched into her solo on the radio. 'Woah woah woah woah woah let's realize... that a change can only come.' It wasn't the exact melody that Lionel Richie and Michael Jackson had crafted, but it was her Boy George moment; just as he had gone a bit rogue in the middle of Band Aid, she did the same on the US charity song for Ethiopia.

"Any luck with the lights sitch?" said Tash as they continued to bounce along the concrete slabs.

"Nearly done it!" said Raymond, still frantically flicking at switches.

The orange indicator lights alternated left, right, and then left again. Next, all four flashed as the hazard warning lights came on. Then the horn blasted loudly and refused to stop.

Finally, the lights dipped before being fully extinguished.

"Done it!" shouted Raymond.

But the horn was stuck on.

"Stop beeping the horn!" said Maureen from beneath her spare wheel.

"Yes, I'm trying," said Raymond, thumping at the round button in the centre of the steering wheel. "Can you smell burning?"

"You've pressed the cigarette lighter in!" said Maureen, pointing at the little plastic knob, far closer to her reach than him.

"Did I?" said Raymond. "Right over there? Are you sure it was me?"

"It can't have been me; I don't smoke."

"I don't smoke."

"Stop being clever just because we're abroad."

"Sake, I can't see a fucking thing," shouted Tash as the sound of the wheels of the C5 on the hot ground was drowned out by the horn right behind their heads.

"Turn the horn off!" shouted Jamie, in a state of darkness-and-noise-hell.

"Who are you beeping, Raymond?" asked Maureen in the darkness.

"Not actually beeping anyone," said Raymond, sweating like crazy and thumping the horn again.

"Turn it off!" shouted Tash, madly steering into the darkness.

Raymond slowed them all down and then came to a stop before turning the key and removing it from the ignition.

The horn continued to beep.

"Nope, that's not done it," said Raymond.

The distant lights of the tiny airport terminal were to one side of them now, but far brighter were the thousands of stars above, devoid of any light pollution.

Jamie climbed out of the C5 and instantly realised that his legs weren't up to it. The incessant bouncing of the Sinclair on the concrete had turned them to lead, and he dropped to the ground. Not that anyone could really see.

"Jamie, are you OK?" asked Tash. "Where are you?"

"Down here. Legs gone to sleep."

For no apparent reason, the horn stopped.

"Thank goodness for that," said Raymond climbing slowly out of the VW, the Dalek head still attached. "It's a long song this, isn't it?" he said as an ensemble of eighties American pop stars sang 'We Are the World,' for the millionth time.

Tash realised she could see him a little better, and Jamie too.

And the C5. In fact, everything was slowly brighter.

And what was that noise?

Four seconds later, the Britannia Airways departure to East Midlands Airport lifted into the air from behind the parked campervan, and Tash swore she could see the look of horror on the face of the pilot.

"Move again! Fuck sake!"

"We're still on the runway!" shouted Maureen.

"Yes, thank you, darling," said Raymond. "That would explain the plane."

"Swap places," said Tash, dashing to the campervan, gently holding her sleeping son's head close to her chest. She was terrified but euphoric too. If he could sleep through this, maybe life would be okay for her as a single mum.

Tash sat herself down next to Maureen and felt for the keys. They weren't there.

Raymond sat behind Jamie, who had managed to right himself and find the driver's seat in Grandad's time machine.

"Keys!" shouted Tash through the window.

"Oh God, yes, sorry," said Raymond standing up and attempting to climb out of the C5. He failed. Maybe it was the Father Christmas outfit or his portly size, but he slammed down face first into the runway, his feet still trapped in Grandad's seat. A piece of Dalek rolled out into the Menorcan darkness.

"Are you alright?" asked Jamie.

"Is anyone else hot?" asked Raymond trying to right himself.

He started to fumble again in his pockets and then ran to Tash to hand the keys over. She grabbed them and hysterically felt for the ignition slot.

At first, it was hard to tell, but soon everyone realised that Raymond wasn't rushing back to his seat behind Jamie. Instead, it was almost as if he was punching himself. Slowly at first, but then faster and harder, his opened palms crashing down onto his Dalek helmet.

"Raymond, what are you doing?" said Maureen.

"Are you alright?" said Jamie.

He was running backwards and forwards whilst hitting his head.

"Raymond?" shouted Tash. "What the fuck?"

"Wasp!" he shouted. "Wasp in my crash helmet!"

Tash surprised herself. Even though she and her child were currently parked on the flight path of an international airport, the sight of the silhouette of a Dalek man dressed as Father Christmas whilst punching his own head was just too wonderful a moment to pass by. She just watched.

"Take it off!" shouted Jamie.

"Really?" replied Raymond, still doing his wasp dance.

"Of course, why not?"

"I don't want to get bitten by a mosquito. They come out at night."

"You're thinking of vampires," said Jamie.

"I'm thinking of mosquitos!"

"Wow, now there's a dilemma," said Tash. "Share a helmet with a pissed-off wasp or share the whole universe with the chance of a mosquito bite."

"They carry rabies!" said Raymond.

"He's right. We've seen the posters. Mosquitoes and Alsatian dogs," said Maureen.

"Really?" said Tash. "Just take it off, Raymond!"

"There's a choice we're making, we're saving our own lives," sort of sang Bob Dylan.

"I always wondered if this part was a muppet? Is this a muppet singing?" said Tash.

"It's true we make a better day, just you and me," continued Dylan.

He was actually mimicking Stevie Wonder mimicking him. Dylan struggled to find what the producer Quincy Jones wanted from him, so Wonder went to the piano and did an impersonation of how Bob Dylan would sing it – to Bob Dylan. Dylan then copied it pitch perfect for the recording.

"Sounds like Beaker," said Jamie. And he was a little bit right.

"Hang on!" said Raymond. "I think it's a bee."

"What?" said Jamie.

"In my helmet," said Raymond.

"What makes you say that?" asked Maureen.

"It stung me but stopped buzzing, so pretty sure it was a bee! Great news."

"The best news," said Tash. "You have all the luck. You gonna sit down so we can live? Or do you need to check for vampires?"

Raymond stumbled to Jamie and tried to get in but missed the seat. He tried again and failed.

"I think the bee venom is affecting my balance. Is anyone else hot?"

"We're all hot; it's July in Menorca! Get in here," said Tash.

Raymond joined his wife, and Tash started the engine.

"I need to make a plan," said Tash, and with this, she pulled the indicator stalk, illuminating the full beam. The airfield was like daylight as far as the eye could see. To the right was a dilapidated windmill, long since abandoned and built on scorched earth. It was as far away from the terminal as Tash could see.

"Jamie," she shouted from her opened window.

"Yes?"

"Head for the windmill over there."

Jamie started to look in completely the wrong direction, as he had done his whole life when anyone tried to point out an object of interest.

Every holiday he'd ever been on, he'd missed the paraglider.

Every trip to the Peak District, he'd missed the peacock.

Every summer night, he'd missed the hot air balloon.

And now he was staring in the opposite direction to their salvation.

"No, over there," said Tash patiently.

"Yep," said Jamie. His gaze hadn't moved.

"No. Where I'm pointing," said Tash urgently; she was mindful that the VW lights were in full view of the authorities in the airport.

"Got it," said Jamie, looking somewhere else again.

"Look where I'm pointing. How the fuck are you supposed to see what I can see if you don't look where I'm pointing?"

Maureen started to open her door.

"Where are you going?" said Tash.

"I'm not listening to you swearing all day."

"Did I swear?" said Tash.

"Yes, you did. You said the F word," said Raymond.

"Don't you say it!" said Maureen.

"Sorry, Maureen," said Raymond. "The bee sting has turned me into an animal. I don't even know who I am anymore."

"I can't see where you're pointing cos the headlights are in my face!" said Jamie. "But if you dip them so I can see where you're pointing, I won't be able to see where you're pointing cause the headlights are dipped."

"It's a fair point," said Maureen. "I can't believe you haven't planned this through."

And then she topped this insult by folding her arms. You really couldn't beat that.

"Planned it through?" said Tash. "Did I miss the planning meeting? Who took the notes? Was it on Zoom? Maybe I missed the invite!"

"There's no reason to be facetious," said Maureen. "What's Zoom?"

"They do smart a bit, don't they? Bee stings," said Raymond, lying on the bench seat, rubbing his crash helmet like it was his head. He was struggling to get comfortable.

"These cushions are terrible. Just full of lumps."

Jamie climbed out of the C5 and ran over to the camper.

"I think we're all a bit stressed. We came here for a good reason. We're all good people. Let's try to remember that. We shouldn't argue. Let's just reset and plan what to do next."

He looked around them and up to the sky.

"Is this still the same song?" said Maureen,

"Yeah. We've not had the key change yet," said Tash.

"Is it Stevie Wonder?" said Maureen. She liked 'I Just Called to Say I Love You', so she was familiar with his voice.

"It's everyone – ever," said Jamie.

"Oh, my word, who's this shouting?" she replied.

"That would be Bruce Springsteen," said Jamie.

"Who?"

"Really?" said Tash. Had she really no idea who that was? "Bruce Springsteen!"

"This?" said Maureen, listening to yet another chorus.

"Well, not now, no. This is Ray Charles," said Tash.

"Kill the lights, sis. No planes are landing or taking off. Let's just think of what we need to do next. We have a bit of time."

Tash did as he suggested and turned off the engine. For the first time, they all heard the cicadas that magically filled the unfathomably hot night air.

And then another noise presented itself.

The siren of the Guardia Civil.

Chapter Sixty-Three

The green and white Renault 4 had some distance to cover before reaching the illegal immigrants on the opposite side of Mahon airfield. They also needed to comply with appropriate routes to circumnavigate the runway, regardless of air traffic – or lack of it.

"I'll steer!" shouted Tash from the C5, handing her son to Jamie, who dashed back to the campervan and gently passed his sleeping nephew to Maureen in the passenger seat.

Jamie stepped up into the driver's seat and started the ignition.

"Give me one more flashlight!" shouted Tash.

Jamie flashed on the headlights, and then Tash shouted again.

"I'm good! Turn them off, and let's go!"

Jamie switched off the lights and gently accelerated forward. He wound his window fully down and kept leaning out.

"Tash, are you OK?"

"I'm fine, but take your hands off the wheel, Jamie; you're making this too hard."

It was a bizarre experience to accelerate in a vehicle in near darkness with your hands off the wheel.

"Keep talking to me, sis!"

"What?"

"Keep talking to me!"

"Turn the radio down!"

'We Are the World' really was a very long song.

"I don't know how – it seems to be..."

They all stopped speaking as the van seemed to drop by a metre or so, shaking them all crazily in their seats.

"Are you OK, Tash?"

"Sake!" she shouted, having come off the end of the runway and into a sun-baked ditch of frazzled grass.

Unfathomably, they continued onwards.

"They don't seem to know where we are," said Maureen, straining to look over her shoulder at the red lights on the rear of the Renault, zig-zagging in the distance, trying to illuminate the uninvited plane spotters with their yellow headlights. Instead, they simply saw concrete and pine trees, the sound of the siren getting quieter as they moved into the distance.

"Bump!" shouted Tash with a faltering voice as the C5 slid up a discarded timber gate, followed by the roaring German van just inches from her head.

They were both in the air, mimicking yesterday's planes that launched into the skies as they departed the airport and headed north over Villacarlos harbour.

But these British passengers were heading in another direction, eastbound towards the small town of Sant Lluìs.

Until they landed, of course. Which would be in just one and a half seconds.

Chapter Sixty-Four

Surprisingly the VW landed first, dragging the C5 down with it. Maybe it was the weight, although Jamie wasn't sure as he thought the law of gravity applied to all things equally. Other than his Grandad's balls when they'd showered at Don Valley swimming baths in the early nineties. They were very much each doing their own thing. He'd declined a hot dog on the way home that day; the Wagon Wheel from the vending machine was more than enough.

"Brake, Jamie! Brake!" shouted Tash.

Jamie applied the brake as best he could, and the two vehicles slid to a halt in a rising cloud of red dust or, given the darkness of the night, dust.

Maureen clutched baby Raymond close to her chest and peered beneath her helmet to see if he was awake. The clear moonlit sky shone down, and a serene and oblivious squidgy face snored back at her. Not for the first time, she felt very privileged to be trusted with this precious cargo.

Tash was at her window in no time, spitting out the mouthful of baked earth that had filled it on landing.

"Is he alright?"

"Fast asleep," said Maureen gently, handing him to Tash.

"That was a better landing than Dan-Air," said Raymond.

Maureen cautiously removed her helmet and passed it to Jamie, who opened his door and threw it into the ground.

"Won't we need that?" said Tash. "In case we get a puncture?"

"Oh yes, sorry," said Jamie, climbing into the moonlit field to retrieve it.

They were shielded from the airport by a derelict stone building with the remains of a windmill projecting with faded grandeur into the warm breeze. The walls were tumbling down through years of neglect, and the gate that had acted as their launch pad leant on the other side, forming a convenient ramp.

"Have you taken off your helmet, Maureen?" said Raymond, sitting in the back of the van under his Dalek helmet. "Don't forget the mosquito risk."

"Oh no! I'd forgotten about that!" said Maureen.

Tash clipped baby Raymond onto her chest sling and delved into the passenger glove box.

"Panic over," she said and retrieved an aerosol can, then sprayed it straight into Maureen's face. She started to spit and snort.

"What on earth's that?"

"That's it, all protected from the flies now," said Tash, sliding open the side door and helping Raymond remove his Doctor Who prop.

"Off it comes, Raymond," said Tash, recoiling a little at his double-sized nose, illuminated by the modest interior light that flickered on when the door opened.

"Christ, that bee did a good job," she added before spraying more De-Icer into his face. Clearly, Jesus had been preparing for winter in London when he stocked up his van.

"Does it look bad?" he asked.

"No, not at all," lied Tash, flicking off the interior light. "Not if I turn this off and look the other way."

"Are we in the right place? Where are the banks?" said Maureen.

"It's a good question, Maureen," said Tash.

"It's two questions," said Jamie.

"It is two questions, Jamie. Well done for spotting that," said Tash. "I'm gonna go with *No,* and *I have no idea* for my answers."

"Is anyone else hot?" asked Raymond, trying to lean outside the increasingly hot van.

"That's a symptom," said Maureen. "Oh, my goodness, what on earth have we done?"

"What?" said Raymond.

"Don't come near me! Don't bite me!" said Maureen.

"He's not got rabies, for Christ's sake," said Tash. "He's only been here two minutes, and he's been banging on about being hot all day."

"Does anyone have any water?" said Raymond.

"That's another! Thirst!"

"Maureen, calm down," said Tash. "He's dehydrated 'cos he's been dressed as a Smurf all day, and now he's in the middle of the Mediterranean in July!"

"I can't keep track of this space travel nonsense. It doesn't suit me one bit. You know where you are with normal travel. A couple of barley sugars and 'I Spy', and you're there. No, this isn't for me. Take me back, please," said Maureen.

"It doesn't quite work like that," said Jamie. "For a start, the police are looking for us over there."

They turned slowly to peer around the tumbledown shack; sure enough, the Renault 4 was still doing confused laps of Mahon airport. They watched for a moment until it came to a halt under the watch tower.

"Look at that," said Raymond with a dismissive tone. "They've given up already."

"What do you mean by that?" said Tash.

"We found them an indolent people, didn't we, Maureen? When we came to Salou."

"Everything's mañana mañana," said Maureen.

"That means tomorrow," explained Raymond.

"What?" said Tash.

"Mañana mañana, means tomorrow," said Maureen.

"Okay. Two things," said Tash. "One, no, it doesn't; it means tomorrow tomorrow. And two, are you saying that every single person born in Spain or one of its islands has the same character traits as one another?"

They considered this, and then both answered together.

"Yes."

"Oh my God," said Tash.

"They're different to us, you see. They eat their tea at bedtime and sleep at lunchtime. You can't tell me that's normal behaviour?"

"You really are xenophobic, aren't you?" said Tash, disappointed at her brother's foster family.

"I'm not sure what that means?" said Raymond. "Is that where you cut yourself, and it doesn't heal?" He examined his hands to see if he was bleeding.

"That's haemophiliac," said Jamie.

"Raymond does get nosebleeds more than most people, but he's not got that," said Maureen.

"It can be very embarrassing. I once got one at an ice cream van, didn't I, Maureen?"

"Nightmare," said Tash.

"They thought he'd squirted his own strawberry sauce. They were quite rude to start."

"They wanted five pence for it! I had a nosebleed!" said Raymond.

"Isn't it raspberry sauce?" said Jamie. "Chocolate or raspberry, at an ice cream van?"

"Now that's a fascinating question," said Raymond, rubbing his chin.

"Not, it's fucking not!" said Tash. "And anyway, being xenophobic means you don't like foreigners. Sort of."

"Nonsense!" said Raymond. "We went to see *ABBA The Movie*, didn't we, Maureen?"

"We did," she replied. "Although we didn't like that Australian chap in it."

"Very rude man," agreed Raymond. "But that's Aussies for you."

"And we both love Swiss Roll," said Maureen. "So, what do you make of that Little Miss Accusations?"

"Okay, I might kill myself in a bit, so let's change the subject," said Tash.

"Yes, let's change the subject! This is no way to start a holiday, is it?" said Raymond. He liked playing peacemaker.

"Holiday?" said Tash.

"Well, you know. A trip abroad, as it were."

"Is there a toilet?" said Maureen.

"What?" said Tash.

"Is there a toilet around here? I mean, most airports have toilets. Or don't the Spanish wee?" said Maureen assertively. "Excuse my language, Raymond, but she made me say it."

"Jamie, can you take over? I need to go and smash my face against a wall," said Tash.

"Well, don't try that one; it's fallen over," said Maureen pointing to the wall they had all travelled over. "That's Spanish builders for you. Is this still the same song?"

It was. 'We Are the World' came in at just over seven minutes, and we were getting it all.

"I have an idea," said Jamie, attempting yet another Ctrl Alt Del.

"Thank God," said Tash. "Let's hear it." She sat down on a particularly uncomfortable stone and breathed in the scent of pine needles and arid earth.

"We need a plan," said her brother.

Everyone agreed with lots of...

... "Yes, a plan,"

... and "Good idea that, actually,"

... and "Champion," type remarks. The latter from Raymond, of course.

They waited in silence as their eyes grew accustomed to the darkness, and Jamie cleared his throat.

More silence followed, but for cicadas.

"Well?" said Tash.

"We need a plan," repeated Jamie.

"Oh, it's that thing where you say we need a plan, but you don't have a plan? Again?"

"Er, yes," said Jamie.

Everyone muttered their disappointment with things like...

..."thought he had a plan,"

... and "I expected some kind of plan,"

... and "Shame that, real shame that, on the plan front" type remarks.

"At the risk of being shot down in flames again," said Maureen, "I think it's fair to say that whatever town you typed into your little go-kart, this isn't it." She gestured at the wasteland around them.

"Can't argue with that, Maureen," said Tash. "You got me there."

"We typed in Sant Lluìs. The Sinclair only offered us one place," said Jamie.

In fairness to Grandad's computer program, it was partially correct. Sant Lluìs airfield had closed in 1969 and shifted all commercial flights west by one kilometre to the new Mahon terminal.

"Let's head for the town over there," said Raymond, pointing to the amber glow from a settlement a kilometre or so ahead.

"We can't keep travelling like this," said Tash. "We're going to destroy the C5. That's my route home."

Yet again, Jamie chose to ignore her choice of words.

"Can't we leave it here, inside that?" said Raymond, pointing at the remnants of the stone building, mostly tumbling walls and dilapidated terracotta roof tiles.

"No," said Tash. "We are never, ever, *ever* letting this out of my sight."

She could see Jamie's hand rise.

"Jamie, you've been talking all night. Why are you raising your hand now to ask a question?"

"I don't know," said Jamie, with his hand still in the air. "But it is cooling my armpit."

Raymond copied. "Oh yes, it does, doesn't it? How lovely! Very refreshing, you should try it, Maureen."

"Ladies don't sweat, Raymond. How dare you."

"No, sorry," said Raymond, trying to ignore his wife, who

was now casually lifting her arms away from her body to see if it was indeed more comfortable, and it was.

"Well, as I see it, we can just about fit the C5 into the back of the campervan, so it can travel with us," said Jamie.

Tash looked at the C5 and then at the van.

"How do we get it up there?" she asked.

Jamie looked around and then pointed towards a pile of broken pieces of gate and roof timbers.

"As we did at the hospital, we make a ramp into the side door and then wiggle it in."

"You sure it will fit?" asked Tash, but she wasn't convinced.

"Bet you fifty quid," said Jamie.

Chapter Sixty-Five

"You can transfer it to my banking app when we get home," said Tash. "Unless you have the cash now?" She had remembered the pantomime of assuming they would both go back to 2020.

Three planks of sun-dried pine wood had formed a capable ramp into the side of the borrowed VW, and together they had successfully forced Grandad's time machine into the opening.

For about three feet.

Then it got stuck, and the extended seat that had been so lovingly bonded onto the rear of Sir Clive's original design was well and truly still outside and floating in the air.

"It's almost in," said Jamie.

"Well, it's not at all in any way whatsoever, really, is it?" said Tash.

Jamie tilted his head to one side to try and get a more precise take on the situation.

"Quick vote?" said Tash to Raymond and Maureen. "Is this smaller vehicle here," she tapped the C5, "almost inside the larger vehicle, here?" she tapped the VW. "Hands up for agree?"

Raymond and Maureen looked pained as they kept their hands by their sides. Jamie had only been trying to help.

"Why don't we take some of the furniture out of the van to make more room?" asked Raymond.

"The furniture that's fixed in the campervan with screws and bolts?" said Tash.

"Er," said Raymond, seeing the flaw in his plan.

"And do we abandon that here, or do you want to tow the furniture behind us?" said Tash.

"I thought we could put it on the roof rack," said Raymond.

Tash looked up.

"Jamie, there's a fucking roof rack!"

Chapter Sixty-Six

The pretty, white-washed town of Sant Lluìs was indeed the glow they had seen across the dark sunburnt fields behind the airport. The French constructed the buildings in the late eighteenth century in a chequerboard layout, and they remained unspoilt. The mostly two-story facades were all lovingly maintained and coated in matching whitewash and painted green shutters to block out the brutal summer heat from the modest dwellings and businesses within. Locals had seen the now-famous windmill in all its working glory long before being turned into the modest museum that remains today, whether your today is 1985, 2020 or beyond. They had seen horse trotting races here, the only Spanish location to host the sport. They had seen the steady influx of tourism in the 1960s as the world became enamoured with their August Feast of St Louis Festival, and the Menorquìn version of boules that gently passed the time on so many balmy afternoons.

And this evening, had anyone looked up from their late-night Fino sherry or cool glass of Estrella, they would have seen Father Christmas and his pissed off elves driving a German campervan through the bunting festooned streets with a moon buggy strapped onto its creaking roof and Stephen Tin Tin Duffy singing 'Icing On The Cake'.

"It's very pretty, isn't it, Maureen?" said Raymond in awe.

"You say that Raymond, but try getting some proper English sausage around here," replied Maureen, utterly unaware of the childish titters this prompted from Jamie and Tash.

"Play your cards right, Maureen," said Tash, "the night is young."

"What do you mean?" she replied before turning to Raymond. "What does she mean?"

"Is that a bank?" said Raymond, pointing to a red sign in a closed shop window.

"Keep your hands on the wheel," instructed his wife.

"Carnisseria," he read as the VW idled past. "Is that one of the banks, Tash?"

"I think the picture of the chicken is a bit of a giveaway, don't you, Raymond?" said Tash, bouncing baby Raymond on her knee, much to his delight.

"The chicken bank? What? A bank for chickens?" said Maureen.

"It's a butcher's," said Tash. "Mind you, you might get yourself some sausage!"

"Slow down, Raymond. I can't see all the shops; you're driving too fast."

"I'm trying, darling. The brakes aren't responding too well; maybe they're hot?"

"And, by the way?" said Jamie.

"Yes?" said Raymond.

"Well, there's no rush, but they drive on the right over here."

"Oh, sweet Lord!" said Raymond before swerving to the other side of the remarkably narrow street.

"Banco!" said Tash, pointing ahead down the road. "Banco Central!"

Everyone seemed delighted to see the modest shop front approaching on the right.

"It's got a road down the side," said Jamie. "It could totally have a back door, too."

"Slow down, Raymond, let's have a good look," said Tash.

He didn't.

"Erm," was all he said.

"Raymond," said Tash. "Slow down."

"I'm trying," said Raymond.

"Try that other pedal," said Maureen, "maybe they're on the wrong side too!"

"No, that's the accelerator, I'm sure of it."

"Try it!" demanded Maureen.

"I'm pretty sure it's the accelerator," said Raymond.

Maureen clambered over to straddle between the front seats, then clumsily stretched her foot over to the accelerator, across the top of Raymond's hot legs and slammed her foot on the pedal.

"Just give it a try!"

The van lurched forward.

"See!" said Raymond, struggling to stop the camper from mounting the curb and wiping out an elderly couple sitting in timber dining chairs outside their front door.

"No!" said Tash, "this isn't right!"

"They've failed!" said Raymond. "The brakes have failed!"

"Don't panic," said Jamie. "It's late; the road is empty. Just keep steering until we come to a stop."

"Okay, okay," said Raymond. "Good idea, Jamie. Everyone calm down."

His voice sounded very shaky now.

"Everyone just stay calm, and I'll just steer until we stop by ourselves. Everyone stay calm. Nice and calm," muttered Raymond. "Calm. Nice and calm."

They hummed along the charming white streets listening to Raymond.

"Everyone stay calm. Just stay calm."

They did until they each spotted crossroads up ahead. Every one of them clenched their teeth in the unspoken hope that no other traffic would be hoping to cross the junction in front of them as they sailed through. Well, until Raymond spoke.

"Just stay nice and calm."

"Stop saying be calm!" shouted Maureen. "We're *being* calm. Everyone's very calm!"

The van sailed through the crossroads without a problem,

and everyone breathed a sigh of relief. Then the straight road ahead ended abruptly with a white wall.

They had to turn sharp left.

There were no other options.

"We have to turn left," said Raymond. "I've never turned left at thirty miles an hour before."

"It's thirty kilometres an hour," said Jamie, pointing at the speedometer.

"Is that faster or slower?"

"Slower," replied Jamie.

"Oh. Well, that's something then, isn't it?" said Raymond before shouting, "Brace!"

And with that, he swung his left arm down, and the van bounced around the corner, clipping the cracked clay paving stones as it nudged over them. On the roof, the C5 slid fully over to the opposite side and then teetered over the edge. But Jamie's rope knots were too good, and the mad spider's web of nylon rope held the Sinclair at an impossible angle – half on and half off the rack.

"I'm going to gently ease the handbrake on now to see if that helps with our little predicament," said Raymond.

"Well, why didn't you do that before?" asked Maureen.

"Because I only just thought of it now," replied Raymond.

"Thinking of it before would have been a better idea. Think on, next time!"

"Think about something before I think about it?"

"Exactly!"

"Careful," said Tash, clutching baby Raymond close to her chest. He loved his bouncy ride, blissfully unaware that his co-passengers were hiding dread and fear.

"It's stiff again," said Raymond. "This happened on the bridge, don't worry. There's a little knack to it."

He squeezed the button tightly and pulled with all his might.

"If I just..."

The handbrake handle lifted clean off its housing into the air, with a snapped cable dangling beneath.

"No, that's not worked."

"That's come off in his hand," said Jamie.

"Thanks, Jamie. Let us know if we crash," said Tash.

"Could we just turn the engine off?" said Raymond.

"Good idea," said Maureen, starting to flick any switch she could find. The windscreen wipers came on, and the radio volume doubled. Phil Collins' drum fills were teasing the epic intro to 'Easy Lover'.

"No, don't do that. The steering lock will come on," shouted Jamie over Phil. "We won't be able to steer at all."

He tried to turn down the music.

"I'll just stick with the plan," said Raymond, "keep steering until we stop. Bound to happen soon."

They all looked through the window as the van bounced up a kerbstone and across a roundabout, over a sprawling, white-washed ornamental road sign set into the ground reading "Sant Lluìs" and scraping Raymond's wing mirror on a rustic stone monument beneath a weather cock. They didn't see the monolith smack one of the rear wheels of the C5, nor did anyone witness it bounce onto the ground and roll in the opposite direction. The camper sprung back onto the road on the other side.

"You can still steer, Raymond," said Jamie. "I think it's best to steer still. Especially on roundabouts."

"Yes, of course, sorry," replied Raymond. "Binibeca."

"Pardon?" replied Tash.

"I don't know. I was just reading the road signs."

"And they still drive on the right," said Jamie.

Raymond swerved again, and they all banged heads, then heard the C5 above slam back into position in the centre of the roof.

"Sorted!" said Raymond.

"Why aren't we slowing down?" said Maureen. "We should be slowing down by now?"

"There must be a very gentle descent on the roads, darling," said Raymond. "It's nothing to worry about. You often see this sort of thing on apparently flat streets. It's nothing to fear."

The vehicle continued moving forwards, and the unlit road ahead suddenly fell away and gave a breathtaking view of the moon reflecting on the gently shimmering Mediterranean Sea, just one kilometre ahead.

Down the hill.

At the bottom of it.

The hill they were at the top of.

"Anyone else hot?" said Raymond as the VW picked up its pace.

Chapter Sixty-Seven

"Could we try sticking it in a slower gear?" said Jamie as they pelted down the tarmac that lay between impossibly black spaces on either side of their ride. In the daytime, they would have seen freshly laid cul-de-sacs cut into the rock and scrubland as developers started to build a township of single-story villas in the expanding resort of Binibeca. This evening Jamie and Tash just saw the bobbling sweaty heads of Raymond and Maureen, and beyond them, the approaching twinkly windows from villas and apartments that stood between them and the warm sea.

"It's not in gear," shouted Raymond in despair, trying to be heard over Phillip Bailey's falsetto warning that *you better forget it, you'll never get it*.

"I know," said Jamie, "but if we could stick it in second or first, it would slow us down."

Raymond squinted at the gear stick in the darkness.

"What are you doing? Keep your eyes on the road!" said Maureen.

"I'm looking for the gear stick numbers, " Raymond said.

"Well, I can't see those in this light," said Maureen, and she reached up to the cluster beside the mirror that controlled the internal lights and flicked them on. They were quite a contrast to the darkness they'd grown accustomed to.

"There," said Maureen, pointing to the gear knob.

"That's very helpful, darling, but I can't see anything at the moment. Any chance you could turn that light off?"

She did with a huff, and Raymond realised he was now driving half on the kerb.

"I'm going to steer us off the kerb to start with, and then attempt the first gear suggestion from Jamie."

"Moped!" shouted Tash as a 50cc Vespa appeared ahead.

Raymond spun the wheel, and the campervan mounted the opposite kerb and entered the cleared scrubland. Everyone heard the C5 slide across the roof rack and held their breath for the sound of it hitting the rocks behind. But it didn't come.

"I seem to be approaching a dwelling, so I'm going to take a different direction," said Raymond as a three-story villa came hurtling towards them.

They all heard the C5 slide the opposite way as Raymond mounted another dark section of rock, and they bounced madly towards the only apartment block in the resort.

To the left, drinkers and diners enjoyed the late-night respite from the July sun in the Palomino bar. Next door, another cluster of ex-pats were nursing San Miguels in El Contrabandista, known locally as The Smugglers pub.

Next to that was an opening cut through the building. An oversized walkway, but maybe, thought Raymond, maybe, enough for a VW campervan.

They bounced across the road, steered expertly by Raymond, and slid through the gap in the apartment building and onto the grass beyond before coming to a stop, helped in no small part by a small pine tree lodged in one of the headlamps.

"Is Raymond alright?" was the first thing Raymond said.

Maureen turned too, and Jamie looked over the moment he picked himself up from the floor.

Baby Raymond looked back at everyone and displayed the biggest grin he had yet to perform in his five months on earth. His soother moved back and forth in his mouth as he sucked.

"He's fine," said Tash, kissing him gently on the forehead.

"That could have been a lot worse," said Jamie.

An unpleasant scratching noise started to get louder, followed by a thud, as the C5 slid down the windscreen, cracking the glass perfectly from top to bottom. The Sinclair bounced onto the carpet-like grass lovingly tended by the resident gardener before rolling on two wheels to the edge of the pool and gently lowering itself into the shallow end.

"That's a bit of a setback," said Jamie. "It's fallen in the pool."

Chapter Sixty-Eight

"We don't really allow inflatables in the pool," shouted Alistair McDermott from the covered first-floor terrace of Apartment N.

Tash looked up to see an impossibly tanned Scotsman leering down at her. Over his shoulder, his wife and numerous other party guests looked down their noses, too, as Phyllis Nelson gently suggested they all 'Move Closer' on the soiree's cassette deck, set at a reasonable volume level of 3 out of 10; this wasn't a party after all.

"Good to know," said Tash as she strained to lift the front of the C5 into the air whilst clutching her giddy son in the other. The shallow depth of the child's end of the pool had stopped the Sinclair from sinking, and Tash had beaten all land speed records to jump in and prevent the Pye cube, Sinclair Spectrum, and former iPhone from going under.

Jamie was trying to pull the rear of the seat back onto the flags around the pool's edge, and Raymond was standing alongside Tash, secretly loving the cool water nearing his house keys.

"Can you get around that side, Maureen?" said Raymond.

"Don't rush me; it's cold," she replied.

She'd opted for the steps in, as she hated getting her hair wet in the pool and was also surprised how chilly it felt.

"It's lovely when you get in, darling," said Raymond, with

just the merest suggestion of urgency in his voice. A stranger wouldn't have noticed.

"Stop shouting at me in a foreign country, Raymond!"

"Sorry," said Raymond.

"Sometimes you've just got to rip the plaster, Maureen," said Tash.

"What does that mean?" she replied. "Rip the plaster?"

"When you know something's gonna be shit for a bit, get it done. The bad stuff soon passes! Rip the plaster!"

"Don't you start ganging up on me! You're in the shallow bit. It's colder over here."

"But you don't need to get in over there. We need you over here," said Tash.

"I say, we don't really allow inflatables in the pool," shouted Alistair again.

"Is this yours?" shouted Tash before showing him her middle finger.

"You mustn't tolerate that, Ally," said his wife.

"They seem to be dressed as *Noddy* or something?" said Alistair, squinting at the bizarre foursome.

"It looks like *We Are The Champions!* The kids love that," said his wife, and everyone giggled through their Cinzano Biancos and Noilly Prats.

"Problemo, problemo!" said a voice rushing towards them.

A wiry Spaniard with a chef's apron covering his Farah slacks and cheesecloth shirt rushed over to them. He placed his lit Fortuna cigarette between his lips and stood alongside Jamie at the rear of the C5, and pulled with instant effect. The Sinclair rolled out of the pool and onto the grass.

Wow, thought Tash. He looked 5' 8" and nine stone tops, but he had some strength.

"Oh my God, thank you so much!" said Jamie as he doubled over to catch his breath.

"No problem. You have a bad day!" said the man, gesturing at the abandoned VW.

"I'm sorry," said Jamie. "We'll move that."

"You get in, yes?" said the chef.

Jamie suddenly felt eleven years old and did as he was told. He walked to the van, climbed in and started the engine.

"But it has no brakes," he remembered to shout as the chef started to push the van safely away from the pool. It struggled to gather pace, despite the baked solid red earth and scorched thick blades of grass and soon rocked to a stop at the foot of path steps. Jamie climbed out and walked over to the chef, clutching the snapped handbrake in his hand.

"Thank you so much. We're new here and didn't quite know the lay of the land."

"We're having a bit of a bad day," said Raymond, rolling out of the pool like he had rolled onto the cart in London. They all waited whilst he tried to stand up, with the sound of dripping pool water cascading around his feet from his red cloak.

The chef took a drag on his cigarette before throwing it into the bushes. He pulled the crinkled red and white paper packet of Fortuna from his shirt pocket and offered one to Jamie, but he politely declined.

"Julian," said the chef, lighting another cigarette and offering his sweaty palm. It was the first time Jamie had seen just how hot this man was. Jamie offered his usual limp handshake back – these were never his strength. You never knew if you would get the whole hand, a thumb or a finger. He found handshakes overrated. And on this occasion, he was happy that most of the shake missed; Julian was a very hot man.

"He's Jamie," said Raymond, filling in the pleasantries. "I'm Raymond."

He offered his hand and regretted it, wiping the sweat from his palm on his sodden cape soon after.

"Raymond Claus, yes?" said Julian with a twinkle in his eye, as he kicked a rock behind the rear wheel of the van. It had no direction to roll now.

"What? Oh! Yes!" said Raymond. "It's a long story."

"He's very capable, isn't he?" said Tash.

"You sort them out, Julian!" shouted Alistair from Apartment N, as he and his guests applauded the display in a very British way. Less Glastonbury, more cricket match. In fact, it was so genteel that they could still hear the synth intro to Kool & The Gang's 'Cherish' from the cassette player.

Julian nodded politely and turned to whisper to Raymond before nodding up to the Scotsman.

"This guy is a erm, how you say..." He started to discreetly gesticulate what any reasonable human being might identify as *wanker*.

Raymond nodded. "Yes, well, this is it." He hoped this man would stop this gesturing very soon.

"What is this word, eh?" said Julian, still gesturing and drawing deep again on the cigarette in his tight lips.

"Well, erm," said Raymond, trying to turn his back to his wife as casually as possible. "I'm trying to think, actually."

"What name is he? He is..." and again Julian gestured whilst drawing on his cigarette.

Tash loved this, Jamie too.

"What is the word, Raymond?" said Tash.

"You know?" said Julian. "This guy, this man. He is – what do you say?"

Raymond wanted to help this kind man improve his English, but as Maureen's stare burnt a hole in his back, he realised he was stuck between a rock and a very hard face.

"What's he saying?" said Maureen, still half in and half out of the pool.

"Are you residents?" said Alistair, catching sight of Maureen on the aluminium steps. His cigar tip glowed in the warm night air.

"Help me, yes?" said Julian to Raymond. "Gilipollas? The word in English?"

"I think it's erm, is it..." said Raymond before lowering his voice as far as he could... "Is it erm, is it..." then he couldn't believe that he whispered, "toss pot?"

Tash snorted.

"No, no!" said Julian.

Maureen was frozen still, like a gazelle spotted by a leopard. Surely blending in with the pool would make her invisible to the rude man above.

"Excuse me, I'm up here!" shouted Alistair.

Raymond took a deep breath and leaned into Julian's ear before swallowing, then whispering.

"Yes! Wanker!" said Julian with sheer glee.

"What do you say to that man?" said Maureen.

"Thank you," said Julian before shaking Raymond's hand. With that, he took another draw on his cigarette and made for his sweatshop kitchen. Raymond wiped his hand clean again, and started to undo his soaking cloak, surprised he'd only just thought of it.

"Excuse me, do you know the banks? In Sant Lluìs?" said Jamie to the departing chef.

"Si," said Julian. "I must work now. Come and see me. Palomino. Acqui." He gestured at the bar wrapped around the side of the building from the front, then went back to work, muttering happily to himself.

"Wanker. This guy is wanker." Another day, another English word.

"Thank you!" shouted Raymond, Tash and Jamie in unison.

Julian caught sight of Maureen as he walked past her.

"Gracias," she muttered, still half in and half out of the unlit pool.

"You speak Spanish! Muy bien!" said the smiling chef. "¿Quieres nadar?"

Maureen glared at him. "Just a little. I mean, I don't know what that means."

He had asked if she wanted to swim and was more than familiar with the restrained manner of many middle-aged Brits and their reluctance to let life in, especially at the start of their holiday. And judging by the pallor of her skin, she was at the very beginning of her holiday. He placed his cigarette in his mouth and, with both hands, gently shoved her into the pool.

"Diviértete! ¡Estás de vacaciones!" He laughed and walked on.

She didn't want to *enjoy herself*, and she certainly wasn't going to *enjoy her holiday*, but how was he to know? Maureen's shriek could have been heard fifty kilometres across the sea on the northeast coast of Mallorca. Julian assumed this was all good fun and continued to his kitchen furnace.

"Oh my God, he's shoved Maureen in!" said Raymond, dashing towards her, finally discarding his Father Christmas cape as he jumped in.

"Help! Help!" shouted Maureen, water splashing in all directions around her. "He attacked me!"

Raymond's face appeared above the surface, and he realised he could easily touch the bottom. He waded over to her.

"Just stand up, Maureen!"

"I'm going to drown! He tried to kill me!"

"He was having a bit of fun! Just lower your legs."

"What about jellyfish?"

"It's a swimming pool."

"So? It's dark. How do you know there are no jellyfish?"

"Or piranhas," said Tash.

"What?" shouted Maureen.

"Or pirates," said Jamie.

"Tread water then," said Raymond.

"How do I do that?"

"Open your legs," said Raymond.

"Don't be disgusting, Raymond. People are listening."

"Put your feet down."

"What do you mean?" said Maureen, swallowing mouthfuls of chlorinated water.

"You're in the shallow end. Put your feet down."

And she did. When she finally straightened up, the pool water stopped at her hips.

"We don't really allow night swimming!" shouted Alistair.

"Oh, buzz off!" shouted Maureen. Blimey, she'd finally lost it and wasn't proud of herself.

"Pardon my language, Jamie," she said.

"No problem," he replied.

"Pardon my language, Tash." Maureen was still regretting her indiscretion.

"Of course, we quite understand," said Tash.

They waited. But she had finished her apologies.

"What are you looking at me like that for?" said Maureen to her husband.

"No reason. I just thought you were going to apologise to me too."

"No," said Maureen. "It's your fault that I'm standing in stagnant water. I swallowed half of it."

Raymond reached over to help her up the steps.

"Sorry, yes. But I don't think it's stagnant. People swim in it."

"Do you want to drink some?"

"No, thank you."

"Right, well, take my word for it. I'll need a tetanus when we get back home. How am I going to explain that to Dr Varma? Hmm? My husband took me into space, and a criminal assaulted me?"

"It's not space, darling. It's Mallorca."

"Menorca," said Jamie and Tash in unison.

"And he's not a criminal; he's a chef. He's going to help us."

"I think I might be getting sunstroke. I feel very queer," said Maureen.

"We haven't been in the sun, Maureen. It's been dark since we got here."

"Don't be clever about weather, Raymond. It doesn't suit you."

Chapter Sixty-Nine

"This is mad hot. We haven't thought this through," said Tash, sitting in the opened side of the camper with baby Raymond on her lap, clutching Gabriel in his tiny hands and between his lips.

Her holdall was filled with all the supplies she might need for twenty-four hours away with a baby, but her water supplies were getting warmer by the minute. Alistair's balcony provided a soundtrack courtesy of David Cassidy's 'Last Kiss' now, although it was George Michael's backing vocals that spilt out into the warm night air. Alistair really did enjoy his ballads.

"Can't we open all the doors and windows, then you and Maureen can sleep in here with him?" said Jamie, rubbing his nephew's cheek.

Maureen was lying on the long bench seat and was having as much trouble as Raymond getting comfortable.

"Maybe that chef can give us some cold water?" said Raymond.

"At least everyone's dried quickly," said Jamie.

They had. These balmy Menorcan nights were relentless and brutal to sleep through. Tomorrow, if they were lucky, they may find one of the banks had air-con, but none of the resorts did, and the holidaymakers around them had every window and door wide open. Some better-off holidaymakers might have a pedestal fan or two to blow the hot air around.

"I'd prefer it if he gave us a bed," said Maureen, thumping her fist into the hot vinyl cushion that spanned the plywood day bed.

"I could murder a beer," said Tash.

"I'm not so sure he'd be so keen to hand those out," said Raymond.

"Can't believe we didn't bring any Euros," said Tash.

"Any what?" said Raymond.

"Euros," she replied, then remembered. "I mean pesetas."

"Do they change their money?" said Raymond. "In the future? The Spanish?"

"All of Europe does," said Jamie. "Single currency. The Euro."

"Never," replied Raymond, genuinely shocked.

"Oh, my goodness, no!" said Maureen. "What about the Queen?"

"We don't join," said Tash. "We wanted to be in Europe – but refused to bin off the pound."

"Rule Britannia!" said Maureen, suddenly very happy.

"Although we just voted to leave the EU," said Jamie.

"What's that?" said Raymond.

"The EEC," said Tash.

"How do we do that?" said Maureen. "We can't move the whole country. Where on earth do we go?"

"No, we leave the European Union but stay in Europe. I can't believe you're making me explain that part," said Tash. "Did you think we towed Britain further up the North Sea?"

"I'd hope to go further south," said Raymond. "I don't fancy any more rain."

"But we couldn't go much further south before we hit France, Raymond!" said his wife.

"Oh yes, I forgot about France."

"We don't move anywhere!" said Tash. "Sake!"

"Can this chef man get us some proper cushions?" said Maureen.

"You're confusing me for someone who lives here," said Tash. "We all arrived together. Besides, the chef man has a name."

"Oh yes," said Jamie. "What was it?"

They all thought for a moment and muttered as Tash watched in amazement.

"It was a Spanish name, I think," was followed by someone else saying, "I wouldn't know how to spell it," and then, "was it something to do with Manuel?"

"Julian!" shouted Tash. "He was called Julian! Bloody hell!"

They looked back at her for a moment.

"Someone's paying attention to the hot Spanish guy," said Jamie.

"Do you mean hot or hot?" said Tash. "Cos I'm not sure what you're implying."

"Well, I just meant hot, but now you mention it, maybe you meant hot."

"Will he give us some drinks do you think?" said Maureen.

"Maybe he'd accept sterling? Have you got a few quid, Raymond?" asked Jamie.

Raymond started to feel in his pockets.

"Raymond," said Maureen. "Raymond!"

The urgency in her voice was alarming.

"In here. Now!"

"What is it?" replied Raymond, trying to step past Tash. "Is it a lizard? It won't hurt you." He was already removing his shoe, ready for a reptile fight.

"It's not a lizard! It's an emergency! Hurry! Now!"

Chapter Seventy

"Why does it have Julio Inglesias on it?" said Maureen, never too worried about pronouncing his name correctly.

"Well, he's famous, isn't he?" said Raymond, lifting the bundle into the moonlight. "We have Florence Nightingale on ours. They have pop stars on theirs."

The Spanish 5000 peseta banknote shared the same brown colour as the British tenner in 1985 but little else. And at this moment, Raymond had a fat bundle of them in his hands.

"It's Juan Carlos, their king," said Tash, squinting up at the treasure.

"He looks like Julio Inglesias," said Maureen.

"Is he Enrique's dad?" said Jamie in the back of the van. He had continued to unzip the bumpy vinyl cushion and was extracting bundle upon bundle of Spanish currency before tossing it onto the van floor.

"Who?" said Maureen.

Upstairs, Bowie was singing 'This Is Not America," and he was right. They were unmistakably surrounded by Spanish currency.

"It's not going to be legit, is it?" said Tash.

"You mean fake?" said Raymond lifting a single note to the moon to examine the watermark.

"I mean dirty."

"All money's dirty," replied Raymond, sniffing it. "It's been in people's pocket's all day."

"Stop licking money, Raymond. Dirty!" said Maureen.

"I sniffed it! I didn't lick it!"

"No. I mean, he was handling a lot of stolen cash, wasn't he? This is probably on a wanted list. All the serial numbers will be known to the police," said Tash.

"How much is one of those worth?" asked Maureen.

Tash delved into her distant history of economics and thought for a moment.

"Maybe twenty quid."

"What?" Maureen looked like she'd won at bingo. Not that she went to bingo. Well, not that she'd ever admit to it.

"There are about fifty notes in each bundle," said Jamie, flicking through a stash in his hand. "And there's got to be a hundred bundles in here. That's like, that's like..."

He started to do maths in his head.

"About a hundred grand," said Tash.

"Pesetas?" asked Raymond.

"Pounds," replied Tash.

"One hundred thousand pounds?" said Jamie before Tash shushed the hell out of him whilst checking for eavesdroppers in the pool vicinity.

"Oh my God, we're smugglers!" said Maureen. "We didn't know. None of us knew! Did we? None of us knew! Because we didn't! We didn't know! That's our cover story!"

"No," said Jamie. "It's not."

"What do you mean no, it's not?" said Maureen. Was he mad?

"It's the truth. It's not a cover story. It's totally the truth. We didn't know."

Maureen breathed a slight sigh of relief and did a tiny waft of her arms to cool the sweat that gathered underneath them. They stood in silence before Jamie raised his hand. He had to lean out of the van door for this to be seen by the others.

"Question from the smuggler with the sweaty forehead," said Tash. "Unless you're cooling your armpits again?"

Maureen dropped her arms to her side; surely no one had seen her do the same thing?

"They won't miss a few of them, will they?" said Jamie.

"Jamie! You're no criminal!" said Maureen.

"No, he's not," said Raymond. "But he has a point. Doesn't he?"

They all fell silent.

"But," said Maureen. That was all she could manage before stopping herself.

They fell silent again. The smell of flame-grilled chicken from the Palomino kitchen danced across the pool and under their noses. They stared at the ground, listening to the lapping of the Mediterranean Sea as it broke gently on the rocks behind the low-rise villas across the other side of the pool.

The cork from a bottle of Cava popped and flew off the balcony of Apartment N, followed by rapturous applause from the crowd waiting to taste its chilled bubbles.

Another waft of seared poultry smoke filled the VW.

"Shall we take a vote?" asked Tash.

Chapter Seventy-One

"I do think a vote can be very much overrated," said Raymond as crisp brown chicken skin and moist white meat tumbled out of his over-filled mouth.

"Don't speak with your mouth open," said Maureen, carefully trying to load up the back of her fork with small pieces of fluffy baked potato. She'd once seen Meg Mortimer do this on *Crossroads* and was pretty sure it was *de rigueur* in society ever since. Meg should know; after all, last year, she'd left the motel to go on the QE2, and it doesn't get more regal than that.

Raymond considered this as he chewed. She watched to make sure he swallowed in full before attempting his apology.

"I always speak with my mouth open," he said.

"Don't behave like a child, Raymond."

The Palomino bar was half inside and half out, and given the night's heat, they had opted for a square aluminium table beneath the stars. Opus' 'Live Is Life' was on the stereo, as it most probably was in every Spanish bar this summer. Three hi-ball glasses of San Miguel were half empty, and cool condensation dripped down their sides into a pool on the metal tabletop. Maureen had tried to order a Babycham and lemonade, but these idiots had never heard of it, so she asked for a glass of sweet white wine, which was far from sweet when it arrived. How on earth these people hadn't heard of Blue Nun was beyond her understanding. The waiter Paco had smiled patiently as Raymond mimed "sweet" to him before eventually nodding his understanding and bringing a 1981 Rioja Blanco. They didn't really serve wine by the glass, but he was used to the quirky demands of the Brits, so he would simply cork up the bottle and hope she ordered more.

She wouldn't be doing that. Anyone could tell this was terrible wine.

Well, that was Maureen's take on things.

It was only worth 500 pesetas, although if she had the foresight to lay a bottle away, this Vina Tondonia would fetch £750 in 2020. 1981 was their best year. Happily, Maureen didn't need to play the wine markets now that she had £100,000 in stolen Spanish notes.

"Leave the salad, Jamie," said Maureen before depositing more potato into her mouth.

Jamie was about to hurl a fork full of the stuff into his face but aborted with inches to spare.

"What?"

"Leave the salad. They don't wash it," she replied.

"Of course, they wash it," said Tash, with a tinge of doubt. She was a little distracted as she'd positioned her chair so she could see the C5 by the pool.

"In tap water?" said Maureen confrontationally. "The tap water you can't drink?" She'd won this one, she was sure of it.

Jamie looked at his sister, who shrugged back at him. He knocked the salad off his fork and cut into the chicken instead. Tash lovingly rubbed her son's forehead as he drank from a freshly warmed bottle of formula milk. He was wearing just a nappy and seemed happier than the baby on the table next to them, who'd been travelling since breakfast time, including a three-hour delay at Luton airport. She was refusing anything her parents tried to soothe her.

"I join you?" said Julian, removing his apron and using it to wipe sweat from his forehead. He dragged a spare chair across the warm flagstones to their table.

Maureen looked like this chef had just asked if he could shit on her plate.

Staff?

Sit with us?

Whilst we eat?

"Of course," said Raymond, sliding along to make space for the knackered chef to join them.

"Raymond!" said Maureen.

"What?" he replied, oblivious of the inner turmoil his wife was fighting – the shame of it.

A long table of two families looked up and smiled at Julian, and a few shouted his name.

"Hola!" he waved back at them.

One of the kids – a teenager dressed head to toe in white cotton – stood up clutching a C90 cassette. He walked inside and handed the tape to the English landlady behind the bar. She thanked him and placed it into a dusty silver cassette deck above rows of Larios Gin and silver bottles of Poncho Caballero brandy liqueur. She turned off Opus on the radio, clicked the play button on the deck, and the homemade mix tape filled the bar and terrace with Nick Rhodes' stabbing intro to 'A View to a Kill'. Duran Duran ensured that 1985 was the year Bond themes were cool again.

Paco followed the chef with a tray expertly balanced on one hand before carefully serving the diners. Another San Miguel for Raymond, Tash, and Jamie, and another glass of wine for Maureen before placing one final San Miguel in front of Julian.

The waiter smiled and gently rubbed baby Raymond's forehead with his hand, then went back to work serving drinks.

"Gracias," said Julian, followed by other versions of this from his table mates.

"We didn't order these," Maureen whispered to Raymond. She was furious. "I hope they don't think we are paying for them."

Julian heard. They all did.

"The wine is no good?" said Julian, extracting a Fortuna from his pocket and lighting up with a single click of his lighter.

"Pardon?" said Maureen.

"The wine. Is no good? This is my gift to you," explained Julian, exhaling deeply in Raymond's face. "Welcome to Binibeca!"

"He's buying us some drinks, Maureen," said Raymond, coughing through the smoke.

"I finish my shift now. At last! Very hot!" he fanned his face with his apron. "How is the pollo?" said Julian.

"This is delicious," said Jamie. He meant it.

"It's amazing, gracias," said Tash, leaning over to scoop up a piece as demurely as possible. For a sweaty, short man, he was managing to confuse her a little. Happily, Jamie had cut Tash's up when she started feeding baby Raymond so she could fork pieces with one hand. He'd done it without being asked or without it being expected. The fact that he wasn't great with cutlery did however mean she looked like she was placing roadkill into her face every few minutes.

"Very nice indeed, thank you," said Raymond, loud and clear. "Isn't it Maureen?"

Maureen nodded, not that she'd touched hers.

"It reminds me very much of chicken," said Raymond, very slowly as if Julian were deaf. "It's a meat we have back in England." He mimed an aeroplane when he said England. Then added, "chicken."

Tash and Jamie shared a glance.

"Good," said Julian. Was he smiling, too?

"Do you wash the salad? Maureen says you don't?" said Tash, resting her fork back on the plate.

Maureen's face went through all the pink and red colours on the Crown Plus Two paint chart before settling on Pottery Red. Julian laughed and gulped deeply on his cool drink.

"She likes to joke!" said Julian. "I think you need mecánico, yes?"

"We need lots of things," said Jamie, "but that would be a great start. Do you know one?"

"Yes, this is no problem. Where do you stay?" he replied, tapping ash onto the floor.

"Oh," said Raymond. "We thought we might sort of sleep in the campervan, sort of thing." He mimed a campervan to help the Spaniard before adding "Camper? Van?" loudly.

Julian looked confused. "All of you?" He looked at the serious faces and then gestured at baby Raymond. "El bebé?"

"He's called Raymond," said Jamie.

"Raymond?" asked Julian. Even he seemed surprised.

"Nothing's certain yet," said Tash, which was news to the others.

"We came here by mistake, actually," said Raymond. "Well, we didn't plan it."

Julian rubbed his chin as he thought. As the Brits stared back at him, he took another long draw on his cigarette. Even the baby in Tash's lap seemed to have his eyes locked on the olive-skinned man.

"I speak to my boss," said the chef, standing up, grabbing his beer, and walking inside the bar, his black espadrilles flipping onto his heels.

"He's going to kill us," said Maureen.

"What?" said Tash.

"I don't like his tone one bit. Get me out of here."

"His tone? He's speaking a foreign language!" said Raymond. "Which is more than we can do."

"Why do you think that?" said Jamie, amazed at Maureen's claim.

"I've seen *The Godfather*," said Maureen. "It all started like this."

They all thought for a while before replying in unison.

Things like...

... "no, it didn't,"

... and "*The Godfather* didn't start like this,"

... and "You're wrong there, Maureen. Not *The Godfather*, no."

Then Jamie took decisive action. "If you think he's trying to kill us, there's only one thing for it."

"What?" said Tash.

"Steady on," said Raymond. "Don't do anything silly. We don't have our E111s."

"Our what?" said Jamie.

"A certificate of entitlement to urgent medical treatment during a temporary stay in another member state of the EEC," said Raymond.

"Wow, we should hang out more, Raymond. You just keep bringing the gold," said Tash.

"Jamie. What are you suggesting we do?" asked Maureen, still concerned.

Jamie looked at them individually, then spoke calmly but with great authority.

"I'm going to try the salad."

And he did.

They watched as he slowly chewed and finally swallowed.

He then let his tongue probe inside his cheeks and teeth before swallowing again.

"Nope. Doesn't taste of Novichok. I think we're safe."

"Taste of what?" said Raymond.

"Oh, things go next level with poison in the 21st century, Raymond. You lot are just playing at it."

"You say that, but I once had a bad spell after some iffy salmon," Raymond said.

"That's because it was fresh," said Maureen. "Anyone with half a brain knows you should only eat salmon from a tin."

"When do we pay?" said Jamie.

"When we're done," said Tash.

"They're a very trusting people, aren't they?" said Raymond. "I mean, if this were the Poseidon Fish Bar in Brixton, you'd have to pay upfront, especially for haddock. They're sticklers for that."

Tash stared at him.

"They put a little star next to it on the menu, and you have to order – and pay – when you walk in." Raymond shared this fact with the solemnity of a grandparent betrothing a family secret to a descendent.

"There's a lot to be said for human trust," said Jamie, going in for more salad, then continuing to speak as a tomato pip slid slowly down his chin. "It makes you feel better inside. Essentially, everywhere you go, anywhere in the world, you find we're all good people."

They all considered Jamie's speech and let it warm their hearts.

"So, who's gonna pay with the stolen money?" said Tash.

Chapter Seventy-Two

"Oh my God, he is a terrorist!" said Maureen.

They were standing one behind the other halfway up a painted stone tread staircase, and things were suddenly pitch black.

"Un momento!" said Julian before running up the stairs past them. Even if he hadn't spoken, they would have known it was him from his Agreste aftershave, which he regularly used in his kitchen to mask the smell of cooking oil and his own sweat. The undertones of tobacco added a beguiling something that Tash found herself equally repulsed and fascinated by. Very confusing.

The light returned and a ticking timer illuminated the stairwell, indicating they had another fifteen seconds before darkness would return. This wasn't an eco-friendly attempt to minimise the carbon footprint of the apartments' communal staircase; more of a decision driven by fiscal economy from the landlord and the desire to minimise the invasion of mosquitoes into the open windowed building.

At the top of the stairs, Tash held her baby close and watched Julian extract a key from his pocket and slide it into the hole inside the round aluminium knob on the door marked *Apartamento P*. The frame above the door had a round green peeling sticker which read: 'If you're going places, travel Woodcock Travel.' This instantly turned into an advert jingle in Raymond's head.

Julian paused after unlocking the door to gently rub the downy hair on the back of baby Raymond's head. "Un chico guapo," he muttered before smiling at Tash. "A handsome boy."

She took the compliment and, for a moment, wondered if she might be blushing but put it down to the warm winter clothes and elf hat (which she quickly removed), not to mention the thirty-two-degree heat inside the building.

"And this? This is mouse?" he held up Gabriel before placing him gently back.

"He was my Grandma's. And my dad's. And then mine. And now he's his."

All the time she spoke, she was hearing her voice in her head:

Shut the fuck up, Tash, you pathetic cow.

"And you'll check around the pool again?" said Jamie.

"Give him a moment, Jamie!" said Tash.

"Si, no problemo. It will be found, is okay."

Tash had been horrified to see a C5 wheel was missing when they started to move it. Jamie was convinced it would have come loose as it fell into the pool, but a late-night inspection was fruitless. They had agreed on a daylight search in the morning, but Julian had reassured Tash he would have another search with his torch.

He opened the door, hit another timer button, illuminating a further ascending staircase inside, smiled at the Brits, and gestured to go in.

"Welcome."

As they shuffled through one by one, it was merely bad luck that the initial timer clicked off as Maureen reached their good Samaritan. Her shriek was involuntary, but Julian pressed the light button again and smiled at her, indicating as best he could that the switch was a bit like a clock. She was having none of it and raced past him, only to find the light on the inside was about to click off too. Another shriek was followed by Julian leaning in and pressing the timer switch for her benefit.

"You are welcome," he said to the back of her legs which dashed up the staircase behind the others.

"Oh, by the way," said Julian into the apartment void that rose above him. "The note you paid with."

The footsteps stopped. Maureen's sharp intake of breath was the last thing everyone heard.

"Yes?" asked a very pathetic-sounding Raymond. "We found it, actually. It's not ours. Where did you pick it up, Jamie?"

"I didn't pick it up. It was Maureen!" said Jamie.

"Everyone shut up," said Tash.

"This is too much; you need change," said Julian.

There was an audible collective sigh of relief.

"That's alright, Julian, you keep that. Our tip," said Tash.

"Really? No, no."

"Really," said Tash.

"You are very er, generous."

"We know," said Maureen, continuing up the stairs just in case he did turn out to be a kidnapper.

Apartment P was more of a duplex. Off the first landing were a twin bedroom, a bunk bedroom, a bathroom, and a door into an open plan kitchen, leading to a dining and living room with a balcony overlooking the pool. Another staircase rose to a double bedroom with an extra spare bed, ensuite bathroom and vast roof terrace, also overlooking the pool but the vast darkness beyond suggested a stunning view of the sea when the sun or moon could be bothered.

"We have family here at erm," Julian did some English counting in his brain, "nine o'clock?"

He held out nine fingers.

"Si," said Raymond.

"What did you just say to him?" said Maureen, suddenly very suspicious.

"I said si; it means yes."

"Well, don't. He can understand us," she replied. "You'll just confuse him with your Spanish."

"Sorry," said Raymond before turning to Julian. "Sorry."

Julian smiled.

"You can rest, but tomorrow you must leave, yes?"

"Of course, yes," said Tash. "We're very grateful."

Julian smiled at Tash a little longer than he thought he would. He wasn't leering; the last thing he wanted to do was live up to a British stereotype of Spanish single men. But this lady had a warmth to her and an effortless maternal instinct. He might have felt a little differently if he'd discovered just how often she'd accidentally left her baby on trains, buses, libraries and supermarket tills. Still, for now, he was enjoying her company.

"This place is massive," said Jamie walking back down the stairs from the top floor.

"It's very kind of you. You must let us pay you," said Raymond.

"We talk tomorrow. Rest, yes? And tomorrow mecánico aqui, si? Meet him here..." with this, Julian walked through glazed doors onto the balcony and gestured down at the pool. "Aqui, at erm," he did more maths in his head, "half to nine, yes?"

"Half to nine? What does he mean? Ask him what he means, Raymond?" said Maureen, swiping her finger across the white tile-topped breakfast bar that separated the kitchen from the dining table and examining it for Spanish dust.

"Can't you ask him, Maureen? He's right next to you?" he replied.

"I don't speak the language," she replied.

"He's speaking English."

"I knew you'd be like this when you had that second beer," said Maureen. "You're drunk."

Jamie glanced over at a plate on the wall, which cleverly – or hideously – doubled up as a clock. He mimicked the hands on the face until he and Julian agreed that he meant half past nine.

"Muchos gracias," said Jamie, reaching out to shake Julian's nicotine-stained hand.

He gladly accepted and smiled at his temporary guests.

"Dormir bien."

He started to leave, and as Tash stepped to one side to let him pass, he did the same. They laughed and moved again, each time blocking one another.

"I'll stand still, and you move this time," said Tash, with a giddy smile.

She did, and he did.

Then he was gone.

"I'll stand still, and you move this time," said Jamie, in his best Tash voice.

"Shut your face, you knob," said Tash.

But she knew what everyone was thinking.

"Who's taking shift one?" she said, hoping to change the subject.

"No one's going to take it from the bottom of the stairs," said Jamie. It's late, and we'll be up before anyone else."

"It's non-negotiable, Jamie."

"Well, you can count me out," said Maureen. "I didn't want to come in the first place."

"Three hours each, then. Me, you and Raymond. Who's first?" said Tash.

Chapter Seventy-Three

This mad little go-kart was something to behold. It was cracked and dirty and smelled of sweet poultry, yet it seemed pretty solid with its additions of extended seating and odd contraptions bonded onto the front.

The light went out, and suddenly everything was dark.

A match lit the bottom of the stairwell, followed by the glow of Spanish tobacco. It struggled to illuminate the rear of the Sinclair but was enough to hold his attention for a moment.

The light came on once more, and he heard Jamie chatting to himself and the sound of his footsteps descending from above.

"Don't know why I've bought a sheet," said Jamie to himself before laughing. "Should have brought a pillow, though. Maybe you can be my pillow, Mr Sheet?"

Probably better to leave now, thought the curious man. It had been a long day. He took another drag on his smoke and stepped outside onto the crazy paved path.

When Jamie reached the C5, he was oblivious to the smoke in the air. He climbed into the back seat, rested his head on the painted wall to one side, screwed the sheet into a ball and rested it by his neck for comfort.

The chances of his sister tagging him in three hours to mind the C5 were minimal, but he didn't mind. He was still getting a buzz about her being back in his life.

Sure enough, when Tash eventually took her turn, the sun was rising, but it did give Jamie an hour or so on an actual mattress.

Chapter Seventy-Four

You'd think they would all be used to the sound of Maureen screaming by now, but they weren't. Maybe it was the relentless, intense dry heat that made sleep a short-lived descent into transient pockets of sweaty slumber, maybe it was the slim mattresses, or maybe it was the deafening cicadas from the dark hillside that faced the apartments. But they all felt jet-lagged the moment Maureen's horrific shriek viciously awoke them.

As Raymond opened his eyes, he instinctively sat up, smacked his head on the ceiling, and immediately regretted taking the top bunk when they chose beds last night.

Beneath him, Jamie sat up and swung his legs across the damp nylon sheets until he was sitting on the edge of his mattress. One moment later, he was struck in the face by Raymond's feet, who had done the same thing.

"Bloody hell!" said Jamie.

"Sorry, Jamie," said Raymond, fumbling for the ladder.

Jamie examined his nose for blood, but it seemed OK so far. Raymond hadn't been so lucky; he had an Artex-shaped scratch on his forehead that was filling with scarlet, which was toning well with the bee sting that still glowed on his nose.

"Do you know where the ladder is?" said Raymond.

"Help!" shouted Maureen. "Help! What's Spanish for help?"

"We're English. You don't need to shout in Spanish," said Jamie.

"Help!" she said again.

"That's it," said Jamie.

"Where are you, Raymond?"

"We're just finding the ladder," said Raymond.

"What is it?" said Jamie, climbing from his bed and onto the landing.

"There was someone in my room!" said Maureen, trying hard to cover herself from Jamie's innocent eyes as he peered in her door. She'd dragged the cheap sheets and dubious bedspread with her as she leapt from her double bed, so his innocence remained intact.

"I don't think so," said Jamie. "You might have been dreaming."

"Found it!" shouted Raymond.

"Found what?" said Maureen.

"The ladder," said Raymond.

There was a smash from the bunk room.

"No, I didn't," said Raymond.

"Did you let him take the top bunk?" said Maureen.

"He wanted it!" said Jamie, walking back to check on his roommate.

Raymond was in a heap on the floor. He'd tried to descend the small wooden ladder but had mistaken part of the bed frame for the steps and hurled himself onto the tiled floor from six feet in the air.

"Are you alright?" said Jamie.

Raymond lifted his face to force a smile.

"Just a little knock," he replied before gesturing at his shoulder. It had a lump where the joint once was, and his arm was hanging loose below. A dislocation if ever Jamie had seen one. Which he hadn't until now, and he didn't like it one bit. Jamie felt himself starting to faint, so he lowered himself down the scratchy plaster wall, knocking a decorative plate of Ciutadella harbour onto the floor with a smash.

"What the fuck is happening in there?" said Tash, standing at the bathroom door as the toilet flushed, her baby son giggling in her arms.

"I'm okay," said Jamie. "Don't look at Raymond's shoulder."

"Christ," said Tash.

"Someone tried to get in bed with me!" said Maureen.

Tash arrived at the top of the stairs and glanced Maureen up and down in a very judgemental way.

"Come on, love. We all exaggerate from time to time, but that's pushing it."

"They did!" said Maureen. "They did! And then there was a clatter at the top of the stairs!"

"That was me," said Raymond through the pain.

"Before that!" said Maureen.

"I thought you were minding the C5?" said Jamie to his sister.

"We're allowed a nappy change!"

"Someone tried to get in bed with me!" repeated Maureen.

"Okay! Okay! Calm down, calm down, Maureen," said Tash before sitting on the floor next to Jamie. She smiled at her and tried her best to reassure her.

"Even your husband doesn't want to sleep with you," said Tash kindly. "Why would anyone else?"

"There was someone in my room," said Maureen.

"Hands up, who was in Maureen's room?" said Tash.

No one raised their hand.

"See? You just had a dirty dream," said Tash.

"I did not dream anything!" Maureen was getting cross now.

"Okay, okay," said Tash before turning to Jamie. "You ok, Jamie?"

She placed a hand gently on the back of his neck. He nodded.

"How are you doing, Raymond?" said Tash, peering into his room.

"I feel a bit sick on account of the shoulder bother. Which incidentally prevented me from raising my hand in the earlier question and answer session, but I can confirm I haven't been in Maureen's room."

Tash nodded. "Good to know."

"My arm's hanging off sort of thing. It should be up here, you see?"

"TMI," said Tash before rubbing Jamie's neck again.

"Can you describe this person, Maureen? What did they look like?"

Maureen nodded and took a deep breath. "Pure evil."

Tash nodded patiently.

"I was thinking more hair colour, and age, that kind of thing. Number of eyes, just a ballpark figure."

"I have a question," said Jamie, his hand in the air, unlike Raymond's.

"What is it?" said Tash.

"Aren't we supposed to be meeting a mechanic?"

"Shit," said Tash.

Chapter Seventy-Five

They dashed past the C5 and out through the main door to the apartments, then took a left, avoiding Bini Boutique selling beach balls, brown glass Sangria jugs, postcards and Menorcan leather sandals, instead taking the steps to the abandoned VW. Madonna was singing 'Material Girl' somewhere on a poorly tuned AM radio.

"What time is it?" asked Tash.

Raymond glanced at his watch. "Do you mean what time do we think it is, or what time is it in Britain now, or what time is it in Mallorca now?"

"Menorca," said Jamie.

"Sake, too many options. I just want to know what time it is here now."

Raymond glared at his watch, which was very close to his face, given his wrist was holding his other shoulder in place. "Erm, I don't know. I didn't bring my bifocals."

"What do you mean you don't know?" said Maureen.

"I didn't alter it when we arrived, and it's coming in and out of focus. But it seems to think it's quarter past ten on Christmas Eve morning."

"Oh, my goodness, I need to get the sausage rolls out of the freezer," said Maureen.

Raymond went into panic mode.

"Can't we bake them from frozen?" said Raymond.

"From frozen?" replied Maureen, in the tune most of us might say, "from outer space?"

"They did on *Farmhouse Kitchen*."

"Is that the show where she always starts in the wrong place?" asked Jamie.

"What do you mean?" asked Raymond, now rocking from one foot to another in worry.

"She always pelts it through from the kitchen after the credits and races to the dining table to start the show?" Jamie had seen plenty of daytime TV since October. Too much, in fact.

"Well, she's setting the scene, so to speak, isn't she?" said Raymond. "I would imagine a farmhouse kitchen is a very busy place. My grandma had puppies in her oven!"

This understandably silenced them all.

"There are too many responses to that, Raymond. We've got jokes about your Grandma's puppies, buns in ovens, eating dogs; I mean, where does a girl start?" said Tash.

"It was an Aga. The vet said to put them inside with the door open."

"Like a slow roast?" said Tash, teasingly.

"No, they used to do it with newborn lambs, too, in the winter. It wasn't on full; it had a back burner."

"Grace Mulligan served frozen sausage rolls on *Farmhouse Kitchen*?" said Maureen. Her day was becoming more baffling by the minute. "I'll not accept that!"

"Said they'd be just as tasty," said Raymond, nodding. "It's worth considering."

"You're not getting this are you?" said Jamie. "It's July the thirteenth. Today is the middle of summer in 1985."

"Where the hell is the mechanic?" said Tash, tiring of Raymond baiting.

"We're late, aren't we? Probably been and gone," said Jamie.

Maureen snorted a laugh. "You must be joking. The Spaniards are never on time. Probably having a siesta or something."

"I was on time," came a voice from the ground.

They looked down to see a pair of almost flared jeans protruding from the front of the campervan. These were followed by many accusations from above in stage whispers, each blaming the other for being rude about the natives. The legs shuffled out to reveal a cream and brown towelling t-shirt with a v-cut collar flanked by wide lapels. It struck Tash that the Spanish were far more laissez-faire about being slaves to fashion, and many of their sartorial choices had roots in the seventies, not the eighties.

In fact, she was about to make a hilarious joke about *Saturday Night Fever* when the rest of the mechanic slid into view. It was Julian.

"Good morning, campers!" he said, quoting the current British humour back to the Brits, a skill many of the hospitality sectors did in these times. It rarely failed to amuse, especially fans of *Hi-De-Hi*, although today was one of those days when it failed beautifully.

"Julian," said Tash.

"They're a very capable nation, aren't they?" said Raymond, struggling to hide the delight in his voice.

"What are you doing under there?" said Maureen, with an accusatory tone.

"Did you sleep well?" he replied, reaching over to a battered transistor radio with a bent aerial. He turned the volume dial down a little, just as King's 'Love and Pride' made itself known with the unmistakable drum fill at the top.

Everyone replied in the affirmative, even Maureen, albeit in hushed tones.

As Julian stood, he wiped his oily hands onto his jeans and pulled a Fortuna from his back pocket. He took a single match from a book of twenty and struck it on the rock by the back wheel. It was all very Clint Eastwood circa 1965, and Tash found herself staring again. He noticed her gaze and assumed she wanted a cigarette, so he offered one. She declined with a shake of her blushing head. Why wasn't he hot in those dirty jeans? Silly jeans.

"Any sign of the wheel?" she asked. "Any luck last night?"

"Sorry," he said, shaking his head. "But this is a small place, and it cannot roll far. I shall keep looking."

Tash did one of her deep sighs and maybe let out a "Sake" under her breath.

"How's the van?" asked Jamie.

"Pipe? Is pipe?" said Julian, making a line in the air, then gesturing beneath the van. "Pipe?"

"Pipe. Yes, brake pipe," said Jamie.

"This is repair, and fluid good again, and handbrake," said Julian. "You drive on rocks?"

The crowd started to look at their shoes or into the bright blue sky as they tried to rekindle a memory of whether they might have gone over a rock last night, accompanied by lots of "erm", "rock?" and "don't think so," type whispers.

"Stick to road, yes?" said Julian with a twinkle in his eye.

"Well, yes, this is it," said Raymond, still clutching his shoulder and trying to hide his excruciatingly painful injury.

"You are hurt?" asked Julian from behind a cloud of smoke.

"What this?" said Raymond, "bit of a bruise, that's all. Got it in the bedroom."

"Oi oi oi!" said Julian, winking at Maureen and slapping Raymond. "Bedroom!"

"No. I was sleeping with Jamie," said Raymond. Like this made everything better. "I was on top."

Julian nodded slowly, trying to piece this jigsaw together. "May I see this?" he asked.

Raymond released his grip, and his arm dropped and swung loose causing him to whimper. Maureen gasped, Jamie fainted, and Julian shouted to a first-floor balcony.

"Mama. Mama!"

It wasn't tinged with any panic or urgency, but there was a definite air of insistence.

"Si?" came a reply from inside the dark room behind the balcony.

"Baja."

"¿Que es?" She wasn't about to come down without him explaining why.

"Baja."

She muttered some frustrated noises, and the apartment exit door slammed, rattling the single glazed panels on the French windows. Or Spanish windows.

Julian was pouring a bottle of 7-Up into Jamie's mouth when his mother appeared. She was even smaller than him and dressed in black with a pale blue cleaning tabard over her cotton skirt. Her jet-black hair was scraped tightly into a bun, revealing sun patinaed skin, and thin expressionless lips. She stepped over to Jamie and glanced him up and down.

"Qué ocurre?"

Julian shook his head and gestured to Raymond, who responded with a self-conscious wave of his good hand. Unfortunately, doing so meant he let go of his shoulder, and his arm dropped again.

"Ay!" said the old lady before setting off to see her patient.

She made Raymond lie down on the scorched grass with his dislocated arm outstretched towards her. She held it tight, with her now bare feet resting against the side of his chest to prevent him from moving towards her when she started to pull.

She spotted the blood on his forehead, the bee sting on his nose, and the talon-shaped scabs down his cheek. He might be the unluckiest man she'd ever come across.

She shouted over to her son in a rapid fashion, and he turned around to translate.

"She pull back and so, and moving will make this erm... pop back. Si?" he explained.

"Oh my God, I can't watch this," said Tash.

"I'd be very happy for her to do it without explaining," said Raymond. "Par favor."

The mother shouted again, and Julian translated.

"She says would you like her to count down?"

"Oh, Er. Yes. Yes, please," said Raymond, his mouth feeling very dry suddenly. He watched a single pure white cloud glide slowly overhead in the perfect sky, then seemingly dissolve in the morning heat.

Again, the lady was talking to her son.

"She says, would you like her to count down from five or from three?"

"Erm," said Raymond. "What does everybody think?"

As ever, this peculiar group started their ruminating out loud:

"Five for me every time."

"Three, I'd say three."

"Does she pull on one or zero?"

"Just get on with it!" said Maureen.

"Yes. I'll leave it up to her," said Raymond, then repeated himself in the direction of Julian. "I'll leave it up to her."

Julian translated for his mother. She turned to Raymond and started to count down.

"Cien, novente y nueve..."

She burst into hysterics, and Julian did too.

"What's she laughing at, actually?" said Raymond, forcing a smile onto his terrified cheeks.

"She is counting down from one hundred!" said Julian, who laughed again, followed by his mostly toothless mother.

"That's a good one," said Raymond. It wasn't. He'd never felt pain like this.

But then she went to work with no more words.

The strain on her body and Raymond's was clear for all to see. Raymond's lips turned inside out as he tried to contain a scream in his mouth. She paused to get a better grip on his wrist and went again. Her twisted toes curled into his rib cage to keep him in position. Raymond's face was positively pumping in time with his racing heartbeat. The strain on the old lady caused her to break wind, but it didn't deter her.

In typical fashion, Raymond took the blame.

"Pardon me," he hissed through clenched teeth.

Eventually, he could contain it no more, and he bellowed a lungful of hysterical screaming that reverberated around the white-washed apartment block and cluster of garden villas.

The nurse stopped working immediately so she could cover her ears.

"What kind of a nurse is she?" said Maureen, unable to maintain her silence.

"Veterinaria," replied Julian.

Raymond took a mighty lungful of warm air and slowly exhaled. "What does that mean?"

"She's a vet," said Jamie, trying hard to hide his beaming smile.

The lady then dropped to her knees, and it was clear for everyone to see that she was now squatting on either side of Raymond's elbow, with her bum in his face.

"Erm," was all Raymond could muster before she started pumping his forearm back and forth like a one-armed bandit.

"I normally have to buy a girl a drink before she'll do that for me," said Jamie.

"Help! No! Help!" shouted Raymond before a sinewy gloopy noise ended the commotion instantly.

"What was that?" said Maureen. "Is he alright?"

"It's a miracle!" said Raymond. "Maureen! The pain has gone! The pain has gone!"

Everyone started to clap in a combination of relief and astonishment.

The old lady was clearly shattered, but after a few moments to catch her breath, she clambered back to her feet and stumbled to stay upright whilst she slid her twisted toes back into her sandals. The result was that each of her legs was now either side of Raymond's head, and his face was accidentally ensconced under her black skirt, with a view of her knitted underpants and other things he couldn't quite identify.

"Erm," was all he could think to say.

"Raymond!" shouted Maureen. "Stop it! Get out of there!"

"I normally have to buy a girl a drink before she'll do that for me," said Jamie.

"That's actually quite funny," said Tash. "Because you did the gag earlier, and it was a bit lame, but it's come around again, so I like what you've done there."

"We must pay them for their help," said Raymond, beneath the black skirt.

"Don't talk inside ladies' skirts!" said Maureen.

"Good point," said Tash before turning to Julian. "What do we owe you?"

He stared at her lips as she spoke, but he was unclear what she had said.

"Repetir?"

"For the van and the happy ending?" said Tash, gesturing at the VW and the elderly lady.

"Nada," said Julian.

"No, we must pay you something?"

"Is your husband better?" Julian was nodding at Jamie, rehydrated after his little medical episode.

"Oh my God, he's not my husband! I'm not married," said Tash, very quickly.

"Sorry!" He smiled at her. "Your boyfriend?"

"My brother! I'm totally single. Totally, totally, totally single."

"That's three *'totally's,*" said Jamie.

Then Maureen screamed again.

Chapter Seventy-Six

"You're dehydrated, darling, that's all. Stop beating yourself up about it."

Raymond was trying his best to appease his wife, but even he was surprised that she'd climbed into the passenger seat of the VW as he steered. He was surprised because Jamie, Tash, Julian and Julian's aged mother were pushing the vehicle along the grass by the pool and onto the road behind.

"I am not seeing things!" said Maureen. "He was on that balcony!"

She pointed to the balcony above the one where the party was being held last night.

It was empty.

Raymond had gassed the engine up when he'd attempted to start the camper, and now the engine was flooded with fuel. He'd explained something about the intense heat and the carburettor to Maureen before she told him to shut up because she wasn't interested and because someone was trying to kill her.

Raymond continued cranking the engine as they finally hit the baking tarmac, and the sound of the engine spluttered to life. As it did, the radio powered on again, at full volume. It really did have a mind of its own. If any holidaymakers in the garden village had been enjoying a lie-in, Sheila E ensured that ended with instant effect, far louder than Julian's modest Invicta radio. Still, it didn't matter because she was *in love, in love, in love, with* 'The Belle of St Mark'. Prince unmistakably wrote the song for her, and 1985 was the middle of his purple patch. Raymond steered towards the kerb side and wound down his window.

"Do you know anything about radios?" he asked Julian while trying to mime all the words simultaneously.

"I know you ran over mine," said Julian looking sadly at his ex-radio on the ground beneath one of the campervan's wheels.

"What?" Raymond didn't understand.

Julian opened Raymond's door and twisted the VW radio dial to no effect. He tried again with more gusto, and the volume dipped to a more palatable level before the knob came off in his hand. He handed the knob to Raymond and smiled.

"Thank you very much for all your help and, you know, your mum," said Raymond.

Julian smiled, and his mum set off back home across the thick, springy blades of grass.

"Woah! Hang on! We're not going yet," said Tash. "We need to get the C5."

"Oh, bum. I forgot about that," said Raymond.

Jamie's hand was in the air. Tash sighed. "Yes?"

"How do we get it back up there?" He pointed to the hot metal roof of the VW, which was already displaying those little heatwaves you see above American desert roads at the cinema.

Credit where credit's due, Jamie would always get to the point, even if it was the last thing people wanted to hear. They all peered around the grass surrounding the pool as if a car ramp might present itself to them, possibly accompanied by a fanfare.

Julian was at the painted green door of the pool plant room that stood on the other side of the deep end, like a miniature villa. He unlocked the door and stepped inside.

Is this man in charge of everything around here, thought Tash. She walked over and surprised herself with the diminutive cough she offered before speaking to him.

"Erm, hi Julian. Hi!"

"Hola!" he replied, lifting a vast bottle of pool cleaner out of the way to reach his PH testing kit. "He has broken the bus already?"

"What? Oh no!" she smiled.

Julian caught sight of baby Raymond and started playing hidey-boo with his hands to the captivated infant. He was a natural.

"You must be a great dad," said Tash.

He smiled.

"Are you?" she asked. Had he understood?

"No children," he smiled. "Where is the time? I cook, si? Always cooking!"

"You must have a very understanding wife."

He either didn't understand or was busy. "Can I help you?"

"We need to get the C5 back on the roof of the van," said Tash, humiliated that her line of questioning had been blocked. "The bus."

"Excuse me?"

"The moped thing. The go-kart."

Julian looked out of the door at the van.

"Why?"

"I need to keep it safe; it's valuable."

"Valuable?"

"Well, not valuable. Just valuable to me."

Julian thought.

"Where are you going?"

"Sant Lluìs, the town up the hill. We're kind of meeting someone at lunchtime."

"And you come back to here?"

Tash looked around and thought for a moment. Shit, she hadn't considered this, but maybe. They would probably want to eat something, drink something, and perhaps freshen up before returning home.

"Yes, I think so."

Julian seemed happy with this answer, and a smile spread across his stubbly face.

"Excelente."

He gestured into his pool plant room. It was a glorified hut made of bricks and a solid red clay tiled roof. In 2020 London, it would probably sell for two million quid as a detached studio commanding views across the water, and the potential to add a toilet subject to the necessary permissions and consents.

"I move these, and you keep it in here."

Tash felt her heart sink. This man had been generous in every way, but now he was offering something she simply couldn't accept. She trusted him, but she didn't trust any other bugger that might walk by this rundown chicken shed.

"Oh, well, that's really kind, but I promised someone I wouldn't leave it."

Better to blame someone else for this decline of hospitality, she thought.

"You don't trust me? Strange man from Menorca?"

"Of course, I trust you. You've been lovely, but..."

The silence was broken by Julian lifting a key. "You take the key; I have food to cook!"

He was smiling, not upset.

She thought.

Then thought again.

Then thought a little more.

Christ, it was hot, and she needed to make a decision quickly.

And Christ, it really was really hot.

Like, really hot.

And didn't he have nice teeth?

Chapter Seventy-Seven

"I think I might change my mind again," said Tash.

"Are you kidding me?" said Jamie, making no effort to hide his despair.

In his defence, the doorway into the pool plant room was in the centre of the wall, making it far more challenging to steer the C5 inside without rocking back and forth.

They joked about how similar this was to Raymond's new girlfriend rocking his elbow back and forth before showing him her wonderland. Then Jamie and Tash had done their "pivot!" jokes whilst impersonating David Schwimmer – this had gone over Raymond's head. In fact, of the three of them, he'd probably worked hardest but laughed least whilst trying to hide the Sinclair.

Maureen had opted to stay locked in the VW in case her stalker returned.

"Jamie, this is a big deal. This is our ride home!"

"You have the door key. What would anyone do with this? Everyone just wants to swim. What could go wrong?" Raymond had made an excellent argument for sticking with the plan.

"Asteroid," said Jamie.

"Asteroid?" said Tash.

"That's the only thing I could think would be likely."

"Define likely?" said Tash.

Raymond started to look outside at the sky.

"Tsunami," said Jamie.

"In the Med?" said Tash.

"You did ask what could go wrong," said Jamie.

"I was speaking metaphorically," said Raymond.

"Well, as I see it," said Jamie, "we are in a tranquil holiday resort in the middle of summer. Unlike last time, the C5 isn't listed as stolen, and unlike last time, we don't have a weird American with a gun, so things are pretty much on our side. I would say the risks remain, asteroid, tsunami and lizard."

"Lizard?" said Tash. "How would a lizard be a threat?"

"There's a lizard," said Jamie, pointing at the wall behind Tash.

She was the first out of the building. In fact, Raymond and Jamie had to force the door open to get out themselves as she was trying to close it the moment she was safely away from the reptile.

"That's a big one," said Tash as she trembled to turn the key in the lock.

"That was a big one," agreed Raymond. "Can we all agree we won't mention that to Maureen? I told her they don't have lizards on Mallorca."

Jamie and Tash glared at one another, then back at Raymond.

"We're on Menorca," said Tash.

"Can we just agree, please?" said Raymond.

"Agreed," said the siblings.

Tash placed her fist into the middle of them all. Jamie copied and rested his on hers.

"What's happening?" said Raymond.

"It's what Madonna does before gigs," said Tash.

"Is she still going in 2020?"

"Yes, and she's wearing even less," said Tash.

"And why does she do that?" Raymond was staring suspiciously at the siblings with their arms outstretched.

"If you've got it, flaunt it," said Tash.

"I mean, why does she do that?" Raymond pointed at their arms.

"It means we're all bonded and on the same page," said Tash.

"Like the Power Rangers," said Jamie.

"The who?" said Raymond.

"Like the Three Musketeers," said Tash.

"What do I do?"

"You put your hand on Jamie's, and then we say something about God or something, and then we do it."

"Do what?"

"Oh, fuck sake, forget it," said Tash and walked off.

Chapter Seventy-Eight

Raymond stared nervously at a bundle of peseta notes in his trembling hand.

"I'm not sure I'm the best person for this."

"Well, I'm not doing it; I've got my seat belt on," said Maureen.

"It doesn't have any seat belts," said Raymond.

Maureen responded by placing index fingers into each ear. It was challenging to normalise sitting comfortably in a greenhouse on wheels in July, let alone on the island of Menorca, but she was doing well. She was cooler than might be expected as, over the last ten minutes, Maureen trained Raymond to waft her perspiring brow with a creased copy of *El Pais* newspaper that she'd found in the footwell. It was dated 10th December 1984 and had cost Jesus Morón forty-five pesetas. It was hard to tell if he or his family had purchased it to read or to swat flies on the windscreen and use the corners for discarded chewing gum, as all these things had happened. But as Maureen had refused to touch it, on the off chance it was carrying rabies, she'd insisted Raymond use his spare hand to waft her, and it was becoming second nature to him now, despite the pain in his shoulder.

Jamie stared at the hand-written note Martha had hurled at his head before her arrest.

"Well, don't look at me. I'm doing mum things," said Tash, glancing at baby Raymond sleeping on her lap.

"But he's asleep," said Raymond, which was a fair observation.

"No ovaries, no opinion," replied Tash.

"Well, what sort of thing does everyone want?" Raymond looked beaten. "I'm not really a clothes shopper."

"It's hardly Primark, is it?" said Tash, nodding at the tiny shop beneath the apartments.

"I don't know what that means," said Raymond.

"Look, we can't spend another day dressed like Will Ferrell if only cos it's so fucking hot!"

She gestured at Maureen's improvised elf suit and Raymond's pared back Father Christmas outfit. Jamie and Tash had rolled up their trousers and sleeves from their respective eighties and twenty-twenty outfits, but the material was winter thick, and the style was bizarre. Jamie's Smart-R's jeans would only roll so far, and his wool sweater was cumbersome when itchily rolled up to his elbows. Tash had almost cried as she rolled up her Hollister jeans, they were new, and her French Connection cardigan was ruined beyond repair.

"I don't know what that means either," said Raymond.

"He plays an elf," said Jamie helpfully. "They filmed it with forced perspective rather than CGI. Old school. He really looks like way bigger than Papa Elf. Camera trick sort of thing."

Raymond stared at Jamie, his tongue hanging out of his mouth, hoping it might catch a tiny taste of sense coming his way.

"Beg pardon?"

"What?" said Jamie.

"Who's Papa Elf?"

"Bob Newhart," said Jamie.

"Oh, we know him, don't we, Maureen!" said Raymond, pulling on his wife's shoulder.

"I can't hear you. Go and shop before one of us boils to death!" said Maureen.

"Right, yes. Sorry."

Raymond climbed out of the van, then realised he was still

wafting the newspaper, so he leant back to pass it to Maureen, who declined it with disgust. He placed it on his seat, climbed out once more, and then slammed his door shut. Next, he rolled up his sleeves, now stained red from the wet red cloak that covered them yesterday and knocked on his window.

Tash leaned out of the opened side door behind.

"Why are you knocking on the window when this is open?"

"I'm not sure. Can I ask a couple of questions?"

"No."

He did, anyway.

"What if they realise this is dirty money?" he whispered, waving the pesetas in the air.

"It's only a few notes; they're hardly Interpol, are they? They sell plastic buckets and spades."

"Can I ask one more question?"

"No," repeated Tash.

And again, he ignored her. Not through belligerence, he simply couldn't hear her above the ringing in his ears. He hated stressful experiences; they made him anxious.

"What sort of thing should I buy?"

Tash sighed loudly and stared at the hot box ceiling above her head.

"Anything! Just make us fit in!"

Chapter Seventy-Nine

"I suppose I should have asked for your sizes, really, shouldn't I?" said Raymond, with one eye on Jamie.

The 'I love Menorca' t-shirt he'd chosen for Jamie was what Maureen might call snug.

The print style was one of the latest trends on the island and used the letter 'I' next to a large red heart, above bold letters spelling MENORCA, which spilt over two lines beneath. Very trendy. Or on trend, depending on which decade you were from.

The white cotton blend clung to Jamie's chest and arms with little scope for movement and happily/unhappily came to an end just above his navel. A loose piece of thread from the fabric was distracting him so much that he'd already unravelled a good half inch from the bottom of the shirt whilst trying to snap it off. Beneath, a pair of yellow Bermuda shorts fitted snugly and boasted an eye-catching print of parrots and palm trees in neon pink. They also had a logo which said Rockstar, which was a shame.

"They didn't do shoes," said Raymond.

"No," said Jamie, glancing down at his boots; he wasn't too fussed. "But did they take the money, OK?"

"Yes, and I got change too," said Raymond, sounding suddenly upbeat. "The whole transaction very much reminded me of shopping, in a way."

"You were shopping," said Maureen.

"Yes, but it was shopping abroad and shopping with, you know..."

"Stolen money," said Jamie in his usual loud voice.

"Shhh!" came a cry from the others.

Jamie took this on the chin but still hated being silenced by people, let alone groups of them.

"She gave me this, too!" said Raymond, holding up a hand-carved wooden-handled corkscrew.

"Oh, my days!" said Maureen. "Put that away!"

"It's a corkscrew!" he replied. "We own one now! Do you like it?"

"It's a, it's a..." said Maureen, struggling to get the words from her mouth, but as he held it proudly in the air, she pushed herself on; "It's a ...ding-a-ling!"

Raymond stared at the phallus corkscrew in his hand. "Is it?"

Tash and Jamie smiled at one another. Tash mimed the word "ding-a-ling" at her brother to maximum effect.

Raymond wasn't convinced. "Is it?"

Tash took the freebie from him and examined it.

"Yep. Sorry, Raymond. She gave you a one-eyed Pete, for sure," said Tash.

"A what?" he asked.

"You know. Third leg. Pocket rocket. Rumpleforeskin."

"Can you stop that now, please?" said Maureen, folding her arms for effect and then regretting it as her new dress seemed to have an 'instant-sweat' facility.

Tash handed it back to Raymond, who took it suspiciously like a bomb before placing it gently inside the van.

"The fuck is this supposed to do?" said Tash, holding up the end of a hand-made lace wraparound dress that was barely covering her Nike sports bra and warmest winter knickers.

"Er," said Jamie, taking the flap of material from her and peering around to assess her options.

He opted to tuck it into the back of her H&M pants, which she wasn't expecting.

"Get off, you freak!"

"I'm trying to help!" said Jamie, slightly offended at the *freak* tag.

"Let's see you then, Maureen," said Tash, itching her arms as the prickly lace slid around her.

"I'm not getting out," said Maureen.

"Come on, let's see you," said Tash. "We're all in this together."

"No."

"Come on, Maureen. We need to be a team," said Jamie.

The passenger door slammed, and a loud clomping noise accompanied Maureen around the front of the van. She stopped before she came into view.

"If anyone laughs, I am going home, and I mean it."

"Good luck with that," said Jamie. "We've locked the time machine in a pigsty, and we need to catch a murderer first."

"No one is going to laugh," said Tash, pulling her lace dress out of her knickers and her knickers out of her bum. Christ, it was hot.

Maureen clipped around the tarmac into view, and suddenly everything was clear.

A middle-aged and mightily pissed off flamenco dancer stood before them.

A red and black spotted dress hugged Maureen's body to mid-thigh, and then countless ruffles of flamboyant material flared out at all angles around her knees. This was the type of nylon fire hazard souvenir that families would purchase for "loved ones" back home, and evidently, the largest teenage size had been a perfect fit for Raymond's wife.

Tash's nostrils flared, and her teeth clamped tightly shut. There was no way she could look at her brother. He struggled to keep tears in his eyes as his chest wobbled from holding in his hysteria.

Eventually, Tash broke the silence.

"I thought you said they didn't sell shoes, Raymond?" She pointed at Maureen's feet.

"Well, they only sell flamenco ones," he replied from his open window. "You'd look daft in flamenco ones."

"Actually, now you put it like that, yes," said Tash. "I would. I would look silly."

"They look great, Maureen," said Jamie, staring down at her black patent flamenco shoes.

Maureen returned to her seat, the tap shoes announcing her every movement.

"I think we'll blend in quite well now, actually," said Raymond, stepping out of his door.

Sadly, the Bermuda shorts rail didn't hold Raymond's size, so he was in a pair of large white Speedos with a double-knotted bow in the rope around the top. Beneath them were his milky white legs, then his brown cotton socks tucked into a pair of flip-flops, with creases in the polyester around his big toes.

"Were flip-flops an option, Raymond?" said Tash. "I wasn't aware of the flip-flop situation?"

"No, I found these in the van," he explained.

"Mmm," said Tash. "They sound clean."

As he stood up straight, everyone saw his splendid new white t-shirt for the first time.

"Frank Says Relax!" was printed in bold black letters across his chest.

"Who the fuck's Frank?" asked Tash.

"I'm not sure, actually. It was a lady that worked there. Maybe her husband?"

"It should say Frankie," said Jamie. "You bought a counterfeit top."

"A what?" shouted Maureen from the other side of the van.

"Don't panic!" said Tash. "He won't be the first or last. What time is it?"

Raymond looked at his watch. "Do you mean now, or do you mean..."

"Let's sort the watch sitch, please! Now!" shouted Tash.

"What do you mean? Like synchronise it?" asked Raymond.

"What?"

"Synchronise the watch, like on the telly?"

"Don't you need two watches to synchronise them? Or more?" said Jamie.

"I just want to know the actual time!" said Tash.

Raymond glanced into the perfect blue sky.

"Well, the sun is nearly overhead, and it's what, mid-July, so I would say..."

"Thanks, Raymond Mears, but I'm gonna ask someone with a watch. A proper one."

With that, Tash wolf-whistled a gardener across the driveway separating a cluster of single-story villas. He glanced over.

"Hola!" said Tash. "Do you have the time, please?"

He stared back.

"Erm, hora?" said Tash, staring back at her brother. "Is it hora?"

"Quelle hora, et il?" said Jamie, very loosely in the direction of the native.

"That's French, Jamie."

"Hora is Spanish," he said.

"But the rest was French."

"Isn't hora, egg?" said Raymond.

"We don't want any eggs," said Maureen. "That's how Spanish flu started."

"That's oeuf," said Jamie.

"And it's still French!" said Tash, marching across the road to the bewildered worker. She tweaked the lace out her pants again and then clenched his wrist to pull his watch to her face. He wasn't wearing one. She tried the other wrist, but nothing. He stood up, walked across to the VW campervan, and pointed at the small clock on the dashboard.

"He's showing you the clock in the camper," said Jamie. "We should have thought of that."

"It's twenty past ten," read Tash. "Set your watch to ten twenty, Raymond."

"Tash, you didn't thank the man," said Jamie, waving at the gardener as he crossed back to his work.

"Yes, I did."

"No, you didn't," replied the others in unison.

"Sake!" shouted Tash before turning to the man.

"Thank you," she shouted in a tune that a child might use after begrudgingly being made to thank someone by a parent.

"Right," said Raymond, tweaking his watch. "Eleven twenty."

"Ten twenty," said Jamie.

"Kill me now," said Tash as she clambered into the campervan, scratching her itchy arms as the lace slowly cut into her baking hot skin.

"Yes, but I'm thinking about Franco and the Nazis," said Raymond.

"Bloody hell, that took a turn," said Tash.

"Should I explain?" said Raymond, desperately wanting to.

"No," said all the others together.

He didn't seem to hear.

"General Franco ran this country until the mid-seventies when he died."

Tash leant to her brother.

"If I ever tell you that you are the most boring man on earth, always remind me of Raymond. Promise?"

Jamie nodded.

"He was on Hitler's side in the war, so set the Spanish clocks to the same time as Germany, and no one ever changed them back," said Raymond, tapping his Casio, which was getting very hot in the sun.

"Raymond, some of your stories creep up and bite people on the arse, cos they're so interesting," said Tash.

"Thank you," he replied.

"That wasn't one of them."

"Why the history lesson?" asked Jamie.

"Because the campervan is on London time, so we need to add one hour to get local time in Mallorca!"

Tash waited for him to realise his error, but she realised she would be waiting a long time.

"Do we have everything we need?" muttered Raymond, tweaking his watch again.

"I could use some self-respect," said Tash, pulling lace from her armpit.

"I'd like some water," said Maureen.

"Did we get sun lotion?" said Jamie.

"Other than sun lotion and water and self-respect, do we have everything we need?" said Raymond, as Jamie climbed in alongside his sister and slammed the rear door.

"Yes," replied the rest of the Scooby Doo van.

"Right, then off we go."

"I'm so hot," said Jamie.

Everyone looked at one another. It was dangerously hot inside. Each lungful of air was burning hot, and their new clothes instantly stuck to their bodies.

"The pool looks amazing," said Tash.

They all looked at the shimmering white peaks in the pool that twinkled as the tiny waves reflected the sun. Beneath them were inviting depths of azure blue cool water.

"We could have a quick dip in the pool to cool our legs off?" said Raymond.

"Are you joking?" said Maureen, like he'd suggested pissing into it from the roof terrace of their apartment.

"Well, I wasn't actually," said Raymond, as a stream of sweat poured down his nose and into his mouth.

"Instant death, you know, dehydration," said Tash.

"Is it?" said Maureen.

"And we're going out in the hottest part of the day," said Jamie.

"How instant?" asked Raymond.

"Work with me on this one, Raymond," said Tash.

"But we need to be in Sant Lluìs by midday," said Maureen.

"Two minutes, tops," said Tash.

Chapter Eighty

The VW struggled in second gear up the hillside, and Jamie was delighted to hear Dario G's 'Sunchyme' on the radio yet confused at the same time. This was 1985, surely? Wasn't 'Sunchyme' released in '97, the year he started secondary school? The penny dropped when he heard a verse he'd never heard before. So, 'Sunchyme' was sampled. He reserved judgement on the original by Dream Academy for a while, but slowly 'Life in a Northern Town' was winning all of them over.

Well, all but one.

"I've never been so humiliated in my whole life," said Maureen.

"We didn't know about the chlorine, did we?" said Raymond. "How were we supposed to know?"

"Well, the signs he'd put up were one way of knowing," said Jamie.

"But we didn't see them," said Raymond. "And they were in Spanish."

"You didn't see them? Or they were in Spanish?" said Jamie. "How would you know they were in Spanish if you didn't see them?"

"We all got in!" said Raymond, slowly running out of protest ideas.

"Shouted at by a cook!" said Maureen.

"He was looking out for us! We shouldn't have been in there," said Jamie.

"He didn't need to yell like he was selling wet fish at Billingsgate," said Maureen.

"Maureen doesn't really like being shouted at," said Raymond trying to neutralise the quarrel.

"Well, I think he's a good guy. He was just trying to do the right thing, maybe went the wrong way about it," said Tash.

This silenced them for a moment.

"No one's perfect," she said. "Even Jesus didn't bring enough food."

"What on earth are you talking about?" Maureen was most displeased by the sudden comparison to Him.

"Well, he wasn't perfect, was he? He didn't bring enough food! One fish and one loaf for five thousand people! Come on!"

Maureen refused to discuss the bible with people like Tash. Jamie thought it might be his turn to try to reset the mood.

"Well, we shouldn't take everything literally, sis. That was a probable."

"Parable," said Maureen.

"What?"

"You said probable. The word is parable." Then she folded her arms again.

"Oh no. Have I been saying that wrong my whole life?" said Jamie.

"No, not your whole life," said Tash.

Jamie nodded. At least she had his back.

"Just until now. You'll get it right for the rest of your life."

They all sat in wet clothes as the campervan headed inland towards S'Uestra on the way to Sant Lluìs, rocking gently from side to side as it bounced over the potholes in the narrow road.

"Good job we had that newspaper to sit on," said Raymond, trying to clear the air.

Nobody replied.

"We can thank Jesus for that!"

Everybody glared at him.

"Don't take his name in vain," said Maureen.

"No, I mean the baddie, Jesus, who owns this van."

"Thank the prick who tried to kill you and caused all this shit in the first place?" said Tash.

"Well, he didn't cause all this, did he?" said Raymond. "We're here to help Martha because someone stole her money."

They considered this.

"Actually, he's right, and she wouldn't even exist if you hadn't come into our life," said Maureen. "So, it's all *your* fault."

She made no attempt to hide the fact that she blamed Tash solely for this, rather than Jamie too, although it had been the two of them that accidentally travelled back in time and nearly killed Bob Geldof.

"I don't want to be here anymore than anyone else!" said Tash. "This has been a very long day for me. My body is very confused."

"I understand that," said Raymond.

"What's that supposed to mean?" said Maureen.

"Well, you know, international travel. It brings its problems, you know," he replied.

"What problems?" asked Maureen.

"You know."

"Stop saying *you know*. I don't know. What are you talking about, Raymond?"

"Tash said her body was confused. It happens to us all."

"Still making no sense to me," said Jamie.

"Well, your holiday can't start properly until you have your first poo."

"Raymond!" said Maureen.

"It's true," said Raymond.

"I meant my body is confused because it's not slept properly since December the 23rd. 2020, which my brain thinks was something like three days ago."

"Oh," said Raymond. That shut him up.

"But now we know your bowel habits and what Maureen calls your old fella."

Maureen folded her arms yet again, and they listened to 'We Close Our Eyes' for a while.

"Sant Lluìs," said Jamie at a road sign up ahead. "Soon be there."

Chapter Eighty-One

"What kind of prick unpacks for just one night in an apartment?" said Tash, leaning forward to lift Raymond's hand off the steering wheel. His body was blocking her view of the clock.

"Ow!" he shouted involuntarily; his recently reattached shoulder was still sore.

"Twenty-five past," read Tash. "When were you planning on telling us about the camera?" she asked Jamie as she slumped back into her seat.

They were driving back to Binibeca, having been parked in the shade of a side street in Sant Lluìs and debating whether to get ice cream, when Jamie realised he didn't have his allocated camera for his Jason Bourne assignment.

Julio Iglesias was singing 'Feelings' from his 1976 album *En El Olympia*, further proving that Spanish DJs didn't give a shit, and in fact, they had a lot to teach the world. You were never more than six feet away from a Julio song in Spain throughout the seventies and eighties, and it was a better place for it.

"We always scan a room before we leave, don't we, Maureen?" said Raymond.

"No one wants to get home and find they've left their foot cream in the bread bin," she agreed.

"That one might need some explaining," said Tash. "But don't feel the need to get me involved."

"When we rent a caravan, we always place our essentials in one place," said Raymond. "It means that we know where everything is to take home again when we leave. And also, the last place burglars would look for valuables is in the bread bin."

"I'm guessing foot cream theft really died off in the nineties," said Jamie.

"You don't need to be clever with me, Jamie," said Maureen. "It's you that left your camera in your bedroom."

"I left it at the top of the stairs, so I didn't forget it."

"How did that work out for you?" said Tash.

Jamie turned to look out the window at the waxy green foliage that miraculously sprouted from the arid ground on the hillside.

Tash held her camera up. "You both have yours, yes?" she asked the driver and co-pilot.

"Yes," said Raymond. "I fetched them from the bread bin right after Maureen spotted that ghost."

"You unpacked too?" said Tash.

"It wasn't a ghost," said Maureen. "It was a murderer."

"You unpacked too?" repeated Tash. Was anyone hearing her?

"Maybe I need to get locked up in an American prison before anyone pays any attention to me!" Maureen was feeling ignored. "Maybe the threat of corporate punishment would make you pay attention!"

"Not at all, Maureen. I always pay attention to you," said Raymond.

"Next right," she said. He ignored her.

"Isn't it capital punishment?" said Jamie.

"You missed it. I said that right," said Maureen, folding her arms over her flamenco dress.

"I thought corporate punishment was like rulers and slippers and stuff," said Jamie.

"Killed by a slipper?" said Raymond, looking for the next available right. "That would take ages. Is that legal?"

"No. Capital punishment is execution; corporal punishment is what they did in schools," said Tash.

"*Did*?" said Maureen. "Don't tell me they get rid of that!"

"Oh yes, the spanking with a ruler has gone now, Maureen," said Tash. "It goes like this: Warning, blame the parents, exclusion, then firing squad."

Maureen glanced over her shoulder briefly. She couldn't read this woman at all but was 95% sure this was her idea of a joke. The camper turned a sharp right and soon took another into a parking space outside the Palomino bar.

"Be quick, Jamie," said Tash as she slid the door open for him.

"I don't have the key. I gave it back to Julian," he replied.

Tash looked at him, then at the others. She handed baby Raymond to her brother.

"I'll fetch it."

"It's alright, I'll go," said Jamie. "I know where the camera is."

"You said, top of the stairs. And I'm halfway out now," said Tash before dropping down to the ground. "And now I am out, so I may as well go."

"Oh my God, you have the hots for the chef," said Jamie.

"Like *you'd* know! Virgintarian!"

"You do!" Jamie was delighted as he watched his sister run over to the bar.

She raised both middle fingers behind her back as she went.

"What's she doing?" asked Maureen.

"I think that means she'll be two minutes," said Raymond.

Chapter Eighty-Two

Annie Lennox was doing impossible things with her voice, and Stevie Wonder worked his magic on a harmonica. Even Raymond was tapping his fingers on the steering wheel to 'There Must Be an Angel' as they stared through the windscreen.

"What's she laughing at?" said Maureen.

Tash had disappeared into the restaurant before she and Julian reappeared and walked to the main apartments entrance. They reappeared again three or four minutes later with Tash clutching Anthony's camera case. She was finding Julian's banter hilarious. The throw your head backwards type of hilarious.

Except Jamie knew she wasn't finding it as hilarious as everyone else thought.

"She's flirting," said Jamie. "She's doing that thing where she plays with her hair and crosses her legs over one another."

"Michael Aspel crosses his legs; it doesn't mean he's flirting," said Raymond.

"He flirts on *Aspel and Company*," said Maureen, disagreeing. "Legs or no legs."

Raymond considered this.

"Oh yes, I suppose he did with Lulu," said Raymond.

"Why are you thinking about Lulu? Stop thinking about Lulu."

"I wasn't thinking about Lulu. You mentioned his TV show."

"He interviewed Mrs Thatcher, but she didn't pop into your head, did she?"

"But," said Raymond. But he couldn't think of how to calm this escalating situation.

Outside, Julian pocketed the apartment keys and smiled at Tash.

"You are busy tomorrow night?"

"Pardon?" She wasn't expecting that. Not one bit.

"You are here? Tomorrow night? I buy you dinner."

"Here? How would that work?" She pointed at the Palomino and considered why he wanted to cook her dinner. He'd be sweating in the kitchen.

"Is my day of no work? My mother cook tomorrow, and I have erm, day off?"

She wasn't ready for that either. Christ, he was asking her on a date. She wasn't even planning on being here tomorrow. Unless she hung around for an extra day. Wait, what the hell was she thinking? She lived in England. In 2020. Then Madonna started singing 'Crazy For You' on the Palomino's stereo. She was a sucker for that song. In 1991 when it was re-released, she'd received it on single as a gift on her seventh birthday, and she'd listened to it non-stop for a month. It got her through the sadness of *Bread* ending on BBC1. She sort of liked the sitcom, but mostly liked being allowed to stay up to watch it.

"She's going red," said Jamie. "He's asking her out."

"How do you know that?" asked Raymond.

"Oh, you're getting tips now, in case you bump into Lulu," said Maureen.

"He's kissed her!" said Jamie. "OMG, he kissed her!"

And he had. Admittedly it was on the hand, but he'd had no choice, as Tash had agreed to date him tomorrow night, and this was him sealing the deal.

So that was something she hadn't seen coming.

"OM what?" asked Maureen.

"G," replied Jamie.

"What does that mean?" she replied.

"OMG," said Jamie. "It means Oh My," and then he stopped. She was a God-fearing lady and wouldn't like this flippant use of His name. He stared at her for a moment, then spoke.

"Gooch."

She nodded as she let this land.

Jamie was initially pleased with his quick thinking, then started to regret his word choice. However, he reassured himself that he hadn't blasphemed, and the chances of Maureen knowing gooch meant that little area between the anus and the genitals were slim.

Chapter Eighty-Three

"That's the one we saw last night before you broke the brakes!" said Maureen, pointing through her window at the Banco Central and the side street alongside it.

"I don't know that I actually broke them," said Raymond, slowing the van down to a stop.

"You were driving, Raymond," said Maureen.

"That's a fair point," he replied.

The Eurythmics had made way for The Colour Field's 'Thinking of You' as Jamie slid open the side door and climbed out. "I'm just going to see if it has a back door."

He set off down the slender road between the bank and a poultry shop with chain link fly nets covering the fan-cooled interior.

"This is all very much like that scene in that show, isn't it?" said Raymond with a tinge of excitement and nerves in his voice.

Maureen ignored him and wafted her new skirt to cool her legs. They both suspected she was doing it in the style of a flamenco performer but were too scared to mention it.

"Probably," said Tash.

"You know the one?" he asked, turning in his seat to look at her.

"Is it the one where Bucks Fizz get trapped in a shitty van?

And Cheryl Baker plays a cop who goes undercover as a flamenco dancer that only eats food she can peel?"

Raymond considered this.

"No, I've not seen that one. Who's in it?"

Jamie was back in no time, and the morning heat had raised beads of sweat on his receding hairline. "Back door, for sure. But looks locked and unused."

"Still, we shouldn't ignore it," said Raymond.

"It's hot, isn't it?" said Jamie taking a can of Kas Naranja from his sister and spraying her thoroughly in the face with it as he struggled to remove the ring pull.

"That will be the weather," said Tash, drying her face on the back of her hand.

"How the hell do you get these off?" said Jamie. He'd only drunk from bottles since he'd been in 1984, and these metal triangles that actually came off the top of cans seemed lethal.

"Shall we identify the other bank before we pair off?" said Raymond.

"So, we're looking for another bank that might be called Sa Nostra?" said Tash, helping Jamie to neutralise the threat from his can top.

"Like that one," said Jamie, pointing to the other end of the block, then taking the drink back from his sister and drawing deeply on the can.

"That was quicker than I thought," said Raymond.

"Time?" said Tash.

"Time now here, or time in London now or..."

"I don't want to be me anymore," said Tash. "Anyone want the job? You just need to make some terrible life decisions and then get trapped in the past?"

Jamie leant in to pick up his camera.

"Good idea; let's synchronise cameras," said Raymond.

"You can't synchronise cameras," said Tash as she lifted hers.

"No," agreed Raymond, suddenly fiddling with his.

Jamie twisted Kenneth's 35mm SLR, and the flash went off, then a whirl of an auto advance film movement confirmed it was indeed good to go.

"Okay, let's decide who goes where," said Tash.

"One sec," said Jamie, and he blinked to regain his eyesight, temporarily blinded by the flash bulb, which hummed as it recharged itself. "I can't see anything."

"That will be the flash that went off in your face," said Raymond. "Happens to you every time you get your passport photo done, doesn't it, Maureen?"

She didn't like this revelation. "I don't remember."

"You do! We had to borrow that wheelchair to get you out of the kiosk in Boots? The queue was backing up."

"I don't remember."

"The manager made you lie down next to the verruca plasters, and she lifted your legs above your head?"

"I said, Raymond, I don't remember."

"You do! When the photos came through, you were blinking on them all, so you had to close your eyes when we went through passport control to prove it was you?"

"She doesn't remember, Raymond," said Tash, tiring of the story. "Shall we go over the plan one more time?"

"You can't go over a plan one more time if you haven't gone over it the first time," said Jamie, his vision slowly returning.

"Great point. We're really making progress. OK. What's the plan?"

"Well, we agreed that we would each take a door to the bank and each take a photograph of anyone that looks like that baddie coming in or out with loads of money," said Raymond.

"I'm actually getting used to the word baddie now," said Tash. "It kind of fits with us being in a Scooby Doo van and everything."

Jamie raised his hand and immediately regretted it after it smacked into the campervan ceiling. "Ow!"

"You don't need to raise your hand, Jamie," said Tash.

"If we get a photo of this woman, how will the police know that we took it today and not last year?"

"What would it matter?" asked Maureen.

"We're trying to prove that she didn't die in a fire last October. So, we need to prove it's today."

Jamie had a point. Unlike 2020, a photo didn't have a location and date virtually attached to it. They could have faked the whole thing.

"We use a newspaper!" said Raymond. "We use Jesus' newspaper!"

"The one we're sat on?" said Maureen.

"Yes," said Raymond, extracting the front page from beneath him.

What had once displayed a baffling array of Spanish headlines and a photo of two men you wouldn't want to meet on a dark night was now a shredded pulp. What wasn't in his hands was now imprinted in reverse on his white Speedos.

Tash was next to retrieve hers – with the same result, then Maureen too. Jamie's wasn't there; he must have taken his with him and lost it on his little recce.

"Does anyone have a copy of *Grazia* or this week's *Angling Times*?" said Tash.

"It's dissolved with all the pool water," said Jamie.

Raymond turned around and caused the siblings to recoil. His face was blotchy red, and his arms and neck matched it.

"I have an idea!" he said.

"Are you alright?" said Tash, causing Maureen to look at her husband for the first time since poo-gate.

"Raymond, you've turned into Frankenstein!"

"Frankenstein's monster," said Jamie.

"Not now, Jamie. It's not a good time."

Raymond pulled down his sun visor to see the mirror, and a spider fell into his lap.

"Spider!" said Jamie calmly.

"I look like Frankenstein!" said Raymond.

"Frankenstein's monster," said Jamie.

"Still not a good time," said Tash.

Maureen removed her flamenco shoe and smashed Raymond in the groin.

Twice.

And then a third time.

"Got it," she said, examining the underside of her shoe before handing it to her husband. "Get rid of that."

He was frozen from his attack but silently took the shoe and opened his window to flick the spider off. He didn't check his mirror, so didn't see the cyclist that bounced off his fist and slid along the melting tarmac of Carrer de Sant Antoni.

"Cyclist," said Tash, a little too late.

"He's a pedestrian now," said Jamie.

"Can I have my shoe back, please, Raymond? Stop messing about," said Maureen, as Raymond stared in disbelief at the man on the tarmac, his arm still hanging out of his driver's window. "Is anyone else hot?"

"That will be the chlorine burns," said Jamie, examining his arms and then his sisters.

Happily, they both seemed fine.

"He's always had susceptible skin," said Maureen. "He got psoriasis from the Pontins showers at Prestatyn."

"We don't know it was from the showers, Maureen."

"Twelve hours on a coach, and all we come home with was a bag of Kwik Save fudge and athlete's foot," said his wife.

If she could have folded her arms again, she would. But they were already folded, and a double fold would have been impossible, especially in that dress.

"Britain's first Kwik Save!" said Raymond with a massive smile and knowing nod to the passengers in the back. "Prestatyn! Opened 1965!"

"I'd clap, but we'd both know I was faking it," said Tash with an unimpressed glare.

"Is anyone worried about the man on the road?" said Jamie, straining to look between the front seats.

"He's up!" said Tash, and she was right.

The elderly gentleman shuffled towards the campervan before stopping to pick up his bike. It hadn't fallen onto its side as it was attached to a two-wheeled cart which it dragged behind. This grey-haired local looked like he might live in it; it held two decrepit tartan fabric suitcases and a blanket. On top of these, a solitary orange had survived the impact of the collision. Thirty-nine others, and a sign *Para La Venta,* littered the street.

"Sorry about that," said Raymond out of his window, still pained from the groin assault. "Spot of bother with a spider."

The man stared at him and grimaced, showing a massive gap in his upper teeth, so Raymond tried his best spider impression, which made the man hurry to collect his spilt fruit before pedaling away very quickly.

"There's a shop down there," said Jamie, pointing along the road to the next junction. "I bet that sells newspapers."

"Jamie, that is a great idea," said Tash. "Off you go, Raymond."

"What? Why me?"

"Because you can ask them if they have any cream for your new disease! It has a green cross look!" said Tash.

"What does that mean?" he replied.

"It means pharmacy," said Tash before turning to her brother for support. "Really? They didn't know that in 1984?"

"Eighty-five," said Jamie. "It's Live Aid day."

Raymond considered this as he examined his face again. "I could use some cream."

"And don't forget the newspapers either," said Maureen. "Don't get any tabloids; I wouldn't be seen dead reading those."

"Right, Maureen."

"I'd prefer the *Mail* if they have it."

"No shit," said Tash; Maureen's information source suddenly made perfect sense.

"We don't need to read them," said Jamie. "Just get whatever they have. There might not be much choice."

"Yes, he's right," said Maureen. "Off you go."

Then she leant over to open Raymond's door for him.

As he set off down the road, the sun reflecting off his pasty white and blistered red body, Maureen beeped the horn to get his attention. He turned to walk back in the relentless dry heat, losing the same flip flop twice as he tried to get it to stay on his foot despite the sticky sock.

As he reached his window, he leaned in and smiled, despite his exhaustion.

"What is it, darling?"

"Walk quicker than that; we're in a hurry."

Chapter Eighty-Four

"What did I say about *The Mirror*?" said Maureen, trying to turn down 'White Wedding' on the radio and failing.

"There wasn't much choice, Maureen!" said Raymond. He'd picked up a large bottle of water and helped himself first, which was most out of character, but clearly indicated how he was handling the temperature.

"Well, I'm not holding a tabloid newspaper to save anyone's life," she replied, handing it back to him. "It's not even today's edition!"

"None of them are; they're shipped over here apparently," he replied, handing over two identical copies of *Smash Hits* for her to pass to Tash and Jamie.

"These are the same," said Maureen.

"And?" asked Raymond.

"Why did you buy two of the same magazines?" she asked.

"Because they didn't have four," he replied. It was a simple decision as far as he was concerned.

"You're not listening. Why two the same?"

"We're not going to read them, are we? We're just going to try to incorporate them into the photo we take of the baddie!"

No one even flinched at the word baddie anymore. Their bizarre existence was becoming normalised.

"Is that Boy George?" she asked, with disdain in her voice, glancing at the large photo on the cover.

"It's Lady Di, isn't it?" said Raymond squinting through his closing eyes, which had reacted badly to the chlorinated pool. "It's a lovely umbrella. I like that yellow."

Maureen handed the magazines to Jamie; he kept one and passed the other to his sister, who examined the pop star's face, and the title alongside it. "You were both wrong. 'Howard Jones escapes the British Summer'."

"What's this?" said Maureen taking the final glossy magazine.

"I don't know. The only thing I could find with July on it," said Raymond, flicking through his *Daily Mirror*. *Intasun* were offering two weeks in Corfu for £129. Wherever that was.

"*Cheri* magazine," read Maureen. "A view to a thrill: Under the covers with 007's boldest bedroom beauties."

Jamie and Tash flicked through their magazines.

"Why is she bending over?" said Maureen before flicking to page two and reading from the contents. "Getting wet with the saltiest sea-fairer."

"Is Corfu in Spain?" asked Raymond. "It looks just as unpleasant."

"We're not in Spain. We're in Mallorca," said Maureen, flicking over the page after licking her finger and thumb like the lady in the bank. She always felt this was a sign of a successful employee and made a mental note to do it more in company from now on.

"We're in Menorca, which is part of Spain," said Tash, without even looking up.

"What are Duran Duran up to?" read Jamie.

"Swinging Club Tara lets us inside," read Maureen.

"Green Gartside is a beautiful man," said Tash. "Why don't I know more about Green Gartside? I mean, it's not even an opinion; that is a very beautiful man." She held it up to Jamie, who nodded briefly.

"Shouldn't it be what *is* Duran Duran up to?" said Jamie. "Duran Duran *is* a band."

Then Maureen screamed and hurled her magazine over her head, narrowly missing Tash but hitting Jamie square in the face.

"What is it? Another spider?" asked Raymond, nervously eying up every inch of his wife's dress and praying it hadn't landed in his lap again.

Maureen glared at him, her face glowing red.

"You filthy, filthy man!"

Raymond turned and looked over his shoulder. Jamie had opened Maureen's magazine and turned it on its side to examine the full centre spread. She was called Susie, and she had no hang-ups.

"You can have *Smash Hits*, Maureen," he said without looking up. She took it from him, pausing only to clout her husband over the head with it.

"What time is it, Raymond, and I mean here now in Menorca, today? Now. Here. Now. Where we are. Not New York. Not London. Now. Here," asked Tash.

Raymond squinted through his closing eyes to read the time. "We have fourteen minutes until midday."

"Then we should get into position," said Jamie, turning the magazine the other way around for a moment to better understand what Suzie was doing.

Tash leant in. "You don't mean that position, do you?"

Jamie closed the magazine and smiled. "No."

"Okay, I tossed a coin, and here's where everyone is going to be," said Tash.

"When did you toss a coin?" asked Raymond.

"When you were gone."

"I didn't see you toss a coin," said Jamie.

"What coin? Raymond has the kitty," said Maureen.

"The what?" asked Tash.

"The kitty."

"The hell's a kitty?" asked Tash.

"It's all our spending money, pooled together," explained Maureen. "Whoever never heard of a kitty?"

"I think we're getting distracted a bit. We have thirteen minutes now," said Raymond.

"And how do you get four outcomes from tossing one coin?" asked Jamie. "The more I think about it, I can't see how you could do that with one coin toss."

Tash glared at him. This seemed to silence the others.

"Me and Jamie will do this one," she said, gesturing at the bank next to them, "and Terry and June can do that one." She pointed to the bank further along the road.

"Why is she calling us Terry and June, Raymond?" asked Maureen.

"Well, everybody loves Terry and June, don't they?" He meant it.

"Maureen and me, stay on this road; you two cover the back," said Tash.

Raymond nodded. "Right. Unless you'd rather I took you around the back door, Maureen?"

Tash looked at her brother, and they suppressed a forbidden giggle.

"No, I'll stick with the plan," replied Maureen.

"Right. Discreetly take a photo of anyone that looks like the baddie," said Raymond. He paused for effect here, "And try and get your newspaper or magazine in the shot."

"How will we know when she's been?" asked Jamie.

"Because we'll see her," replied Tash.

"I mean, how will we know if she's been and one of the others has seen her?" he asked.

"Do you mean, how long should we wait until we reconvene?" asked Tash.

"No, but that's an okay question for you to answer."

"How about we have a signal if we see her, so the others know?" said Raymond. "Like a whistle?"

"Other than *The Masked Dancer*, that might be the worst idea I ever heard in my whole life," said Tash.

"Why?" said Maureen, happily able to fold her arms as she had unfolded them a little earlier.

"Let's assume Raymond spots her at his allocated door? She sees a man who looks like he's eaten a bee pizza, waving a dirty magazine at her whilst whistling and trying to take her photo?"

"I thought Jamie was taking the dirty magazine?" asked Raymond.

"I still think she might find it unusual behaviour," replied Tash. "Look, if I stand here, I can see Jamie down there, so if Jamie sees her, he can give me the thumbs up. I can signal Maureen, who's outside that door, and she can gesture to Raymond, who is around the side. We have it covered."

"Okay, I like this new plan," said Raymond.

"It's the first plan," said Jamie. "We didn't have a plan, and now we do. This is the first plan."

"Eleven minutes," said Raymond squinting at his watch.

"How do I use this?" said Maureen, holding up her Instamatic.

"Point and click," said Raymond.

"Does it wind itself on?" she asked. "I can't do winders. They're too fiddly."

"The bank – the door's opening!" said Raymond, pointing at the front entrance of Banco Central. The heavy door cast a shadow over the person waiting to depart, and all four in the van raised their cameras to their eyes, waiting to start papping.

"She's early! Surely, she would be going in now, not coming out?" said Maureen.

A young lady dressed in the bank's corporate colours stepped outside and leaned against the wall before lighting a cigarette.

"It's someone that works at the bank," said Jamie.

"Yes," said Tash.

"She's smoking a cigarette."

"Yes."

"Maybe she's not allowed to smoke inside."

"Maybe."

They didn't notice the yellow Raleigh Burner that pedalled slowly towards them. Or the ten-year-old boy riding it and examining the four people inside the VW campervan.

He mounted the pavement and stopped alongside Maureen's window before knocking on it.

"Oh, my lord, a beggar!" said Maureen. "Raymond, do something."

The boy knocked again.

"Quickly! Do something! Beggar!"

"Like what?" asked Raymond.

"Throw something. I don't know."

"You want me to throw something at a child?"

"He's not a child. He's like one of those small baddies from horror films!"

"Small baddies?" replied Tash.

"Like the man in the white suit!" She was very stressed. "The one that shouts, '*The plane, the plane!*'"

"That's *Love Boat*," said Raymond, "that's not a horror film."

"Are you thinking of dwarfism?" said Jamie.

"No, there aren't six others," said Maureen. "I know exactly what I mean!"

The boy knocked again, and Maureen let out an involuntary squeal.

"A lot to unpack here," said Tash. "But I guess we should start with the fact that he's a child."

Raymond leant over his wife and wound down her window.

The boy's skin was the kind of beautiful colour Tash never achieved in a fortnight of sunbathing. His hair was glossy chestnut brown. The whites of his eyes were electrically bright. All in all, it made her conclude that youth was genuinely wasted on the young.

He held up a ruffled piece of brown paper – possibly ripped from a carrier bag - with a hand-written scrawl across one side in red crayon. Raymond took it from him.

"If he wants directions, he's asking the wrong people," said Jamie, "Tash once had to spend the night in Ikea."

"Those arrows on the floor are bullshit, and you know it," said Tash. "Just designed to keep you inside."

"What does it say?" asked Maureen, "is it in foreign?"

"We're the foreigners, Maureen," said Raymond.

"Don't be absurd, Raymond," she replied. "We're British. Everyone else is foreign."

Raymond held the paper at arms-length until his focal point kicked in.

He couldn't comprehend what he was reading.

Well, he could, as the words made perfect sense, but he couldn't understand why they were on this old carrier bag in newly pressed crayon.

"Can you hear me?" said Maureen. "What does it say?"

Raymond read the words to the rest of the van.

"Raymondo, Jamie, Tish and old lady."

Everyone exchanged glances, finishing on the humiliated flamenco dancer in the passenger seat.

"Who do they mean?" asked Maureen.

Then the child on the street addressed them in a clipped English accent.

"You come with me now?"

He pointed in the direction of the shop down the road where Raymond had just acquired the magazines and newspaper.

"Oh my God, the stolen money," said Maureen. "You've got us arrested!"

"He's about nine, Maureen," said Raymond. "And how would he know our name?"

"That's where I was right, you see! He's a man! A midget one, and he's going to throw us all in prison."

Jamie's hand was in the air, as far as the van allowed.

"You can't say midget, it's offensive."

"Everything seems offensive where you've come from," said Maureen. "Is it possible to exist for one hour without upsetting anybody?"

Jamie and Tash considered this before muttering together, "No, not really."

"Now," said the child. "Par favor? Muy importante!" He was shuffling from one foot to another like he needed the loo. His grey cotton shorts were covered in red dust from playing on the cool ground beneath the shelter of pine trees. His ripped t-shirt was once black, and the logo was instantly recognisable to Tash and Jamie, albeit in a different language, *Regreso Al Futuro*. The DeLorean beneath was starting to peel off.

Raymond looked at the others.

"This is a tricky one, isn't it? How does he know our names?"

"Shall we have a vote?" said Tash.

"On whether he's a man?" asked Jamie.

Tash watched the boy blow an impressive bubble with a Hubba Bubba that he'd been gifted less than an hour ago. Until then, he'd yet to try this American non-stick variant and was now loving every minute.

"The only man I know who looks that young is Ant or Dec, and they travel in pairs," said Tash.

"What about Stephen Mulhern? He looks about twelve," said Jamie.

"Fair point, but he always travels with Ant & Dec. Besides, this isn't Stephen Mulhern. He's not wearing enough make-up. I think we can say this is a boy. Shall we vote?"

No-one answered.

"A vote on having a vote?" asked Jamie.

"I just wanted the one vote, to be honest, Jamie. Do we follow José Krankie? Or do we tell him to do one?

"Par favor?" repeated the boy as he opened Maureen's door. She recoiled again, but they could all see a desperate plea in his eyes.

"Come on then, but we need to be quick," said Raymond, before repeating this in his own version of Spanish to the boy. Which was essentially repeating it all in English but much louder. And adding some hand gestures, which translated better as:

Chest

Wife's chest

Bewildered people in the back

Baby

Let your fingers do the walking through the yellow pages

Helicopter.

He ended by tapping his wrist and then wished he'd tapped the one wearing the watch, but the moment had gone. He did, however, remember to lock the campervan as they set off at a mad pace behind the boy on the bike.

Which was good, as it still contained the illicit bounty of pesetas.

Chapter Eighty-Five

The boy took a right into the shop immediately before the magazine store, and Raymond breathed a sigh of relief, checked his convoy behind him, before following the child inside.

He hated fly screens, but not as much as they hated him. The multi-coloured tassels of this one seemed to loop around each of his limbs and flick their ends into his eyes and mouth. It was disappointing that Maureen, Tash and then Jamie negotiated the plastic screen effortlessly whilst he still struggled to release a bottle green coloured strip from his flip-flop.

Inside was dark, as it was no coincidence that the design of these small-windowed buildings ensured they remained as cool as possible on such baking hot days.

As their eyes grew accustomed to the cool interior, they saw a solitary lady in her sixties spying them suspiciously from behind her chilled fresh fish counter. Her white apron seemed to demonstrate excellent attention to hygiene – besides the blood stains – and sweat was sticking her dyed hair to her temples.

Shelves inside the cool cabinet were laden with white fish, prawns, white bait, and roaming lobster. On the counter behind were rows of Xoriguer gin in flagon-styled terracotta bottles, complete with a small thumb loop. The dusty bottles at the front hid the newer pristine dark green glazed ones behind. Above them, a car radio was wired to a solitary damaged speaker, making 'Axel F' sound like it was being played on a toaster.

"If this kid takes us to his room to show us some Madonna posters, I'm gonna be well pissed off," said Tash.

The boy stood by another fly screen at the rear of the tiny shop, behind which were ascending stone steps. He waited for the elderly lady to finish filling a large plastic bucket with water from a hose and then took it from her, sloshing it across the tiled floor. He gestured for them to follow up the stairs, and they did, taking care not to slip on the water that spilt over the sides of the bucket.

"I think in terms of weirdness, this might be topping everything we've done so far," said Jamie.

"Is this legal?" asked Maureen.

"Is what legal?" asked Tash.

"Aren't we trespassing?"

"Well, no. He's invited us up," said Raymond.

"Has water boarding been invented yet?" asked Jamie.

"Surfing?" asked Raymond, catching his breath as the steep steps took their toll.

"No, it's a way of getting people to say stuff you want them to say," said Jamie. "With water."

"Sounds like *It's A Knockout*. Do they dress up as fruit and fat foreigners?" asked Maureen.

"Jamie, you've started something again. Let's park it," said Tash. "How long do we have Raymond?"

He looked at his watch. "Eight minutes."

"What?" said Jamie. "This is ridiculous. Let's tell him we'll come back later. We're cutting this too fine."

The child opened a door that flooded the gloomy stairwell with brilliant Mediterranean sunshine, and they squinted to save their confused eyes. They continued to walk through it and found themselves on a flat roof, two floors above the shop. He gestured for them to follow as best he could, now using both hands to steady his bucket of water.

"I hope this isn't a lace factory," said Raymond. "We fell for that in Salou."

"A what?" said Jamie.

"They lure you in with a free glass of sangria, then tell you about the history of lace over the past two hundred years. In the end, you buy a dress just so they'll let you out."

"That would explain Maureen's wardrobe," said Tash, following Raymond onto the roof. "Joke!" She added quickly, as things were too confusing to start bickering right now.

Then they stopped.

Sitting on the roof, with his back to them, was a rotund sunburnt man, dressed in a sand-coloured safari suit with loop fastened turned-up shorts. He glanced slightly over his shoulder at the boy and gestured for him to hurry up.

The boy approached the man, then stood with his young legs firmly braced straight and lifted the bucket before emptying the complete contents over the man's head.

"Ahhhhhhhhhhhhhhhh!" sighed the man with utter delight. "Gracias, amigo."

He delved into his chest pocket and extracted a packet of Hubba Bubba, shook it dry and then removed one before tossing it into the air.

The boy caught it with delight, unwrapped it and hurled it into his mouth.

"Señor," said the boy, through his salivating chews, "Los Ingleses."

"Si," said the man, rubbing the water from his chin.

"Aqui," said the boy.

The man turned fully around and leapt to his feet.

Maureen screamed.

"The murderer!"

Chapter Eighty-Six

"Well done, well done," said the man as he extracted a thousand peseta note and handed it to the boy, who couldn't believe what he was holding. He also handed over the remains of his Hubba Bubba packet.

"You must be Raymondo?" said the man, happily holding out his sweaty hand.

"State your purpose," said Raymond, blocking his wife from the curious wet man. Upon further inspection, he looked like he'd been crying and had a split bridge of his nose with blood smeared from it. Tash snorted in hysterics at Raymond's highwayman approach.

"Excuse me?" said the man.

"We're British. If anything happens to us, there will be a search party by sundown," continued Raymond.

"Sundown?" said Tash. "Is this *Brokeback Mountain*?"

"A search party?" said the bewildered man.

"I think by the end of the day is pretty optimistic, given no one knows we're here," said Jamie.

"You must be Jamie," said the man, offering his hand to him now. Jamie waved awkwardly; he wasn't big on handshakes.

"Tish," said the man to Jamie's sister, offering a rejected hand again.

"Tash," she corrected him.

He turned to Maureen. "And I'm sorry, ma'am, I don't know your name."

"She's the old woman," said Jamie, pointing to the piece of brown paper in Raymond's hand.

"How do you know our names, and is this important?" asked Tash. "We need to do something in less than six minutes."

"Six minutes?" said the man. "I apologise. Jeez! How rude of me."

He looked kerfuffled.

"May I ask what?"

"Just something at midday," said Jamie.

"Midday?" said the man looking at his gold-coloured Seiko. "Who says it's midday?"

"Hitler," said Jamie.

The man glared at him.

"Long story," said Tash.

"It's five to eleven," said the man. "I triple-checked. GMT plus two."

They all looked at one another before stepping aside so the boy could go back downstairs.

"Jesus' van is on Spanish time," said Maureen. "Can't believe no one thought of that."

The wet man tried again.

"My name is Lieutenant Francis Duffy. I'm a friend of Martha."

They stared again.

"Boy, it's a hot one!" he said, staring at the impossibly perfect blue sky. "You can call me Frankie. A bit like the guy on your top!"

He pointed at Raymond's 'Frank Says' t-shirt, then glanced at his tight Speedos. He hadn't really taken in what they were wearing when they arrived, so he took a moment to absorb the authentic Andalusian splendour of Maureen's nylon flamenco outfit, then Tash's lace all-in-one affair, then finally Jamie's Bermudas, beneath his I ♥ MENORCA t-shirt which was now two inches shorter as he'd continue to fiddle with the loose cotton strand.

He hated to judge on first appearances, but on this occasion, he allowed himself.

God, the English are a bunch of unfathomable weirdos.

Chapter Eighty-Seven

The four of them, and baby Raymond, stood in a tiny square of shade that the stairhead walls cast onto the flat roof and glanced down at Duffy's colourful map, which lay open on the baking hot tiles.

"How do you know all this?" asked Tash suspiciously. "Martha gave all her notes to us."

"That's an excellent point, Tish. But she only needed to remember the time," said Duffy with a smile. "Midday."

"How do you figure that out?" said Jamie.

"She knew the date, July thirteenth; it's the day her parents were buried. She knew the town; it's the same name as her boyfriend."

"She has a boyfriend?" asked Jamie.

"Not a pleasant individual," said Duffy before continuing. "But that's her business. So anyways, all I needed to do was make enquiries about the banks. I came out last month, right after they set her date."

"They sentenced her?" said Jamie, his voice sounding hoarse.

"Not yet."

"So she's alive? Tell me she's alive?" asked Jamie. Tash took her hand from her son's legs and placed it on her brother's back.

"Of course, they set a date for the nineteenth of this month. That's Friday."

"To... do what?" said Jamie, but he couldn't finish the question.

Duffy shook his head. "A hearing date. She looks likely to lose and they'll sentence her then."

"The death sentence?" said Raymond.

"No! That won't happen!" Duffy kindly laughed and then thought again. "I mean, it might. The death penalty was rescinded, but New York State want it back. They have a crime problem. And they keep trying to bring back the chair or whatever. It won't happen. She'll probably just get fifty to a hundred."

"Fifty to a hundred what?" asked Tash.

"Years."

Everyone tried to take in this information.

"I supposed that's better than execution," said Tash.

"She's innocent," said Jamie.

"I know! But it's better that they don't kill her!"

"They won't do that," said Raymond. "He's just said that. They won't bring back the death penalty"

"I mean, they might," repeated Duffy. "If anyone manages it would be those guys. They got it past the Assembly and the Senate, but a couple of suits usually block it."

"Usually?" said Jamie.

"We probably don't need to worry."

"Probably?"

Duffy started to tear up. "She didn't do anything. She's a good kid."

This made the British awkward, particularly the eighties contingent. Men don't cry.

"That's why I need as many hands-on-deck as I can," said Duffy blowing his nose on a cotton handkerchief, then folding it over and looking awkward.

"That's not worked," he said. "Ooh, that's messy."

He tried refolding the snot-filled material, but it wasn't looking good.

"Does anyone got a Kleenex?"

Tash delved into baby Raymond's bag and cautiously offered a small handy pack wrapped in plastic.

"Thank you so much, Tish, my, that's so very kind." He started to pull them out one by one, and the crowd patiently waited as he cleaned his hands and nose. He stopped as he took another out of the pack.

"These feel a little damp?"

"It's balm," said Tash.

"Excuse me?"

"They have balm in them."

Duffy looked as baffled as Raymond and Maureen at this, but carried on.

"I have a mucus gland situation; the guys at Vermont Medical Center are a little baffled by it. Which is a worry, but it does mean that when they figure out what the hell is going on, I get the condition named after me. So, I guess I have that going for me." He handed the packet back to Tash, considerably depleted of tissues.

"You can keep that," she said.

"No, no, I couldn't possibly," said Duffy, holding out the snot-covered plastic.

"You absolutely could," said Tash.

"So, you have police here, too?" asked Jamie.

"Jesus, no!" said Duffy, immediately stopped in his flow by Maureen's visible flinch.

"Excuse me, is everything alright?" he asked.

Maureen nodded and folded her arms. Duffy continued.

"No, Tish, this is too complex. They're a corrupt bunch!" Then he instantly decided to caveat that remark. "Not me! Gosh no. There are some fine people in the force, but this is too risky to share until I get this sewn up. We! We get this sewn up."

With that, he stood up and waved across the street. Then he attempted a wolf whistle, but lots of spit came out and no sound.

"I have an issue with my saliva glands, too." He attempted again. Just more spit happened.

Tash placed her finger and thumb in her mouth and whistled so loudly that Maureen covered her ears. One block behind the row of shops in front, a thirty-something woman stood up and returned the American man's wave. She was beneath a white baseball cap with a red peak. If they were closer, they would see the *Los Angeles 1984* logo and Olympic rings embroidered on the front. She slunk back down as soon as she'd appeared.

"That's my daughter, Katie," said Duffy. "She's an old friend of Martha."

They all nodded as their confusion set in.

"There's just the two of you?" asked Maureen. "So, the American police are too busy to help? Or do they think she's guilty?"

"I don't trust anybody except family these days," said Duffy. "This whole thing got out of hand. But she spoke very highly of you guys."

Jamie's hand was in the air. Duffy noticed and glanced at Tash.

"Does he need to go to the bathroom or something?"

"He has a question."

"Why did you ask us up here if you have it all covered?" said Jamie.

"Well, I was hoping for some support, to be fair, but as it stands, you have blocked my view of one of the main doors to that bank. So that's the first thing that needs to be done."

"Are you going to arrest her?" asked Raymond. "You know, the baddie?"

"The what?" replied Duffy.

"The corrupt solicitor that stole Martha's money, are you going to arrest her?" asked Tash.

"I have no authority to do so. I can only hope to take photographic evidence of her presence today. I have the front doors covered, and Katie has the rear."

"Being in the air is a smashing idea," said Raymond. "Very much like Jim Bergerac might do!"

Duffy didn't understand Raymond, so he just stared at him for a moment.

"So, what do you need us to do?" asked Jamie.

"You need to blend in, to start with," said the lieutenant.

"Well, we've got that covered," said Maureen in her flamenco outfit. "What else?"

He glanced at her tap shoes and pulled his wet shirt away from his hot chest.

"Do you got cameras?"

They all held up their gadgets, and Jamie held up Anthony's large camera bag.

"May I ask where you acquired that, sir?"

"I sort of got it from a bird spotter. He loaned it to me. He works on Tower Bridge. He makes it go up and down. He works the night shift. He has photos of loads of birds around his office. He's from up north. Newcastle, I think."

Duffy was too polite to interrupt this tome of information, so he nodded politely at each fact.

"He's called Kenneth. He let me stay with him once. I did a poster and stuck it in his office window. We also," but he was interrupted.

"Jamie, Jamie! He's got enough info," said Tash.

Duffy walked to a pile of carrier bags on the roof and moved them to one side, revealing an identical camera case.

"This is yours, I believe."

Jamie stared at the man's bag and his.

Duffy zipped it open and pulled out an Olympus Trip. "This belong to your friend?"

Jamie nodded, and Raymond clapped before saying, "Oh, that's very clever! How did you do that?"

Jamie unzipped his camera case and lifted a Canon F-1, complete with a lens cover. As he pulled it out, two separate lenses fell onto the tiled floor, to the horror of Duffy.

"Careful, careful, careful," he muttered as he pounced to pick them up. He examined the long case that held the zoom lens and carefully peered inside. He breathed a sigh of relief. "We're good."

"Sorry," said Jamie, peering in. "Why do I have all these films too?"

It didn't take Maureen for Jamie to realise what had happened.

"He's the murderer!" she said through bated breath.

"Wow! Is he the guy that tried to sleep with you, Maureen?" said Tash before asking Duffy, "Are you staying in Binibeca?"

Duffy laughed. "My God, that was you?" he exchanged Kenneth's camera case with the one in Jamie's hands. "That's funny! I'm sorry to wake you. I was told the apartment was available from 9am."

"We overslept," said Raymond. "See, Maureen! He doesn't want to sleep with you! We said he wouldn't want to do that! She thought you wanted to sleep with her! I'm so pleased you're not a murderer!"

"You scared me!" said Duffy, laughing. "I dropped my camera, and it was dark, and..."

He gestured at two similar camera cases.

"In fact, our suitcases are still in my car. We didn't have any place to change," he gestured at his clothes. "I've had these bad boys on since Madrid."

"What happened to your nose?" asked Maureen, mindful that his split nose was now drying. "Did you get in a fight?"

"There was an altercation, ma'am. I can't lie about that."

They all stared at him. He was ready to give his backstory.

"The boy with the air con," he explained. He was leaning in for effect.

"The bucket?" said Tash.

"Yeah, the bucket," he replied. "I said I'd give him a piece of gum per bucket." He gestured at a galvanised steel bucket on its side on the roof. "His grip could have been better the first time around."

They all seemed relieved.

"It was the boy and the bucket, Maureen," said Raymond. "I thought he was another baddie!"

"So, we just walk around casually and take photos if we see this unpleasant lady?" said Maureen, pointing to the mug shot of Bee that sat next to the large map.

"She's not stupid," said Duffy. "She might not look like that anymore. I suggest we take photos of anyone we see coming out of that bank. Especially if they're carrying a lot of money."

"What if she kills one of us?" asked Maureen.

"That's highly unlikely," replied Duffy. "She's trying to set up a new life here, probably with a new identity. The last thing she needs is to get arrested."

"How will you see her from up here?" asked Jamie.

"Me and Katie got these zoom lenses." He held up the one Jamie dropped. "We could see a pimple on her nose with these."

"So, we're looking for a pimple-nosed lady?" asked Raymond.

"Figure of speech. But the main thing is, we photograph anyone and everyone."

"Then what?" asked Tash.

"Then we meet up and share the photos. See what we've got."

They all nodded and walked over to examine Duffy's vast map. He was very thorough.

"What's the plan then?" said Raymond, squinting down at the myriad of lines, symbols, and letters. "Where are we on here?"

"Excuse me?" asked Duffy, looking down at the glossy paper.

"This is here, is it?" asked Raymond, "Sant Lluìs?"

"Oh! I see!" said Duffy. "No, that's a map of Disneyland, California."

He leant in to admire it with the others.

"We're thinking of going next month. It's their thirtieth year. They had a two-hour special on NBC. Cool, huh?"

"You're planning a trip to Disneyworld?" asked Tash.

"Disneyland. Disneyworld is in Orlando. It was Katie's idea. Something to take our mind off poor Martha if today doesn't work out, you know?"

They all looked at him in amazement, was he starting to cry?

"I love that kid. She doesn't deserve any of this."

Tash considered resting her hand on his shoulder, but it was wet with sweat and water.

"But it will work out!" he said, perking up. "It will work! Now we have you guys on board too! Probably. I mean, we'd guessed odds of like twenty to twenty-five per cent success; but with you, you know, we've got to be nudging like thirty-five, maybe forty."

They stared again, and he walked to the top of the stairs and yelled down into the darkness through the open door.

"Hey, boy! Agua par favor!"
Then he remembered his manners.
"Does anyone else want a bucket of the cold stuff?"
They shook their heads.
"Boy, it's a hot one!"

Chapter Eighty-Eight

"He's a strange man," said Raymond, reversing the campervan into a side street.

"He's American," said Maureen.

"It feels better to have someone else working on this, " Jamie said.

"In between his holiday plans," said Tash, feeding baby Raymond from a bottle of formula milk she had warmed in a Pyrex bowl of water loaned to her by the fishmonger.

"Good news about the clocks, too," said Jamie. "We could have used all our film up one hour too soon."

"I don't see how things can go wrong now," said Raymond in a very positive manner. "Can you lower your head, Jamie, so that I can see?"

"Do I just click this?" asked Maureen turning around to Tash and Jamie whilst squashing Dudley's Polaroid Instamatic to her face.

"Cyclist," said Tash before a thud struck the reversing van, causing Maureen to accidentally take a photo, flashing Jamie in the face.

"Pedestrian," said Jamie blinking madly.

"Your second cyclist knocked over, Raymond. Shame Anthony's not here; I bet there's a badge for that."

"No, it's not," said Jamie, looking through the rear window. "It's his first."

"Same guy?" said Tash. "You did the double, Raymond! Normally you have to drive around for ages to find the same cyclist to knock over."

"You need to be careful, love. There aren't as many prints in those cameras," said Raymond, gesturing at her clunky Polaroid.

"Says the man who just knocked down a pensioner!" said Maureen, turning back into her seat and flicking the dispensed photo into the footwell.

They watched in horror as the elderly man climbed up off the road and again restacked the remnants of his already damaged fruit onto his mobile home before pedalling slowly past the gap alongside the camper. The passengers averted their gaze as he offered them all his middle finger on his way past. He also ensured that the steel brake handle scraped the entire length of the camper on the way past, an unmistakable sound that they all heard beneath Howard Jones reassuring them that 'Things Could Only Get Better.' As the old man set off onto the main road, his dwindling pile of squashed oranges started to wobble, and some more rolled onto the melting tarmac.

"You see, I'd have a little box to stop them rolling off," said Raymond. "Something to hold them in. Maybe a little timber frame."

"Maybe he'll consider one tomorrow. If he doesn't die in the night from his injuries," said Tash.

"Three minutes," said Jamie looking at the VW clock. "Come on. Let's do this."

Chapter Eighty-Nine

They were in position very quickly, with Tash remaining inside the camper to finish baby Raymond's lunch. She'd nestled his head in her camera-holding arm, and her other hand held his bottle in place.

She looked along the side street to Jamie and saw him standing very suspiciously and fiddling again with his frayed t-shirt.

"Act natural," she said along the empty street.

"What?" he replied.

"Shhh! Act natural, and stop pulling at your t-shirt. It's disintegrating!"

Jamie tried one more time to snap the loose material hanging in a massive loop and then thought better of it. His top had indeed unravelled, and he was now standing down a side street clutching a pornographic magazine and wearing a crop t-Shirt with I ♥ MEN printed across his chest. He took a photo of a stray dog.

"Just people! Take loads, but just people!"

He nodded his understanding.

Raymond was saying his goodbyes to Maureen along the road and gestured as discreetly as he could to Tash that they had two minutes until the ETA of Bee to collect her millions. He did this by putting his camera under one arm, his *Daily Mirror* between his legs and then holding up two fingers. One on each hand, a method she'd never seen before.

Just in case she hadn't seen him or counted his fingers (she had, he was less than fifty yards away), he decided to hold his open hand way above his head and shout 'two' at her down the road. Followed by a thumbs up. Tash nodded as discreetly as possible, hoping he would soon piss off around the back.

He did, leaving his flamenco wife to cover the front door of Sa Nostra bank. Tash caught Maureen looking at her reflection in a bakery window and was delighted to see that she liked what she saw. She had a slender frame, and the dress was absurd, but Maureen was having a moment of self-appreciation, and Tash was delighted to have witnessed it.

Maureen stared down at her Polaroid and tried a few more dummy shots of the bank door whilst holding the masthead of *Smash Hits* 3rd-16th July 1985 in the frame. It was trickier than she had imagined.

"Hola!" came a familiar voice.

Tash spun around to see Julian smiling at her through the open van window. In his hand were countless bags of half chickens, each freshly plucked and butchered.

"Hi!" Tash surprised herself at how loud and giddy her voice sounded.

"Are you broken again? I give you a lift to the apartamentos?"

He gestured at his rusty white Seat parked outside the chicken shop, then bent down to remove the ignition key from the top of the front wheel.

He opened his door and climbed inside. "Until we meet again?"

"Adios!" she replied and giggled again.

He smiled, started the engine, and drove away.

"Giggly prick, shoot me now," said Tash to herself.

She turned to see Jamie photographing a couple of teenagers walking in his direction. She suddenly realised that her heart was in her chest. This was quite an exciting assignment. Why the hell had she been distracted by that chef? This was important. Martha's life could depend on her actions over the following minutes. She hoped Maureen hadn't spotted her giggling stupidly at Julian. She glanced down the road to see if Maureen had crossed her arms at her, but no, she had relocated to a discreet position and was ready to take photos of anyone that passed through the bank door at any time.

This felt good. Tash was finally doing something that felt right. Not only was she hoping to save a life, but she was also righting a wrong and working towards a lifetime of happiness for her brother. She also realised how much she was enjoying being part of a team. That was a new one on her. Then the bank door opened, and the silhouette of a large woman filled the doorway. She raised her camera and waited.

Chapter Ninety

"So, if you see someone walking a dog, but the dog's off the lead, and the dog starts doing its business on the grass behind them... And the owner doesn't see... Do you say something?" asked Raymond, still amazed about what the future held for humanity.

He could see Jamie along the back road, and between casually photographing every person that passed by, they had managed to find a volume level to maintain a chat to fill the time. They were nearing their second hour of work and had found modest areas of shade to protect their skin from the blistering sun.

"Usually, I sort of smile and point behind them, and when they see, they walk back and bag it up," said Jamie.

"And they literally pick it up?" Raymond's expression was pure disbelief.

"Yeah. They carry dog poo bags in their pockets."

Raymond was shaking his head in wonder. "So, what does the parkkeeper do with his spare time?"

"Parkkeeper?" said Jamie. "No, we don't have them."

"Who locks the parks at night then?"

"No one."

Raymond was struggling to imagine this chaos. Then he had a hideous thought.

"What if the dog has an upset tummy?"

"You mime."

"Mime?" asked Raymond.

"Yeah. You open a bag and pretend to pick it up so other dog walkers don't judge you."

People bagging up dog shit in 2020 was mind-blowing for Raymond. The future of his country sounded like another planet.

"And they still show *Dad's Army*?" said Raymond.

"Yes," said Jamie, itching a mosquito bite on his knee. "*Blade Runner* was way off. Although we do have electric cars."

"You're pulling my leg, now!" said Raymond; he was no fool.

"No. We do. Electric ones."

"Well, how far can you go before unplugging it? We struggle on the stairs with Maureen's Hoover, and that's after I extended the cable with a kit from Rumbelows."

"We're done!" came a familiar voice.

Duffy was standing behind Raymond with his camera around his neck. The zoom lens looked absurd in length.

"You found her?" said Jamie from along the back road.

"Who knows?" said Duffy. "We need to see what we all got. But the banks are closing now until Monday."

"I could use a drink," said Raymond, trying to separate his sweaty t-shirt from his ample tummy.

"Great call, buddy," said Duffy. "Meet you both around the front. Take it from there."

Chapter Ninety-One

"We always use Truprint," said Raymond. "Very reliable, and you get a free film with your prints."

"They are worth waiting that bit longer for," agreed Maureen. "They're not very large, but if you pay an extra seventy-nine pee, they make them all bigger for you."

They were standing in a row outside the fishmongers. The American glanced up and smiled as his daughter joined them. She was walking slowly along the road on the shady side, and her flip-flops made the very sound that named them as she got closer.

"Hey Katie, these are our English friends!"

Katie looked hot. She had been in a spot with no natural shade, and two hours of midday sun had burnt her nose. She wore a lemon-coloured t-shirt with rolled-up sleeves revealing white tea-bag styled material in the lining, which contrasted sharply with her lobster red arms. Her pleated white shorts gave way to similarly red legs. The orange sponge ear protectors of her Walkman headphones slid off her head and around her neck. Curt Smith was silenced as she clicked stop on the machine attached to her belt, but he was right; everybody *did* want to rule the world.

"Hey," she said before asking if her father had water.

He nodded and shouted "Agua?" through the fly screen before turning back to the others.

"Raymondo says he has a developer guy for the prints," he said to his daughter.

"What about our man?" said Katie.

"Well, he says he's reliable and quick," he replied.

Raymond was delighted to be someone with a 'developer guy'. It made him feel very important.

"How long will they take?" asked Katie.

"Well, they say two weeks, but they're usually sooner, and postage is included," said Raymond, standing up as straight as he could. God, it felt good to be part of a well-oiled machine. Duffy and his daughter stared at this blotchy Englishman. Suddenly, Raymond felt his speech hadn't gone as well as he might have expected.

"And they give you advice stickers, too," said Maureen. "If you've used too much flash or something like that."

"Yes, or if the subject was moving too much, sort of thing," agreed Raymond.

"Don't they sentence Martha in six days?" asked Tash.

"That is the plan," said Duffy, just as a bucket of water emptied itself onto his head and into his partially opened camera.

"Jesus!" he shouted, spinning around to the child holding an empty bucket. "To drink! To drink! Agua to drink! For the lady!"

Tash's nostril started to flare again as she held in a laugh. She didn't dare look at her brother.

"Hold it up, hold it up!" said Katie, taking the camera off her father to let any water out whilst also covering the film from the sunlight. A Pentax hung from a strap around her neck.

"It is very hot," said Raymond, suddenly looking pale. "Is anyone else hot?" He'd started to see stars.

"Are you alright, Raymond?" asked Maureen, concerned at his draining pallor.

"Sit down, Raymond," said Tash, lowering him down to the pavement. "He's dehydrated. I'll get us all a drink."

She stepped through the fly screen, followed by her brother. Jamie was back outside in a moment with a heavy bucket of ice which he tossed over Raymond's head, just as he'd seen the young boy do earlier.

The ice was mixed with gloopy red water, swiftly followed by fish guts, fish heads and litres of scaley scrapings, which coated Raymond's burnt and patchy skin.

"I see what I've done," said Jamie. "It looked like ice."

"Now that stinks," said Katie.

"I see what I've done," repeated Jamie. "It looked like ice. The fish stuff must have sunk. Underneath the ice. It looked like ice. A bucket of ice. I see what I've done."

A commotion inside turned into the fishmonger remonstrating with these tourists on the pavement before dousing Raymond in water from her hose pipe. She was reluctant to do this as water was scarce on the island, and wasting it in public on idiots was frowned upon.

"Sorry," said Raymond as the fish innards slid down his frazzled body onto the street.

The woman stopped and retired back inside, shaking her head.

"Here," said Tash, handing smoked brown drinking glasses filled with water to Raymond and Katie. They both thanked her and emptied them instantly.

"That's not coming off," said Katie, wiping her mouth and pointing at Raymond's cheeks.

"No, don't worry, that's what he looked like before," said Jamie. "He's got chlorine poisoning."

"No, but there are stripes of fish down his face," said the American.

Raymond laughed. "No, I can see the confusion, miss. But, I was attacked by an owl! They're talon marks!"

"Really?" said Katie, leaning in to inspect his face. "An owl attacked you?"

"Well, he was actually trying to catch some mice. You know, off my face, sort of thing."

"You're the unluckiest man I ever met," she replied.

"Thank you very much!" said Raymond, genuinely delighted to get an accolade of any kind, especially from a pretty stranger.

"Listen, Raymondo, your Rupert photo guy sounds great," said Duffy, "It was Rupert?"

"Truprint," said Raymond.

"Yes, him. But we don't have that kind of time."

"Of course," said Raymond. "I didn't know you had someone in mind. Is he in America?"

"Villacarlos," replied Duffy kindly.

"I don't know what that means," said Raymond.

"It's northeast, on the coast."

"Oh, it's here?" said Tash. "The day continues, lovely. And I thought we'd finished. Quick shower, paella, C5 back to Tower Bridge. But no, never that straightforward, is it?"

"Are you parked around here? We can follow you," said Raymond.

Duffy gestured at a white Seat 127 amongst the plethora of other white Seats along the road. Franco had created an alliance with Fiat in 1948 to enable his Spanish motor company to come to life. Throughout the sixties, seventies and much of the eighties, these Fiat clones were omnipresent throughout Spain and its islands and were invariably white.

"Or maybe that one," he pointed at another identical model. "Or is it that one?" He spotted another.

Katie tried the key in one of the car doors, and it opened.

"This is us," she said before a dog inside started barking madly. She slammed the door shut and watched as the mongrel leapt up and down to the half open window. She moved to the next car. It opened too.

"One key fits all," said Duffy. "But then, why steal one – when it's the same as all the others? That's communism for you."

"They're not communists," said Tash.

"Really? I thought Franco was like a dictator or something?"

"He's been dead ten years," said Raymond.

"But he has a point," said Jamie, suddenly realising the stark lack of diversity in the traffic.

"Quick as you can, then," said Tash, unable to restrain her irritation at Duffy. "We don't want to keep the printer waiting!"

"There's no rush," said Duffy. "They can't see us until ten pm."

"Oh wonderful, time to kill too," said Tash.

"I could use a swim, get me out of these clothes," said Katie, blowing down her t-shirt. It was purely functional but caught Jamie's attention, and Tash spotted it. The prick, weren't we here to save Martha's life so he could marry her?

"I'd love a swim," said Jamie, smiling in the general direction of Katie.

"You can swim in Vermont, Katie! We should immerse ourselves in the local culture, not water! We could check out the donkey sanctuary?" said Duffy. "We got a few hours to fill."

"Apparently, the gin factory is worth a visit, too?" said Raymond.

"I'd like to find somewhere that sells English aspirin," said Maureen.

"English aspirin?" asked Jamie.

"It's an English headache."

Tash stared at the others.

"I'll just keep it simple. Think I'll grab a coffee. Maybe get a tattoo."

Chapter Ninety-Two

The English and the Americans were gathering in the apartments' car park. The sky was morphing into an impossibly pink and blue blanket as the burnt orange sun set over the sea. Finally, they could enjoy the warmth it cast on them with little fear of burning to a crisp. Duffy and his daughter had indeed been allocated apartment P and had kindly offered one of the bathrooms to their new friends to freshen up and change. Sadly, none of the Brits were shrewd enough to explain why they would only do the former, as a change of clothes wasn't an option. Even if Raymond had wanted another crack at acquiring a holiday wardrobe for them all, Bini-Boutique had closed for the day. However, they were undoubtedly refreshed after a cold shower (necessity, not choice), even if they were wearing their curious daytime outfits again.

Duffy held a large *El Corte Inglés* carrier bag from his stop off in Madrid, rammed with their collective efforts of today's 'shoot'. He had brought six additional rolls of film each for him and Katie, and these nestled with the three films from Raymond, Jamie and Tash and the printed-out Polaroids from Maureen (she's managed just three photos but was adamant she'd not missed anyone, so no one complained). Duffy double-checked that he'd counted all the rolls correctly, then took a deep breath and looked at his watch.

"Is it far?" asked Raymond.

"Ten minutes," replied Duffy.

"Why are we leaving so early? I thought you said he couldn't see us until ten?" said Tash.

"He can't, but I made a dinner reservation; we gotta eat, right?"

"Ask him if they do Bernard Matthews crispy crumb turkey steaks, Raymond," said Maureen

"He speaks English, Maureen," said Raymond.

"It's a seafood restaurant," said Duffy. "On account of the island being surrounded by ocean."

"It's a sea," said Jamie.

"Excuse me?" said Duffy.

"The Mediterranean is a sea. Not an ocean."

"Is it wet?" said Duffy.

"Yes," said Jamie.

"Does it got fish in it?"

"Yes."

"So, what's the difference?"

"A sea is smaller and usually surrounded by land. It's often the way out to an ocean."

"Is anyone taking notes?" asked Tash.

"Well, I won't eat anything from the sea or ocean," said Maureen to Raymond. "Ask him if they do Findus crispy pancakes."

"He can hear you; he's listening now," said Raymond.

"You can have salad," said Duffy.

"Tell him they don't wash their salad," said Maureen. "I'll just order a banana. Something you can peel."

"This isn't Bhopal," said Duffy, referring to the horrific Union Carbide India incident last December when half a million locals were exposed to toxins after a gas leak.

"We'll find something," said Raymond. "Maybe Chef will have a tin of Smash."

Duffy felt in his pockets and looked deflated. "Shoot, I left the keys upstairs. Can we travel with you?"

"Of course," said Raymond.

Raymond didn't see Jamie raise his hand when he realised the Americans would be travelling with them. In fact, no one did, so with his arm still in the air, he followed their guests to the VW and waited patiently to climb into the back, seating himself alongside Katie and feeling the warmth of her leg against his. She wore peach-coloured cotton shorts, and one of those white mesh-styled crop vests like Madonna wore in the 'Borderline' video. It did a lousy job of hiding her bikini top beneath, which was fine because that was the point of the current fashion. Tash was the last one into the back, holding sleeping baby Raymond close to her chest. She flicked Jamie's knee, decidedly unhappy with his choice of seat. After all, this was about saving Martha's life, and he was behaving like a fourteen-year-old with his first crush.

"Shift. I'm sitting there," said Tash.

Jamie moved to sit on a floor cushion, still holding his arm in the air. He didn't hear his sister mutter "prick," as he passed her. It was only then that Katie spotted his hand.

"Are you okay?" she asked.

"Do you have a question, Jamie?" said Tash. "Or just a very sweaty pit?"

"Oh," he lowered his arm, forgetting it was raised. "No, it doesn't matter now."

The interior was dimly lit from the setting sun and amber streetlight, but Tash could tell from his demeanour that he was lying.

The moment Katie and her father started to squirm on the bench seat, the penny dropped.

"What the hell is this made from?" asked Duffy, fumbling between his legs at the seat pad filled with stolen Spanish currency. Soon this bruised sky would be filled with countless twinkling stars, and Duffy struggled to peer in the darkness to see if he could find a zipper to investigate.

Raymond turned the key in the ignition, and instantly Hall and Oates started spelling 'M.E.T.H.O.D.O.F.L.O.V.E'. It was the fastest Raymond had ever reversed from a parking space in his whole life and was enough to distract Duffy. Raymond crunched into first gear and raced off into the darkness towards the hillside road that would take them to Villacarlos.

As they travelled the correct way around the roundabout that had ripped the underside of the van the night before, it was a shame that baby Raymond hadn't yet learned to speak. Not that anyone would have expected him to at five months old or twelve months if he had spent seven more in 1985, which he hadn't. But he saw something very familiar that no one else did. And that something was travelling around the opposite side of the round-about at great speed.

Chapter Ninety-Three

As the campervan idly rocked through the beautiful streets of Sant Lluìs, the serenity of 'Slave to Love' on the radio and the warmth of the summer night was causing eye lids to droop.

Bells, sirens and flashing lights suddenly shattered the calm. Up ahead, three Policía Nacional cars were racing towards them and showed no signs of slowing down.

"Raymond! The money!" shouted Maureen. "They're onto us!"

Raymond did his very best handbrake turn into Carrer de Sant Esteve, and all his passengers but his wife were hurled against the side of the camper. Miraculously, Tash sat up straight and was delighted to hear her son burp and continue sleeping.

"They're driving past. We're okay," said Raymond, his heart in his mouth, as they watched the first two drive by.

"No. They're stopping," said Jamie.

And he was right. Well, sort of.

The third was smaller than the others; it turned until its headlights filled the inside of the campervan. Despite the blinding beams, they could see a policeman step out of his door and yell at them.

"Calle du un solo sentido!"

"What does he mean?" said Raymond, locking his door. "They carry guns, you know."

"Don't say a word, Raymond. We're allowed one phone call," said Maureen.

"It's a one-way street," said Katie. "We were going down a one-way street."

"We were only going one way," said Maureen, "and we were there first!"

"Calle du un solo sentido!" repeated the officer with a stern glare. Then he walked back to his Seat Ritmo, opened the light brown door emblazoned with the Policía Nacional badge and climbed back in. The car ignition fired, and he set off to follow his colleagues. The road was moonlit again, and the bunting overhead gently flickered shadows from the amber streetlights as far as the eye could see.

"What money?" asked Duffy, pulling his safari shorts out of his arse.

Everyone ignored him.

"You said, *'Raymond, the money'*. What money?"

Raymond started up the engine again and muttered something about travellers cheques.

Chapter Ninety-Four

"How could we forget about *Live Aid*?" said Jamie, nursing a cool glass of San Miguel and staring at a 14-inch black and white portable TV placed outside Restaurante Trebol. The venue was a matter of feet away from the sea in Calas Fontes, a small bay in Villacarlos. Holidaymakers walked idly past, gazing at the sailboats gently dipping up and down in the moonlit ripples of the Mediterranean. The twinkling lamps on the promenade infused an idyllic glow that covered every inch the eye could see, and the modest breeze from the gentle inlet to the sea struggled to cool the humid night air.

The venue had been featured in a 1970s British 'sex-comedy' featuring Leslie Phillips called *Spanish Fly* and remained relatively unchanged. Whitewashed cave walls revealed carved-out windows into a cool restaurant, with rustic chairs and tables outside. *Live-Aid* on channel National 1 was met with indifference from most holidaymakers. Still, Jamie peered into the tiny set and spotted Elton John in a very warm-looking full-length jacket made of a carpet or something. He was singing 'Don't Go Breaking My Heart' with Kiki Dee, and even on the black and white set, it was plain to see that most of the band were dressed in white. This was very 1985.

Crockery rattled, and cutlery scraped as tables of sun-kissed families enjoyed their flame-grilled seafood dishes with clinking bottles of deep red Faustino or jugs of brandy-laced sangria.

"This is happening now!" said Jamie.

The Wembley show was about to enter its final hour before handing over to Philadelphia, and London was in darkness, but 72,000 people in the audience made it clear that the gig was ticking all their boxes and more.

"What's wrong with these people?" he said, amazed that the tourists around him didn't seem to care, leaning further into the screen to get a better look.

"What *is* wrong with them, Jamie? Look at this shithole," said Tash, nodding over his shoulder to the magnificent panoramic vista of rustic stone-fronted buildings, housing bars, restaurants and shops. Lights twinkled on larger yachts anchored further out, unable to reach the shallow waters that moored countless timber sailing boats.

Despite herself, Tash was more interested in *Live Aid* than she thought she would be, if only because the weight of Elton's hat was making his ears fold perfectly in half from the top; so she sat with one eye on the sea view and one on TV, cradling her sleeping son, and sipping Xoriguer gin and limon. She'd taken her eyes off Elton momentarily to enjoy the theatre of Zander, the waiter, pouring the local gin from a great height into her highball glass until it covered the blocks of ice and lemon, and then continued further up and up the glass. The splash of Fanta limon seemed like an afterthought. She'd sleep well tonight, she thought, whenever tonight came, and whichever year she found herself in.

Jamie was distracted from Elton by Katie walking back to join their table. She'd just paid a visit to the "bathroom", as she'd called it, which had taken some translating to the staff. Her glowing sun-scorched skin seemed to have settled into an agreeable tan that glistened with coconut-scented after-sun lotion. She'd removed her Madonna-style mesh t-shirt in the loo and was simply wearing a peach-coloured bikini top. The aroma of her Ysatis perfume momentarily replaced the scent of paella in Jamie's nostrils, and he was instantly in love. With her, not the paella. However, he had thoroughly enjoyed that. So had everyone except Maureen, who had negotiated a jacket potato with the waiter. She returned the first one as they had cut it open for her, and she reminded her husband that unless they could serve food previously frozen by a British manufacturer, she would only eat something she could peel.

"It's just so hot," said Katie as she dragged an aluminium bistro chair from beneath their table and sat alongside her father.

Maureen had never before sat at a dining table with someone primarily undressed in the bosom area, so overcompensated by looking in every other direction than at this vulgar American hussy.

"I think that's Crete, Raymond," she said, looking across the sea to the coastline. Her geography was a little off, given they were looking at more of Menorca across the inlet to Mahon, and Crete was five hours' flight away to the east.

"Raymond," she repeated and clipped him around the head, causing him to spill his lager-shandy down his 'Frank Says' t-shirt.

"Sorry, yes," said Raymond, averting his gaze from Katie.

"Not there, there," said Maureen. "You're not even looking where I'm pointing."

Raymond wasn't, and he knew it.

"Sorry, no. Yes," said Raymond. He tried to look somewhere else.

Duffy looked at his watch. "We should head over in a minute or so."

In his lap was his carrier bag loaded with all the film rolls from everyone's efforts earlier in the day.

"I ordered you a glass of wine," said Jamie, not looking at Katie. "You were having a wee. And the man asked."

There was a confused silence.

"He's talking to you," said Tash.

"Oh, thank you," said Katie with delight and reached for a glass of white Rioja that pooled cool drops of condensation onto the tabletop. She downed it in one go, something that Jamie steeled himself to watch. "Right, let's go."

Whether you liked a drink or not, this was quite a sight to behold.

"Oh God, it turns out I like her," whispered Tash to her brother.

"This guy, I admire for his musical talent, more than anything else..." said Elton in between songs, as he introduced his final song, a duet of 'Don't Let The Sun Go Down On Me'.

Jamie glanced at the television. "This is George Michael. He's going to introduce George Michael!"

"Is he the Wham! guy?" said Katie, wiping her wet lips with a napkin.

"Yes," said Jamie.

"How do you know he's going to introduce him? Isn't this live?"

"Just a guess," said Tash, trying to simplify things as they all stood up to leave.

Duffy walked ten feet across the pedestrianised cobbled road to the edge of the delightfully lapping water. Boat after boat were moored on the quayside and disappeared as far as the eye could see around the horseshoe bay like pure white stepping-stones, gently undulating in the calm swell. Ahead of Duffy's size-eleven sandals was an aluminium walkway onto one of them. He turned to the others and proudly spoke to them. "This is us!"

The boat was originally from Alicante but had spent five of its six years here in Menorca. The Furia 33 was an impressive-looking vessel and had the main sail tightly wrapped up like a body in a bag suspended horizontally above the deck. Raymond made this joke as an observation to his wife and then instantly regretted the day he learned to talk.

The 'Reina Betty' was named after the 1979 Spanish entrant for the Eurovision, Betty Missiego, who the original boat owner felt was cheated by only coming second, so he reimagined her as a queen, and subsequently named his boat in her honour. She was larger than most other boats that clung around the bay but still a modest size compared to the yachts Duffy had seen in Mahon and Ciutadella when he did his initial recce of the island in May.

A moped broke the peaceful silence and screeched to a halt

just inches from Duffy's legs. The helmetless driver leapt off and swung a tote bag from around his back. He set off to the boat, accidentally blocked by a bewildered Duffy.

"Excuse," said the driver.

Duffy stepped out of his way.

"Carlos!" shouted the driver setting foot onto the deck. His beckon was met by the opening of the cabin doors and an older man dressed simply in black linen shorts peering out; then, the flash of a match illuminated his face as he lit a cigar. Sweet smoke rose from his mouth. He gently placed the cigar on the roof above the cabin doors and silently disappeared inside before reappearing again, holding sixty large cardboard posters and muttering to the rider. "S'Uestra y Sant Lluìs."

"Gracias," said the driver, emptying his bag into a bucket on the deck and four camera rolls of 35mm Kodak film clanged into the galvanised steel. He placed a lid on the bucket and used both hands to take the posters from the old man.

"De donde. Despues de estos?" asked the boat owner, looking at the bucket, and retrieving his cigar from the roof.

"S'Algar y Punta Prima," replied the photographer.

"What's happening, Raymond?" asked Maureen. "Ask him what's happening. Is it drugs?"

Duffy heard and turned to explain.

"This young man is a photographer; he's been to S'Uestra and Sant Lluìs to take photos of the tourists, and our friend Carlos has developed them for him."

He turned to the moped driver, who was now shuffling back onto the quayside, and asked, "Puedo?"

The flustered driver reluctantly nodded, and Duffy lifted the top poster from the pile to show his audience.

"This is a seven-by-five of a lady dining in resort tonight, and this guy took a photo of everyone at the table after they placed their meal order." He squinted in at her plate. "The shrimp looks good."

Then he moved his hands to reveal the top of the poster and smiled at his audience.

Wanted Dead or Alive

"Like in the movies, see?" said Duffy, unable to keep his laughter inside. The photo had been stapled into a large, coloured poster that mimicked the bark of a tree, with a wanted poster in the centre. "Like a Western an' all? This gets me every time."

"That's very funny!" said Raymond. "And they're not actually wanted? They're not in trouble?"

"Brenda from Newcastle doesn't look like she's tooled up, does she, Raymond? She's not even managed to find her mouth with her fork. Look."

It wasn't very charitable of Tash, but it was a long shot that Brenda – if that was her name – would buy this when the photographer returned. It wasn't her best angle.

"Folks love all this; he reappears just as they finish their meal, three or four glasses of sangria in, then they hand over their pesetas!"

"Par favor?" said the impatient driver, taking the poster off Duffy and sliding them all carefully into his bag. He was on his moped seconds later and on his way to deliver his goods.

Carlos stood up on deck to straighten his aged back and spotted Duffy. "Hola."

Duffy was in raptures that he'd been recognised so soon and that the plan was going so well. "Buenos dias, Señora!" said Duffy, calling him a lady by mistake.

Carlos had heard it all before. He slowly paced to the opposite side of the boat and started pulling up his slouched shorts.

"Tengo que mear," said Carlos over his shoulder at Duffy and stared in anticipation of a response.

"Dammit, I know this one. Tengo kee mare," said Duffy, turning to Katie.

"I think he's going to have a piss," said Tash.

"Is this something to do with the camera roll? How many exposures in each one?" Duffy asked Katie, who responded with a shrug of her shoulders. "Think, Duffy, think!" He delved into his memory banks, "I teng, you tengo, we ting, is it ting?" said Duffy. "Where the hell is my phrase book?"

"Yeah, he is," said Jamie, watching Carlos at the end of the boat.

"Yeah, he needs a piss," said Tash.

Sure enough, Carlos pulled down his zip, fumbled inside his shorts and then unleashed six bottles of Mahou lager into the Mediterranean.

"Look away, darling," said Raymond.

"Oh, my word, you don't get this sort of thing at Scarborough," said Maureen, turning her back to the display. "You ate fish from that sea. I'm glad I ordered potato."

The waterfall continued.

"I mean, I find that really impressive," said Jamie. "Cos I can't go if anyone's looking. I've been known to mime at the communal urinal if there's no cubicle in the gents. Just to save face."

"You mime a pee?" asked Katie.

Jamie nodded; he'd forgotten she could hear.

"You mime the whole thing?" asked Tash.

"Even the shake and the zip going up again."

"What about when you wash your hands?" asked Raymond.

"Stay out of this, Raymond. Stop showing off," said Maureen.

"No, I wash for real," said Jamie.

"So, it's like stage fright?" asked Katie. "Stops you going?"

Jamie nodded again.

"But no other issues down there?" She smiled.

Jamie blushed, and Tash looked furious.

"Don't you leave the loo needing, you know, to go for a pee?" asked Raymond, mouthing the final part like the word might get them shot.

"It's not a choice; it's a glitch in my wiring," said Jamie, "we shouldn't judge people."

"He's right, Raymond; you shouldn't judge people," said Maureen, still facing the restaurant. "You wee sitting down."

The crowd were astonished by this little revelation, and their remarks of "a man sitting down to wee?" and "now he knows how we feel" and the like, were only interrupted by Raymond's explanation to his wife.

"That's because you say I'm too loud standing up!"

"I don't want toilet talk anymore," said Maureen, but clearly, she couldn't leave it there. "But we're attached, and Mrs Denton thought we'd got a burst main last New Year's Eve! And she's twelve inches through the wall! You sounded like a racehorse with diabetes!"

Luckily, or unluckily, depending on how you felt the evening was going, Carlos was able to put an end to this by emptying all the gas from his bowels as his wee came to a halt.

All but one of the spectators turned and joined in with Jamie's involuntary clap. Obviously, Maureen didn't, and Raymond stopped when he spotted Maureen glaring at him.

"Rollo de la cámara?" said Carlos, walking towards Duffy with his hand outstretched to shake. He had no idea why these sunburnt foreigners were clapping.

Duffy reluctantly shook his hand and then cleaned it on his safari suit trousers whilst handing over his bag full of undeveloped film and, for some reason, Maureen's Polaroids.

"Dinero?" said Carlos, without looking in the bag.

"De Niro?" said Duffy before asking his daughter. "De Niro?"

"He's an actor, isn't he?" said Raymond.

"He's saying you look like him," said Tash.

Raymond looked delighted. "Is he?"

"No," said Tash.

"It means cash, doesn't it?" said Jamie.

"Cash! Of course, yes, yes," said Duffy.

Carlos peered into the bag and spotted more rolls of film than he had anticipated.

"Ay!" he announced as he placed a hand over his forehead in shock.

"He's haggling," said Maureen. "We saw this on *Wish You Were Here?* Someone tried it on with Judith Chalmers in a market in Marrakesh. Walk on. We'll find another one."

"Another one?" asked Raymond. "He's a skilled film developer."

Carlos belched and rammed his index finger up his nose.

"I can see that," said Maureen.

"This isn't Morocco, ma'am," said Duffy. "We need a quick turnaround, and Carlos is our man."

Duffy looked over at Carlos before fumbling inside one of the many pockets in his safari suit jacket. Eventually, he extracted a bundle of one-thousand peseta notes secured in a silver money clip and started to flick through them with one eye on Carlos, who responded with a shake of his head for each proffered amount.

"Oh, for goodness sake, this is taking forever. Take this," said Maureen, shoving Duffy to one side and handing over four of the five-thousand peseta notes from the campervan. Duffy's eyes registered amazement, but not for long as Carlos had pocketed these before anyone could blink. Maureen was less happy with Carlos kissing her hand and sitting her down on a cushion at the top of his cabin steps. "Raymond, Raymond!" was all she said as she glanced over her shoulder in despair.

"I'm here, darling. Well done on the money, by the way, you handled that very well."

"You don't mess with these people. They're ruthless."

"Well, he's a fisherman who loves photography," said Duffy. "Maybe he's ruthless with fish!" No-one laughed. "We're tired. It's a little late. I get it."

Carlos picked up the bag of film rolls and sidestepped past Maureen to descend into his cabin. He was a chivalrous man and hated to turn his back on a lady, so Maureen felt the zip of his shorts followed by his hairy tummy on her nose, a moment only bettered by the body odour that accompanied his arms pits down into his make-shift dark room. The heat that rose from inside was palpable, as was the smell of inks and developing fluid. Maureen could make out countless lines of string and clips that created a miniature Mardi-Gras scene around the inner cabin walls, all glowing deep red.

Carlos appeared briefly at the door with another full bottle of Mahou lager. He clipped off the top with an opener and ceremoniously filled a colossal wine glass to the brim with the chilled beer. It easily took most of the litre bottle, but what remained sloshed back down into the bottom of the amber glass. He raised a glass to Maureen and handed her the inch in the bottle before slugging half of the glass in his hand and placing his cigar on the roof again. He slammed his cabin doors shut and slid a black curtain across the tiny window. Maureen looked like a lady who'd been handed a fresh turd and passed the bottle to Duffy. He copied Carlos's manoeuvre past Maureen, muttering his apologies and then knocked on the door.

"How long, Carlos? How long will this take?"

"Qué?" came the reply from inside.

Duffy was from the Raymond language school, so he repeated his question more slowly but at twice the volume. He got no reply.

"Cuánto tiempo?" shouted Jamie. "It means how long?" he explained to the others. "I think."

"Say it again?" asked Duffy.

"Cuánto tiempo?" said Jamie.

"Say it again?" asked Duffy.

"Cuánto tiempo?" said Jamie, patiently.

"Say it again?" asked Duffy; he needed to get this right.

"Cuánto tiempo?" said Jamie.

Duffy repeated this as best he could after knocking again.

"Ehhhh, dame una hora," shouted Carlos.

"One hour," said Jamie.

Tash looked around. "What, we just wait here for an hour?"

"I wish I'd had a wee at the restaurant now," said Jamie.

"I was thinking the same," said Raymond.

"Now I have bathroom guilt," said Katie with a smile.

"Jeez. Now you said that, I could use one," said Duffy.

"Feel free to piss in the sea, guys. Carlos won't mind," said Tash.

"We could ask to use the restaurant loo, couldn't we?" said Raymond, "We've only just left."

Chapter Ninety-Five

"I can't believe they didn't recognise us!" said Duffy, over his shoulder. "I tipped them too!"

The sound of Duffy's piss hitting the sea was soon followed by Raymond's on the opposite side of the deck. They had both edged down to the front of the boat, as far away from the quayside as possible. Jamie had taken the furthest point from the pedestrians and had made a joke about Jack and Rose in *Titanic* as he'd taken his position, but only Tash understood, and she didn't find it funny.

"Why don't we just go and get a drink someplace?" asked Katie. "Use their bathroom."

Maureen had elected to stand on dry land with her back to the boat. If she didn't approve of something, she either crossed her arms or turned her back on it, much like a dog when a family photo was taken. "I don't want another drink, thank you very much, and it's the last thing they need," she said.

"Are you miming, Jamie?" asked Katie, trying to spy him in the darkness.

"Yep," he replied.

"Okay, let's get a drink," Tash announced loudly, ensuring her little brother got to empty his bladder.

Duffy and Jamie walked around their side of the boat, and Raymond failed to walk around his. His foot caught on a gallon drum of developing fluid that Carlos had stored out of the way. Happily, it simply knocked over onto its side and not into the sea. Raymond too, fell onto his side, but given his girth was more significant than the drum, he did fall into the sea. The sound of his impact was synchronised perfectly with a round of applause from one of the restaurants as someone blew out their birthday cake candles to a rapturous response from their family. Tash, Jamie, Maureen, Duffy and Katie all turned to see where the noise came from and joined in with the applause; it seemed the right thing to do on such a balmy and idyllic evening.

Raymond didn't join in as he was using both hands to stay afloat and didn't hear anyway as his ears were full of warm salt water. Lab tests might possibly prove they contained Duffy's urine too, but Raymond didn't want to bother scientists at this time of night. He'd just try to get out of the sea without drowning and then hopefully wouldn't smell of piss. Either way, Maureen would be livid.

Chapter Ninety-Six

It was all too familiar for Raymond to be half on and half off something. He was now dripping wet and clutching onto the nylon rope on one of the side fenders that protected the boat from others. But his body was in the same position it had been last night in the apartment pool, and earlier yesterday as he tried to clamber onto the cart in London. Dragging yourself out of the sea seemed trickier as the boat was gently moving, and he had nowhere to get any purchase on his feet. Miraculously, he had found another rope that ran around the vessel's perimeter and managed to jam his heel onto it. His eyes were stinging with salt water, but happily, one of his ears had just cleared with a pop, and he was suddenly able to hear Menorca again. With a rocking motion, he pushed countless times until an almighty effort successfully dragged all but one of his shoes out of the water. He lay motionless, gasping for oxygen. His chest started to palpitate quite madly, and he was convinced this was the end. His heart had taken too much. The fear of passing alone in a strange country was unbearable. He started to feel faint, and his peripheral vision went fuzzy and grey before closing in further.

Was that it? That was his life?

What had he achieved? What had he left behind?

Would he be missed by anyone other than Maureen?

Would he be missed by Maureen?

Why were the fruit gums in boxes shaped like fruit, but the ones in tubes just round?

Then he realised the problem.

He was holding his breath in fear.

He finally exhaled and drew in the fresh air, and the symptoms passed in moments. He closed his eyes and started to count like Jamie often did. Seven eleven breathing it was. In seven and out eleven. Or was it the other way around?

Raymond pulled himself into a sitting position, leaning on the raised walls of the boat cabin, and then looked around for the others. They were nowhere to be seen.

Oh, God. How long had he been missing?

He slid his back up the side of the boat until he was standing up, terrified he might slip in again. To avoid further risk, he held every single rope, handle, cleat and steel bar he could find as he clambered over the cabin roof before jumping down to the cockpit outside the double doors. Despite his muffled squeal after landing on the side of his ankle, the doors remained closed. It helped that Carlos was getting every single note wrong as he attempted to hum along to DeBarge's 'Rhythm of the Night' from the boat radio. Raymond took one more deep breath, rubbed his salty eyes, and then made for the quayside, pulling the white speedos from his arse as he went. His walk was cock-eyed as he was now wearing just one flip flop, and his other stockinged foot was starting to swell to twice its size.

Chapter Ninety-Seven

If Raymond had been worried that his absence had traumatised his wife, he needn't have been. None of them had noticed he wasn't walking with them along the quayside. Tash and Maureen had broken new ground over the comfortable Menorcan shoes displayed on racks alongside yet another seafood restaurant. Locals and tourists wore the Avarca sandals, and the impossibly comfortable handmade leather footwear now adorned Tash's feet as Maureen handed over another five thousand note to the surprised shopkeeper. She hadn't purchased any for herself as she was a very wide H fitting, and that fact was a secret she had only ever shared with Gina from Freeman Hardy & Willis in Peckham. Jamie and Duffy had been captivated by a supersized boat moored in darkness but for one dim lamp inside.

"Sorry to keep you waiting," said Raymond, still limping and dripping wet as he approached the two men.

Jamie looked Raymond up and down but didn't acknowledge his wet clothes and missing flip-flop. Nor the quickly drying footprints behind him.

"This is a big one," said Jamie.

"Yes, I suppose it is," said Raymond, before rubbing his salty eyes again and trying to remove the water that still blocked one of his ears.

"You had a swim?" asked Duffy.

"Er, yes, I suppose I have, in a way," replied Raymond.

"Dangerous to swim so soon after a meal," said Duffy.

"Well, it wasn't my idea, actually," said Raymond to the back of the American who walked off to meet his daughter next to some head scarves.

"They sell shoes here," said Jamie, looking at Raymond's feet. "But I bet you'll have to buy two."

Raymond's foot was so badly swollen that he had been unable to get it to fit into the largest of the Avarca sandals. When Maureen had seen him trying them on, she had been entirely unimpressed by the explanation of his missing flip-flop. All in all, it hadn't been a great few minutes or so for Raymond, but they found something that fit as an interim measure until his ankle settled down.

The group set off in the direction of a bar, with Raymond following slowly behind. One foot in a flip-flop, one in a flipper. He carried the other flipper under his arm.

Chapter Ninety-Eight

"You guys named this place first," said Duffy, taking a deep draw on a large glass stein filled to the brim with San Miguel. "Georgetown, after one of your people. Did you guys have a famous George sometime?"

"If it was in the seventies, it might have been *George and Mildred*," said Raymond.

"No, this was centuries ago."

"King George, maybe?" said Tash, halfway down another Xoriguer and limon. She'd chosen the seat beneath the solitary olive tree by the quayside. They were further along the bay, nearer a concrete ramp into the sea that allowed fishermen to access the water with their modest boats. It gave a clearer view of all the vessels. Tourists' chatter blended with the lapping of the Mediterranean.

"Then the Spanish kicked your asses out and named it Villa de San Carlos. Which became Villacarlos," he said.

"Except now they're changing the signs to Es Castell," said Katie, pointing to a street sign where a street artist had opted to paint out the word *Villacarlos* with white paint and then spray *Es Castell* over the top in red.

"Why are they calling it that?" asked Raymond, trying to catch the straw in his Coke between his lips and tongue. He failed, so tilted his head to come at it sideways. That didn't help.

"It's an interesting fact," Duffy said before being interrupted.

"Always on a hiding to nothing when you prefix any story with that," said Tash. "No pressure."

Duffy didn't quite understand what she was getting at, so he continued.

"The mouth of the Mahon port along the coast had a castle on it, and the Spanish call a castle Es Castell."

He paused, waiting for a reaction.

"See?" said Tash. "Every time."

Jamie walked back from the loo looking far more comfortable than when he went in. He sat behind his smaller beer and was soon distracted by the movement of tourists idling back and forth past the beautiful boats, bars and restaurants.

"Another interesting fact," said Duffy before being interrupted again.

"I think the jury's out. This might be the first one," said Tash.

"The monastery in the centre of the island is on a mountain called El Torro. And you can see Mallorca from it," said Duffy proudly.

Everyone slowly nodded.

"I think it's called El Torro. Maybe it's Los Torro. Or is it Del Moro?" Duffy looked less confident now. "It's one of those."

They nodded.

"And now I come to think of it; you can't see Mallorca from it."

"So, it's a place with a name we don't know, and its USP is that you can't see Mallorca from it?" said Tash.

"It's US what?" asked Duffy.

"Although, there are loads of places I can't see Mallorca from," said Jamie, "so that's not really a selling point, is it?"

"He's right," said Maureen, holding her piña colada with utter suspicion. Duffy had ordered it for her, and she had yet to partake. "I can't see Mallorca from here, so why would I climb up a mountain so I couldn't see it from there?"

"They have a bull," said Duffy.

"Oh, well, a bull is something, I suppose," said Tash.

"They had a bull," said Katie.

"Bulls don't last long around here," said Jamie sadly.

"No, they didn't kill it. It led some monkeys to Mary, and there's a statue up there," said Duffy.

"Monkeys?" asked Raymond.

"I think it was monks, Dad," said Katie. "Not monkeys. Monks."

"That makes more sense now," said Duffy as the penny dropped.

"Who's Mary?" asked Tash.

"*The* Mary," replied Duffy.

"Berry?" said Tash.

"J. Blige?" asked Jamie.

"Mother of Jesus," said Duffy.

"Oh!" said Tash. "Lost, was she?"

"Monkeys are Gibraltar, aren't they, Maureen?" said Raymond. "Gibraltar? They have monkeys and Marks and Spencer's."

Maureen nodded and sniffed her drink; it was getting the better of her curiosity.

"So, it's a big hill, with no bulls or monkeys, but there's a statue of Mary at the top?" said Tash.

"Jesus, not Mary," said Duffy. "I think. It has long hair, and he's standing more Jesusy than Mary would. So, I'm guessing it's a statue of Jesus."

"You should definitely think of getting a job as a tour guide," said Tash, before pointing at his trouser suit, "you know, if this safari job doesn't work out."

"And you can see the top of the mountain from the bottom," said Duffy. He nodded to confirm that he wasn't exaggerating. "Really!"

This landed slowly around the table.

"That's all mountains, isn't it?" asked Maureen.

They all slowly started to mutter their agreement.

"Well, listen. If, for some reason, we all have to move over here, and spend the rest of our lives on the island," said Tash. "... after I've visited every single bar, restaurant, beach, shop and museum, twice, I might give your little mountain thing a go."

Duffy nodded and swigged more beer. "It sounds pretty good."

"They have guidebooks next door," said Raymond, gesturing at the shop next to their bar. Racks of postcards were being slowly spun around by sun-kissed tourists pondering which family members were important enough to receive a holiday update by post. These would arrive five or six days after they returned, but that was utterly irrelevant. "I had a flick through one until the shop owner pointed to a sign which said: 'please don't read the books'; it was written in a few different languages and everything."

"What are you supposed to do with a book if you're not going to read it?" asked Maureen.

"I thought that," replied Raymond. "They're a very curious people."

"It means don't read it before you've bought it," said Tash.

Raymond and Maureen absorbed this news. Then Raymond offered a little-known fact to the silent table.

"I did read that where we are now is the most eastern part of all of Spain. So, it gets more sunshine than anywhere else! In the whole of Spain!"

"Why would it get more sun just because it's the most eastern?" asked Tash.

"Can't argue with a guidebook," said Raymond. "It's printed and everything."

"Did it not say it gets the sun *before* the rest of Spain? Not *the most* sun?" asked Jamie.

"Yep, the sun sets in the east and rises in the west, so that's most likely what it said," replied Duffy with some authority.

"Other than the fact you got that completely the wrong way around, does anyone want to join me with a bit of shushy time?" said Tash.

"That man's waving at us," said Jamie, waving back.

"Don't wave at strange men, Jamie," said Maureen, pushing his hand down.

"It's the boatman," said Jamie.

And it was.

"He's finished early!" said Duffy, emptying his glass and screeching his aluminium bistro chair across the stone flags before leafing through his money again. "I know you guys are going to protest, but I absolutely insist that these drinks are on me."

Jamie raised his hand.

"No, Jamie, no. I insist. You guys have been a tremendous help, and this is something I want to do as a token of my appreciation."

No-one protested.

"His boat's on fire," said Jamie.

And it was.

Chapter Ninety-Nine

Raymond had no idea what Carlos was shouting at him. Locals connected hose pipes from their restaurant fronts and showered precious water supplies onto the boat. Soon a capable team of fishermen had approached from the rear and configured a highly innovative contraption to squirt seawater onto the roaring flames.

"Ellos!" shouted Carlos, sitting with his head in his hands on the quayside. He muttered something to Jamie, who tried his best to interpret his fury from his limited memory of A-Level Spanish.

A young waitress had joined in with their conversation, and she caught Tash's eye.

"He says you are to blame. You spill something to his cigar," said the lady, distracted by Raymond struggling to stand straight with his flippered twisted ankle.

"What?" said Tash; she was having none of this.

"You spill liquid. Alcohol," repeated the lady, trying to keep up with Carlos.

Amongst the dying flames, the spilt barrel nestled alongside the melting cabin. Raymond stared in horror and had a flashback of the moment he sprained his ankle when he reached out to the cabin roof to catch himself. Jamie watched as Raymond quickly glanced at his hand. In the centre of his palm was the imprint of a cigar burn.

He'd kicked over the rinse fluid and then knocked off the cigar. The isopropyl alcohol had slowly trickled to the lowest point and met Carlos's Villiger Robusto long after Raymond had left the boat.

"We didn't touch a drop," said Maureen, folding her arms and stomping her feet in fury. The effect was enchanting, given she was wearing a flamenco dress and shoes. If she could keep this up for ten minutes, she might draw a crowd.

"The photos," said Duffy, staring inside the cabin as smoke replaced the flames.

"Martha!" said Jamie, suddenly realising the impact of the fire. He leapt onto the boat only to be restrained by Duffy.

"You can't go on there, boy; you'll kill yourself."

"But Martha!" said Jamie. His eyes started to water and a knot tied in his stomach.

Duffy stared into the cabin.

"We had a chance! We could have saved her," said Jamie.

Katie was crying now. "Daddy, what the hell are we gonna do?"

Duffy looked at her and realised he was crying too.

"I don't know, Katie. I just don't know. Jeez. How the hell did this happen?"

Raymond clenched his burnt fist tightly closed.

"Señora," came an assertive shout from down the quayside.

An officer of the Policía Local walked keenly towards them. Alongside him, a flustered shopkeeper was trying to keep up. The official held a five-thousand peseta note in the air and pointed at Maureen. Raymond's brain processed the situation in an instant. Maureen had been busted. She'd spent stolen money, and now he had to do something to save his wife from trouble. But what could he do?

Luckily, he was soon distracted by the almighty pain in his shoulder, then his ankle. Duffy had reached out for help as he dropped like a boat anchor onto the ground. His grasp on Raymond's arm hadn't lasted long, and sixteen stones of American now rested on Raymond's flipper. Duffy moaned loudly as he clutched his lower side.

"Daddy are you alright?" said Katie as she dropped to his side. He whispered in her ear, gasping for breath.

"What is it? What's wrong?" asked Jamie.

"He's on my poorly ankle," replied Raymond.

"He didn't mean you, Raymond, and stand up straight; you're slouching," said Maureen.

"Sorry, Maureen," he replied. "I think my shoulder's popped out again."

Jamie looked at Raymond's arm, which hung very strangely, and sure enough, Jamie fainted again.

"Jamie!" shouted Tash, struggling to catch his head before it struck stone.

"Qué está mal?" asked the policeman, distracted from his initial mission, he was now facing a medical emergency.

"Spot of bother with my shoulder, and there's a man on my ankle," said Raymond.

"Him," said the officer, pointing at Duffy.

Katie looked up with tears in her eyes.

"His appendix, I think it's burst!"

"Mi dinero," said the shopkeeper, trying to get the policeman back on track about her money.

He gestured for her to return to her shop and explained that the latest developments took priority.

"Más importante," he said.

She sauntered away, staring at Maureen.

Chapter One Hundred

"That's a lot of ice cream," said Katie.

Duffy scraped the empty bowl with his finger and sucked off the remaining *La Menorquina* iced lemon dessert, which had somehow evaded his spoon.

"It's good; you not eating yours, Raymondo?"

Duffy's hospital bed was alongside Raymond's, who was bandaged around the shoulder and cast in a pot around his broken ankle.

"I can't hold the bowl and use the spoon," he replied, glancing at the bowl on the small cupboard between their beds. He nodded to his unusable arm.

"That's too bad. They should get you a straw," said Duffy, glancing up at a passing nurse. "Straw? Se*ñ*or? Straw?"

Maybe Nurse Gabarro didn't understand the word straw, or perhaps she didn't take kindly to being called a man, but either way, she just shrugged and continued along the ward.

"Look at that. She speaks no English. That's too bad," said Duffy, his eyes falling on the ice cream again.

The ward fell silent for a moment. Then, the opened windows suddenly filled with the sound of a convoy of ambulance sirens outside the hospital building.

"Because that ice cream is just gonna melt, and I hate to see wasted food, you know? My mom always told me that food waste is bad," said Duffy, raising his voice to be heard.

Raymond nodded.

"That's just gonna sit there and melt and then go in the trash," said Duffy.

"Would you like it?" said Raymond.

"Oh no! No, I couldn't take that. That's yours."

"Take the fucking ice cream," said Tash. She was changing baby Raymond's nappy on the empty bed alongside Jamie. "Sake."

Duffy's mood was already good, but it visibly improved as he reached over and tucked into Raymond's ice cream, muttering as he went.

"Too bad about the straw. That's just a real shame, Raymondo. Real bad."

"So, it wasn't your appendix?" said Jamie.

He was eating his ice cream on the bed on the other side of Duffy.

"Well, it comes, and it goes, you know?" said Duffy, without breaking his impressive pace of scooping spoons into his mouth without taking a breath.

"A more cynical person might think you faked it to get that police officer off our case," said Tash. "Which impressed the hell out of me, by the way," she said.

"A more cynical cop might ask where you got a handful of stolen pesetas."

This silenced them but for Duffy's slurping, which was thankfully soon disguised by the arrival of footsteps. Each of them tried to establish if these were the cushioned soled sandals worn by the friendly medical team or the rugged leather of the Policía Local standard issue brogues.

"You'd think hospital toilets would have a proper flush," said Maureen, appearing at the foot of Raymond's bed. "There's a little rod sticking out of the top. I gave up in the end. No idea."

"You pull it up," said Tash.

"I'm not going back there; it smelt of drains," she replied as she climbed back into the single wardrobe next to her husband's bed and closed the door on herself. No one blinked.

"I don't think you need to hide anymore, darling," said Raymond.

She continued talking from behind the veneered door.

"I'll make that decision, thank you," she said. "It's filthy in here. Are we going to be much longer?"

"The nurse checked them all out," said Katie. "They're good to go."

"We're just waiting for a chair for Raymond," said Tash.

"What does he need a chair for?"

"Well, he's broken his ankle," said Jamie.

There was a pause.

"And?" said the wardrobe.

"So, he needs a wheelchair," said Tash.

"Well, he got here without one."

"But the pain did make him pass out," said Katie.

There was another pause whilst the wardrobe pondered this.

"Did they ask to see the E111?" said Maureen.

"Not yet," answered Raymond.

"What's that?" asked Katie.

"It covers the health–care cost," said Raymond, blushing. Their E111 cards were in Brixton and may have expired for all he knew.

"Shoot, our insurance is in the apartment," said Duffy.

"Maybe we could pay cash, Maureen," said Raymond avoiding eye contact with the Americans.

"You are talking to a wardrobe?"

Everybody looked to see the arresting officer, standing with a sombre expression at the foot of Raymond's bed. He strolled to the wardrobe and opened it. Maureen stared at him for a moment.

"I was trying to find the toilet."

He peered in the tiny cupboard. "Did you find it?"

She shook her head.

"Did you check everywhere? What about there?" He pointed into a dark corner by her feet.

She nodded slowly, wishing the ground would swallow him whole. Him not her, of course, because he was the problem, sticking his nose in.

The officer stepped backwards so Maureen could climb out.

"You are lucky," he said. "We are too busy with real criminals this evening. And we need these beds. You are free to go."

"Thank you very much, Detective Inspector," said Raymond, adding a speculative "Sergeant?" at the end to cover all bases.

"And remember, you must not exchange your pounds anywhere except a banco, si?"

He held up the iffy five-thousand pesetas note, evidently assuming they were victims of crime too. These sunburnt tourists weren't money launderers.

"Well, this is it," said Raymond. "Sorry."

"Buenas noches," said the officer and gestured to the door. Everyone who wasn't standing soon was, except Raymond.

"I'm just waiting on a wheelchair."

In a moment of serendipity, Nurse Gabarro arrived, wheeling one and helped Raymond into it.

"Thank you, miss," he said.

"Sir, we need to get my insurance documentation from our apartment. Can we come back and show this to you or somebody? Full disclosure, I have one exclusion clause for a mucus issue. It's pre-existing but nothing to do with what happened here. And these guys have some card or something?" said Duffy.

Maureen looked like she might explode with fear.

"Please just go. We need the beds, and we are very busy tonight," said the officer, gesturing to the ward doors. This was not a matter for further discussion.

"Jeez, that's very kind, sir. Very kind. May I ask where you get that ice cream?"

The officer stared blankly back at him.

"No? Well, that's okay."

As they set off down the ward with Jamie pushing Raymond's wheelchair, it became apparent that the largest of his left wheels had a squeak.

"Sorry about the squeak," said Raymond.

"I can't be listening to that. You'll have to walk," said Maureen.

So, he did.

Chapter One Hundred and One

"So, you got a few bad five-G's from some back-street dealer?" said Duffy.

"I don't want to talk about it," said Maureen.

"I didn't see you change any money. Where was this guy?"

"Tell him I don't want to talk about it, Raymond," she replied.

"She says she doesn't want to talk about it, if you don't mind," he stopped to try and rub inside his ankle cast.

"You can't drive like that," said Tash, watching Raymond limp towards the VW.

"Good point. Shall I drive?" said Jamie.

Tash glared at him.

"No, let Frankie do it," she replied, smiling at Duffy.

"Me?" he asked.

Jamie looked quizzically at his sister, then realised she was casually nodding at the rear of the camper and its vault of stolen money.

"Yes, you!" said Jamie, a little bit too assertively.

Duffy took this instruction and climbed into the driving seat.

"You sit with your dad," said Tash, opening the door for Katie.

Katie looked at the masses of papers and junk that remained from Jesus in the footwell.

"Is there room?" she joked.

She scooped up the litter, climbed in, and then Tash shut the door.

"What is this, a trash can?" asked Katie as she peered in the darkness at the newspapers, crisp packets and empty drinks cans.

"Some stuff we picked up on the way," said Jamie, climbing into the back followed by Tash, baby Raymond and then the Man from Atlantis with his flamenco wife. Duffy searched for the interior light and flicked it on so he could find the slot for the ignition key.

"Who's the mad man?" said Katie, smiling at the Polaroid at the top of the pile of rubbish in her hands.

Maureen looked very awkward. "That was just a test photo we took earlier."

"Is that the cyclist you knocked over twice, Raymond?" said Tash.

"He rode under me," said Raymond.

"Poor man was only trying to sell oranges," said Jamie.

Duffy took the Polaroid and looked at the moment captured in the frame: A gap-toothed pensioner's fearful face hitting the rear windscreen of the VW that morning. He smiled for a moment, then stopped and lifted the photo closer to the interior light.

"When was this?" he asked.

"Just after we met you," said Maureen. "He's fine; we saw him pedal away."

"His oranges were a bit bruised," said Jamie.

"That's not code," said Tash.

"Do you know who this is?" said Duffy, suddenly looking more alive than his daughter could ever remember. Even brighter than when he doubled up on *La Menorquina* in hospital.

Duffy held the photo of the pensioner at the passengers in the back. Jamie raised his hand.

"Great, first guess from Jamie," said Tash. "Go."

"Is it Bee?" he asked.

Tash looked at her brother and back at the photo. "You think that looks like a middle-aged black lady?"

"He said she might be in disguise; that's why we took photos of everyone."

"He did say that," said Raymond.

"We saw him get up. It was his own fault, really," said Maureen, more concerned about blame.

"And they can do all sorts with CGI and stuff," said Jamie, squinting at the photo, still believing this might be their lady.

"With what?" asked Katie.

"That's *after* they film stuff, Jamie. Did you see Maureen fumbling around with a MacBook Pro after she took it?" said Tash.

"Are they still talking about the photo?" Duffy asked his daughter, who shrugged. She wasn't sure.

Duffy cleared his throat.

"Ladies and gentlemen. Today we spent the afternoon trying to prove that Ms Barbara Fernandez: Attorney at Law – also known as Bee – was alive and well, and the perpetrator of grand theft, murder, arson and faking her own death..." He waited to add some tension.

"This is like *I'm A Celebrity*," said Jamie. "He's teasing us. He's going to go to the ad break next."

"Not to mention perverting the course of justice and framing an innocent young lady," Duffy was carrying on.

"But all our photos got burnt," said Tash, ignoring the sudden squirm this remark brought on in Raymond.

"Not this one," said Duffy.

"But that's not a black lady," said Maureen before turning to Tash. "Is black offensive?"

"Can I finish, please?" said Duffy.

"Yeah, but speed it along a bit; you're losing us," said Tash.

"Do you know who this is?" asked Duffy, holding the photo closer to the others.

"We already did that part, didn't we?" said Jamie.

"Is it you?" asked Raymond.

"What?" replied Duffy, looking at the photo and then himself in the rear-view mirror. "I look this old?"

There was silence, which upset him further.

"How old do you think I am?" he asked.

"I dunno, sixty-eight?" said Tash.

Katie held her face in her palms, half through horror and half through hilarity.

"Sixty-nine?" said Jamie.

"I think you go down after you offend someone," said Raymond.

"Sixty-eight?" asked Jamie.

"That was my first guess," said Tash.

"Sixty-seven?" asked Jamie.

"What?" said Duffy, looking in the mirror again and feeling the crows' feet around his eyes.

"Are you going to tell us who it is on the bloody picture or not?" said Maureen.

The whole campervan fell silent at this brutal use of the English language from the least likely candidate. Duffy looked shocked and berated, so he decided to quit the game.

"Harvey Eikenberry," he said slowly and with purpose.

The van went quiet again.

"Who?" said Maureen. She was getting irritated now.

"Harvey Eikenberry," said Duffy, nodding slowly, hoping for the penny to drop.

"Is he the chocolate factory man?" asked Maureen.

"That's Charlie," said Raymond.

"No, it was Willy Wonka's factory," said Jamie. "He gave it to Charlie."

"He's right, the book was *Charlie and Chocolate Factory*, but it belonged to Willy Wonka," said Tash.

"Can someone explain what's happening?" asked Maureen.

Then someone knocked on the side of the campervan, and a torch lit up the inside.

"Problema?" shouted the policeman outside. The same policemen who had just released them. He was peering in with interest.

Jamie looked between his legs to see a bundle of five-thousand pesetas notes peeking out of the unzipped cushion; he slammed his knees together and shouted, "Drive!"

"We're going, señora," said Duffy, fumbling around for the keys.

"He means señor," said Jamie to the passengers inside.

"Got it," said Tash.

Duffy fired up the VW and set off to Binibeca with Mai-Tai telling him their love was 'History'.

Chapter One Hundred and Two

Eikenberry tilted his bike as far as possible to ensure his brake handle gouged a deep groove into this bastard's VW T2. It was one thing to be knocked off his bike by the driver's hand but another to be reversed off his saddle by a campervan.

He set off slowly to ensure no other traffic would surprise him and then let the lay of the land drag the bike comfortably down the hillside to the most eastern side of the island and into the resort of S'Algar. He allowed himself a smile as the wheels gathered pace and periodically looked back to ensure it was only oranges that fell off his little cart.

Hotel San Luis in S'Algar was pretty unique on the island of Menorca. It had been one of just a handful of multi-story hotels constructed during the tourism boom of the sixties and seventies before the authorities put a stop to high-rise buildings. Subsequently, only a few coves and bays on the 112 miles of coastline around the sleepy island were blighted by a blip in the skyline. Apartment blocks were typically two or three floors high, and most developments were single-storey villas. The downside of this was they didn't enjoy the same view that eight-year-old Ronnie was enjoying from her sixth-floor balcony over the resort below and the Passeig Maritimo spanning the shallow turquoise sea that lapped the rocks by the bathing area. She was wearing her new *Care Bears* swimming costume and sat alongside a green bottle of 7Up on top of the wicker framed table. She was fiddling with a red circle of plastic caps, methodically removing one to insert into the miniature gun she had purchased in the hotel shop on her arrival. The sliding patio doors behind her were open, and the sound of Ultravox performing 'One Small Day' to the Wembley Live Aid crowd played loudly inside.

Happy that she had inserted her cap into the chamber correctly, the fun began. She stood up from the wicker chair and walked to the slotted steel balcony to seek her target. On the ground to one side, sun-kissed tourists lay on plastic sun loungers around the vast swimming pool, occasionally looking up from their Danielle Steele or Stephen King novels to scold their children for getting the pages wet. But the angle was too tight, too far to the right, and she wanted to copy the *Dukes of Hazzard* and lean on something. Her mum let her stay up for the show, and she'd even allowed Ronnie to record the show's finale at the start of the year. She could quote it word for word.

What about the cleaners on the balcony three floors down? She could get a clean shot, but again, she wouldn't be able to lean on the balcony, which would look so cool. Then her eye was attracted to movement on the road approaching the hotel, and she smiled.

Perfect.

She steadied her wrists on the balcony and closed one eye as she took aim. It was challenging as the target was moving, but happily, it was getting closer.

She took her time.

Not now.

Not yet.

Wait.

A little closer, and she would be able to make out his face.

When she could, she smiled and pulled the trigger.

The pistol fired, and the unmistakable cloud of smoke and aroma of sulphur rose into the skies. The crack of the cap was pleasing to her. Not so much to her mother, who stepped out onto the balcony.

"Let's quit it with the shooting for a little, honey. You're gonna be out of bullets!"

"I shot Uncle Harv!" replied Ronnie, pointing down at her target.

Approaching the hotel, the elderly man pedalled his bicycle, towing a solitary orange on a trailer. It rested on a blanket, covering two suitcases, each holding one hundred and seventy bundles of bank notes. Each bundle held one hundred notes. Each note was worth five thousand pesetas.

And these were totally legit.

In a way.

Harvey pedalled beneath them and waved up, before continuing around the back to the main foyer. Ronnie giddily waved back and slurped her 7Up. Her mother stood still behind her, overcome with joy, before shouting down to her partner.

"I'll come down," shouted Bee.

Chapter One Hundred and Three

Maureen peered behind her into the Palomino interior and reached through the window to point the HiFi speaker away from her. Depeche Mode sounded like a building site to her, and she had no interest in anyone singing about a disease. The whole thing was most unnecessary, especially as it was gone midnight. Far gone.

Katie allowed herself an unseen smirk before Maureen turned back around and continued examining the Polaroid.

"I can't see the likeness. He looks more like Captain Peacock," said Maureen, glancing between the photo and the newspaper image of Harvey Eikenberry that sat on the table. His picture had been alongside Bee's on the front page of the *Canadian Gazette* but had long since been folded over as everyone assumed they were looking for her, not him.

"I don't know that name," said Katie, taking another sip of her San Miguel. "Peacock? Was he like the Falkland war or something?"

"Grace Brothers," said Maureen. "Firm but fair. And it was a conflict, not a war." She stared at the Polaroid. "He's got a tooth missing here, can't be the same man."

"That will be the one they found after the fire," said Katie. "He helped Bee plan the whole thing. They'll have removed it.

His poor wife. She thinks he's dead. And poor Martha. She's been through hell."

At the other side of the table, Jamie and Raymond were deep in conversation as they stared at the moon that hung perfectly in the clear night sky.

"I know it's not a big thing, but it's always been our pipe dream," said Raymond, sipping his very first glass of Fundador, which he'd elected to dilute with Fanta Naranja after it made him sneeze merely by sniffing it.

"I don't know many men that don't dream about that, to be fair," said Jamie, finally realising he and Raymond had a shared ambition. "For me, and I know it's a cliché, I'd want a red one. They have to be red."

Raymond nodded in contemplation. "I'm not sure about red, but we'd like it to have some decent storage for boots and stuff."

"Storage?" said Jamie. "They're not about storage!"

"Well, yes, I know that, but there's no reason they shouldn't have plenty. You know, somewhere for an umbrella and such the like."

"You know you can get a four-door version now?" said Jamie. "Well, for the last ten years or so, to be fair. You know, in 2020. Which is quite a wait for you. If you live that long, of course."

Raymond glanced at Jamie as this observation seemed brutal but realised Jamie was just speaking as he saw it.

"We'd only want two doors," said Raymond.

"You need to dream bigger, Raymond," said Jamie.

"Maybe."

They sipped their drinks and contemplated life and dreams.

"I mean, we'd definitely need it to be double glazed."

"A double-glazed Porsche?" said Jamie.

"Porch," said Raymond. "I've always wanted a porch."

Jamie nodded. "The umbrella makes sense now."

"Raise your hand if you're a hero!" said Duffy, arriving from the path that led to the road. They all looked up and, mainly being British, didn't.

"We're not a big nation of hand raisers," said Tash. "Other

than my brother."

Jamie knocked over his drink, and Katie instantly righted his glass and pulled back her chair from the ensuing spill.

"Sorry," said Jamie.

"You were quick," said Tash to Katie. She wasn't sure if she was impressed or wanted her to piss off out of her brother's life.

"I had a lifetime of training. Martha used to spill half of everything she ever ordered."

Tash felt a warm surge of joy in her tummy.

Jamie was badly mopping up his San Miguel by mostly moving the spill around in circles with a saturated napkin.

"Señor," said Paco, intervening with a cloth whilst balancing a tray of drinks in his other hand.

"Thank you," said Jamie.

Duffy started to sniff, and then snorted noisily. This was followed by a hacking cough that seemed to last for hours until he was happy that he had cleared the mucus from his throat. He was left with the dilemma of how to dispose of this from his ample mouth. A disgusted Paco leant forward to the chrome napkin dispenser and handed him a handful of them whilst staring in fascination at this strange man. Duffy nodded his thanks and then noisily filled the collection of serviettes. Every face around the table glared at the floor. It seemed to take forever. Eventually he spoke.

"I have this condition," said Duffy, smiling at Paco, before scrunching the napkins into a ball, and handing them to the waiter, who accepted them in horror. Duffy spotted one final glass of beer on Paco's tray and took it before sitting down.

"You read my mind," said Duffy before emptying the glass in one. Paco raised his eyebrow philosophically. He thought the Brits were the drinkers, not the Americans. "One more for the road, please, Paco. Gracias señora."

Paco ignored the error, lowered the tray for Duffy to place his empty glass down and then disappeared into the bar, still holding the napkin ball at arm's length.

"Sorry, I was a while. I changed again," he said, gesturing at his clothes.

Everybody looked at his identical attire.

"You changed?" asked Tash. Why would anyone buy this outfit twice?

"Sure," said Duffy. "Why?"

"No reason."

"You made the call, then?" asked Jamie.

Duffy nodded and released an almighty lungful of breath. "Seven thirty over there. My guy was just finishing his shift. Not pleased to hear from me. Until I broke the news, of course!"

"He believed you?" asked Jamie. "He believed Harvey's still alive?"

"We don't know who is in on this," said Duffy. "This evil could go high up in both states. So, my guy's off radar now, for his own sake. He's headed straight to the Governor; they went to high school together. They're like brothers."

"They are brothers," said Katie.

"There's that as well," said Duffy. "We got that going for us. So, this won't get buried."

"This is very much like the ending of Scooby Doo, isn't it?" said Jamie. "When you say everything's going to be alright, and all the baddies get arrested, and the goodies get released from prison?"

They all sort of laughed, and Paco arrived with another beer for Duffy. He was now wearing rubber gloves.

"Hey, Paco. Will you take a photo of us all?" asked Tash, surprising herself with her need for a memento.

Paco nodded and placed his tray on the table, looking for a camera.

"Use this one," said Maureen, mindful that her camera had been used the least all day. Paco took the Polaroid, flicked it open, which wasn't easy in his gloves, and then stepped back to get the whole group into his viewfinder. They all strained to lean forwards, backwards or sideways to see the little man and his camera. It flashed, and everyone relaxed again. Paco offered the camera back as the photo slid out of the front. Tash took the print and gestured Paco back into position.

"One more," she said.

"Why do we need one more?" asked Jamie.

Tash was reluctant to admit that she was hoping to abandon him in the eighties and wanted each of them to have a matching photograph for the remainder of their lives.

"For these guys," said Tash, pointing at the Americans.

"That's so kind," said Duffy. "I got a feeling we made friends for life here, Katie!"

Everyone smiled, in a way, depending on how they felt about the sentiment.

"Not to mention you two!" said Duffy, winking and nodding at his daughter and Jamie. "I might be an old man, but I can see you guys have been hitting it off!"

"Dad!" said Katie in protest.

This was news to Jamie. He was always last to know what people thought about him. Tash was horrified. "Just take the fucking picture, Paco!"

Paco retook his position, and the crowd repeated their pose, albeit with some more stern faces.

"Thank you," said Tash, taking the Polaroid back from the waiter. Duffy held his hand out for his memento.

"What?" she asked, taking the latest photo and wafting it around in the hot air, hoping it would help it to develop. A fallacy that remained throughout the camera's popularity.

"I thought that one was for us."

Tash stared at him for a moment. "It is. I'm just developing them both." She started to shake them both.

Duffy nodded and became distracted by Maureen's photo from earlier in the day. "Such an amazing shot!" He said before laughing. "This guy thought he was having a bad day when you ran him down! Wait until he sees what the morning brings."

"The morning? They'll be that quick?" said Maureen. "That's very impressive."

"Well, speaking figuratively," said Duffy. "We need to find him, and hopefully her, first. The airport will have their details within the hour, but this place has two major harbours and a hell of a lot of coastline. Then we need to deport them, then prosecute them. We'll need your help, of course."

"What?" said Tash.

"Beg pardon?" said Raymond.

"Say again?" said Maureen.

"We might need to call you as witnesses, given that you were in the van that knocked him down."

"Twice," said Jamie, taking the photo from Duffy to have another look at this baddie.

"Jamie!" said Tash. "TMI."

"He got up!" said Maureen. "He was fine!"

Duffy continued. "We'll need to let the local police seize the van and lock it away. It's a big enquiry. Don't worry; we can arrange transportation for you. But I'm gonna need a copy of your passports and all, you know, just so they know we're the good guys!"

Maureen started to squirm in her seat, Raymond choked on his drink, and Jamie raised his hand. Duffy glanced at him and nodded.

"But Martha won't face prison, or, you know? Death? She'll be released?" Jamie looked very anxious. Tash slowed down her photo wafting and handed one to him. "Put it in my bag?" she whispered and gestured to baby Raymond's holdall. She'd somehow give Jamie his own copy when she abandoned him later; she was confident Duffy wouldn't ask for it; he was too preoccupied.

"That's a given, young man," said Duffy. "And we thank God for that. Unless there's some failure of the system, and she gets sent down for life. Or she fries. But that's not gonna happen. That's a very slim percentage point. Very slim indeed. But we still want to nail these bastards, right? They stole over eleven million dollars, faked their deaths, and were gonna let someone fry for that! Let's take these guys down! Now, who's with me?"

He raised a glass to his band of brothers and sisters. They fell silent, and then the muttering started, all at the same time:

"Passports? Now, where did we put the passports?"

"It's not our van; to be fair, someone loaned it to us."

"Can we get back to you on that?"

"I need to make a trifle."

Chapter One Hundred and Four

"Are you okay down there?" shouted Duffy from the upstairs bedroom of apartment P. Katie turned over in her single bed to look at her father. Something had disturbed him, and he stood in the doorway looking down into the darkness of the floor below. The door at the bottom of the stairs opened very slightly, and Raymond's head appeared from his room.

"Sorry, yes, we're just having a bit of a disagreement about who goes on top. Jamie says it's his turn, but I liked it so much last night that I'd rather go on top of him again."

"You're talking about the bunk bed, right?" asked Duffy.

"Yes." Raymond thought he'd made that quite clear. "What did you think I meant? Pardon?"

"Alright. I sleep a little light and wasn't sure if the cops were here. They said morning, but you never know, right?" He yawned, placed his hand down the back of his boxers and scratched, and lifted the other arm to glance at his watch. He twisted it to the light from the evening sky that leaked in from the terrace doors. "It's gone two; you should get some rest."

"Yes, of course. Good night," said Raymond.

Duffy nodded and closed his door before climbing into the double bed adjacent to his daughter's and starting to snort again.

"Good people," he said. "Strange people. But good."

"Get some sleep," said Katie before turning her baking hot pillow over to the relatively cooler side and closing her eyes.

Downstairs, things weren't quite as Raymond would have them believe. Jamie's hand was in the air, in a way, as he was sitting on his bottom bunk alongside his sister.

"Jamie," whispered Tash, "you must whisper, you must try, please be as quiet as you can. What is it?"

"Can you not sit on my pillow, please?" he replied.

Tash pulled the pillow from beneath her and tossed it onto the floor. Raymond moved his plaster cast foot out of the way and leant on the bedroom door.

"I am not staying here one moment longer than we need to. We did what we said we would," said Maureen from the top bunk. She was sitting in her side saddle style, looking very demure.

"We need to fix the wheel! The wheel came off when we arrived!" said Tash for the hundredth time. "But now he's got the police coming to impound the van and take our passports which we don't even have!"

"You still have the key to the little shed thing, don't you?" asked Raymond.

"Yes," said Tash, holding up the key. "This is how we get home!"

"Well, we're going to have to fix the wheel now and then leave," said Raymond.

"It's the middle of the night," said Maureen.

"So?" asked Tash.

Jamie's hand was up again.

"Stop raising your hand all the time. What is it?" whispered Tash.

"Well, I was wondering," Jamie started to say before the other three interrupted with a communal "Shhh!" He recoiled in shock and tried to finish as quietly as possible. "How? We don't have a wheel!"

"We borrow one," said Tash.

"Borrow?" asked Maureen. "How do we bring it back?"

"Alright, steal then, for fuck's sake! But we have no choice."

"Where do we *borrow* one from?" asked Raymond.

"How big is the wheel on Duffy's Fiat?" asked Tash.

"Seat," said Jamie, followed by another "shhh!" from the ensemble.

"It is a bigger wheel, but it might work," said Jamie in his best attempt at a whisper.

"How do you suggest we get that off?" asked Raymond.

"They all have a jack in the boot, don't they?" said Tash. "There'll be some pliers or whatever you use in there."

"It'll be a nut wrench," said Jamie, his volume back to normal, "not pliers."

This time, Tash simply placed her palm over his face to silence him.

"How do we get his keys?" asked Raymond.

Chapter One Hundred and Five

"It's one of these," whispered Tash, "it has to be."

All but Raymond crouched on their knees, fumbling around the many wheels of the many Seat's parked outside the apartment block.

"That's a Renault," said Jamie to Maureen.

"Shh!" said Tash as Maureen huffed and moved on to the next car.

"Found it!" said Raymond, followed by a metallic clink as the car key fell to the ground. "Dropped it!"

"Bloody hell, Raymond, don't bend any further," said Tash rushing over to him, followed by Maureen and Jamie.

The three of them started to feel around the dusty tarmac beneath the front wheel of the car, next to Raymond's damaged ankle.

"Are you not going to help?" asked Maureen, watching her husband's idle stance.

"Bit of bother with the old arm," he replied. He was bent at right angles from his hips up.

"Bother?" replied Maureen.

"Stuck," said Raymond.

"Are you kidding?" Tash asked as she continued searching for the tiny key.

"It's trapped between the top of the tyre and the underside of the wheel arch," he replied.

"Just pull it out and stop being silly," said Maureen.

"I'm not being silly," said Raymond as politely as possible.

"Found it!" said Jamie, followed by another group 'shhh!'

He held up a tiny key that glinted in the moonlight.

"I think it's the t-shirt material," said Raymond.

"Well, you're going to have to take it off then," said Tash.

"He'll do no such thing," said Maureen.

"We don't have a choice, Maureen," said Tash. "I'm sure you can keep your hands off him until we can get him covered up again."

They started to undress Raymond by squeezing his t-shirt up from his ample tummy and then squeezing his free arm loose. His head was next, and then they agreed to take a breather.

Maureen should probably have thought better of sitting down on the bonnet. The sound of the Seat wheel arch lowering over Raymond's arm made an unpleasant snapping sound, followed by the highest pitch squeal they'd ever heard him make, and he'd made a few.

"Off the car!" said Tash.

The moment Maureen leapt up, Raymond gave an almighty tug, and his arm was free.

Way too free, to be fair.

It hung limply by his side, just like yesterday. His shoulder had popped out once more.

"Lie him down," said Tash, gently moving her sleeping son to one side, tucked perfectly inside a crib she had fashioned from his sleeping bag.

It took a while to get Raymond on the warm ground, as his ankle was out of use, too. When they managed, he was staring at the thousands of night stars, unable to distinguish which were real and which were the product of his hysterical brain as it struggled to contain the pain inside his chest and not allow it to unleash itself around the balconies of the sleeping tourists inside.

"What did Julian's mum do?" asked Tash, flapping Raymond's elbow up and down.

"He's making a lot of noise. How can we help?" asked Jamie, as quietly as he could.

Maureen glanced at Raymond's ripped and abandoned t-shirt hanging from the wheel arch and started to tug. With a pathetic rip, it came loose, leaving the remnants of the cotton fashion fail in her hands. She began to twist it into a curious bundle, and Tash watched in awe. This woman had survived the war, survived losing her parents, survived the shit that a life with Raymond had thrown at her, yet nothing phased her. Nothing at all. Now she was making a sling from a discarded piece of cotton, and it was amazing. Maureen squeezed the material a little tighter and then into a ball, and then surprised them all by forcing it into Raymond's moaning mouth.

"Oh," said Tash.

"That's quieter," said Maureen.

Jamie started replicating some of the other manoeuvres he remembered from yesterday, each one creating a higher pitch from Raymond's gagged mouth until a single click ended Raymond's pain.

"Mem mum mamie," muttered Raymond.

"What does that mean?" Tash asked Maureen, who shrugged.

"Maybe you should take it out of his mouth now?" said Tash.

Maureen pulled the cotton from Raymond's mouth. He choked in some much-needed hot oxygen before speaking.

"Well done, Jamie."

Jamie smiled and held up the key again. "Shall we just take one of Julian's wheels as we're here? The keys all work on any car."

Tash absorbed this suggestion. "Jamie, you know I love you very much, but I really need you to be quiet. Especially whilst I think."

She turned to look at Julian's car and made a mental list:

He'd been so kind to them.

He'd been so generous.

He'd repaired the VW.

He'd saved the C5 from the pool.

He'd loaned her a safe place to store it.
He'd asked her on a date, and now she couldn't go.
He made her tummy feel a bit funny.

She turned to look at Duffy's hire car at the other end of the row.

He'd helped, yes, but now he was making things very difficult for them.

He wanted their passports.

He wanted to impound their campervan.

He made her tummy feel funny, but in a wrong way; it was a little repulsed if she was honest, especially the way his jaw clicked when he ate, and now she thought about it, maybe he should shower more.

"No. Let's stick with the plan," said Tash.

Chapter One Hundred and Six

The key had worked on Duffy's car, as they all suspected, and now Jamie and Tash were taking turns to try to force the cross-wheel wrench to loosen the last wheel nut from the front of the jacked-up 127. Maureen was singing something very quietly into baby Raymond's ears, and Raymond stood at the open boot of the car.

Then Tash realised he was licking his lips and squinting a bit, a typical sign he wanted to say something.

"What is it, Raymond?" asked Tash.

"Why don't we just take his spare?"

He pointed into the boot.

Chapter One Hundred and Seven

Tash tried to force the key into the pool store door with trembling hands.

"Don't snap that key," said Maureen.

"One, I won't," said Tash, "and two, when has anyone ever saying *don't do something*, made someone change how they're doing something? You're just stating the obvious."

"You are being a bit rough with it," said Raymond.

Tash glared at him.

"Although it is quite dark, so maybe it's just my eyes," he said.

Jamie followed up the rear, wheeling the Seat spare wheel as he went.

"And since when did keys snap in locks anyway?" said Tash. "Is that like a 1950's thing or something?"

She didn't even get to "or something," before the key snapped in the lock.

"Sake."

Maureen passed baby Raymond to his older name's sake and started to cross her arms but was interrupted.

"Don't you fucking dare to cross your arms at me! We're all in this together," said Tash.

"There's still a bit hanging out," said Raymond, "all's not lost. I don't think we need to fall out about things."

With this, he handed baby Raymond to Tash and started fumbling with the snapped key in the lock.

"Just need to give it a bit of a wobble, show it a bit of love sort of thing," talking more to himself than his audience, but sure enough, the remaining bit of metal slowly wobbled free.

"There we go!" He was very proud. He looked again at the object in his hand. "Isn't this the car key?"

Tash became instantly hot and fumbled in her lace pocket for the correct key. Shit, yes. It was there. She held it aloft and slowly spoke.

"Right, let's assume that I have apologised, and you have all accepted my apology, and we have all moved on, alright?"

They all sort of nodded; maybe Maureen didn't, and then Jamie took the key and unlocked the door. And despite everything they had been through together and everything they feared and hoped for, not one of them could have predicted what was inside.

Chapter One Hundred and Eight

"It has all its wheels," said Jamie.

They were all so confused that they didn't even try to silence Jamie.

He wheeled the C5 carefully out of the storage room, edging it gently over the stones that gave way to the swimming pool beside them.

"It looks just like the others," said Raymond, examining the replaced wheel.

Tash looked over at the apartments.

"Julian," she whispered. "He found it and fixed it."

"Looks like he cleaned it. It looks like a brand new tyre!" said Raymond.

"He likes you," said Jamie.

"I broke into his car," said Tash, with a pang of guilt rising in her chest.

"And snapped his key," said Raymond.

"It's like that film," said Maureen.

"Which film?" asked Tash, one eye still on Julian's dark apartment.

"Chitty Chitty Bang Bang," replied Maureen. "That had a rubbish little car. Can we get on, please?"

Tash turned to the others; she had something on her mind.

"Do we all need to go back?" The moment she said it, her eyes dropped to the floor.

"What?" replied Maureen.

"Of course, we do," said Raymond.

"What about you, Jamie?" said Tash, still casually looking at the pool. She clenched her teeth. How the hell would this chat go? She could really do with making things as simple as possible for herself. This way, Jamie wouldn't need to hang around Gaywood Close for the first seven months of 1985. Maybe he would go straight to America with the snot machine and his daughter? Start his life with Martha straight away? Jamie stared at his sister. What the hell was she talking about?

"I don't understand."

"I just wondered if you wanted to hang around for a bit and check that Martha's alright? Check that Frankie's got her off the charges and stuff?"

"How the hell would that work?"

"I don't know," she replied, her voice fading.

"We've locked my mate in a cage with an owl. We have to go back. What are you talking about?" said Jamie, at his normal volume.

A light came on inside Apartment N.

"Alright!" whispered Tash.

Then a light came on above in Apartment P, followed by the relentless hacking of Duffy's throat.

"Sake!" said Tash.

"So, what's the plan? We need to connect the pole to both vehicles and then find a hill again," said Jamie.

"How about we tow that back up to Sant Lluìs?" said Raymond, pointing to the C5. "Then we turn things around to come back down the hill *behind* it? Like on Tower Bridge"

"When we all nearly died?" said Maureen.

"Yes," said Raymond happily.

"That won't work," said Jamie.

"Why?" said Maureen.

"His ankle. I'll drive."

"Shhh!" said Tash.

Chapter One Hundred and Nine

As the VW Campervan climbed the hill, Jimmy Nail made a beautiful sound from his unconventional face, covering a Madonna cover of a Rose Royce song. Jamie took one last glance at the sign for Binibeca in his rear-view mirror. They had passed through S'Uestra and were now approaching the outskirts of Sant Lluìs. This would be enough of a descent to get them home with no fear of interruption. He felt a pang of regret that he had not been able to say goodbye to Katie. And felt embarrassed to have needlessly vandalised Duffy's hire car without a word of explanation. But the outcome was the best they could have hoped for. Martha would live, and that was an almighty thing.

Maureen guiltily toyed with the bundles of five-thousand peseta notes that tumbled out of the bench seats and struggled with an inner voice: *How many would they miss if they accidentally made their way home to Gaywood Close?*

Raymond was sitting in the passenger seat alongside Jamie and regretted destroying his 'Frank Say' t-shirt. It was one thing feeling your paunch wobble every time you drove over a bump but watching your hairy nipples bouncing every hundred yards was a bit much.

Tash almost regretted her insistence that she sit in the C5 as the VW towed it slowly up the hill, but the motion was causing her son to fall asleep, and the cicadas in the night air were making her eyes close too. This didn't last long as Jamie swerved madly, and the C5 rocked wildly to one side then managed to drive on two wheels before dropping back down onto three.

"Sake, Jamie!" she shouted.

"Get off the fucking road!" shouted an angry lady in the darkness.

Tash strained to look over her shoulder and could just about make out the silhouette of three people walking down the road to S'Algar.

Chapter One Hundred and Ten

"It worked last time, so it will work again, have some faith," said Tash, punching the return destination into the Sinclair Spectrum keyboard, now covered in sand from the dry air that warmed their skin, despite the ungodly hour.

"I just don't want to get this wrong. We did an amazing thing, and I don't want anything to change," said Jamie, squeezing his sister from behind.

"Forget the handbrake this time, Maureen," shouted Tash. "Just use the footbrake and follow my lead."

"What does she mean?" said Maureen, now in the driver's seat. "I can't do this!"

Kirsty MacColl on the radio was causing a big distraction to the new driver. The driver with feet that worked. This time, she was wearing the spare wheel from the Seat as a helmet, as she'd felt she looked slightly silly wearing the spare VW one. Happily, Raymond didn't have an opinion. He'd been told that as she helped him place that one onto his head.

"You'll be fine. Just keep an eye on Tash, and when she lifts her arm, we let off the brake and roll down the hill. You just need to steer," he replied.

"I don't know where we're going!"

"Just stay on the road!"

"Why is the steering wheel on this side?" Maureen's voice was frantic now.

"Have you only just noticed that?"

"Don't be clever," she replied, revving the engine madly.

"Little less gas, darling," said Raymond.

"Gas? Gas? How do I turn on the gas?"

"I saw two shooting stars last night, I wished on them, but they were only satellites," sang Kirsty.

The Pye TV screen on the C5 was flickering with all the return journey data on its multi-coloured screen.

"Is everybody ready?" shouted Tash. "Well, whatever, we're going."

She hit ENTER, and the wheels started to spin.

"Pardon?" shouted Raymond from inside his makeshift helmet.

"Stop talking, Raymond. I'm trying to look at Tash," said Maureen. "I can't listen and look! Where's the gas?"

"It's American for petrol."

"We're in Mallorca, not America."

Jamie leant into his sister's ear and tried to whisper to her, but it came out full volume as ever.

"We're going home!"

She raised her hand, and the cavalcade set off down the hill into the darkness, gathering speed quickly.

"Oh my gooch!" shouted Maureen.

Chapter One Hundred and Eleven

Miss Kaye was a spinster and had waited all her life to visit London. When she read about the guided Christmas tour of the capital city in the Yorkshire Post, she'd walked from her Whitby cottage to the post office to buy a first-class stamp and a fresh pad of Basildon Bond unlined paper to write a letter of interest and enclosed a cheque in full payment for the three-day trip.

She'd been overwhelmed with emotion to drive past the iconic gates to Buckingham Palace, she'd been delighted to see the cosmopolitan bright lights of the Ritz, and she'd been awestruck to see the astonishing height of Nelson's Column. But nothing could have prepared her for the wonder of the sight she was seeing now. Not from a trippers' coach but from her very own hotel bedroom window.

The bold concrete monolith that was Tower Thistle Hotel clung to the Thames on the northern side of Tower Bridge, and half of its many rooms had an uninterrupted view of the world-famous bridge. The others looked over St. Katharine Docks. Miss Kaye had requested a river view and had got one.

Having allowed herself a Tia Maria coffee at the end of her three-course meal, she was surprised that she hadn't slept soundly through the night. Maybe it was the caffeine, or perhaps it was her full bladder, but she found herself standing at the window in the dark, gazing out into the December night, only to discover that the mighty bridge was being raised.

Initially, she had been concerned to see an unusual van parked on the lower raising deck, but it clung perfectly to the bridge until it was almost vertical. Now she watched with her heart beating in her chest as the rear lights flickered, and the vehicle suddenly descended the near vertical drop, pushing a tricycle ahead of it.

Curiously, she didn't see it continue down the road along the rest of the bridge. Instead, there was a modest flash, and then the bridge started to lower again to reveal nothing. She thought she must have imagined the vehicle, but couldn't reconcile it in her head, as she could describe it clearly to anyone who might ask. Not that she saw many people.

As the two decks lowered further, the flash occurred again, and the van was back, this time travelling the same stretch of road it had just departed, then disappeared into the darkness beyond. She rubbed her chin and pulled the dressing table chair over to the window. Maybe it would happen again.

It didn't.

Chapter One Hundred and Twelve

"Kenneth, I'm so sorry," said Jamie, running to the office door.

Kenneth was enraptured by the owl, who hated the song about doves that Prince was performing on Radio One.

"I thought you'd forgotten about us," said Kenneth.

In fairness, he'd only been in there for nine minutes. That was how long it took them to travel to Tower Bridge and back (ignoring the trip to the Balearic island inbetween).

Jamie opened the door and dropped to the floor as the owl flew straight at him and then out into the night. The concrete floor felt cold on his stomach beneath his ripped t-shirt.

"We can explain everything," said Raymond following Jamie into the warehouse. Kenneth glared at his patchy skin and inflamed nose. Why was he wearing just speedos? Wasn't he freezing?

Tash walked past them and into the office, clutching her son in the baby carrier. She started to fumble through filing cabinets.

"What are you doing?" Jamie asked his sister.

"Putting the camera back," she replied. "We never took it, did we?"

"Where's my one?" asked Kenneth.

Jamie handed it back, and Kenneth examined the rear.

"There's no film in it."

"We sent it to be developed for you," said Maureen.

Kenneth stared at the flamenco dancer.

"Early Christmas present," said Raymond. "Sort of thing."

"Really?" said Kenneth, double-checking his camera. "You hardly know me?"

"Well, we feel like we do, don't we?" said Maureen.

"We've heard a lot about you, Kelly," said Raymond.

"Kenneth."

"Yes," said Raymond.

"But I haven't got yous anything."

"We don't give to receive, Kenneth," said Maureen. "Now, if you'll excuse us, we need to lock up for the night."

Kenneth glanced at the knackered shutter.

"I guess I'll be off then," he said. "Merry Christmas all of yous."

"Pardon?" said Maureen, distracted by something behind the campervan.

"I said Merry Christmas."

"Yep, bye," said Tash, her head buried in a draw.

Kenneth made to leave and stopped himself. "Would it be rude to ask when I get my photos, like?"

"Erm," said Raymond. "How long do you usually have to wait?"

"About three days or so."

"Might be a little longer," said Jamie.

"No worries," said the Geordie. "What with Christmas and all that, like?"

"Sort of," said Jamie, struggling to look his friend in the eye. "Yes. That."

"See you soon, then."

And he was gone, confused by this final exchange. His euphoria had turned into a disinterested farewell.

"We need to put the van exactly where we took it from," said Jamie.

"I can do that," said Tash, leaping up and grabbing her son.

They stepped outside together.

"Where was it?" asked Jamie.

Tash looked at the ground where the police had sprayed paint onto the cobbles around the perimeter of the van. She waited for the penny to drop.

"What?" said Jamie, unsure as to why she was staring at him.

"Well, it's there, isn't it? There's a fucking outline!" Her voice sounded strange.

"Are you ok?" he asked.

"Yes," she lied. "You look cold."

"I'm not cold," he replied.

She rubbed his bare arms to get the blood circulating, and then rubbed his back. To anyone watching, it might even look like a cuddle.

"Oh, Jamie," said Tash. "Here's that photo. Can you take it? I spilt milk in the bag."

She handed him the Polaroid of the six of them outside the Palomino bar. He placed it in the back pocket of his shorts, climbed into the van and then screamed.

"What is it?" shouted Tash, uncoupling the C5 from the front of the VW with a spanner she found in the filing cabinet, she was careful to keep the mains cable connected to the van battery. That was a Jamie job.

"There's someone in here!" replied Jamie.

He felt around for the interior light. When his fingers eventually flicked it on, Maureen's face lit up inches from Jamie's. "It's you!"

"I was looking for something," she said.

"I thought you'd got out?"

"I got back in again. I dropped my earring," Maureen said, holding up something that Jamie couldn't see.

"We're putting the van back where it was," he said, attempting to fire up the engine. On the fourth attempt it growled to life and the radio started playing.

"Well, let me get out then," said Maureen, leaning towards the side door. Jamie couldn't hear her clearly as a bizarre song was filling the van. It sounded like a mix of Frankie's 'The Power of Love' and Band Aid's 'Do They Know It's Christmas?'

Maybe the DJ was pissed.

"I said let me out!" shouted Maureen as the van started to wobble backwards.

"Can you just lower your head, so I can see?" said Jamie, straining to look through the back window.

"Sometimes you just gotta rip the plaster," shouted Tash from outside.

"What?" said Jamie.

The van briefly filled with light. Then it was dark again.

"What the hell was that? Did you just take my photo?" said Maureen.

Jamie stopped the van and turned to Maureen. He held his hands up. "Do I have a camera?"

She looked dissatisfied with his reply.

"Did your sister take one?" said Maureen squinting through the windscreen.

Jamie turned to look too. He couldn't see her from where he was sitting, so he climbed down and peered around the front. Happily, only Holly Johnson was singing now. The sad amber streetlight illuminated the cobbled road and the steel brace that had connected the C5 to the campervan.

"Tash?" said Jamie.

"What was that flash?" said Raymond, standing in the warehouse doorway.

"Tash?" said Jamie, looking at the tools on the ground, and the separated tow bar.

He knew straight away.

The way he knew Adam Simpson wouldn't invite him to his tenth birthday party like he'd said he would.

The way he knew Jess Ward wasn't coming to Cineworld that night she'd agreed to.

The way he knew the producer at his X Factor audition wouldn't be in touch despite what she'd told him.

He'd had a gut feeling he wouldn't be going home with his sister. Something had changed.

Then he heard his own voice, reciting his sister, "when you know something's gonna be shit for a bit, get it done. The bad stuff soon passes. Rip the plaster."

His warm tears dripped down his sunburnt cheeks and gathered on his trembling chin. He leant down to pick up Tash's discarded elf hat. That was wet, too. It had been used to wipe his sister's tears before she'd hit ENTER.

Then Maureen clicked past with fifty five-thousand peseta notes poorly concealed beneath her flamenco dress.

Chapter One Hundred and Thirteen

"I'm just tired, Mum, that's all," said Tash, as she continued crying over her Christmas dinner.

"She looks a funny colour," said Andrea, pouring herself more Sauvignon Blanc. "Look at her, George, she's a funny colour. That's your liver, isn't it?"

The irony of her remark whilst topping up her own alcohol wasn't lost on Tash, but she wasn't in the mood for quips.

"She looks brown, have you overdone the fake tan?" asked her father, George, before forcing a perfectly stacked fork of cold turkey, chipolata, roast potato, stuffing and cranberry sauce into his mouth. This was particularly impressive as the final few inches to his mouth were from memory as his purple paper hat slipped over his eyes.

"Oh, my Christing hell! Can everyone stop looking at me and just eat?" said Tash.

"Natasha! That's an all-time low from you! And on His birthday!" said Grandma, Dot. "You take that back!"

"I wasn't looking at you," said George, trying to pull his hat back up his head and failing. "These always rip. Why do they always rip?"

"Big head," said Dot. "It's a Summers thing. Your father's the same. That's why he's come up with those stupid things."

Sure enough, Grandad Ernest was currently wrestling with

gristle in his dentures from beneath a split yellow paper crown hat with an elasticated golden band around the middle keeping it in place. He tapped the band and, after finally swallowing, explained.

"Hat fixers, I'm going to offer them in three sizes and six colours. I reckon I could get them into Poundland or sell them direct to the cracker manufacturers."

"What colours?" asked George.

"Gold and silver, obviously," said Ernest. "Then red, green, erm, did I say gold?"

"Yes!" said Tash.

"Hmm," said Ernest, oblivious to her irritation. "Oh! I remember now. Brown and grey."

"Not very festive colours, those," said Andrea, slowly pulling a piece of turkey apart to examine a pink patch.

"Well, I figured that if no one goes for the hat fixers, I could sell them to Pets at Home," said the old inventor.

"That's silly, Ernest. Pets don't wear Christmas hats," said his wife, buttering a slice of bread, ensuring the surface was fully covered up to each crust. No bread was visible when she was done.

"No, but these would work perfectly to hold back rabbit's ears when they're eating," he explained.

"Hence brown and grey?" said George.

"So, they don't feel silly," said Ernest. "You'll barely see them on if they match their fur."

"Are you being serious?" asked Tash.

Ernest wasn't sure what she meant, so he just looked back at her quizzically.

"Since when have rabbits' ears got in the way of them eating?" she asked.

"I wouldn't want those massive things flopping in my soup," said Dot. "It's not such a bad idea."

"Soup?"

"Good to have a strategy if the crackers people don't work out. Top marks for that, Dad," said George. "Not sure if rabbits are the way to go, though."

But Ernest was distracted by the TV now. The Queen's speech was beginning with a thoroughly British image: The Mounted Band of The Household cavalry played instruments sitting on regally dressed horses in the grounds of Windsor Castle.

"I'm going to have a bath," said Tash. She pushed her chair back from the dining table and walked out of the room.

"But I've not served my Aldi dessert," said Dot.

"Ooh, sounds exciting," said Andrea. She didn't mean it.

"It's a ... Ferrero Rocher inspired chocolate and...." said Dot, gazing up at the mistletoe hanging from the Dunelm chandelier; she often did this when she was trying to remember the name of things. It didn't need to be mistletoe, just something above head height. "Chocolate and... phenelzine dome,"

"I like the sound of that!" said George.

"Phenelzine? That's what they give depressed people," said Andrea.

"Look at him twatting them drums next to that horse's ears," said Ernest staring at the TV. "I wonder how he'd like it if someone did that next to his ears."

"There's something wrong with that girl," said Dot, glancing at the empty seat at the table.

"Is Jamie still running?" shouted George to the hallway. "Shall we plate him something up?"

The door opened, and Tash walked in again.

"I told you! Yes, he's still running!" she shouted before grabbing the fullest bottle of Shiraz she could find amongst the festive fare and walking out again. She wasn't happy with how the door slammed the first time, so she opened it and slammed it again.

Baby Raymond didn't blink an eyelid as he slept in his crib alongside Andrea.

"Have we lost you, Ernest?" said Dot to her husband, now glazed over as he stared at the TV and images of animals grazing on a royal estate. "What are you thinking?"

Ernest turned to his wife, then his son, then his daughter-in-law, and then finally his great-grandson.

"You don't want to know," he replied before taking a slug of his wine.

"Yes, we do. What are you thinking?" asked Dot.

"I was wondering if a cow had ever had it off with a horse," he replied.

The room went quiet, but for the ticking of the grandfather clock and George Michael singing "December Song" on the Echo speaker, four years to the day since he left the earth.

"See? I told you didn't want to know," said Ernest.

Andrea looked at her husband, but his loyalty to his father meant he opted to examine a stuffing ball on his plate instead.

"Do you mean bull?" said Andrea.

"Praline!" said Dot. "I mean chocolate and praline dome."

"Ah! That makes better sense," said George, who was immediately silenced by Dot.

"Quiet George, she's about to speak; turn that off." Dot turned up the TV to listen to Queen Elizabeth II, and George silenced Alexa as instructed.

"Look at her lovely smile," said Dot. "I don't know what we'd do without her."

Chapter One Hundred and Fourteen

Tash sat on the candlewick bedspread in the same room where she had fallen asleep alongside her brother last night, and her tears dried. She had an exceptionally crisp towel wrapped around her, struggling to absorb the remnants of her bathwater. Her Grandma wasn't a believer in fabric softener, so the family had to settle for drying themselves with sandpaper. She flicked slowly through an album of family photos that Grandma kept beneath the bed.

Turning through each page was an event, as each was protected from the other by an elegant paper insert, much like a vintage wedding album. Tash wasn't too proud to drink wine from the bottle, so she was set for the next hour or so.

She smiled; there she was, aged three standing alongside her newborn baby brother; she looked proud and irritated at the same time. Nothing had changed.

She flipped over the pages and stopped at another of her sixth birthday party, blowing out candles surrounded by delighted school friends and Jamie, beaming a bigger smile than anyone.

Then Jamie's tenth birthday. Just him and her, but his smile was joyful as ever.

Over the page was Tash's thirteenth birthday party, horse riding with her schoolmates, and Jamie at the rear. He'd fallen off more times than the instructor had ever known, but his spirit remained undiminished. Tell Jamie he couldn't do something, and he'd spend however long it took to prove you wrong.

Then another of Jamie's birthdays. Maybe his twelfth. Just him and his sister.

She found herself crying again. Why hadn't she seen this before? She'd effortlessly been surrounded by so many friends her whole life. He'd only ever had her.

And she'd just abandoned him in 1984.

And never mind him, what about her? He was her best friend. He was her rock. He was baby Raymond's uncle. And more than this, he was supposed to be downstairs eating a fake Ferrero Rocher dome. What was she supposed to say? He couldn't be running forever. Maybe she could confide in her Grandad. He might have an idea. Or not.

Christ, she had a lot of thinking to do.

Her eyes flooded with burning hot tears again, and she struggled to focus on the wine bottle before it met her lips. Her timing was off, and her sudden onset of hysterical snotty sobbing sprayed the Shiraz back down into the green glass, down her legs, and onto Grandma's carpet. She placed the bottle safely to one side, hurled herself on the floor and wept.

She knew she had to release this grief and let it have its moment, like a bee sting or root canal. It passed sooner than she feared as a wave of mental clarity swept through her head.

She remembered why she'd abandoned him.

This morning, he'd proudly visited her as a pensioner to prove he'd lived a happy life with Martha. That was all she'd ever wanted for him. The unconditional love you're only guaranteed from your family. The unconditional love she'd yet to find for herself. She closed the album and smiled, then whispered to herself. Moving her mouth made her temples ache; her head was so full of remorse.

"You did what he told you, Tash. Yes, you went the long way around, but that was his fault too, the prick."

"Don't spill any wine on that carpet!" shouted Dot, from downstairs.

Tash glanced at the burgundy-coloured puddle by her legs.

"I'm not stupid," she shouted back, knocking the bottle on her knee and splashing another inch on the Axminster.

"Balls."

"And bring Gabriel when you come down, you know he gets grouchy if he wakes up without him," said Dot.

"Alright!" shouted Tash, struggling to hide her irritation. How hard was it to get some 'me-time'?

She started to unpack the baby bag she'd taken on her mini tour of Menorca. She placed the nappies alongside the box on the floor, the nappy sacks beside them, and the formula milk on the chest of drawers. She'd taken more baby-grows than she'd needed, and bibs, and nappy sacks, but that's holidays for you.

As she delved deeper to find the family heirloom, she removed the final sachets of Calpol and tubes of Sudocrem, and spotted the Polaroid photograph that Jamie had slid into the bag for her. Not in the side panel, and not wrapped in anything to protect it, where she might have placed it, but face down in her sports bra. She laughed as she recalled Jamie removing Martha's.

At least he'd spent his life with a memento that matched hers. The photo, not the bra. She would need to hide this well, but what a wonderful keepsake.

She was home. Her son was home. Both grandparents were alive; and her brother had met the love of his life after she was released from jail on or soon after July 14, 1985.

She couldn't hope for more. She had done the right thing for once in her life, and it felt terrific.

She googled altruism.

"Yep, that's me," she said as she reached for the bottle, spilling it once more.

"Sake."

THE END

Epilogue

"Does it change anything?" asked Katie, ripping into some country bread and smearing pure white salted mantequilla across the chunk in her tanned hand. She was already regretting her denim shorts; the temperature was rising fast. Duffy swallowed his mouthful of café con leche and shook his head.

"Changes nothing, honey. We'll get her outta jail, but it's just strange, is all. They seemed like good people. And I thought he was carrying a candle for you."

"Stop it, Dad," said Katie, without letting on whether she was upset or relieved that Jamie had vanished. She took a deep mouthful of impossibly sweet, freshly squeezed orange juice.

"Just seems strange to leave the one thing that meant the most to the baby," she said, staring at Gabriel, now sitting on their table, covered in sand.

"Must have dropped him when they got in the van," said her father.

"Why are they taking so long to visit us?" she asked, looking at her watch.

"Who?" asked Duffy, attacking his full English breakfast with cutlery that seemed too small for his chunky hands.

"The local cops."

He rammed half a sausage into his mouth.

"Damn, that's hot...."

He blew out hot air as saliva trickled down his open lips. He chewed for a moment and replied.

"There was a targeted attack last night, someplace on the island. They don't ever get that kind of thing over here. This place usually sleeps."

"Sounds nasty," said Katie, smiling at Julian as he walked past and nodded his salutations.

"They'll get to us. We just might need to hang around a little longer."

"I can live with that," she replied happily, smiling at Julian. What was it about this unlikely Lothario?

Someone dived into the pool, and the sound of an approaching moped completed the perfect Spanish holiday scene. Paco turned on the stereo, and John Parr sang 'St Elmo's Fire' from the speakers resting inside the opened timber framed windows. Paco nodded his head to the brass section. Had Jamie been here, he would have told Katie that Parr was from Worksop, near his grandparents, and still lived close by in Doncaster. And that he'd met him on Fargate in Sheffield when Parr re-recorded the song for a local kids' charity. He'd hit all the original high notes too. A lovely man. Lots of hair.

But Jamie had gone, so Katie would never know this.

Duffy looked up from a greasy slab of bacon as the rasping moped grew closer and pulled into the parking space next to their table. The driver climbed off; then slowly gaffer taped a poster onto the side of the international post box, before discarding a smoking cigarette stub onto the path.

The top of the flier was stencilled in Spanish:

Querido por la policía

Beneath was a black and white photograph of a shocked balding man in his fifties. Below was a warning not to approach the suspect – but to contact police if spotted.

It was a photograph of Ernest Summers.

A Small Favour...

I hope that you enjoyed "Wish You Were Here Yet?"

As an independent author, I rely solely on Amazon and Audible reviews to enable me to continue writing. I would be extremely grateful if you could find the time to leave a review for this third instalment.

(As ever, I shall keep you updated on book four on my newsletter - there's a link on my website jamescrookes.com)

Thank you for your continued support, it really does mean the world to me.

Warm wishes.

James Crookes

PS: I spent some very happy times in Menorca in 1984 and 1985, and a great deal of the locations and venues mentioned in these pages were real (and some still are). Apartment P remains in my heart forever. I hope that you enjoyed me showing you around, you've been great company.

Acknowledgments

First and foremost thank you for reading. I am overwhelmed by the messages of love and affection for the family of characters in these books. Sincere thanks for staying with Tash, Jamie, and their extended families. As ever, it's a privilege to share these moments, and relive some of the happy times from the eighties with you.

Thanks to Sinéad Fitzgibbon, as ever for diligent and supportive editing.

Thanks to the amazing Scott Readman.

Thanks to Richard Dew. It was wonderful to walk with you through the head offices of the Midland Bank and computer department in the eighties. Thanks also to Janina Tomlinson, Patricia Winfield and all your friendly colleagues on the Midland Bank Poultry and Princes St. Facebook group.

Thanks to Sarah Lines, a friendship formed on email during the first lockdown, we still hope to finally meet you in Menorca. Thank you for connecting me with David Nutall and thank you David for your superb memories from the magical island in 1985.

Thanks to Sally Bull, not just for your equine advice, but for many happy holidays in Binibeca in the eighties.

Thanks to Christian Mitchell, your extensive Met knowledge was more than I could have hoped for!

Thanks to Kim Marks, my friend for over forty years, despite being a thousand miles away, your airport memories were perfect, and added so much.

Thanks to John Parr for your amazing memory, you're a lovely man. (And for one of the best songs of the eighties!)

Thanks to Wes Butters for help and encouragement and a stunning website.

Thanks to John Harrison and Steve White for your support through all of this.

Thanks again to Dominique and Julian for your keen eyes and unfaltering faith in me.

Thanks to Nikki for making me laugh every day, and keeping me sane through this difficult year. I'm lost without you.

Made in United States
Orlando, FL
19 December 2024

56084849R00295